THE ENDLESS SHADOWS
OF PETE

THE ENDLESS SHADOWS OF PETE

A HUES NOVEL
BOOK FIVE

J. L. JACKOLA

Library of Congress Control Number 2023904742

Paperback ISBN 978-1-960784-07-0
Hardback ISBN 978-1-960784-08-7
Electronic ISBN 978-1-960784-09-4

Distributed by Tivshe Publishing
Printed in the United States of America

Cover design by Dark Queen Designs
Map design by Worldwyrm

Visit www.tivshepublishing.com

ALSO BY J. L. JACKOLA

AUTHOR'S NOTE

You made it to book five! I had such a blast writing this series, and especially writing this final book. As I like to do in my series endings, I've turned things on their head and completely disrupted the status quo of my characters. Don't worry, there's still a happy ending—it just might not be the one you were expecting!

As with the first four books, book five consists of characters who are mature and sexually confident. Please be aware of possible triggers.

This book contains intense and explicit sexual scenes, language, mmf/mm/mf scenes, violence, and death.

I hope you enjoy the end of the adventure. If you'd like to leave a review, that would be lovely. And follow me on social media for news on my upcoming projects.

J. L.

KANTENDA
DRANTH MOUNTAINS
FETTERRED FOREST
CHENTHOM

ELTANDER
NENOCHIN
APENDIA

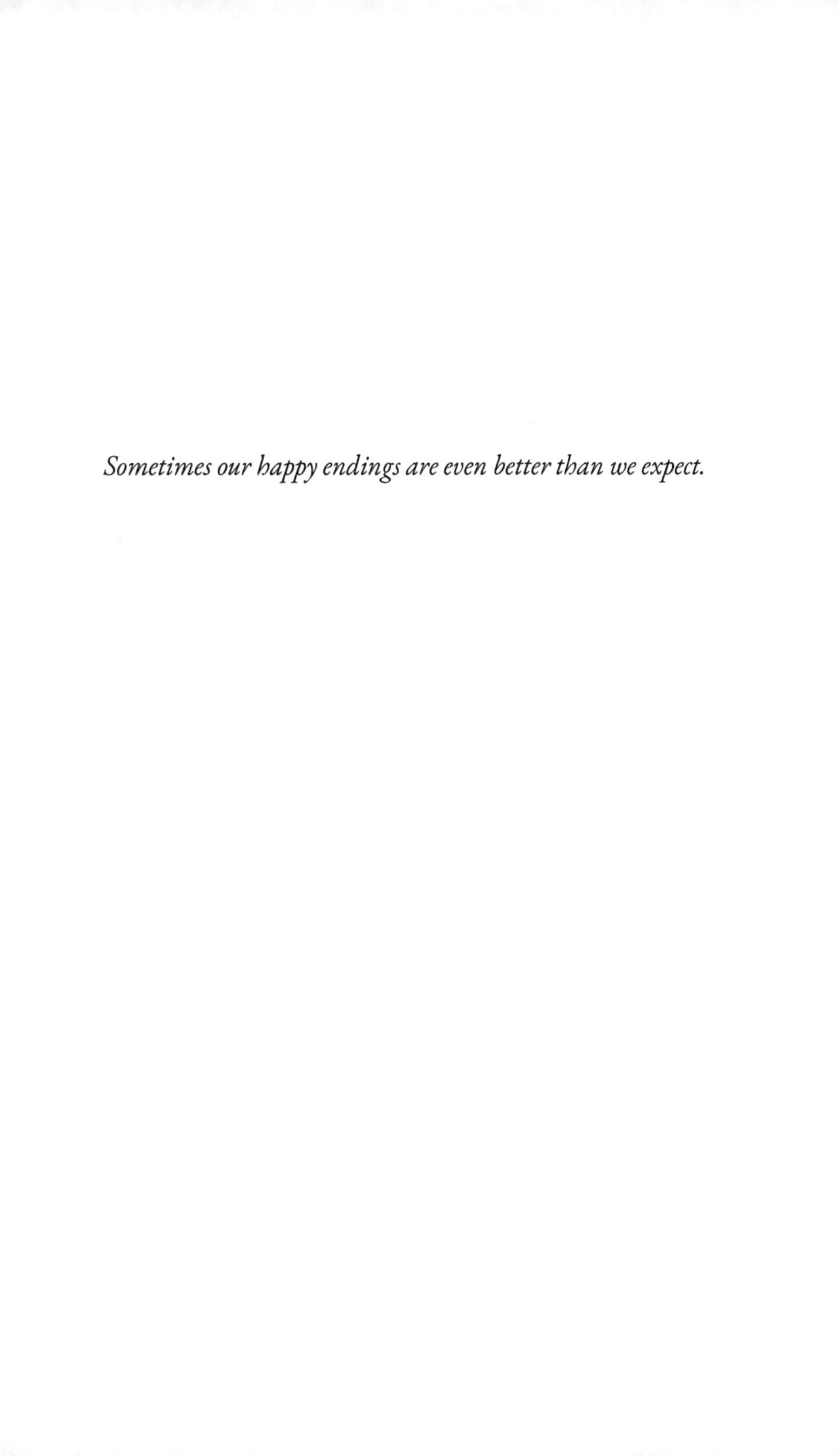

Sometimes our happy endings are even better than we expect.

PETE

The clash of metal permeated the air, sparks of magic coloring the sky gold, white, gray, and black. It made a visual effect that would have been fascinating to watch had Pete not been fighting for his life and that of the others.

"Enough!" a male's voice boomed, and their opponents pulled back.

Pete steadied his drawn shadows but kept them present. The others stepped back in defensive stances, even Crimson, who looked like a dark angel. Wisps of hair the shade of deep ruby had fallen loose, and her eyes were a lush green rife with seduction. He'd noticed her seductive power in the last wave of her magic, several soldiers falling prey to it before falling to Bormick's fatal blow.

Bormick cut down the closest soldier right as they'd stopped fighting.

"Bormick," Pete chastised.

"What? Why are we listening to some random command?"

It was a good question. Pete glanced at Skye and Mark, who shrugged. A web of deep colors encircled Skye, like ribbons dancing around her, a distinct stream of gold within them. Shimmers of it bounced through her auburn hair, so that she looked like a goddess standing among them. The golden flecks in her eyes sparkled, a sight that juxtaposed the deadly intent they carried, and as always, he was glad he was on her side.

"You followed my command because it saved you."

The fighters parted for a tall, toned man with blonde hair and golden eyes to walk through. Like the king Bormick had just killed, he reminded Pete of someone who'd spent his days surfing on the California shores. A gold robe adorned his shoulders, the tight white tunic below left untied to reveal his tanned chest. It was an arrogant look that irked Pete and caused him to dislike the man instantly.

"I beg to differ on that," Bormick said, looking at the piles of bodies that had accumulated.

The man stopped, glancing past Pete's shoulder after giving him an appraising look.

"I must thank you. I've been trying to find a subtle way to kill my father for ages, and you've done it for me. And in such an elegant fashion, very fitting for the old man."

Elegant? Pete thought, glancing back at the blood-soaked floor splattered with half the man's organs.

"Elegant is an interesting term," Crimson said, voicing his thought.

The man's eyes turned to her, taking her in. Pete noticed Bormick tense, he doing the same.

"And you must be Crimson. Fiery hair, seductive eyes, and lips any man would want around him."

Bormick growled, stepping in front of her.

"And Bormick of Digremile, renowned thief and killer. Now protector of the Kingdom of Apendia and lover to the queen."

"Who are you, and how do you people know so much about us?" Skye asked, turning his attention.

"And Skye, daughter of the greatest Mage Warrior before her, true daughter of Death's Mistress. Power to rival any others. I do apologize for my father's mishandling of you recently." He stepped closer to her, but Mark blocked his way. "I won't hurt her, Markhem, Commander of the infamous Elite, first of his line to mate with a Mage Warrior. Your strength is unparalleled because of it. But she"—he looked around at Skye again—"has changed. There is gold in your eyes, my dear, gold that belies the true power you now have."

"No thanks to you and your people," Pete said. "Now answer her question."

The man's eyes narrowed at Pete, then studied him. "I am Taenom, next in line for the throne of Upendum, which you have just handed to me, Peter, lost heir to the Digremile Kingdom. Found only recently with his distant cousin. The true son of the Death God, lover to the Crimson Queen. All three of you tied by blood that makes you indestructible when together, yet incredibly vulnerable when you are not. Well, at least the two of them. You are a king bowing down to the others."

The words were simple yet powerful and true. They all knew it, and it was a tightrope he and Bormick walked regularly.

"Content to stay hidden in his shadows when he rules those shadows."

"Why did your father attack our kingdoms?" he asked, ignoring the comments.

"Come, I'd like to show you something." Taenom turned, the soldiers and mages all scattering as he walked by confidently.

"We don't follow commands from you," Mark said, his weapon still drawn.

Taenom looked over his shoulder. "Please, follow me. I promise you no harm."

"Says the man whose army attacked our realms and annihilated an entire race," Bormick muttered.

"What do we do?" Crimson asked.

"Go home," Bormick said.

Pete glanced at Mark and Skye, knowing they were likely thinking the same as he was.

"I think we need to follow," Skye said, the gold in her eyes bouncing in the navy, the sight calling to that part of him that needed to fix it.

"Agreed," Mark added. "As much as I dislike the idea, we need answers."

Pete lowered his power further but left it active. He knew the others could still see it in his aura, and that he was making a clear statement. He took the first step, leading the others out and following Taenom. The prominent white walls and gold features followed through the building, irritating his senses. Strangely, it was like an affront to his magic, to his shadows.

Taenom led them through what appeared to be a great hall, then out onto a wide terrace. The long gold robe he wore dragged behind him in waves.

"He pushes one of us and I'll take his head," Bormick said, no humor in his tone, something Pete would have found strangely sexy if he weren't so tense. He would let Crimson relieve his tension later, if there was a later.

"This is Upendum," Taenom said, gesturing at the glorious city before them.

Buildings of white and gold lay scattered throughout the city, spreading out into the countryside. From this vantage point, it seemed they could see for miles. Everything was lush with life. The sky was still cloudless, almost idyllic. The kingdom was a little too perfect. To their right lie sandy beaches, aqua water sparkling in the sun, a gentle surf pushing against the shore. It really was beautiful.

"Is that the ocean?" Crimson asked.

"Yes," Pete answered. "Have you never seen an ocean?"

"No, never. Your kingdom and Theodore's landlock mine, and I never bothered to explore your kingdom."

The look on Bormick's overwhelmed face led Pete to think he

had never seen the ocean either. After having spent every summer at the shore growing up, the thought of never having seen the ocean seemed strange, but this was another world, one where families didn't pack up the car and go to the shore for the week.

"This is beautiful, but what does it have to do with us? And how does it explain why you viciously attacked our kingdoms?" Skye asked, the sound of her voice strangely melodic. It stoked something in him that gave him pause before he pushed it aside.

"Do you know where we are, Skye? Do any of you, for that matter?"

"No, I followed the memory of leaving this place from when you and your people so kindly kidnapped me and manipulated my magic. The portal brought us here."

"As I presumed. We have watched your realms as far back as anyone can remember. Watched as the magic of your world thrived, waiting for any threat."

Pete raised a brow in surprise and caught Mark's reaction to the words. They confirmed what Taenom's father had spouted from his ugly mouth before Bormick had killed him.

"Your magic was weaker, your Mage Warriors a minimal threat. As the royal line developed, however, the gifts grew with each generation until they flourished with your mother. We paid more attention then, knowing her abilities were the strongest, but she did not appear to be a danger to our realm, and so we remained vigilant, prepared in case she changed. We watched as your world tore its magic apart with war, your mother confirming with her last spell that we'd been correct. She saved you all that day. You see, we knew of your birth, Skye. We knew the power you held; we could sense it. Realm Walkers recognize other Realm Walkers."

"Realm Walkers?" she asked.

"Those who can traverse the realms, defying the veil between those realms. You are a Realm Walker, and with your return, we took notice. We considered your world to be no threat when you disappeared. You were locked far away, your gifts imprisoned until you returned, cracking the veil and destabilizing it."

"Why not attack then?" Mark asked.

"My father wanted to, but I persuaded him to have patience. Her act served a purpose, putting the Death God in his place and, for a time, things went quiet. For years, there was nothing. But we continued to watch, knowing the Death God had claimed his Mage Warrior."

Pete saw Mark bristle.

"Knowing that with each visit to the Shadow Realm, her power grew. She was crossing the veil. Moving through with ease to his realm and to the human realm."

"How could you know all that? No one but Mark knew I visited Crimson and only a select few knew of my time in the Shadow Realm."

Pete could feel the anger in her, it sat like a faint crest of power over her, caressing his own.

"We have our ways."

"What's the point to this story other than to inform us that our security is lax?" Mark asked gruffly.

"The point is, we have taken notice. These two have changed the tide for you. I was able to placate my father before, but now your power has tipped. The Death God and his shadow gods have too much influence and the power you hold is now a threat to the realms, a more lethal one."

"Why are we a threat?" Pete asked.

Taenom eyed him before turning to look upon his kingdom. "The divide between the realms is a fragile thing. One that almost collapsed the two times Skye bled your realm. The Upper God does not like his brother in the Shadow Realm. When the Death God and his mistress created your realm, our god created ours."

"Our god? We have the same gods," Bormick said.

Taenom laughed. "Our god disliked his brother so much he created our realm within a separate veil. You are no longer in your world, you are now in mine. Her ability to traverse the realms is so strong that none of you even noticed the trip through the veil."

"A different world?" Pete asked, his mind spinning.

Taenom turned back to them. "The Upper Realm bridges our world and the one above it, our realm sits between the Upper Realm and yours. Your realm is a divide between the Shadow Realm and us. The Shadow Realm is situated behind the veil of what your human world calls hell where their brother sits, and so on. Each layer of worlds is separated by a veil that only she"—he pointed to Skye—"holds the power to traverse and to destroy. A pure bloodline from the Death God."

"No, I'm Eliana's daughter, not Derrant's."

"So familiar with the gods that you use their names? Even more reason for us to worry. You know your statement is false. Death's Mistress may have created your line, but the Death God has marked you. He has manipulated your magic. The Shadow King's magic sits within you as well, claimed and owned by your powers so that his shadows are now married to yours." Married was a strange term to use, and Pete didn't like the implications the man was insinuating with the statement. "Alone you posed a threat that warranted extermination but with two of you, it was guaranteed." He stepped closer to Pete. "Two direct lines, one from the mistress but claimed by the Death God, one directly from the Death God. Even on your own, Peter, you need extermination."

Pete furrowed his brow. "Why? Because you fear what you don't know? I pose no threat to your realm, nor does Skye."

"Nor do I," Crimson added.

Pete hadn't meant to leave her out, to only include Skye with himself, and furrowed his brow, pondering why he had.

Taenom glanced at her. "No, you don't. You are no longer direct lineage. The gods stripped your line of its original magic and what you now hold within you is a warped version of the magic you took from Skye. Your magic does not come directly as theirs does. Well, as theirs did."

"You changed Skye's magic," Bormick said. "That's why you took her."

"Sharper than you look. Yes, we flushed out her connection to the Death God, replacing it with the magic of the Upper God."

"You thought you did," Skye said, crossing her arms. Pete couldn't help but notice how the move accentuated her breasts.

"We were wrong, his grip was too strong, your tie to the others too close but now you no longer have pure, undiluted magic from the bloodline."

"What did you do to her?" Mark asked.

"I'd like to say we did that, but we didn't. Your body clung to some of the magic we gave you, diluting your connection to your sire's magic, morphing it into something we have not seen. The addition of the shadow magic that rescued you makes your magic potent."

"And now I'm a threat again?"

"Very much so, as is the only remaining pure blood. Peter."

"But Bormick is from the same line," Pete argued.

"Warrior blood runs through his veins, not the shadow blood that passed through your line."

"So if Skye and Pete are a threat, why are you talking to us and not fighting us?" Mark asked.

"Curiosity, I suppose. We have watched from afar. We had the ability to learn, especially when we captured Skye, but my father insisted we annihilate your realm, that we make her a weapon, that we would kill her once the rest of your people were dead."

"That seems more of a Death God approach than the Upper God," Crimson noted.

"Yes, it was, but you must understand, Realm Walkers are a threat to every realm created. Ours are not the only gods. Each world has its own, some with just one or two gods, some with multiple, like ours. The gods across all worlds have an understanding that the veils are not to be crossed. If so, it is a threat to every world and every god's creation."

"I can't traverse realms like Skye can," Pete said.

"And I can traverse them," Crimson added.

"No, you cannot. You have access to the Shadow Realm, but only through the Death God's mark. Your mate, however, has the ability. He simply has yet to access it."

Pete didn't know what to say. He knew there were many aspects of his magic he had yet to explore, but that hadn't been one he'd considered.

Taenom leaned back against the rail and crossed his arms. "I suppose we should be grateful the two of you didn't mate."

"Us?" Pete said, gesturing to Skye.

"Yes. Imagine a child with direct blood from both the Death God and his mistress. In our form, it would put your dragons to shame. It would be an interesting thing to witness indeed."

"I guess it's a good thing then," Mark snapped. Pete could tell the comment had grated on his nerves from the grimace on his face. It hadn't exactly settled right with Pete, either.

"I think we've heard enough," Mark said sharply. "Your realm attacked ours without provocation."

"Oh, but I assure you there was provocation. You should thank your gods that I had my father's ear, else you all would have died years ago, and the Shadow King would have remained in the human realm, trapped and powerless. As it is, I saved all of you."

"Thanks, I guess? That still doesn't bring the kingdom you slaughtered back or the wizards you murdered."

"War has a cost, Markhem. You, of all people, should know that."

"We're leaving," Bormick muttered.

"I beg to differ. You are guests and as so will stay with me as we...work out a peaceful agreement."

"Agreement?" Crimson asked.

"That is what you came here for, correct? Or did you come with the intent of killing my father?"

It was true, they'd come to negotiate and set some sort of treaty. Bormick had crossed the line and taken the king's life.

"We did," Skye said.

"Well then, I will have you shown to your room, and we will convene for a meal once you've rested."

"I don't think we need to rest," Mark argued.

"Perhaps not, but I have my father's dead body to deal with and a kingdom to take control of. I need time."

He gestured to a soldier behind them.

"Take them to the guest wing. Oh, and I would advise against trying to portal home to your realm." His eyes grew a shade darker. "You'll find that ability is dampened here."

He brushed past them before any of them could respond. The soldier walked on to lead them, but they remained in place, looking at each other.

"Do we follow?" Mark asked.

"I don't think we have a choice," Pete answered.

"Agreed," Bormick said.

Against every instinct, he followed.

MARK

Mark's instincts were on edge, his muscles taut with nerves. His one hand gripped the hilt of his weapon, the other Skye's hand. He couldn't figure out how things had turned so quickly. This was meant to be a quick visit, to show they had the upper hand, and to suggest an offer of negotiation and peace. Perhaps that had been naïve, but with Skye's enhanced power and Pete and Crimson, they'd thought for sure this would go in their favor. But everything had turned. He didn't know whether to beat the shit out of Bormick for killing the king or thank him. Taenom was questionable, and Mark didn't trust him. At least he seemed more agreeable than his father. Seemed, but Mark was tense knowing appearances could be deceiving and he didn't trust the man. It was unlikely that his realm had declared war on theirs and suddenly he'd had a change of heart.

The guard showed them to a spacious room, depositing the five of them and leaving.

"We're sharing a room?" Bormick asked. "This might be fun, after all."

"We're not sharing a room," Mark said. "Skye, Pete, can either of you create a portal?"

"He said we wouldn't be able to," Pete answered. "I've been trying since he left us."

"Shit. Skye, anything?" he asked.

She drew hues from their clothing, the room too bland and white. They circled her body, but each time she tried to focus them to create a portal, they scattered.

"Nothing," she replied, returning the hues.

"We're trapped," Bormick said. He looked out of the window. "And there's no way down there. We're too high."

"How did we get so high?" Pete asked, joining him.

"Magic," Crimson answered. "Can't you feel it, Pete? It's all over my skin, like it's in layers throughout this place."

"I feel it," Skye said. "It must be why we can't get home."

Mark glanced around the room. "I wonder if it's something in the building or their entire realm?"

Bormick walked to a chair and sat, propping his feet on the trunk before him.

"Looks like we're stuck together. What do you say we put some stains on this pretty white furniture?"

"Is that all you think about?" Mark asked, confounded by his lack of concern.

"Most of the time. I know what you're thinking, Mark. You and I have the same warrior mentality, it's what makes us good soldiers. There is no way out of this until we know more. And they're not giving us more. So, for now, we play their game."

Crimson hiked her skirts and straddled him. "Sounds good to me. I like games."

"Really?" Pete said, shooting them both an irritated look.

"Really, Pete. I'm a bit spent from all the killing and could use a refill," Bormick replied.

Mark rolled his eyes, but not before they caught the curve of Crimson's bare leg as Bormick slid his hand up her dress. The sight caused a reaction with which he wasn't entirely comfortable.

"This reminds me of a hotel suite," Skye said, drawing his eyes away, the pair ignoring the others in the room. "Do you remember the one we stayed in that time we all went to Florida?"

"How could I forget? I had to listen to Sam and you each night. Not sure why I agreed to subject myself to that," he grumbled, not caring to think back on it.

"You had to listen to her with another man? Yet you won't share her with us?" Bormick asked, his hand now down Crimson's dress.

"Different situation, Bormick," Skye said. "Besides," she said, leaning into Mark, her eyes dusky, the gold specks sparkling, "it was you I thought about each time."

"So, if you fuck me and think about Mark, it'll make it all right?" Bormick tried again.

Skye threw him a look, and Mark couldn't help but laugh.

"So, there are two rooms, and this is like a common room," Pete said, ignoring them all. He was looking into one of the separate rooms.

"What if she fucks Pete instead? Will that be easier? What was it that weird guy said? It's good the two of them weren't mates? Makes me curious to watch."

"Oh, I was thinking the same thing," Crimson added, her eyes lighting with excitement.

Mark gritted his teeth.

"I love how you both pawn me off as if I'm nothing to you," Pete said, and Mark could hear the frustration in his voice. Mark sensed something more that layered his voice but couldn't quite put a name to it. Taenom's words had irked Mark, and he hadn't liked the implication in them—the thought of Skye with Pete.

Crimson stopped kissing Bormick and rose, Bormick giving a disappointing grunt. She moved to Pete, the arm of her dress still pushed down, the curve of her breast exposed. Bormick licked his fingers and gave Mark a sly smile, his erection proudly pushing against his pants. For a moment, Mark wondered what she tasted like. He'd never tasted her, an act that had seemed too intimate.

He pushed the thought away, feeling Skye lean into him and hoping she hadn't sensed his reaction. Unsure where the thought had come from or why it had stirred his arousal, he wrapped his arm around her waist.

"Pete, you are everything to me—to us," Crimson purred, pushing against him.

He gave her a look of doubt that was quickly erased when she kissed him.

Bormick jumped up. "All right, we're going to rest as they instructed us to do. If you two care to play, you know where to find us."

He grabbed Crimson by the waist and hoisted her up.

"Hey!" Pete protested.

"Come on, Pete," Bormick said, taking her in the room, Crimson's giggles prominent. "I'll let you have her fist, and then this curvy ass is mine."

Pete rubbed his face, seeming torn for a moment before glancing back at Mark and Skye, his gaze lingering a split longer on Skye. He shrugged and closed the door behind him.

Mark looked at Skye. Her brow was pinched, and he could see she was thinking about something. He didn't know if it was their situation or Pete's lingering gaze that had her puzzled. The latter had Mark concerned, and he didn't like the possibilities that gaze, or her reaction to it held.

"Skye?"

Her blue eyes met his, rich and heavy with emotion. He brushed a strand of her hair back, wondering at it, then at the strange thought he'd had about Crimson. His hand slid below her hair, and he pulled her to him, his lips meeting hers.

"What do we do now?" she asked, dropping her head.

"I suppose I take you into that room and make love to you, ignoring the surrounding threat and...praying you don't have another man's face or body on your mind while I do."

She picked her head up, narrowing her eyes at him.

"Just saying, since Pete's apparently your perfect mate."

"Are you serious right now?"

"Absolutely. You heard what Taenom said."

"And because of that, you now think I'm better suited for Pete, that it's not you I love, you I want?"

"He's more like you, Skye." She pushed at his chest. "You can't tell me you haven't thought about it."

"Why are you doing this, Mark? Because I can call you out on every gaze that drops to Crimson's breasts or follows her curves when she walks. Do you really want to go there?"

"So you do—"

She placed a finger on his lips. "We've been through this and we're not going through it again. There will be no sharing, no swapping, not any of that."

"Didn't answer my question, Skye."

Her eyes held a lethal quality that stirred his blood.

"What is going on with you?"

"I don't know. Maybe it's this place."

"Well, stop."

Crimson's cries broke past the door, sending an unexpected rush of stimulation through him. Skye's brow furrowed, and he knew she sensed it.

"Are you trying to alleviate your own attraction to Crimson by making there be something between Pete and me?"

"No," he said quickly, not sure what was wrong with him.

She pushed her body against him. "Do you want her again, Mark?"

"No, I don't. I only want you." But he heard the slight lie behind the words, knowing she was right and that his eyes had strayed. He gripped her waist tighter, anger burning in him for his reaction to Crimson's cries. That anger was at its height, having grown since the insinuation Taenom had made earlier and from the look Pete and Skye had shared. It was churning through him like a vicious storm looking for release.

Skye's eyes were dangerous, the dark of her own irritation in them. The look broke the hold he had on his emotions. He pulled her lips to his and kissed her with a fierce passion, feeling the angst in her as she kissed him back. Slamming her up against the wall, he ground into her, spreading her legs roughly with his thigh, his fury releasing.

She didn't object, her own moves aggressive as she ripped at his shirt, pulling it over his head. She grabbed at him, her nails digging into his skin and further stimulating his arousal. Capturing her mouth again, he roughly ripped the ties of her dress, exposing her breasts, the dress falling as he lifted her. His skin met hers and a moan tore from him. A fire was blazing through him, one only she could calm.

She'd undone his buttons, freeing his length that had been pressing to reach her. Her strokes were firm and needy, and they sent the flames within him soaring. In a frenzy, he lined himself up and thrust into her, grunting at the wetness that greeted him. Her cry was loud and uninhibited, urging his pounding on. The emotion between them was heated, brought on by their conversation. His moves were fueled by that emotion, bringing an intensity to them that burned through him like a raging inferno.

She dropped her head to his, kissing him with a demanding force. The wall shook each time he drove into her, pounding her hard against it. As her legs tightened, she clenched around him; the feel inching him closer until she climaxed suddenly. Her body shook, spasming around him in a way that broke him. Release raked him so powerfully that he could barely move, his mouth stifling the scream she'd had as his own groan reverberated in his chest.

He rested his head against hers while they caught their breath.

"Gods, Crimson said you two were intense, but that's hardly a good word for it," he heard Bormick from behind them. "Nice ass Mark. Skye, those legs could bring an army to its knees."

Mark met her eyes, and she shook her head. They both looked over at him.

"Jesus, Bormick," Skye whispered, dropping her head again.

He was buck naked, his hand on his very erect dick.

"What? Pete sent me out to check on the loud crash." He gestured to a pedestal that had been against the wall. The stone figure on it was smashed to pieces on the marble floor.

"Oops," Skye said.

"Hey, if you want to wrap those pretty legs around me and relieve this, I won't object," he said. "I'd let Mark watch."

"Go have Crimson relieve it, or better yet, Pete," Mark muttered, lifting Skye a little more and walking her to the other room, her legs still clinging around him.

"She already did, and Pete's busy. Oh, well, guess I'll have to push my way in. Too bad, Skye. I pound harder and rougher."

Mark slammed the door with his foot and tossed her on the large bed centered in the room. She laughed and gestured for him, her eyes ravenous.

"Do I need to worry about Bormick now, too?" he asked, climbing atop her. "You look awfully hungry still."

"Did you ever think I'm hungry for you?"

"All the time," he said, grunting as she wrapped her hand around him and stroked him back to his full length. "But I wonder if you're not thinking of tasting off the menu."

She squeezed him, and he flinched. "And I wonder if you want me to, so you have an excuse."

He glared at her.

"Is that what it is, Mark?"

"Why do you always push toward that, Skye? We've been through this before."

"We have, but you're pushing an awful lot today. What's going on?"

"Fuck," he said, moving from her. "There goes my hard-on."

"Really? It still looks pretty big to me," she said, climbing onto him. "What's going on, Mark?"

"Nothing, Skye."

She narrowed her eyes. Shifting downward, she kissed his neck, then his chest, licking his nipple and pulling it between her teeth. Her tongue slid across his abdomen, licking each indent.

"Talk to me, Mark." Her hand encased him again, firmly with ownership, and he groaned. "Are you thinking about Crimson, Mark?"

"Shit, Skye—" She moved her mouth lower. Her hand continued its motion while her tongue tormented him, making its way down his body.

"Tell me the truth." Her tongue dipped lower.

"Only if you do," he replied, gritting his teeth at the mounting pleasure. "Were you thinking about Pete?"

She stopped, her eyes lifting. "Why do you want me to think about Pete?"

"Because I saw how he looked at you. He has power that matches yours. He's good-looking, built, and powerful."

She sat up, and he instantly regretted saying anything, missing her touch. He longed for her mouth to return to his skin.

"You're all those things."

"And you're everything that Crimson is, yet you still asked me. Why do you want me to think about Crimson?"

Her expression changed, a slight sadness behind her eyes.

With his hands wrapped around her hips, he said, "Skye, we went through this, remember?"

"I don't want to share you, but a part of me wants you to have her, to get her out of your system."

She couldn't be serious.

"And what happens if I do? What happens if we trade? You spend a night with Pete; I spend it with Crimson. What does that accomplish?"

"Where does Bormick go?"

"Nowhere near you!"

Her eyes lightened with her laugh. "But you're okay with Pete touching me?"

"I trust him more."

She rolled her eyes.

"You didn't answer my question, Skye?"

He was hoping she'd move past it so he could. They'd been through this so many times, and each time he thought they had put it behind them. And it had seemed that way...until they'd stepped into this realm. Now the thoughts were back.

Thinking about having sex with Crimson was keeping him hard. The temptation was there—where it hadn't been since she'd forced herself on him and had broken him. It bothered him that the thoughts had rooted in his mind, and he couldn't seem to free himself from them. He wanted her body, wanted to take her aggressively, just as he had all those years ago. But he didn't understand why. There had never been a sexual longing there; he'd hated her for so many years. But maybe that hatred was because he'd hated himself for cheating on Skye and for enjoying it. Because the truth was, he had enjoyed it.

Dammit, he thought to himself.

Skye still hadn't answered the question. Maybe it didn't need an answer. There was a possibility that he was pushing her to Pete because he was feeling guilty about these new thoughts. But no, he'd seen it, seen her reaction when Taenom had said they should have mated. There was a catch to her breath. He'd seen the way Pete's eyes took her in each time they saw him. No matter how much any of them denied it, it was there.

He couldn't blame him. Skye was gorgeous, breathtaking even. Most men looked at her and desired her, but she was his. No other man had posed a threat, until now.

"It wouldn't accomplish anything," she finally said. "Tell me you love me, Mark."

He furrowed his brows. "You need to ask? I love you, Skye. I will always love you, have always loved you. You are my mate. There is no other who will ever hold my heart."

She smiled, leaning down to kiss him, his body responding to her immediately as it always did.

"I love you, Mark. No matter what happens, no matter what trials we face, I will always love you."

"And your heart?"

She laughed against his lips. "Is yours as it always has been."

She kissed him again, then proceeded to retrace her original path until her mouth found him. She brought him to climax again, and as always, nothing he'd ever experienced before her compared. All thoughts of Crimson faded as he took her again, making love to her. Their bodies were as one, trembling against each other with each climax then repeating as if they couldn't satisfy their hunger for each other.

BORMICK

ormick chuckled as he watched the door slam. Mark and Skye were on another level, their emotions making them almost volatile. There was no coming between the two of them, just as there was no coming between him and his mates. But there was a shift in the air, the auras that had finally settled upon Pete and Skye were shifting. Crimson's had settled and remained unchanged, but there was something happening to the other two and Bormick didn't know how to read it.

Bormick could tell Mark sensed it. But he didn't know what exactly it was. He hadn't noticed a difference until they'd been talking with Taenom. That man was another matter to deal with, as was the predicament they were in. There was a chance that a connection existed between Taenom and what was going on between the others, but he didn't have any proof to substantiate that suspicion.

Returning to his room, he found Pete and Crimson still at it. Pete was in a mood, his aura surrounding him, but that strange drift toward Skye was still there, the same he'd seen in Skye. They were pulling toward each other, and Bormick wasn't certain why or what it could mean for the five of them. Their draw to each other had clearly disturbed Mark, and Bormick was thankful Mark didn't have his ability to see the auras or things would be even tenser.

Pete pounded into Crimson. She was in the midst of crashing from her orgasm, and Pete was taking her hard. He'd been demanding the entire time, refusing to take the submissive role he usually took with Bormick. Bormick had been the aggressor earlier that morning, even if Pete had left him trembling in the shower. The prick had made him come back-to-back, something he'd never experienced but had thoroughly enjoyed.

Pete cried out, his magic enshrouding the room as Crimson climaxed with him again. Bormick watched in anticipation, ready for a turn. He'd give Crimson a break, maybe play with Pete a little more. He liked him when he was aggressive. The magic in the air clung to him, heavy and thick with darkness. It was more charged than normal. He watched as the magic gathered, pushing at the door.

Pushing toward Skye.

The door rattled as Pete shook with the force of his orgasm. Bormick stepped further toward the door, studying it. The shaking increased until, with a blast, it burst open, exploding at the same time as the door to Skye and Mark's room shattered. The two forces culminated in a ray of dark magic that danced with hints of gold, shards of the doors floating within it until they settled to the ground.

He looked back at Pete, whose eyes were large, a hint of fear behind them. Crimson was still below him breathing hard, but Bormick noted the concern in her expression. He turned back, staring at the debris, his mind reeling at what it signaled. Upon glancing up, he caught Mark's eye as he surveyed the damage, a sheet covering his still-present arousal. Bormick could see the shake in his muscles from his release.

"What was that?" Crimson asked from behind him.

He didn't answer, feeling Pete move next to him. Skye walked behind Mark, a blanket held against her, one that failed to hide the curves below. A spark hit her eyes, something passing through them as they met Pete's.

Mark's face hardened, and he shook his head, backing away and forcing Skye back into the room with him.

"Fuck," Pete muttered.

"Yeah," Bormick said, not sure what else to say or what to make of it. Whatever this was, it wasn't something any of them could control, nor had it been anything he'd seen coming.

OTHER THAN THE clink of silverware, an occasional cough or uncomfortable grumble was the only sound that broke the awkward silence among the five of them as they sat eating with Taenom. That silence had hovered over them since the door-shattering moment and Taenom seemed to be enjoying it as he yapped about his realm. Bormick knew he should be paying attention, but he couldn't get his mind from what had happened and the sight of the auras that were reaching toward each other. Still reaching, hanging in a strange stasis as if trying to touch the other but waiting for something.

Glancing at Mark, he noted the tension, but something else. Mark's eyes flickered toward Crimson, a look of lust in them. Crimson's eyes met Mark's, a gleam shining within them. Her tongue slid along her top lip in a way that would have seduced even the strongest of men.

Bormick stared at them, trying to contemplate what in the gods' names was happening.

Mark averted his eyes quickly, his grimace returning. Bormick wanted to smack Crimson for taunting Mark. It was clear that whatever was happening to Pete and Skye was impacting Mark. He'd been stabbing his food and throwing death stares at Pete the entire time. With Crimson, Bormick couldn't tell what she thought of the situation, although she'd been craving a go with Mark since Bormick had met the man. There was a warped there that had served as a barrier to the five of them working together, but it had lessened over time. They'd developed a comfortable rapport, looking past their histories until now.

He looked over at Skye. She was pushing her food around on her plate, her eyes not moving from it. Pete—sitting next to Bormick—was doing the same thing. For once, he was the odd man out and was thankful for it. Whatever was happening, he was the sane one of the bunch.

He couldn't figure out what had changed between the morning and now. The only variable was this place and Taenom's words about Pete and Skye.

Bormick put his fork down. "Why are we still here?"

"You came to us—"

"Yes, with a simple request to leave us the fuck alone, and now we're stuck in this place."

"Are you?" Taenom asked.

"You made it clear we can't portal home, which we can't. And you have more guards in this castle than any I've seen."

Taenom turned his lips up in a suspicious smile.

"You want us to fight our way out? Because we've been playing nice so far, and I don't much like nice," Bormick continued.

Taenom sat back and clasped his hands. "You are free to leave whenever you want. Well, you three are."

Everyone's head rose at his words.

"What three?" Mark asked.

"You, Crimson, and Bormick."

"I don't think so," Mark said.

Taenom stood. "You came into my realm, murdered my father, slaughtered my troops, and you expect no punishment?"

Mark's chair screeched back as he stood. "You and your father raided our lands, annihilated an entire race, kidnapped my wife, and played with her power. I think that gives us every right to reciprocate."

"As I said, you may go. The purebloods stay with me."

"Purebloods?" Pete asked.

"Yes, you are the direct heir of the Death God, she of his mistress, and I am the direct heir to the Upper God. You see, my father and his line while descended from the gods were not direct relation to the Upper God. I am. My mother's line descends directly from the Upper God."

"So, what do you need us for?" Pete asked.

He didn't answer right away and Bormick could see him thinking. "On second thought, none of you may leave. It's clear you're all tied to one another. It would be a pity to see that break. Sleep well. We can start negotiations when the morning comes."

"I don't think so," Bormick said.

"Tell me, Bormick. What is it that holds the five of you together? I sense tension that has lingered for a long while. Whatever binds you is teetering on that very precariously positioned tension. Do you feel it tingling?"

He walked away, leaving the five of them, his guards following. Bormick crossed his arms, his mind stewing. The man was playing some kind of game that Bormick couldn't grasp. There was more to all of this, and they were playing right into his hands.

Taenom's words hung in the air long after he left, the five of them sitting quietly. Bormick didn't know what to say. Taenom was right, there had always been tension that sat precariously positioned. One tip and they'd either be at each other's throats or in each other's beds. Taenom's observations left him with the overwhelming thought that this place, and whatever the reason for their being here, was the tipping point.

Skye was staring at her plate again, but Mark met Bormick's eyes.

"What is it you feel, Bormick, that we don't?"

"I think you know exactly what I see and feel, Mark. It's the same reason those doors shattered, the same reason your wife won't lift her eyes from her plate. The same reason you're having trouble keeping yours from Crimson—"

"I'm not—"

"Yes, you are. Those two are the key here, but you two aren't unaffected."

"There's no key, Bormick," Pete argued.

"Always in denial, Pete. I hate to tell you, but that denial will not work any longer."

"I'm not denying anything."

"The hell you're not," Mark said, slamming his cup in an angry motion. Liquid splashed over the rim in sloshes.

"Mark—" Skye tried, finally lifting her eyes.

"No. I want to know why he was so keen on keeping the two of you here, and why he's obsessed with the notion that you two are purebloods, somehow connected."

"Because they are, and this place and whatever is going on here is calling on that connection. I just haven't figured out why."

"You think there's something …" Skye started, her eye wide as she looked up at him.

She didn't finish, but Crimson did.

"Something driving you two to fuck?"

Skye's cheeks turned a delicate shade of pink which made her even more alluring. For a moment, jealousy slithered through him, his teeth grinding at the thought that fate was drawing Skye to Pete and not to him. But then it faded. As much as he'd love to pound that glorious body, Skye was too delicate for him. There was something otherworldly about her that left him with a sense of awe and a need to protect her, to guard her. Ever since he'd jumped to save her that day, it had been present. No, he would never have the satisfaction of touching her, but he would die protecting her, just as he would for any of his mates.

Silence hung in the air. Crimson's words were like a strange reality check that spoke a truth none of them could avoid. No matter how he feared it would reshape their lives.

SKYE

Skye stared at her plate, unwilling to lift her eyes for fear of meeting Pete's. She didn't know what was happening, but she couldn't bring herself to look at him. She was afraid of the reaction it would stir in her.

Crimson's words were like a slap that had jarred something in her. She'd never thought of Pete in that way, never thought of anyone but Mark in that way, but now she couldn't get the thought of his lips on hers, his body on hers out of her mind. Sure, she'd thought he was sexy and had eyed him at times, had been drawn to his power and the way it seemed to caress her when it met her own. She remembered the feel of his magic when she'd claimed it, and how she'd let it pull her from her prison as it had embraced her. Pete's magic had layered the kiss Crimson had given her. She'd craved more, seeking the essence of Pete within it. There had been a need to experience the real touch of his kiss, of his hold through the magic.

Perhaps there had been something there, but not anything she wanted to admit or own. No matter what had been there before, this was something on an entirely different level.

Mark was tense beside her. She'd caught the look at Crimson earlier. There was more to this tension than Pete. She gnawed her cheek, wondering what was going on with them and not liking where her thoughts took her.

Mark rose, and Skye lifted her eyes, inadvertently meeting Pete's. That wave of arousal swept through her again. His eyes reflected the same until he looked away. She forced her eyes from him and they landed on Crimson whose eyes were following Mark.

Crimson! she yelled in her head.

Crimson turned her eyes to Skye. *What?*

Stop lusting after Mark.

Crimson's lips curved upward deviously. *Only if you stop ogling Pete.*

I'm not—

Are you lying to me or to yourself? I'm always up for a trade, Skye. I would love to feel Mark's cock inside of me again.

Skye glared at her, but Bormick came behind Crimson, scooping her neck up to look at him as he gave her a deep kiss. His hand cupped her breast as he did. "Stop tormenting Skye."

"But it's so fun," she cooed.

"Save the tormenting for me."

He kissed her again, his fingers digging below the fabric and eliciting a low purr.

"We should go," Mark said, and she tore her eyes from them to meet his, noting the guilt behind them. She flicked her gaze lower, spying the bulge in his pants, and raised a brow. They had just talked about this. Yet it wasn't just him. She was just as guilty.

Crimson's words still hung in the air, no one daring to address them, as if ignoring them would erase them.

Skye rose.

"I think that would be wise," she said, walking to him, his attention now solely focused on her.

Desire was in his eyes, desire for her. As she hooked her hand around his neck, bringing his lips to hers, there was no question he was hers. Thoughts of anyone else in the room faded. His hand palmed her lower back, bringing her against him. And just like that, everything was right again.

"Agreed. Whatever Taenom has planned for us is bound to be soon," Bormick said. "Come on, Pete, let's play some."

Mark pulled from her kiss at the mention of Pete's name, his jaw tightening.

"These two need a room again while they work out their issues," Bormick continued. "Unless you two want to see me make Pete a man again."

A flicker of need climbed through her at the thought, but she pushed it aside.

"Fuck you, Bormick."

"Don't worry, Pete, you will."

Mark ignored their banter and opened the doors. Skye's mind continued grappling with images of Pete and Bormick, not certain why the idea turned her on so.

Crimson's voice echoed through Skye's mind. *It's fun to watch them play.*

Mark stopped and turned to her. "What was Crimson tormenting you about?"

You're in trouble now, Crimson teased.

Don't make me hurt you, Crimson.

He crossed his arms, waiting for an answer.

"Really, Mark?" Skye said.

"Agreed. Why don't you two take this to your room and break a few more pieces of furniture?"

"Shut up, Bormick." She wondered at the tone of Pete's voice, at the mix of annoyance and jealousy.

"Really, Skye. If you won't tell me, I'm sure Crimson will."

"Oh, I can tell you all kinds of things, Mark."

Skye shot her a look.

"Oh, get over it, Skye. She was yelling at me for eye-fucking you and I was teasing her for doing the same to Pete."

Mark's jaw tightened, the muscles in his arms tensing. He looked from Skye to Pete, narrowing his eyes. Skye glanced at Pete, who hadn't flinched. His glare at Mark was just as intense.

"That's one way to make this more interesting, Crimson," Bormick said, breaking the silence. "Mark, let it go. Pete, stand down. We're going back to the room so the two of them can fuck their aggression out and the three of us do what we do best. Move Mark. You can think of Crimson while you're pounding Skye, and Pete can think of Skye while his tongue is sinking into Crimson."

Pete broke the stare off and grabbed Bormick, punching him. She didn't have time to see any more. Mark grabbed her wrist and dragged her, catching them up to the guard who was waiting for them.

She heard Crimson scolding the two of them, most of it toward Bormick as they followed the guard. When they were back in the room, no one spoke. She used her magic to repair the door, Pete doing the same. His magic drifted over her skin, leaving the same sensation it always did but heightened.

Mark didn't give her a chance to make it through the door before he was staking his claim on her again. He took her roughly, anger and jealousy fueling his moves and something else that read like guilt. She matched his intensity, the same emotions pummeling her. This time their door stayed intact, although she couldn't help but notice it shake violently again as her climax tore through her.

She lay in Mark's arms long after they were spent, listening to his soft breaths. Finally, tired of waiting for sleep to claim her, she rose, throwing on Mark's shirt and leaving the room. She walked to the open window and stared out at the city below, dark and sleeping, the moon above making long shadows of the buildings.

"You know, if you walk around like that, you'll have me lusting after you, too," she heard Bormick say from behind her.

Jumping slightly, she turned to see him rising from a chair.

"I thought you already lusted after me," she teased.

Since the time they'd been captured together, they'd formed a bond. It was a comfortable friendship where his comments no longer bothered her, and she sometimes played back.

"True. I would never turn down a chance to bend you over and show you how a real man should take you."

"And who says I'm not already shown that?"

"Hmm, I'd say tonight was one of those nights. Mark's anger drive that cadence tonight?"

She cursed the slight flush of her cheeks, thankful for the lack of light in the room.

"Yeah, it did, didn't it?" he answered for her.

She turned back to stare out the window, and he moved next to her.

"There's something not right about this," he said. "Do you feel it, Skye?"

"I don't know what I feel, Bormick." His gaze snapped to her. "Ever since we arrived here, it's all a jumble."

"You love Mark?"

"Of course I do. With every fiber of my being."

"And he loves you. Don't confuse lust for love. You want Pete."

"No, no, I don't—" She heard the lie in her voice. She wanted Pete with a hunger that was growing.

"Yes, you do, and he wants you. He loves Crimson and me, nothing will change that, but he's drawn to you, just like you are to him."

"Just like Mark is to Crimson," she muttered.

"No, that's different, but I haven't figured it out. Those two are definitely feeling some draw to each other, but it's nothing compared to what's happening between you and Pete. It's just strong because the two have a past and both want to experience that again. It's not them I'm worried about."

She let his words sink in, validating what she knew to be true. Mark wanted Crimson—wanted to sleep with her again. It hurt to think about, but she had no place to feel hurt. She wanted Pete to take her, to touch her. She wanted to feel what it was like to have his body against hers, to have him filling her.

"Mark loves you, Skye. That's not at stake. That love will never change, just like it won't for you. Even for the three of us. No matter what happens, there's no breaking the bond me, Crimson, and Pete have."

"Nothing's going to happen. We're going to leave tomorrow, and all of this will go away."

"You can't run from it, Skye. Your world is no longer perfect."

"When has it ever been perfect? There's always something that tries to tear us apart."

"And has anything succeeded?"

She sighed. "No."

"Exactly. Get some sleep, Skye. I have a feeling tomorrow is going to be even harder than today was. Taenom is up to something, and we need to be prepared to fight it, regardless of the fact that we can't portal."

He turned to go, but then glanced back, his blue eyes shining as they took in her exposed legs and the silhouette of her body below Mark's shirt.

"And if you wear something like that again, it won't be Pete that Mark needs to worry about. I promise you I'll fuck you so hard you'll never want to go back to Mark's bed."

He walked away, the comment leaving her breathless. Bormick scared her. He wasn't a gentle man; she knew that from sharing moments with Crimson. He liked it rough. A shiver went through her. She enjoyed it when Mark was rough like he'd been tonight, demanding and forceful. But she had a feeling that would pale in comparison to Bormick. At the thought, she ran back to her room, discarding Mark's shirt and snuggling close to him. His arm automatically found her, protectively wrapping around her and guarding her.

Bormick was right, nothing could ever change the way she and Mark loved each other. Nothing had, not Crimson, not Derrant. Through it all, their love had been constant. And it would remain that way, no matter what they faced.

CRIMSON

Morning came, waking Crimson earlier than Bormick and Pete. She did a long cat stretch, smiling at how Bormick's arm rested on Pete's chest. She turned toward Pete, watching as he slept peacefully. Gods, how she loved this man. Her man...and Bormick's.

He was her soft lover, the gentle one who made her feel like she was his world. But his eyes had wandered, his attention drifting to Skye, and she wasn't certain how she felt about it. She teased to cover the envy. She'd never admit she was jealous. There was no question Skye wanted him. Crimson had noticed it before. The glimpses, the longer eye contact. She'd seen the same in Pete, but he had never admitted it, always denying any attraction to Skye. But now there was something happening between the two of them, and maybe that was what bothered her.

She laid back down and stared at the ceiling, thinking of Pete with Skye. If it made him happy, she'd share. She shared him with Bormick regularly. The more she thought of it, the more she decided it wasn't the act that had her envious. Pete was a god in bed. Why not share that with Skye, as long as she didn't get greedy? It hadn't bothered her when she'd sent the demon Ash to her men, and this didn't bother her.

No, what she didn't like was the strange tie she could sense. Something more than physical need was drawing them to each other, and that gave her pause. Not that anything the two felt mattered anyway. There was no way Mark would ever let Pete touch her. Although Mark's eye had been wandering to Crimson. The thought made the warmth between her legs grow. She wanted Mark again. He'd been equal to Pete and Bormick, even when he'd been pretending. She thought back to him, his body on hers, his length deep within her. A shiver of pleasure drifted across her. Yes, she wanted him again, and that had only intensified since they'd been here.

She rubbed her eyes and looked over at her men. Her body was aching for release after the thoughts of Mark.

Time to take care of that, she thought, climbing atop Pete and urging him awake with her tongue.

He moaned as he grew in her mouth. His hand came to rest on her head, fingers weaving through her hair. Bormick grumbled at the disturbance until he realized what was happening.

"Well, well, someone's thirsty this morning." His hand caressed her ass, his finger exploring her wetness and causing her to buck forward, jerking Pete with her lips.

"Jesus, Crimson," Pete grunted.

She loved when he cursed with his human words. He'd explained them to her, so she knew their significance in that world. Even though they held none here, it still turned her on to hear them.

Bormick mounted her, letting out a pleasured sigh as he slipped into her more gently than he usually did. The grip he placed on her hips was not gentle, however, and she knew he wouldn't be going easy on her. She didn't mind. Where she loved Pete's gentleness, she craved Bormick's power, and he held power in their bedroom. Although Pete hadn't been gentle the previous night. He'd taken her like Bormick and had brought her to the cliff multiple times. His aggressive side didn't come out often, but when it did, she took everything she could from it.

He threaded his fingers into her hair, bringing her attention back to the length she was still holding in her mouth. She took Pete with possessiveness as Bormick slammed into her. As he and Bormick came, her own orgasm flooded through her. It only intensified when Bormick yanked her hair back, forcing her mouth from Pete to his, his tongue taking in the flavor that remained.

The move sent her body lurching in response. She loved the brutal side of him, the one that matched her own. She pulled away, licking Pete clean, then climbing atop him with a wicked grin. His hands caressed her playfully before he reached around her neck, pulling her down to kiss her. It sent her heart soaring, and, once again, she was reassured that whatever happened, he was hers.

She rode him as he and Bormick played, unable to resist the first climax that settled through her while she watched, a second as Bormick could no longer contain his, then another when Pete took her until he could no longer contain his urge for release and joined her.

As she watched him dress, she asked, "Are you going to think of me when you're filling Skye?"

His look of shock quickly transformed to one of annoyance, Bormick's laugh not helping. She dropped her eyes, trying to figure out the strange clothing that had been left for her by Taenom.

"I'm not doing anything with Skye," Pete grumbled.

"Question is, will you be thinking of him while Mark is filling that pretty mouth of yours?" Bormick teased.

"Mmm, probably not," she answered honestly, causing Bormick to laugh harder.

"And you're not touching Mark."

"I touch her," Bormick said.

"That's different," he snapped before storming from the room.

"You're mean, Bormick."

He pulled her close, nipping at her ear. "I just see things the way they are and you're the one who started it. Do I get to watch when you finally get your hands on him?"

"That's never going to happen, Bormick. Skye and Mark won't allow it, nor will Pete. Now stop."

"It will. Those two can't help it, and you two are caught up in whatever it is that's forcing that."

His words stopped her. "You think something's causing this?"

"Yes."

She relaxed, his words diminishing the headache this situation had been giving her. They'd worked hard to get over the past, to put it behind them. This was a stumbling block no one had foreseen. Or maybe they had. There was a sexual tension that surrounded them and heightened when the five were together. Perhaps this was simply forcing things along.

"You two done in there, or are we going to leave without you?" Mark's voice came from the doorway.

Bormick helped her slide the dress on, slipping a few extra feels in as he did, and causing her to giggle. As they left the room, her eyes fell on Skye. She looked gorgeous. The same style dress, wispy and partially see-through at the bottom, sat upon her delicate frame. Light straps held the top up, her cleavage enhanced by their positioning. Her hair had been piled up as Crimson's had been the day before, long brunette locks falling against her neck where her birthmark sparkled violet below the black webs of Derrant's mark. Her eyes were a dusty blue, the golden sparkles highlighted by the rich blue of her dress.

Crimson was tempted to go to her and take her in front of them all—she looked so appealing.

She glanced over to Pete, who was against the opposite wall, staring at the floor, but she knew he'd reacted just as she had. Skye looked like a goddess, like Eliana herself.

She caught Mark's eyes, which were taking in her own appearance, and she saw the shimmer of need. Her dress was identical, but a rich green she knew made the green of her eyes pop and the darkened hue of her red hair more prominent. Where Skye exuded beauty and elegance, she knew she exuded pure sex, the neckline just low enough to enhance her already generous cleavage.

"I see your dress was gone this morning as well," she said to Skye, forcing her eyes from Mark's.

"Annoyingly, yes. Why are you and I dressed similarly?"

Bormick rubbed his hands together. "I think the game is about to begin."

He opened the door, and a chill passed through Crimson at his words. They insinuated there was a reason she and Skye were dressed alike, and that thought sent a mix of fear and excitement through her. She didn't know what awaited them once they left, but if it meant she had to give Pete up to get a taste of Mark again, she'd gladly play the game.

PETE

Walking through the door, Pete kept his eyes on the ground. Mark had purposely positioned himself between him and Skye. The reaction Pete had when he'd first seen her had been unstoppable. The drop of his jaw was unavoidable. She looked like the goddess they'd seen, the same that had tempted him. Only her eyes were a lusher blue than Eliana's, more seductive. He'd leaned against the wall, hoping his erection wasn't too obvious, the thoughts of feeling her lips around it too clear. He was losing it. That had to be it. He'd taken Crimson, making love to her the night before, sharing her with Bormick. That morning, he'd been satisfied multiple times, yet it hadn't stopped the craving for Skye.

He didn't know what had come over him, but all he wanted was to shove Mark out of the way and take her hard against the wall. He wiped his hand over his face, trying to determine what was wrong with him.

They followed the guards down several corridors and finally into a long room. Taenom stood at the end in front of a massive set of open windows. He turned as they approached, the guard standing beside him. Pete's instincts were screaming. Taenom was too calm, too expectant. Pete drew his power, pushing past the others, brushing against Skye and ignoring the sensation that tingled within him.

"Enough of the games, Taenom. We're going home, and you are releasing whatever hold you have on our ability to create portals."

"Impressive, Shadow King. So bold yet still not as powerful as you could be. Your shadows are no threat to me."

"My weapon and his shadows are," Bormick said.

"Against my father, yes, but not me. I guarantee you will regret drawing that weapon."

Pete could feel the tension streaming from Bormick., his adrenaline elevated. Mark, who stood stoically observing, hand on his weapon, gave off the same impression. His muscles were taut, and Pete could see the strain where they pushed against his shirt.

"The gods have determined that judgement is due. The Upper God does not trust you, daughter of the mistress. Nor you, son of her lover. Neither of you is to leave until you have passed their tests and satisfied them."

"Tests?" Crimson asked.

"I gave the three of you a chance, but you refused and now those tests pass to the three of you as well...some of them, at least. Your freedom falls on the shoulders of the Shadow King and his mistress."

A wall rose before them, separating them from Taenom and plunging them into darkness.

"Fuck," Bormick said.

"What the hell?" Skye muttered.

But Pete didn't have time to react before Mark pinned him to the wall. "What did he mean by 'mistress'?" he growled.

Pete stared him down, knowing instinctually what Taenom had meant and not entirely uncomfortable with it.

"He meant me," Crimson said. "Now let him be."

"No," Skye said, her voice barely audible, "he meant me."

Her voice, along with the confession, sent a rush of arousal through him. Mark punched him and Pete's power flared, but he held back, knowing the danger if he let it go.

"I haven't touched her, Mark," he grunted.

"Mark, you know he hasn't," Skye added. "Let him go and use your energy to help us figure a way out of here."

Mark pushed against him once more, then let him go.

Pete shoved him, glaring back at him.

"Skye's right. Pull yourselves together, both of you. You're both guilty regardless of whether this rests on Pete's shoulders. We need to find a way out of here and then you can beat the shit out of each other," Bormick said.

Mark didn't move, and neither did Pete. He could barely see his silhouette in the darkness, but the tension was palpable.

"Can one of you make light? I'm trying, but nothing's working," Crimson said. She sounded flustered, and Pete wondered if it was Skye's words or Mark's aggression that had caused the reaction.

Mark wiped his face before looking back at Skye, then at Crimson. Pete could see the conflict, his eyes now adjusted to the dark completely. He knew what was going through Mark's mind. It was the same that dominated Pete's thoughts. The same conflicted desire laden with guilt and envy.

Mark walked away, brushing past Skye and Crimson to take the lead with Bormick. Walking away from the conflict, the confusion, and leaving Pete with Skye. He turned from her gaze and met Crimson's, her eyes sparkling in the darkness, a glint of excitement in them. So, it had been Mark's reaction that had flustered her. She wanted him. That was who she was. Sex was her power, and this was fueling her. The thought of him with Skye didn't seem to bother her, the thought of getting at Mark again driving her.

She walked over to him as Bormick and Mark walked on and kissed him.

"I love you no matter who touches me and I know you'll love me no matter what," she whispered before skipping away to catch up with the others.

That left Pete alone with Skye. Her eyes were harder to discern in the ebony of their surroundings, the gold flickering in them, but he could sense her arousal, the yearning behind her eyes.

He ran a hand through his hair. "Come on, let's catch up before Mark comes back to kill me."

He took her hand to move her along, the contact washing through him like a current. She pulled her hand away at the same time, her expression one of surprise. This went deeper than any of them realized, and that scared him enough to look away from her. Whatever was happening—if allowed into fruition—would change the five of them forever. He had no doubt about that fact.

Pete pulled the shadows from the space as they walked, letting them encase him, their touch comforting him. It left a dim gray to the space. He moved Skye ahead of him so he could protect her from behind, his eyes falling on the way her dress hugged her hips, her long legs as they moved below the translucent material. A hunger surged through him—a hunger that encouraged him to reach out and slide his hand around her waist to pull him to her, to feel her body against his. He gripped his hands to keep himself from acting on the urge.

He watched as she pulled ribbons of the gray, filling it with a light glow of gold that illuminated the space with a softness. Their powers seemed to complement each other, her ribbons dancing with his shadows until succumbing to them, drawn into them as if they had no choice but to be one with them.

Mark glanced back, scowling.

"Pete, that magic of yours is freaky," Bormick said.

"Well, so are you, Bormick," he replied, wishing the banter would lighten the mood.

A growl cut through the silence that followed.

"What was that?" Crimson asked.

The lit path only encircled them, moving with their movements. It left them blind to what they faced a few feet ahead.

"Maybe that was too much light, Skye," Mark said. "Can you dim it and send some ahead so we can see what that is before it tears us to shreds?"

He drew his weapon, Bormick doing the same as Crimson drew her power. Skye called the grays back from Pete. Her magic left a warm sensation along his skin, like her hands were caressing him. He bit back the catch of his breath, his eyes locking with hers. A delicate pink filled her cheeks only managing to drive his need for her.

Her eyes remained on his as she let the grays flow back to the space, the golden light returning to her. The blue in her eyes sparkled when the gold in them settled. At that moment, he only wanted to kiss her, to push her against the wall, and feel her as he took her. It was an overpowering sensation, and he struggled to clamp it down. No one else noticed the exchange, the growl growing more menacing.

"What the fuck is that?" Bormick asked.

But Pete couldn't look, his attention only on Skye. Her lips parted, lips he wanted to slide his tongue over, then nibble on.

Pull it together, Pete. You're losing it.

Another growl from behind him broke his trance. He swiveled from her, hearing Bormick, Mark, and Crimson fighting ahead of them.

"Pete," Skye whispered, the two of them now separated from the others. "What is that thing?"

"I have no idea."

The growl had come from a doglike creature, fangs as big as Pete's forearm, drool falling from its mouth. It stood on four legs, almost reaching Pete's six-foot, two-inch frame. Its feet were the size of a head, claws barred and ready to maim. Its hide was a deep gold.

Crimson's magic flashed around them as the others fought.

"I guess this one's ours," he mumbled.

The creature moved to pounce, and Pete drew his power, sending his shadows forth. They slammed the creature back to the ground, only to anger it. He hit it over and over, enshrouding it in his power. Skye's magic tingled on his skin, entrancing him, calling to his own magic when it reached under his shadows and pulled at the golden color of the beast.

The beast roared, fighting to escape the prison Pete had created, a stream of gold climbing from it. He watched as the hue darkened the closer it came to Skye, feeling the beast weaken until he finally released his hold on it, and the beast collapsed. With a final bleeding of its hues, it turned to ash.

God, she was powerful. The thought of just how strong she was would have been overwhelming if it weren't such a turn-on to him. Pete heard the collapse of the other beast and turned to see Bormick's weapon impaling it.

"Well, that was fun," Bormick said.

He moved to the beast, drawing his weapon from its hide. Pete and Skye moved to join Mark and Crimson. Mark was standing awkwardly apart from Crimson, and Pete could only guess that similar sensations had occurred with them during the fight. He didn't think it was on the same level, but it was there, and he would have been jealous if not for the arousal that was still not quelled in him.

They were almost to the others when a wall appeared, dividing them. He caught the flash of one separating Mark and Crimson from Bormick as well. The shimmer of a second one drew his eye, and he grabbed Skye from its edge. That tingling sensation coursed through him again along with a heat that formed in his chest. He let her go quickly, looking around.

"Ahh, this can't be good," he heard Bormick say.

"Are you guys still there?"

"We're here, just all separated," Mark said. "Rather conveniently."

"Can you get out, Bormick?" Pete asked while Skye groped around the walls of their prison.

"No, I'm boxed in."

"So are we," he replied. "But the walls aren't that thick if I can hear you so clearly."

"They're thick enough," Mark groused. "I can't penetrate them even with my weapon."

"Nor can I," Bormick added.

Pete tried using his magic, but nothing worked.

"So now what?" Crimson asked.

"I'm not keen on tight spaces," Bormick said.

"Yet you fuck Pete," Mark said snidely.

Pete noticed Skye shudder beside him.

"Nice, Mark. You aiming low now?" he bit back, intrigued by Skye's reaction.

"When I can," he answered.

Pete raised a brow at Skye, who was clearly aroused by the comment. She looked away quickly, leaving his curiosity piqued.

"Wait, there's something happening to my wall," Bormick said.

"Oh, ours, too," Crimson said, excitement in her tone.

"Look." Skye pointed to the wall opposite him. Golden sparkles were lighting shapes, like something was being burned into the wall.

"Words are forming on the wall," Bormick said as Pete noticed the shapes forming letters.

"Will need to be fulfilled," Crimson said, and Pete assumed she was reading the words in the space where she and Mark were.

"I've got the word 'desires'," Bormick said.

"Desires will need to be fulfilled for freedom to be gained," Skye read their words with the others.

"Shit," Mark muttered.

"Seriously?" Pete asked.

There was silence until Bormick said, "Guess I'm the odd man out on this one. Damn, I can't even watch."

"There's nothing to watch," Pete insisted.

"Agreed," Mark said.

"I don't agree with that," Crimson purred.

"Crimson!" Skye yelled.

Crimson's only response was a laugh.

"I don't think you have a choice, any of you. Mark, time to fuck Crimson again. Pete, well, you know what to do with Skye."

The three of them erupted.

"Fine, then don't."

"I'm not touching Skye, Bormick."

"Damn right you're not," Mark replied.

"I love that the two of you get to make decisions about my body," Skye said, putting her hands on her hips. Damn, she was even hotter when she was angry.

"Are you kidding me? You want to fuck him, Skye?" Mark yelled.

"I didn't say that, Mark!"

"You touch her, Pete, and I'll kill you."

"I'd like to see you try, Mark. Besides, you've got my girl in there. You think I want your hands on her again?"

"Don't worry, Petey, I'll play nice with him."

"You're not touching Mark, Crimson," he commanded.

"No, you're not," Skye added.

"You know what they're doing, right?" Bormick interjected. "This is what they want."

The bickering stopped.

"They want us to fall apart. Shit, that's what this has been all along. That's the reason you've had heightened feelings for each other this entire time."

"What are you talking about, Bormick?" Mark asked.

"He gave the three of us an out, then changed his mind. They want to weaken us. We're too strong together, and they know it. All five of us. They know a lot about our past. Why wouldn't they know about the past between you and Crimson, Mark? It's an undercurrent to our relationship, an unstable one. That's what he meant. Our strength lies in us getting along. What better way to weaken us, especially Pete and Skye, who seem to have some magical connection, than to tear us apart? And what better way than with the sexual undercurrent that never fades?"

"There's no sexual undercurrent. There never was until we got here," Pete said, although he wasn't as convinced as he sounded, remembering the words Eliana had whispered through his mind.

"They took what was there and pushed it. This would have happened at some point. It was inevitable."

"No, it wasn't," Skye argued.

"No? Crimson has wanted another piece of Mark since I met her and Mark, as much as you tell yourself you don't want her, you do. All that anger at yourself wasn't because you cheated, it was because you enjoyed it."

Skye's head dropped slightly.

"Shut up, Bormick."

"It's true. Damn, Mark, she's addictive, and no matter how much you love Skye, Crimson will taunt you. Don't you see? The three of you are central to this. All of it rests on you. Crimson and I are the outliers. I don't care if she fucks you, Mark. In fact, I wouldn't mind taking a seat to watch that. Crimson doesn't care if Pete takes Skye, neither do I, and that's definitely one I want to watch. We're both secure in our relationship with him. He doesn't love Skye, and Crimson doesn't love you, Mark. That's why I don't mind, and she doesn't. He'll come back to Crimson because she holds his heart—he's claimed, just like Skye will return to you. The two of you are unbreakable. That's what those fools don't understand. Look at the shit you've been through.

You've already slept with Crimson. Skye's been sleeping with the Death God for years, but you always come back to each other."

He paused, then added. "And Pete, as protective as you are about Crimson, she's still sleeping with the Death God and sending us your tree nymph. It won't hurt us at all. And it won't hurt the two of you."

Silence ensued, and he looked over at Skye's eyes finding acceptance there. A hint of lust was mingled with it, and his breath stuck in his throat at what it signaled.

"Take her, Mark," she said.

Pete's heart pounded in reaction, and he gripped his hands to keep from grabbing her and kissing her. Her eyes never left his, their steady gaze further increasing his heart rate.

"What?"

"You heard me. Take her, kiss her, fuck her. Just do it. I know you want to."

The way she'd said fuck turned Pete on entirely too much and caused a subtle throb in his dick, as if it sensed the turning of the tide.

"I don't want her—"

"Yes, you do. You always have. We joked about it early on and then ignored it as the years went by. I saw the looks, the side glances, even before this. The closer we've gotten, I've seen it. And who can blame you? She's beautiful and alluring with curves in places I don't have them."

She couldn't be serious. Her curves and those long legs could bring a man to his knees.

"You're assuming I'm okay with this," Pete said.

"Ha!" Bormick laughed, causing him to grit his teeth. "How long do you think telling yourself Skye reminds you of your sister will work? I've seen your sister and trust me, no offense, but she is nothing like your sister. You lie to yourself to cover the fact that you want her. She's a fucking goddess, Pete. That's why Mark's so damn overprotective of her. He knows that every man loses control when she walks into a room."

"I don't—"

"Yes, you do," he said.

"Is that true, Pete?" Mark asked. "Have you always before now?"

"No...I..." Had he? Her beauty had always captivated him—the eyes, the lush lips, the body that had no end. "Jesus, maybe," he answered honestly, running a hand through his hair.

"Dammit. Skye—"

"Mark."

The next move rested on the two of them. Pete knew it. They all did. While Pete didn't like the idea of Mark with Crimson, he knew she loved him, knew she'd have fun, and that she would be in her element. He shared her with a god. It couldn't hurt to share her with Mark. And if Skye and Mark obliged, he wouldn't hesitate to take Skye, to push her against the wall and pound her into it...or maybe he wouldn't. Maybe he didn't want to be rough with her, but instead wanted to experience her slowly, repeatedly.

"Crimson, be gentle with him."

"Dammit, Skye."

"I will, as long as you make my Pete happy."

"Skye—"

"Mark, take her like I know you want to. Bormick's right, this needs to happen." She walked closer to Pete, his breaths coming faster in anticipation. "Pete and I need to do this, and you and Crimson need to get past the cloud you've both been under all these years. Take her like I know you want to."

"That's enough permission for me, Mark."

"Shit, Crimson, don't—"

Silence followed, and he saw the flinch in Skye's eyes. Crimson had taken the lead, Mark giving in. Now it was their turn.

Moving to her, he brought his hand up to her hair, releasing the clasp that held it and watching it tumble. He ran his fingers through it, the silky lushness of it was like he'd always imagined. His heart stopped, then pounded hard as she pulled his shirt, moving his lips to hers. The world froze around them. Tingling sensations collided through his body, awakening the need for her that he'd ignored since the first time he'd seen her. His arms encircled her, pulling her against him. Her lips parted and his tongue met hers, both dancing in harmony. She tasted like the goddess had, sweet and addictive, feeding the need he had for her.

She pressed against him, one hand sliding around his neck, her fingers in his hair, while the other moved up his arm. Her touch sent currents along his skin. Nothing existed but her in that moment and the way she felt in his arms. His hand brushed along her body, skimming her breast. The hitch in her breathing was tantalizing, and he dropped his hand to her hip, pulling her closer.

There was a shattering sound as the walls separating them came crashing down. He and Skye jumped away from each other, his breath still calming. Her cheeks were flush, and her eyes were needy. God, he just wanted to kiss her again and take her. He didn't care that anyone else was there. He wanted to touch every part of her, taste every inch of her.

"Well, well," Bormick said.

Pete forced his eyes from her to look at Bormick. Crimson was still kissing Mark, whose hands had pushed the sleeves of her dress down. There was no denying his need. Pete swallowed. A myriad of emotions assailed him, all of which left him uncomfortable with the sight. He looked at Skye for her reaction. She had crossed her arms, her lips pursed. She cleared her throat loudly.

Mark pushed Crimson away quickly, looking like a child caught in the candy dish.

"I see I was right," she said.

"Skye...I..."

She put her hand up to silence him.

"You're not innocent, Skye. That's quite a flush you have to your cheeks," Crimson said, wiping the corner of her mouth. "I forgot what a good kisser he was. Gives my Pete a run for his money."

"Does she taste as good as she looks, Pete?" Bormick asked. "It's been a while since she let me have those pretty lips of hers."

"Shut up, Bormick," he snarled. He resisted the urge to punch him for bringing that up. He hadn't particularly liked it when Skye had asserted her control and kissed Bormick that time and he didn't want to be reminded of it.

Bormick walked over to them, pushing past Crimson and Mark.

"Not fair that I don't get a taste." He grabbed Skye and kissed her before anyone could react.

Mark cursed and leaped for him, but it was Pete who pulled him away, punching him.

"What the fuck, Bormick?"

He laughed, rubbing his jaw. "Protective of her, are you? Interesting. I think there's more at work here than just a game."

Pete looked down at his hand.

"Don't worry, I'll be extra rough next time to make up for that," he said, shoving Pete against the wall and kissing him.

"Jesus, you two," Mark muttered.

"I can taste her on you," Bormick whispered.

Pete pushed him away; the urge to punch him again was high.

"So it was only a kiss?" Crimson asked. "I get the okay for some play time and all I get is a kiss?"

"I don't think this is where it ends. The game has started. You two will do it, and those two definitely will. Taenom isn't responsible for this. This goes way beyond him."

"What are you talking about?" Mark said.

"This is the work of the gods. Somebody wants those two paired, whether they were meant to at some point and didn't or this is some new thing, they will finish what they started, as will you two. The Shadow King and his mistress." He walked forward, taking the lead again.

"I think we're all fine with just the kiss," Pete said.

Mark shot him a look. "Are you?"

"I'm not," Crimson purred.

"No, he's not. Pete, you've never once kept me from Crimson, but you punched me for kissing Skye before her husband could. This is bigger than any of us. And it's only begun."

SKYE

Skye's body was on fire from that kiss, and she didn't know how to make it stop. Bormick's kiss hadn't taken the sensation away. She rubbed her arms, unsure about what was happening, feeling like a pawn they were passing around and fighting for. It wasn't a position she wanted to be in. Having Pete finish that kiss, to have his hands on her, his body above hers—that was a position she wanted.

You're losing it, Skye, she chastised herself.

There was no explanation as to what was happening, and she was out of control. Bormick's words flittered through her head. If he was right, and this was bigger than them, out of their control, then there might be no way to stop it.

And she wasn't certain she wanted to stop it. That kiss had woken a part of her she couldn't put back to sleep. Sure, she'd always found Pete attractive. He was almost godlike. But she'd never wanted him. At least, she didn't think she had. She'd looked at him, glancing when she could so that Mark didn't notice. But there was nothing wrong with looking or imagining.

Mark grabbed her hand and dragged her from Pete's side, waking her from her thoughts. As he moved her further from

Pete, she experienced a different emotion, an emptiness of sorts, like she was losing a piece of herself. It was a strange sensation and one she only ever experienced when she wasn't with Mark. With the thought, a trickle of fear skittered through her. She moved closer to Mark, then remembered how he'd been kissing Crimson and the hurt returned.

Yanking her hand from his, she stopped walking.

"Come on, Skye," he complained, but he wouldn't look her in the eye. "We need to get out of here."

"I don't think it's that easy, Mark," Bormick said.

"I don't either," she agreed.

Mark's eyes were hard to read in the dim light, but she knew him well enough to know he was conflicted, just as she was. She brought her hand to his cheek.

"It's okay," she said. He dropped his eyes, then turned them back to her, placing his hand on hers and nodding. "Whatever this is, we'll make it through."

"It would be nice to know what this is," Crimson said. "And do I get more of that, Skye? Because I'm seriously still wet over here."

"That's nothing new, Crimson," Bormick teased her, but Skye could hear the strain in his voice. The usual carefree tone was gone. That kiss had impacted the casual play the five of them had always had prior to that moment.

She glanced at Pete, who looked like he wanted to run from it all. She didn't blame him. She wasn't sure how she felt about any of it. His eyes met hers and, just like she realized always happened, she was drawn to him. All this time it had been there, but she'd denied it. Now it was here, and she wanted more.

No, you don't.

But she did. She yearned to have his hands back on her, to kiss him more.

"Think you two can stop eye-fucking each other for two seconds?" Mark grumbled.

She turned sharply. "Look at Crimson, Mark."

"What?"

"Just do it."

She placed her hand on her hips and waited for it.

"Stop it, Skye—"

"Look at her, Mark."

He scowled, and she knew he was pissed at her, and likely pissed at himself because he knew what his reaction would be. His eyes turned to Crimson, and Skye saw it as their eyes met. The lust that flashed within the hazel, the sexual connection that came alive between the two.

"Fuck," Pete muttered.

"Fuck indeed," Bormick echoed.

Mark tore his eyes from Crimson's, meeting Skye's and dropping them again before he ran his hand over his face.

"This is going to be so much fun," Crimson cooed. Skye shot her a look. "What? I'll please him, Skye. You know I can."

Skye glared at her. She was about to come back with a snarky remark when the ground rumbled below them.

"What the—Do you guys feel that?" Pete asked.

"Feel what?"

The wall near Pete shimmered. Skye could feel the magic in the air. An unseen force ripped Pete from where he stood, and his body flew toward the wall, disappearing. The shimmering stopped, and the magic dissipated from the air.

"Holy shit," Mark said as Bormick scrambled to the wall.

Skye stared at it. The strange feeling that part of her had been torn away with Pete swam through her.

"Where did he go?" Crimson asked frantically as Bormick pounded on the wall.

Mark pulled Skye to him, holding her so tight he was almost crushing her.

"Mark, stop, you're hurting me."

"No. Whatever took Pete can take any one of us, and I'm not risking it."

"I don't think you'll have a choice," Bormick said, turning and scratching his head. "If they want her, or any of us for that matter, there's no stopping it."

"Where is he?" Crimson asked again.

"I have no idea, but wherever he is, it's likely another test. Another trial he has to face. Taenom said he was to be tested."

"He said Pete and I were to be tested," Skye said, hearing the shake in her voice. This was becoming real entirely too fast.

Mark tightened his grip on her.

"Breaking her hip won't keep her here if they want her," Crimson said.

"No, it won't, but maybe it's only Pete's test. She's still here," Bormick observed.

"True. So, what do we do to keep our minds from worrying about him?"

"I'm not worrying about him," Mark snapped.

"Imagining him dying wherever he is will not help the situation." Bormick crossed his arms and stared Mark down.

"No, but it makes me feel better."

"Really?" Skye asked. The thought of Pete dying was like a knife to her chest.

She shoved Mark's hands from her waist.

"He just made out with you. I can imagine him any way I want. It's better than the way you're imagining him. Were you imagining him last night? After you said you weren't?"

She wanted to smack him, but she bit back instead. "You just made out with Crimson and had your hands down her dress. Don't lecture me, Mark."

"You two need to stop. Mark, get over it, it's happening—"

"Not if he's dead."

"Are you kidding me?" She stopped, feeling a strange tingle in her body. Meeting his eyes, she saw his expression change, the understanding there before her body was torn from where she stood. The magic in the wall hit her, and suddenly she was free-falling, the world flying by as she dropped. The scream that ripped from her only fled in the open expanse that surrounded her. She was plummeting to her death, and there was no way to stop herself.

MARK

Mark lunged, trying to grab Skye as the same unseen force that had taken Pete yanked her from him. Her body flew through the wall before he could stop her. He pounded on the wall as Bormick went back to frantically searching for a way through. His heart was beating out of his chest. Moments ago, he'd been hoping Pete had been pulled to his death, but now Skye was facing the same fate.

Bormick stepped back. "Still wish Pete was dead? Because if I were you, I'd be praying he's alive and can protect her."

Mark rested his head on the wall. She was gone. Wherever she was, there was no getting to her. No saving her. No guarding her like he was meant to. Now her fate rested in Pete's hands, if he still lived. He was the one who would need to protect her.

Mark turned and leaned on the wall, defeated. Sliding to the floor, he lowered his head to his hands. The world was falling from under his feet. Just a day ago he'd been happy, content in his marriage, with a wife who only had eyes for him. Now, all of that had changed.

Crimson's hand touched his, and he looked up, seeing that she'd stooped down in front of him. Her green eyes were layered with worry. They were large and sparkling in the dim light. She was beautiful; he could admit it freely now. Whatever was happening to them was opening the wounds—the buried emotion they'd all promised was behind them. Perhaps he had been lying to himself all this time. Telling himself he hated her. In reality, he'd been denying his attraction to her, burying it under anger.

She gave him a small smile. "Pete will keep her safe."

He sighed. "I know. And I don't really want Pete dead."

"Could have fooled me," Bormick grumbled.

"I don't. I'm just angry at him."

"It's not his fault, Mark. Nor is it Skye's."

"He's wanted her all this time. That doesn't bother the two of you?"

"No. He kept it to himself. He wouldn't even admit it to us, even when we pushed. I knew he wanted Skye, so did Bormick. But he wouldn't ever have admitted it because he didn't want to hurt either of you."

"And I'd venture Skye was the same," Bormick added. "There's no way she would ever let that come between the two of you. She suppressed it, just like he did. Now they don't have a choice. Neither do you. You still want Crimson and trust me, she wants you bad. She's never been quiet about that."

There was a shimmer of seduction in her eyes as she licked her lips. His mind went to the feel of those lips against his length, the way that tongue worked him in ways no one but Skye did.

"See? Take the moment. Whatever this is, the tides have turned, and we are all on a new course. I have a feeling none of us will be the same when we get out of here."

Crimson leaned close to him, and his body reacted. "I can't wait to feel you inside of me again," she whispered, brushing her lips against his. He couldn't stop himself and grabbed her neck, crushing her lips against his, letting the tension go, the worry, the fight. She was delicious, and he relented to the fact that he wanted to experience her again. There was a fire to her that sparked the angst in him.

"All right, you two."

He let her go, and she drew back, looking slightly shaken as she stood.

"Damn, Mark. It takes a lot to break her like that. I'm going to thoroughly enjoy watching you ravage my girl. Now, Crimson, you stop teasing him because my dick is hard as a rock over here."

"When is it not?" Mark asked, rising and adjusting his own erection.

"Rarely."

"So, what do we do now?" Crimson asked.

"I could think of a few things."

"No, Bormick. I'm not doing any more than that without Skye knowing. And right now, we don't know what's happening to the two of them," he said.

"Well, that leaves you out of the fun, but she can still satisfy me."

"No. Aren't you even concerned about Pete? You have no idea what is happening or has happened to him," Mark said.

"He's fine. They're not going to kill him off. They need him for something. They're testing him. I just don't know why."

Mark studied him, thinking over his words. They were testing Pete and maybe even Skye. Bormick was right, there had to be a reason, but they had no idea why.

"Let's see if we can find a way out of here while we're waiting for them."

"You want to continue walking? What if we end up meeting more of those beasts and we're down two fighters?" Crimson asked.

"I don't think we will. This isn't about us. This is about Pete, and I have a feeling about Skye as well. Whatever is happening to them is what matters. There won't be a test we need to face unless Pete's present."

"Good point, Elite," Bormick said.

"Back to the nicknames?"

"Your dick is going to be in my girl before this day is over. I get the satisfaction of tormenting you until that time."

"Nice."

"Mmm, it will be," Crimson said dreamily.

He shot her a look.

"What? You are an amazing fuck, Mark. I've told you that and now that I have Skye's permission, I'm going to take full advantage of that and remind you just how amazing I am."

His dick lurched in response, and he cursed the reaction, trying to wipe the memories of her body riding his away.

"Focus, Crimson."

"I'd say you need to do the same judging from that tent in your pants, Elite."

Mark shot him a look and began walking down the hall, realizing only as he left the light of the hues Skye had created that there was no moving on. They were stranded in place, which meant he was stuck fighting the worry and the overwhelming urge he had to take Crimson as a means to keep his mind from it.

PETE

Pete fell with an impact that knocked his breath from him. He should have been hurt from the distance he'd fallen and had patted his body in anticipation that something had broken. Thankfully, nothing had. Bringing himself up, he glanced around. What he found didn't give him confidence. He stood on a patch of rocky terrain, and it was barely a patch. He walked to the edge and peered down, trying to see an end to the darkness that lay below, but there was none to see. Whatever had hurled him here had left him stranded on a circle of rock. At least, from what he could see. A source of light filtered from the rocks beyond that lined the walls of the large cavern he was in.

He circled the space, looking for any clue as to what he was meant to do. There was no sign of anything.

"Fuck," he muttered. "The bastards could have at least given me something to go on."

He tried to use his magic, but it wouldn't heed his call. Each time he summoned it, there was no response. He was powerless. Looking up, he searched for the source from where he'd come. There was nothing but endless open space above him, just as there was below him. Stooping, he touched the terrain which was rocky but unlike any rock he'd come across. Then again, he was still adjusting to this world and finding there was plenty that was unlike anything he knew.

He stared at the brittle pieces of rock as he rubbed them in his hand. His mind wandered to what had happened before the force had yanked him into the endless void he was now stuck in. Skye returned to his thoughts. That kiss had been incredible and had touched him to his core. There was no denying it. He had it bad for her and he had no idea how he'd come to this point.

Sure, he'd wanted her before, but who didn't? Bormick was right, she was a living goddess. The thoughts had been there, the subtle pull to her, but he'd ignored them, his need for Crimson overpowering them when she was present. Ever since the battle, the way his power had touched her, bringing her back, he'd been unable to stop the growing desire to be close to her, to touch her.

Pete squeezed his hand, letting the debris trickle through his fingers. There was nothing any of them could do now. Whatever this place had done to break down the walls he'd put up, the ones he could tell she'd put up, he couldn't rebuild them. He didn't think he'd want to if he could. Kissing her had been like heaven, a completely different experience from kissing Crimson, and he wanted more of her now that he'd had a taste. But she was a married woman. Mark was an obstacle he couldn't surmount and one he wouldn't want to. Just like he still loved Crimson, he knew Skye's feelings for Mark hadn't changed. Nor had Mark's, even after he'd been given permission to fulfill Crimson's long-standing wish to have another piece of him.

Shaking his head, he stood and stretched. Crimson wouldn't stop now that Skye had given the okay, and he had no doubt Mark's irritation with this situation would cause him to drift to her. For a moment he was envious of Mark, but then a shiver of excitement went through him because he knew with that drift, Skye would be in his arms.

"God, Pete, stop it," he told himself.

The sound of Skye's scream ripping through the silence disrupted his thoughts. He looked up quickly to see her falling, but she was too far out to land where he was.

"Dammit," he cursed as he ran to the ledge just in time to grab her arm as she slipped past the edge of the rock.

He felt the strain of her arm as she looked up at him. Fear and shock laced her eyes. He gripped her tight, bringing his other arm down to hoist her up. She fell into his arms, her body shaking violently with the terror of the experience.

"You're safe. I've got you," he said, holding her close and running his hand over her hair.

Her body trembled against him, and her arms circled around him. He tried not to think about the closeness of her, the smell of her as he held her tight.

"You're okay, Skye," he said again.

After a few minutes, the trembling stopped, and she lifted her head, her eyes meeting his. He sensed the connection immediately, the draw to her that had gone from a low murmur to a deafening scream. He was lost until she gently pushed herself from his arms, as if realizing how close they were. The move left him missing her touch, an emptiness replacing it.

"Thank you," she said, her voice barely audible.

"I wasn't about to let you plummet to your death."

She gave him a smaller version of her beautiful smile and his heart raced. He wanted to yell at himself for the childish reactions, but he had no control over them.

"Where are we?"

"I don't know, but I can't find a way off of this rock."

She walked to the ledge, looking down and her proximity to it left him nervous. Something told him to pull her away and as he moved to her, he heard a crack. He wrapped his arm around her waist and drew her against him just as a small piece broke off.

"Holy shit," he said. "Stay away from the edge. I don't know if that will happen again, but we don't need to take the chance."

"Agreed," she said, and he noticed she hadn't moved from his arms. Instead, she leaned against him, her head drifting back to lie against his chest. The position seemed natural, like their bodies went together.

Out of instinct, he dropped his head to her hair, smelling the subtle perfume of the soap she used. The lushness of her hair was inviting, and he brought his other hand up to move it from her neck, closing his eyes as it drifted past his cheek. A low sigh escaped her, and her body relaxed into him more. Her birthmark sparkled against her skin, and as he'd always imagined doing, he slid his mouth along it, hearing the light moan that slipped from her.

He was lost to her and didn't want to let her go. Her body was too perfect. His hold on her waist tightened, pressing her further into him, and only then did he realize how hard he'd become.

"God, I'm sorry, Skye," he said, releasing her waist and moving back. "It just—"

She grabbed his hand and brought it back, pulling him to her. "Don't," she said. "I don't mind."

He dropped his head to her neck, brushing his lips along her birthmark again, feeling the stir in his magic as she shivered at his touch.

"What do we do, Pete?" she asked in a hushed tone.

"I don't know," he said against her skin. "As far as I can tell, there's no way off."

He let his hand drift along her arm, brushing the side of her breast and fighting the urge to feel more of it. As he reached for her hand, she took it, and he wondered at how perfectly it fit in his.

"I meant this," she said.

"Ah, this." He raised his head, missing the feel of her skin against his face the moment he left it. "I don't know. I don't even know how this happened."

She twisted her body and faced him, her blue eyes dusty. Her breasts pushed against him, and it took all his willpower not to touch them. "Is it true? Have you always wanted me?"

He inhaled, not sure he wanted to answer that question again, to admit the complications it brought. Of course, things were already complicated.

"Have you?" he asked, turning the question on her.

There was a flicker to her eyes that answered the question for her. So she had. Her lips parted, and he instinctively lowered his head, knowing he wanted to kiss her again, longing for that sensation. They hovered dangerously close to each other.

"I can't," she whispered.

"Can't answer my question?"

"No, I can't let you kiss me again."

"Ever?" he asked as his lips brushed against hers.

She was right. They needed to stop. Mark wasn't here to approve. Neither was Crimson or Bormick. But they had given their approval before this.

Her body pressed further into his, sending a flurry of excitement through him.

"I don't think it will be ever, but not here, not now, not without them."

He dropped his forehead to hers on her last word. She was right, voicing the same thought he was fighting. His need for her was difficult to ignore now. Against everything his body was telling him, he let his hands fall from her, taking a step back and running them through his hair.

"You're right. I'm sorry. Fuck, this is so confusing."

Her eyes held only understanding, as if she were fighting the same feelings, her loyalty to Mark overriding them.

"It's this place. It's doing something to us."

"Is it? Or is it just like Bormick said—waking something that was already there?"

He saw it then, the conflict within her, the one he should have had, but both Bormick and Crimson had given their blessing to whatever this was. Although something nudged at him that this was more than what they saw—that it went deeper, that permission or not, it would happen.

"I—"

A crumbling sound echoed around them, stopping her words. Pete tore his eyes from her and watched in horror as a section of their rock disappeared into the abyss below.

"That's not good," she said.

"No, it's not. We need a way off of this thing now." All thoughts of their prior conversation fled as his mind worked to find any solution he hadn't discovered.

"Did you try your magic?" Skye asked.

"Yes, it won't heed my call down here."

She chewed her thumb, and he couldn't help but smile, having noticed she did that when she was nervous or thinking. It was in such opposition to the strong woman she was, but it was one of the subtle, innocent things he'd always loved about her. Love? He scrunched his eyes at the thought, not knowing where that word had come from and uncomfortable with how it made him feel.

Mark was right, they needed to find their way out of this realm and back to theirs. Something here was seriously messing with him.

"Why did I need to be here?" she asked.

"Because they're testing both of us."

He could see her mind trying to work it out.

Another crack rippled in the air, followed by more of the rock falling away. He pulled her to him again, unsure of which piece would collapse next and not taking a chance. This time, his fear overrode his craving for her.

"The first test was the beasts, right?" she asked.

"Yeah, and the second was the kiss."

He saw the subtle flush to her cheeks and shook his head at the delicacy of it. "You know, you blush beautifully."

Giving him a smile, she said, "I don't think this is the best time."

"Maybe not, but if I'm going to die here, I'm going to tell you how that blush turns me on." It occurred to him that he should take that kiss while he was at it, but decided he'd wait until they were on their last piece of rock to make that move. No sense in pissing Mark off if they did make it out of here.

She looked speechless, and he brought his finger up to close her mouth, seeing the blush deepen. He let it linger, tracing the curve of her lips, feeling the sensuality to them. She parted them and his dirty mind imagined them taking his finger in like it would his length. She had a mouth like Crimson's—lush lips that called to be kissed and used—and he had no doubt she knew how to use it. Mark always appeared too satisfied for her not to be well-skilled in all aspects of the bedroom.

He chastised himself as he drew his finger back.

The only consolation was that she looked just as flustered as he was. The thought occurred to him that she may have wanted to do just what he'd imagined, and the idea did nothing to ease the discomfort in his pants.

"We can't stop this, can we?" she asked.

"I don't think so. Whatever it is, it's here, and it's not going away. The two of us are something together...something none of us saw."

"Together," she mumbled, her brows creasing.

"I know it's worrisome, Skye."

"No, it's not that. Together. The last two tests and this one have been us, together. We defeated the beast with our magic, together."

She put her hand out, and he watched as she tried to draw the hues with no success.

"Like I said, it's not working."

She shifted her body, turning so her back was against him

again and, once more, he had the urge to pull her close and dip his mouth to her neck.

She reached her hand back out, saying, "Take my hand."

He did as instructed, taking the time to slide his hand along the smooth skin of her arm first.

She peered back at him.

"What? It was there, and it's tempting in that dress."

Shaking her head, she said, "I'm going to try drawing the hues and I want you to call your shadows when I do."

"Together," he muttered, understanding now.

"Yes."

He sensed her call the hues and summoned his magic as she did, feeling it heed his call as the light above flowed to her. The black of the abyss below flooded to meet it. The two colors swirled around them. He'd never been within her circle of power when she was controlling the hues and the sensation was stimulating. The breath was knocked from him, her body trembling against him at the same time.

"That's new," she said.

"Definitely."

His shadows swirled before them, then fled to her hues, encasing them, re-enforcing them until they were something different and powerful. He felt her control the direction she fed the magic as it pulled from them and formed a stone in front of them. Her command was seductive. It called to a part of him that he hadn't sensed before, one that wanted to feel her body move against his as their power surrounded them. Somehow, he knew the experience would be nothing like when he and Crimson set their magic free. That this would be like a second skin, another piece of their souls touching. The thought was overwhelming, and it threatened to break his hold on his shadows.

"Pete."

"Sorry, it's just...I'm not really sure how to explain it."

"I know." She didn't need to say anymore to tell him she'd had the same sensation.

Another piece of their stone broke off, bringing him back to the situation at hand.

"Let's make a few more of those stones and get the hell out of here," he said. "Can you command the magic on your own now?"

He had a feeling she could, which was even more frightening because that meant she could command his shadows. Then again, they were a part of her now, having brought her back from the brink of madness. There was a good chance they would take her direction.

He dropped his hand from hers, the magic still swirling before them. She directed it, and just as he'd suspected, it obeyed. Her command whispered along his body; the shadows still connected to him. It was an erotic feeling and based on the slight moan that escaped her, she'd experienced it, too. The sound sent a frenzy of desire through him, and he longed to hear it as she came undone against him.

"That's different, too," he said, trying to steady himself.

"God, yes, it is. I hope that doesn't happen every time we need to do this. It's enough to make me climax."

His jaw dropped, his length jerking in reaction to her words, his mind imagining what she looked like in the throes of her climax.

"It's fine to say things like that when we're in the group, but don't say that now when we're alone and trying to survive or I might be tempted to ignore the impending doom just to experience that."

Her breath hitched, the quiver of her body tantalizing him. A louder crack rumbled below them, their rock swaying.

"I think that will have to wait, much to my disappointment. We're out of time. Can you make those things while we run?" he asked, his mind clearing quickly.

"Let's hope so."

He grabbed her hand, feeling the command she sent to their magic. More stones formed, her control of the power tantalizing him as it drifted around them. There was no time to consider the effect she was having on him any further. They ran to the first stone, the one they were on crumbling away as they left it. A crack formed in the new one and they continued to race from stone to stone. The magic formed new stones seconds before their feet hit. Pete's anxiety spiked with every jump. After the last stone, there was no place to go but a small ledge. He pulled her quickly to it, bracing himself for the impact of his back hitting the wall of stone and flipping her so she wouldn't be hurt. He fell, the impact delayed until his body hit the ground with a force that sent his bones rattling.

Skye was still in his arms, his hold on her tight as he looked up to see Mark's scowl. Bormick's grin was massive. Crimson's was amused.

"Well, I guess we didn't have to worry about them after all," Bormick said.

"So it would appear. Do I want to know why your hands are all over my wife?"

"You did give him permission," Crimson teased.

"For a kiss, not to feel her up."

Pete dropped his head down, trying to catch his breath, the adrenaline still soaring. He could feel the pounding of Skye's heart against him.

"We were running for our lives, not making out, Mark," she said, lifting herself from him.

He reluctantly released his hold on her, that empty feeling returning.

"Running from what?" Bormick asked, helping him up.

"From plummeting to our deaths. Yet another test from Taenom or whoever the hell is running the show here." He dusted himself off, his eyes drifting to Skye as she shook her hair out, pieces of rock falling from it. "Damn, they weren't just collapsing behind us, they were exploding the faster we ran."

"What were?" Crimson asked with a raise of her brow.

"These stones we created with our magic," Skye answered her. "We were stuck in the middle of nothing and the space we were in started to collapse. I created a path with Pete's help, and we ran for it."

"Narrowly making it," he added.

Mark was still grimacing. "How did you help her with your magic, Pete?"

"Really, Mark?" Skye asked.

"Really. You just fell through that wall in his arms—"

"After running from our deaths!"

"Mark, let her be," Pete said in her defense.

"Agreed," Bormick stated. "Even if they were doing something, you gave her permission, and she gave hers. Your eyes were pretty hungry that entire time they were gone."

Pete saw the daggers Skye gave Mark before she relaxed, her expression turning to one of resignation.

"Fuck off, Bormick," Mark griped.

"I'd like to right about now. This place is too small for me, and I haven't gotten a piece of this precious ass for a few hours," Bormick said, squeezing Crimson's ass. "I'm happy to share while the two of them do their thing."

"There is no 'their thing,'" Mark muttered.

"Oh, yes, there is, and you'd best get used to it. I saw that magic around their aura when they fell through that wall—it wasn't distinctly either of their powers, it was a blend. This is happening whether you want it or not."

Pete watched him walk down the hall, leaving his words lingering in their minds, knowing he was right. And now that he'd had a taste of Skye, there was no way he'd be able to survive without having all of her.

BORMICK

ormick turned away from the others, shaking his head. His mind was muddled as he tried to figure out what in the name of the gods was happening. They'd played right into Taenom's trap, but Bormick wasn't certain it was his alone. Taenom was involved, but he was a puppet just like Stavin had been for Bormick. Someone else was pulling the strings, and he was certain the gods had something to do with this.

What baffled him was why this was happening. The gods never interfered with mortal life. Yet the Death God had, and his mistress had fallen in love with a mortal. Bormick knew the story, had listened as Skye and Mark had explained the connection.

The Death God and his mistress were entangled in their lives on multiple layers. The thought struck him that this was yet another layer, one that mimicked their relationship. But that possibility didn't make sense. He rubbed his hand over his face, the silence in the hallway bothering him. He didn't like enclosed spaces, and the lack of their usual bantering was making it worse.

He glanced back. Pete wore a broody expression, walking beside Skye but not close to her. Skye's eyes were trailing the ground, her forehead creased in thought. And Mark's jaw was clenched so tight that Bormick worried his teeth might break. They all seemed to be pouting. All but Crimson who was content. Bormick stopped and turned, studying them.

"Bormick, what are you doing?" Mark asked.

"Trying to figure out what's going on. That spell broke, but it did what they wanted when the Skye and Pete kissed. The two of them survived whatever that last trial was. We may be passing these tests or trials, but I'm wondering if we're really failing. These trials are doing what they want. Fracturing us, and that makes us weak."

Skye rubbed her arms at his words.

"This isn't over. Whatever is coming next will be harder. I suspect the difficulty will continue to build until the four of you face the truth about how you feel. Turning you completely against each other or bringing us together. They want the first, and if that happens, we're all dead."

Mark glanced back at Skye, who was still next to Pete. Bormick hadn't noticed how they'd subconsciously paired. Her eyes were sad. She was torn, as was Mark. But all of this rested on the two of them.

Mark moved to her, pulling her into his arms and kissing her possessively. She melted into him, the heat from it passing against Bormick's skin. There was no denying their love for one another. The two were intense. Pete's eyes were dark with envy, and Bormick furrowed his brow as their eyes met. Whatever this was, it surpassed their own blood tie, casting it aside.

Mark drew back, Bormick's mind still thinking of the ties between them all. He watched as Mark leaned his head against hers, his fingers gently caressing her cheek.

"I love you," he murmured.

"I know, and I love you."

It seemed like a moment they shouldn't be watching, yet somehow should. A picture of what drove them. Their bond ran deeper even than his to Crimson and Pete.

They were quiet, looking into each other's eyes, the intensity of it almost hard to watch. There was something about their love that made it that way. That ensured through everything they'd gone through, their love hadn't faltered and wouldn't. Mark straightened and drew in a breath as if fortifying himself, the commander in him taking over the emotion.

He turned to Pete. "She's yours. Protect her, and you'll continue to have a piece of her, hurt her and I will destroy you."

Bormick noticed the change in the air, watching as Mark brought Skye's hand to Pete's. The air turned again as they touched, a tingle of magic on it.

He turned away from them and moved to Crimson. "Kiss her, Pete, and watch out. She bites."

He pulled Crimson to him and kissed her, Crimson going limp in the wake of it.

Shit, Bormick thought, *didn't see that coming.*

He tried to ignore the way his dick grew at the sight. There was a ferocity to Mark when he kissed Crimson. It spoke of how they were together, and the thought excited him. He didn't like the thought of sharing her, but watching someone as aggressive as himself with Crimson would be worth it. She was a vixen when she was fired up like that.

Skye stared at them, then looked down at the hand that still held Pete's. She glanced back at Mark, who had thrown caution to the wind, his hands running the length of Crimson's body.

Lifting his finger under her chin, Pete turned Skye's head to face him. There was a moment where they simply looked at each other, and Bormick had his own pang of jealousy. This went deeper than lust. That was why Mark had been so against it. He'd had Skye's permission to take Crimson, but the permission he was granting meant giving up more than her body.

Pete stepped closer to Skye, and her eyes searched his. Their lips lingered for just a moment before they kissed again. Bormick perceived the stir in the air, and saw their auras flare to life, encasing them. The way their bodies leaned for each other as though they belonged sent a sharp pain in his chest.

The hallway shook, distracting his attention from them. Mark and Crimson stopped to look at them, Mark's eyes losing the sparkle that had been there moments before.

"Dammit," Mark muttered.

The pair parted lips slowly, the tingle in the air fading. They both seemed stunned, and he wondered if it had been the same with their first kiss. It was hard to say with the barriers that had separated them.

It was clear something tied Pete and Skye to one another. He just didn't know why or what that something was. The Shadow King and his mistress. The words kept coming back to him. Skye dropped her eyes, then looked back up at them. Her eyes were a midnight blue, the gold in them flickering, but with less fervor than usual. The flecks had faded. She let go of Pete's hand and they flickered to life again.

"I'll be damned," Bormick mumbled, approaching Skye and bumping Mark out of the way.

"I didn't give you permission to kiss her again, Bormick," Mark snarled.

"I don't want to kiss her. One punch from Pete is enough for the day."

He tipped Skye's head up, studying her eyes and the gold within them.

"Bormick," Pete warned, bringing his hand to Bormick's arm. His grip was tight, the threat apparent in it.

Yes, Pete was getting very possessive of her.

"I'm not going to do anything. I want to see something."

The gold flickers in Skye's eyes were back in full force, but they hadn't been when she'd touched Pete. They'd lessened, almost to the point where they were gone.

"Take Pete's hand again, Skye."

Her forehead creased as she started to question him.

"Just do it."

With some hesitation, she did as instructed. His eyes widened as the gold shifted just slightly.

"The Shadow King's mistress," he mumbled.

"What?" Pete asked.

He ignored him.

"Kiss him again for me."

"Is this turning you on, Bormick?" Pete asked.

He heard Mark's grumble behind him. Both men were on edge, both staking claim on Skye and ready to attack if they saw him as a threat. It would have been amusing to Bormick, if the situation hadn't been so serious.

"Watching you do anything turns me on Pete, but that's not why. Kiss her for me."

"It turns me on," Crimson cooed.

"Everything turns you on," Mark said.

Bormick turned back and raised his brow. "Nice to see you loosening up, Mark."

"Hard not to when Crimson's hand keeps going down my pants."

Crimson giggled and Bormick flicked his eyes downward for confirmation.

"I can't help it," she said.

He shook his head and caught the death stare Skye gave Crimson.

"What? I can play now, Skye. Don't worry, I'll keep him satisfied while you're busy. Now kiss Pete again because that was a turn-on. I thought you and Mark were intense."

"Not making this any easier, Crimson," Mark said.

"I was trying."

Skye scowled at Crimson then pulled Pete in for a kiss. Bormick sensed the anger in her aura, and noted how the scowl on her face relaxed within seconds as the same magic coursed over the space again.

A low growl came from Mark before Skye released Pete from the kiss.

Pete looked shaken and a bit wobbly. "Shit, I don't know if I like being used as revenge like that."

"Shut up, Pete. You like it no matter how she's giving it to you," Bormick replied, tipping Skye's face to him again. The gold specks were almost indiscernible, then they slowly blinked back to life.

"Gods," he muttered. It wasn't just this place, this game, it was their magic. Hers was calling to his, to make her right, to balance it back.

"Shadows," he said. "Skye, you prefer the darker shades, don't you?"

"Yes, I always have. I told you, I lived in darkness for fifty years. It's comfortable for me."

"Because it's where you belong," Mark said. Bormick turned quickly to look at him. "You live in the shadows. You walk the Shadow Realm with ease."

"Yet you hold sway over the light as well," Crimson said. "Gods, this isn't about you and me, Mark. Bormick's right, this is about them."

"There's a reason you look like Eliana, Skye. Jesus, why you're both drawn to each other," Mark said, the hurt clear in his voice.

"Skye looks like the Death God's Mistress?" Bormick asked. "Oh, shit. The Shadow King and his mistress."

"You keep saying that, Bormick, but why?" Pete asked.

But it was Skye who answered, her eyes widening. "The Death God and his mistress. We are the embodiment of them."

A silence fell over them at the enormity of her words.

"Eliana's magic connects me and Mark, but Derrant connects you and me."

"Two unbreakable ties," Crimson said.

No one knew what to say and, for once, Bormick was speechless. If that were the case, then this was more serious than any of them had imagined. It wouldn't mean just physical attraction, but the one thing none of them wanted, it meant they would fall in love.

Mark walked away rubbing his hands over his face, Pete and Skye stepping away from each other.

"I...I...I can't," Skye muttered.

"You have no choice," Mark said weakly. "God, this is worse than all of it. It was bad enough before, watching you marry Sam, having to share you with Derrant, having Crimson hanging over us, but this." He gestured between the two.

"Mark, I didn't want this either," Pete said.

"We know, baby," Crimson said.

Mark leaned his head against the wall. "So, what now? I just step aside? We all just step aside, and watch the two of you do what? Fall in love?"

"It's already happened," Bormick said.

"No!" they both said vehemently.

"They just don't know it," Crimson said. Mark folded his arms and Bormick could see the denial. "You saw her eyes, Mark. We all did."

"What about my eyes?"

"The gold fades when you touch Pete. The shadows in you both draw to each other," Bormick answered. "They're pushing what's left of the light out. The shadows are overtaking it."

"But that's a good thing, right?" Skye asked.

"Likely. That magic isn't yours. It's foreign."

"Then why is that a sign of anything?"

"Because that doesn't happen when you're with me," Mark said.

"Because Eliana's magic is in Mark, but Derrant's is in Pete. Both sides of you crave both of them, but they need Pete because the bond between Derrant and Eliana is—"

"Unbreakable," Pete finished for Bormick.

"Now I'm bothered," Crimson said.

"Yeah," Bormick said, trying to fathom how to give up another part of Pete.

"Bout time you two feel the way I do," Mark muttered.

"This can't be," Skye said, a quiver in her voice. He saw the fear in her eyes and in the quiver of her lip, and Bormick wished he could alleviate it.

"But it is," Mark said, meeting her eyes.

There was silence again. Bormick didn't know what to say, nor did the others.

"So what happens now?" Skye asked after a few moments of heavy silence.

"We get out of here and go our separate ways," Pete said.

"Can you do that, Pete?" Mark asked. "I've been in love with Skye my entire life, and I can tell you with absolute certainty that forcing myself to be without her is the most painful thing I've ever endured."

"So you want me to fall in love with your wife, and what? Take turns making love to her?" Pete's voice was terse and Bormick could see his frustration.

Mark cringed at his words.

"I think that's exactly what we have to come to terms with," Crimson said, a slight tremble to her voice. "Bormick's right. This is a test, and it hinges not only on the two of you, but all of us. We're the three who get hurt in this if we let it hurt us. Sure, Mark is a great consolation prize, but we don't love each other, we never will. It's physical, no matter how much he denies he wants me again."

"I'm trying to admit it, Crimson, and given everything that's coming to light here, it doesn't seem that bad to admit."

"We're the next test," Bormick said as the truth hit him. "Accepting the attraction was the first. Merging your powers to free yourselves was the second, an acceptance that you belong together. We're the third test. The thing that will break us completely, knowing that the two people we love, love each other."

"I don't love Pete," Skye said.

"And I don't love Skye," Pete said.

As much as it was hurting him, Bormick felt for them. Neither had asked for this situation. They weren't looking to be anything other than what they had been. But what had that been? He'd seen the looks exchanged, knew that Pete wasn't being truthful, hiding his attraction to her beneath a lie, never admitting it. But Bormick thought she was sexy. He'd never hidden the fact that he would fuck Skye in a heartbeat, but that didn't mean anything was happening between them.

"Shadows," he mumbled.

"Shadows?" Mark asked.

That was it. The shadow magic. He looked to Crimson. "There was a reason you were the one who needed to save Skye. You were the conduit. You used that word, calling yourself a Conduit Mage, but it wasn't what we thought it was. You weren't a conduit to hold Pete's magic, but to save her with it. To ensure it touched her magic on a level it never had. Damn, there was no way this wasn't going to happen."

"What do you mean, Bormick?" Mark asked.

"Are you insinuating that I caused this?" Crimson asked, her eyes narrowing.

"No, not at all. It was already starting. You saw it, so did I, and maybe even Mark. Those looks, the way Pete denied it anytime we teased him. It was there between them both. But that event triggered something, making whatever is going on with this place inevitable."

"I felt it," Skye said, her voice barely audible. The vulnerability that was behind her navy eyes was startling. "I sensed Pete's magic, the difference in it, the call to it. It wasn't Crimson who saved me. It was the shadow magic that pulled me free."

"And stayed in you," Mark said. "Goddammit. That's the

reason your magic is darker now. It has nothing to do with what they did to you. I knew that was a bad idea when you suggested it, Pete."

"It saved her," he rebutted.

"Because it was meant to," Bormick said.

Bormick glanced at Crimson, seeing the acknowledgement. "I felt the change, too. I thought his magic had settled with my darker shades, but that wasn't true. The magic I sent to Skye, to seek her out behind the prison she was in, was his shadow magic. It was so free in me, not part of me like the warrior magic that I'd taken from Skye. What returned to me was the power over the light hues, a balance of my warrior magic. Pete's magic left me completely."

"Did you feel anything, Pete?" Mark asked.

Pete looked at his hands and Bormick could see him thinking it through. "Maybe," he said, brushing a hand through his hair. He swallowed, a defeated look on his face. "Yes, there was something. But there's always been a connection between our magic. I feel it each time she wields it or any time it touches mine."

"Do you feel the same way when you touch my magic?" Crimson asked, and Bormick could hear the plea in her voice. She feared the answer as much as he did, as much as he imagined Mark did.

Pete was quiet for a moment before answering, and his delay answered the question for him. "No."

The silence was deafening. Crimson's face reflected the crushing impact that one word had on her before she covered it with a false strength.

"Eliana and Derrant," Bormick said, all the pieces coming into place. "That day set the stage for this."

"Are you saying this was inevitable? Fated?" Skye asked.

"As fated as you and Mark, or us and Crimson, even as fated as Crimson and Mark."

"What?" all but Crimson said.

"Seriously? You and Crimson have the same blood, Skye. If he's drawn to you, he's drawn to her, and she's drawn to him. It's nothing emotional. You hold that place in the tie because you are his mate, but the two are still attracted to each other because of it." He crossed his arms and gave them a satisfied grin.

"You are demented, Bormick," Pete said.

Mark wiped his hand down his face, saying, "I'm inclined to agree."

"He's right. I figured that out when I was saving Skye."

Mark snapped his head to look at her.

"See, Crimson agrees with me," Bormick said smugly.

"Crimson just wants to get in Mark's pants again," Pete complained.

"Says the man, trying to get into my wife's."

"Cut it out, you two. Bormick is right. The four of us are all tied to each other in different ways, but it's there. Whatever is happening with me and Mark started a long time ago and I'd say whatever is happening with you two, started the moment Pete stepped foot in our world," Crimson said with a sigh.

"No, before. You two are meant to be lovers."

"But we don't love each other. This is the most insane conversation—"

"Shut up, Pete. You didn't witness that kiss," Bormick said.

He looked between the two. What he had with Pete was something he'd never experienced with a man. He loved him with a ferocity that equaled the love he had for Crimson. There was a protectiveness that drove his tie to Skye, and he cared about her, even risking his life to save her. She was family now. Maybe that was the key to them getting through this. They were all bonded with each other, had grown to like or tolerate each other, and any of them would place their lives on the line for the other. There was no question of that.

He didn't like the idea of anyone else touching Pete, but if it had to be anyone, then Skye was the one he could accept. He looked at Mark, who was sulking against the wall. Then at Crimson, who for the first time since he'd known her, looked vulnerable.

"This is our test. The five of us are a family, a motley crew, but a family nonetheless now. We can let this break us apart or let it strengthen us."

"And how will this strengthen us?" Mark asked.

"I agree," Skye added.

"Because it's us," Crimson said. "You, me, and Skye share a past, Mark, one that has shaped us but one that can redefine us now that Skye has given us permission to explore it."

"This is different, Crimson, you said it yourself. We don't love each other. In fact, I hated you for a very long time, imagined killing you in countless ways."

"Mmm, enemies to lovers is sexy, Mark."

"Crimson," Pete scolded.

She walked to Mark and leaned into him. "It's Pete and Skye, Mark. If anyone was to steal part of her from you, wouldn't you rather it be him? I trust Skye. I know she won't hurt him. I know she'll make him happy whenever she's with him. It hurts because I love him. It hurts knowing I'll have to let him make room for her where only Bormick and I have been. But I know he won't love me any less."

"You can't be serious. Don't we get a say in this?" Skye asked.

"No," Mark grumbled.

"He's right," Bormick agreed. "You two have already accepted it—"

"No, we haven't done anything except kissed," Pete said, but Bormick saw the flicker in Pete's eyes that told him Pete was hiding whatever had happened when the two had been gone.

Mark moved Crimson back and walked over to Pete.

"Did the world fall out from under your feet when you kissed her? Did nothing exist but the two of you? Nothing but the feel of her against your lips? Was stopping painful enough to leave your heart hammering? Is the thought of never kissing her again enough to shatter you?"

Pete's brow furrowed, and he looked flustered. "Yes," he finally answered.

"Dammit," Mark gritted.

He looked at Skye, who slowly nodded, her eyes heavy with sadness. Bormick's heart hurt for her. She was the one with the most to lose in this, she and Mark. Giving into what was happening meant hurting the man she'd loved for decades. Mark went to her, bringing his hand to her hair.

"I've had to go through a lot with you. I watched you love another man for twenty years. I watched it and it hurt—every second of it."

"Mark—"

"Shh," he stopped her. "Let me finish. You were never mine then. I never got to claim you, to make you mine. But now you are." He sighed and kissed her gently. It was a kiss that held his emotions, one Bormick could see almost knocked Skye to her feet with the power of it. His love stood prominent in it but under the surface, Bormick could see his defeat and the acceptance of what was happening. He could see it in the release of the kiss, the lingering of his lips as he drew from hers. "So this time, I know you'll still be mine and that if you love Pete...God, I can't believe I'm saying that, but if you fall in love with him or already have, I know you'll still be mine, that you'll always return to me. Just like with Sam, just like with Derrant. I don't like giving a piece of you up, but if I have to, if your survival depends on it, if your happiness depends on it, then I will because I can't live without you, Skye."

She kissed him, clinging to him. Pete moved away, Bormick seeing the grip of his hands, the clench of his jaw. He was trying to hide the envy, but Bormick knew him well enough to see it. When she pulled away, there were tears on her cheeks. She looked like a broken goddess, and all Bormick wanted was to protect her from her pain.

"I'm scared," she said, her voice cracking.

Mark kissed her forehead, wiping her tears away.

"I think we all are," Crimson said.

Mark brought Skye against his chest, holding her. Crimson moved to Pete, searching his eyes before kissing him. Pete's hands automatically brought her closer.

"I love you," she said, her hands sliding down his chest.

Pete's eyes were heavy, the emotion reflected in them. "Crimson, I—"

She kissed him again. "I know," she whispered as she brought her kisses across his cheek, then down his neck.

Bormick knew that there was no one who made Pete feel like Crimson did. It had never bothered him. His relationship with her was a completely different one from the one Bormick shared with her. What he felt for Crimson would never be the same as whatever developed with Skye. He could make love to Skye a hundred times and still crave Crimson. They were different and Crimson called to his blood, whereas Skye called to his magic. Each woman answered a different side to him. Maybe that was what this was, just as Pete needed Crimson after he'd given over to his desire for Bormick, Crimson balancing those two sides of him, Skye was the balance to his magic.

He'd always thought Crimson's magic did that, but now, seeing Pete with Skye and the way their magic danced, their auras bleeding into each other, he realized that had never been the case. His magic paired with Skye's, especially now that hers had been morphed.

Crimson left Pete's arms and pulled Mark away from Skye. "Come on, lover, we need to get out of here so I can remind you of the wonders of my mouth."

Bormick groaned. "That mouth of yours is a wonder."

He saw the look of lust on Mark's face, even though his other hand was still holding Skye's as if he didn't want to let go. Skye jerked him back, kissing him before releasing him. Her eyes held a sad look that spoke of a reluctant acceptance.

"Go easy on him, Crimson. I want him back in one piece."

Bormick couldn't believe how brave she sounded. This was it, just like when he and Pete had taken their next step. There was no turning back. She and Mark had given up their holds on each other, handing their love and their relationship to fate and to other people. The move spoke volumes about the two and the depth of Mark's love for her. This one move guaranteed their group would change. The dynamics were now morphed, the sexual tension that had always surrounded the five of them was now released and finding its home. Everything would be different if they survived whatever test this was.

"I can't make promises. Now let's get out of here. You are walking with me. Pete, stay by Skye's side. Let's let them know they can't break us, no matter how they try to hurt us."

Mark snatched his hand from hers and marched over to Pete, pushing him against the wall.

"I'm the only one who gets to pin him like that, Mark. I'm not sharing him with you, too," Bormick teased. He was trying to maintain his own strength, knowing although he was giving up a part of Pete and would now have to share Crimson with another man, Mark and Skye were giving up the most. Perhaps it would all work out and the sacrifices each of them was making would be worth it in the end. He prayed they would be. If not, they were all in trouble and he had a suspicious feeling their world would be lost.

"My threat still holds. You hurt her, and I will tear you to shreds."

"Understood," Pete snarled, glaring back at Mark.

Mark let him go, took one last glance back at Skye, and grabbed Crimson's hand, walking away.

"You need to do that the right way, Mark. You're too aggressive for him. You have to be gentle."

"Fuck you, Bormick," Pete snapped.

Bormick pushed Pete against the wall this time, bringing his hand to feel him. Pete's length rose in response.

"I will. When we're out of here, I'm going to fuck you until you beg me to stop."

"Who says I will?" he replied, grabbing Bormick's neck and bringing him in for a needy kiss. No words were needed. The kiss said it all.

He rested his head against Pete's, knowing there was no way out of this. There was no turning back. Knowing they'd need to make room for Skye to take another piece of his heart—of him.

"Shit," he mumbled, drawing away. He glanced back at Skye, who looked very aroused. "Maybe I'll let you watch, Skye." He left Pete standing there, his erection very evident.

"I'm not sharing Bormick, too, Skye. But I will say you'd find it quite a turn-on. I know I do." Crimson's voice was playful, but he knew her well enough to hear the hurt that still lay below.

Bormick laughed. "We aim to please, Crimson. Go help her walk, Pete. I think she's too wet to move."

That woke Skye, and she shot Bormick a look.

"Hey! I've accepted the Pete thing, but I will hurt you if you don't stop, Bormick," Mark yelled.

"I promise I could hurt you more, Mark, and you might enjoy it. Pete does." He threw Skye a wink as a shudder went through her. Her eyes were lush with sensuality. She was sexy and just looking at her made his balls ache. Pete was one lucky guy.

Pete moved to Skye's side, and they were standing there, looking uncomfortable when the hall shook. Bormick and the others stopped and turned back. A wall appeared behind Skye and Pete, the way before them shifting and splitting into a V. Two paths now stood before them.

"Did we pass another test?" Mark asked, dropping Crimson's hand.

"I'd say we did," he answered. "Question is, what do we do now?"

"Maybe that was the test, and we split up now?" Crimson said.

"You think we're done?" Bormick asked her, knowing they weren't.

"Are we?"

"I doubt it. Let's test it. Mark, take Skye and go down a hall. The three of us will go down the other."

Mark didn't hesitate to take Skye from Pete's side, but as they split up, another wall appeared, barring their access to either side.

"Not over," Bormick said.

"Too good to be true," Mark mumbled. "Go on, go back to him."

"Mark—"

"Skye, go back to him. This is bigger than us. Go. I'll be fine. It's just like the day I watched you marry Sam. It hurts like hell, but it's necessary. And I've got someone to preoccupy me just like I did then." If looks could kill, the one Skye gave Mark in that moment would have crumbled him. "Go, it won't hurt us, and I'll be on the other side waiting for you."

"He'll be very tired, though," Crimson said.

Skye's expression softened, and to his surprise, she laughed. "It takes a lot to tire him, Crimson. If I remember correctly, he left with two women the night of my wedding. You'll have your work cut out for you."

Bormick's jaw dropped. Mark gave Skye a guilty look.

"Didn't think I noticed?" she asked coyly.

"No, but you didn't see the one we picked up in the hotel bar on the way to the room."

"Really?" Pete said. The disbelief in his voice made Bormick chuckle. Although, the admission awed Bormick as well. He knew

Mark was relentless from seeing him with Skye and from what Crimson had shared, but three women at once was impressive.

Mark shrugged, ignoring the daggers poised in Skye's eyes.

"It took a lot to get her from my mind that night."

"Damn, Crimson, you do have your work cut out for you," Bormick teased. "Mark, I didn't realize you were such a ladies' man."

"He was quite the whore," Skye said, an edge to her voice.

"How is it you two have stayed married this long?" Crimson asked.

"Because they have fire and that's what keeps them going. See, if we were home, the two of them would be leaving us about now so they could fuck their tension out."

Skye turned her glare to him.

"I just call it as I see it, Skye. Guess that means Crimson will be getting all that aggression. Try to go easy on Pete, though, Skye. He's a softy."

"Seriously, Bormick?" Pete complained.

"Oh, he is, but there are times—"

"Enough, Crimson," Pete said, and Bormick could see his frustration.

"Yeah, I think that's enough," Mark muttered.

"Huh, it's okay for me to hear about your orgies—" Skye started.

"They weren't orgies."

"If all of us went at it right now, that might be considered an orgy. Maybe that's what we need to do," Bormick said.

The four of them looked at him.

"Way to shut that conversation down, Bormick," Crimson complained.

"It needed to be shut down," Mark grumbled. "Skye, go to Pete, but Pete, keep that aggression under wraps. I'm the only one who gets to pound her hard."

Bormick couldn't contain his laugh as Skye bristled. She was quiet for a moment, then drew Mark in for another kiss, this one was demanding, a sign that she still owned him and Bormick could feel the heat from it.

When she drew back, Mark looked a little unbalanced.

"She that good of a kisser?" Bormick asked, finding it humorous how Pete had looked away, the jealousy heavy in his aura.

"The best," he answered as she walked away and toward the three of them.

"Crimson, your turn to switch sides," he said.

Crimson moved in front of Skye's path. "I suppose after that, this won't be so dangerous." She pulled Skye to her and kissed her. Bormick's mouth fell open at the same time Pete's did, his dick reacting instantly.

"He's right, you are an amazing kisser. It's those lips and that taste. What is that?"

"Honey," Pete and Mark said at the same time. Mark narrowed his eyes and crossed his arms.

"Mmm, that's what it is. Don't worry, Skye, I'll take good care of him. He won't even think about the way you taste, even if you taste that sweet everywhere. I wouldn't mind having a lick. You sure you don't want to join us?" Crimson said seductively.

"I don't know how keen I am to watching you ride my husband, Crimson. I'm accepting this, but I don't think I want to watch." Mark cleared his throat awkwardly. "No matter how much of a turn-on he thinks it is."

Bormick rubbed the back of his neck. "I'd have to agree with Mark, that would be a turn-on. Anything involving the two of you would be."

"Not gonna happen."

"I do believe you said this wasn't going to happen," Pete said slyly.

"As did you," she replied curtly.

"I'm not up for the two of them with you either, Pete. If anyone gets to experience that, it's going to be me," Mark said.

Skye shot him a look.

"I have dibs on that one. I'm the fifth wheel here. You two get to have the fun. I get to have the two ladies," Bormick said.

"No," Pete and Mark said at the same time.

"Oh, my God, just drop it. Crimson and I are not having sex!" Skye said with a frustrated huff.

"Yet," Crimson added.

"Never. There's nothing ..." Her words drifted off.

"Nothing, what?" Crimson asked.

"Nothing there. It wasn't you...fuck."

"Whoa, is she always that sexy when she says fuck, Mark?"

"Shut up, Bormick. What do you mean, Skye?" Crimson asked.

"The kiss, that day you saved me. It wasn't you I reacted to... when you kissed me now, it wasn't the same."

"Because Pete's touch didn't lace that kiss. Goddammit," Mark grumbled.

"What does that mean?" Pete asked naively.

Crimson answered, her disappointment evident in her voice, "When she kissed me back on the battlefield, it was you she was reacting to, not me. Your power, the touch of you through it."

Pete stared at her, his eyes growing wider with understanding.

"So, if Pete hadn't given his magic to Crimson that day, none of this would have happened," Mark said, his voice with a distinct edge to it.

Bormick shook his head. "Nah, Mark. Good try. It was there, it always has been, but that event woke it, and whatever is going on here will cement it. Besides, if it hadn't happened, we'd all be dead now."

Mark leaned against the wall as Pete stared at his hands.

"So, I take it that means no fooling around for us, Skye?" Crimson said playfully, the wound still noticeable in her voice.

"No," she said quietly. She looked lost, like her world had shattered around her, and she couldn't figure out how to pick up the pieces. Bormick understood the feeling, it was hard to avoid given the circumstances.

Mark was the first to speak. "Let's finish this and get the hell out of here so I can strangle Taenom."

"Why isn't this opening?" Skye said, coming back to life. "We switched spots."

"Bormick, go to Mark and Crimson," Pete commanded him.

"Damn, really?" He had been hoping to watch. Pete had a way with Crimson that was stimulating, and he had a feeling that the effect would be magnified with Skye. Disappointment set in. Although it would be fun to watch Crimson tame Mark. He cheered up, wondering how long it would take for Crimson to give in to her need for the man. As he walked to them, the walls lifted.

"I'll be damned," he muttered.

He took one last look over at Pete and Skye. Pete's eyes met his before he looked away and stepped forward with Skye, the wall coming down behind them.

Mark's eyes lingered.

"Come on, no going back now," Bormick said.

"No, there's not."

Mark walked forward with Crimson, Bormick following. He had to give Mark credit; he was taking this well. The man was strong in every aspect, a warrior just like himself, one who didn't show his pain no matter how much he was hurting. Although, as Crimson turned and walked Mark to the wall, Bormick didn't think he'd be hurting too much longer.

"Really, Crimson?" Mark asked as she pawed at him.

"Really. I finally have permission and you are going to give me what I've waited for."

"I'll just take a look further down while you two reacquaint yourselves." He should have been bothered, but given the circumstances, Mark taking Crimson was the least of the two evils.

Mark gave him a look of desperation until Crimson drew his full attention, her mouth devouring his. Her hands found his growing length as he relaxed and returned her kiss. Bormick shook his head before making his way down the hall, wondering how this would all play out after Mark feasted on Crimson, and Pete and Skye made love to each other.

Things were about to get a lot more complicated.

PETE

Pete pulled Skye along as they made their way down the dark hallway. Somehow, everything had become incredibly convoluted. He was heading into the unknown with Skye, Mark with Crimson and Bormick. He and Skye were cut off from their lovers, but he wasn't certain he understood why. It sounded ridiculous to think the reason was so they would become lovers of their own, or to stir the flames of the love that Bormick claimed to already exist.

Pete wasn't in love with Skye. He didn't even want to admit how he craved her, what that kiss had done to him.

"Pete," she said, stopping and tugging at his hand.

"We need to keep going, Skye," he said, not looking back.

"Aren't we going to talk about this?"

"About what?" he asked, turning to her, and regretting the action the moment their eyes met.

"That kiss, both kisses. What happened to us in the cavern…"

"No. We're not. We're going to find our way out and get back to the others."

"I can guarantee Crimson is not looking for a way out right now."

"And what, you want to get even with them?" He hadn't meant for the words to come out with such an edge.

"No, I've accepted it. It is what it is, but I'm confused about this. And you...you won't even look at me."

"I can't look at you, Skye. What do you want me to say?"

"That the kiss meant something. We're all torn apart because of it, because of all of this."

He dropped his eyes, looking at the hand he held in his, feeling the tingle of magic between them.

"I have to keep moving because the alternative is...it's one I'm not certain what to do with."

He looked back into her eyes and saw the hurt. She'd thrown her marriage on the line, and he, his relationship with Crimson and Bormick. She needed validation that she'd made the right choice, that following Pete and letting Mark go with Crimson was necessary. Pete knew Crimson wouldn't hesitate to make the first move on Mark, and that Mark would take her, thinking he'd already lost Skye. Skye knew that as well.

He stepped closer to her, letting his fingers drift along her cheek. "I want to kiss you again. I want to feel you, to taste you, to make love to you. Just as I think I always have." Her mouth parted, and he struggled to resist the temptation to kiss her. "But if it's true, if we really are something more, if we really are destined to love each other like they said, I don't want to take you in a hallway. I want to make love to you the way you need to be made love to. I want to make it so that we have no regrets, that everything we're giving up—everything they're giving up—is worth it."

He took her hand, ignoring the heat of her, the throb in his pants, the overwhelming urge to kiss her, and pulled her along. She stayed silent. Perhaps her mind was spinning like his was. He was contemplating all the times he had lied to himself, told himself he didn't want her, that seeing her didn't cause his heart to race. Brushed off the notion that his reaction to her had been persistent since the first time he'd seen her.

When Crimson had been present, it wasn't so hard. His need for her had always been stronger...until now. This place had sent his attraction to Skye over the line, accentuating it, his need for her now desperate and demanding his attention.

He led her down the hall, stopping as they hit an entryway, only darkness beyond. He glanced back at her, drawing his power.

"What is it?" she asked as he gripped her hand tighter.

"I don't know."

The gold flecks in her eyes sparkled lightly, and he felt her magic touch his, drawing from it as she would her hues. His power didn't escape him as it had with Crimson. He didn't temporarily feel a weight, as it was duplicated. Instead, it was a soft touch that tingled against his magic. His magic opened to her, flowing freely to enshroud her. Her eyes grew closer to navy, and a wave of need crested through him at the sensation of it all.

"Let's go," she whispered.

He searched her eyes again, then turned back, leading their way through the doorway, placing her behind him and feeling her hand on his back. Her touch sent a current of sparks through his body.

Hold it together, Pete, he told himself, unsure if it was her touch or the unknown ahead of them that had him nervous.

Stepping through the threshold, he found a room of gray before them, accents of black adorning the walls. Food and wine sat upon a table in one corner and in the center of the room stood a bed, nothing ornate or fancy, just a bed with throws upon it.

There was a *whoosh* behind them, and the entrance disappeared. There were no windows, no exits, and the message could not have been clearer.

"I guess that's our sign," Skye muttered, letting his hand go to walk toward the wine.

He snatched her back, bringing her against him unintentionally. Loosening his hold, he let her go quickly, the feel of her against him almost too much to handle. He could feel the shake in his hands, the anticipation weighing on his chest.

"No wine. If we're going to do this, we do it sober. I want no thoughts that alcohol was to blame."

She swallowed and gave him a nod.

"We don't have to do anything, Skye."

Her face fell momentarily, and he smiled. She wanted it as much as he did.

"You can't say all those things to me, then not act on them, Pete."

He raised a brow at her. "Do you want me to do those things to you?"

He noted the catch of her breath, the way the gold flitted in her eyes. "Yes."

There was a pull in his heart, a sensation that flooded through him with her acknowledgement, but the sadness behind her eyes kept his need to kiss her restrained. He pushed a strand of her hair back, letting his fingers linger in the softness of it as her lips parted. That hunger in him grew, pushing him to kiss her again.

"I won't unless we're both one hundred percent certain. There's no turning back once we take the step, Skye."

"I know." Her voice was barely a whisper, one underlined with fear.

He understood her reaction—the idea terrified him for multiple reasons. What they were about to do would change everything. It would redefine what he'd understood—what they'd all understood—to be the dynamic of their small family. It had the potential to tear them all apart and, with that parting, he'd lose her. The thought was like a million daggers in his chest, incomprehensible to an extreme that went deeper than even the thought of losing Crimson or Bormick.

"I'm just as scared," he said. "We don't—"

She brought a finger to his lips, the feel of her skin like the delicate touch of silk.

"We do," she said. "And I want you to do all those things to me. I want to experience you and whatever comes after."

"Even if that means what they said?"

"That we fall in love?"

He nodded.

"How is that possible?"

"I don't know, Skye." She was searching his eyes, and he wondered what she saw there. He wondered if it was love. If he'd fallen for her without even knowing it. "But maybe it is."

The gold in her eyes flittered, the navy behind them turning a dusky shade of night. "Take me, Pete."

As she said the words, her magic caressed his skin. The color fled her dress, the material turning to ash that fluttered to the ground around her naked body.

"Christ," he mumbled, taking her in, his eyes lingering on every perfect curve. "Do they not make underwear in this world?" he asked, trying to control himself.

"None that I like." Her eyes were a rich blue the depths of which could drown him. His gaze surveyed her body again, taking in the perfection of her, the beauty. Her hips called for him to grasp them, her breasts were firm with nipples that were peaked in expectation. There was no part of her that didn't make his length jerk in anticipation.

He kicked his shoes off and removed his shirt, going to her and drawing her against him. The feel of her breasts against his skin sent jolts through him. In that moment, it all came rushing back—every glance, every lingering stare, every time he'd looked at her and imagined how she'd feel, how her sighs would sound, her body would look. His attraction to her had been there since that first time he'd seen her in the grove and had grown with every interaction since.

He threaded his fingers through her hair and bringing her lips to his, kissed her sensually. His tongue explored the depths of her mouth as his hands memorized every curve. Taking his time, he let his fingers slowly caress her skin, delighting in the way it felt against his own. With every hitch of her breath and beat of her heart, his emotion for her climbed. He took each one and memorized them, knowing the only other sound that would please him as deeply would be the cry of her falling apart in his arms. He'd never wanted anyone like he wanted Skye at that moment, not even Crimson. He wanted to make love to her, to detail every moan, every quiver, every touch. She was meant for worshipping, and he would worship every inch of her as no one had before.

He moved her to the bed, hovering over her as her hand tugged at his pants to unbutton them. He took her hand in his and moved it above her head, doing the same to her other hand. The complaint she emitted was stopped by his lips. The kiss was sensual, and as she arched toward him, there was no denying that something was changing in him. Drawing back to look at her, he took in the beauty of her. She was stunning, as if she truly were a goddess, Eliana incarnate. The darkening of her eyes leaned on the cusp of an endless night, the blue almost black, the gold specks gone.

"I want to taste you," he said, reveling in the flash of need that passed through her eyes and the slight gasp that escaped her sultry lips.

And he did—he wanted to taste every inch of her and savor it. Kissing her neck, he lingered for an extra moment on her birthmark, causing a rush of his power to meet the tingle of hers. He slid his lips down, grazing her nipple with his tongue. She lifted her legs in response, his hardness feeling the warmth of her through his pants. He wanted her so insanely that he was aching, but he wanted this more, wanted to run his tongue through that warmth, to feel her come undone against his mouth, to lick every inch of her delicious body.

He released her wrists, his hand drifting to her other breast, teasing the pert nipple. His mouth sucked the other nipple until she bucked beneath him, a soft moan escaping. One that set him ablaze.

His hands lowered to her hips, her small waist fitting perfectly in his grip as his lips and tongue found their way down her stomach. She moaned again when he spread her legs, slipping his finger along the dampness that covered her.

It was Pete's turn to groan. Skye was wet, and he'd been the one to cause it. The thought drove him mad. His erection throbbed, begging for release. Instead of satisfying it, he sank his tongue into her, smelling the beautiful aroma of her arousal and tasting her. It was like the nectar of the goddess herself, and he knew there was no turning away from it. He licked as her body arched again, his tongue sinking deep into her. The cry she let out clawed at his arousal. He moved upward to her clit, sinking his fingers into her as he continued to ravage her, all the while fighting the stimulation her writhing body was causing him. Her legs began to tremble, a deep moan coming from her as she arched her back. Within moments, she broke with a cry that sent an uncontrollable fire coursing through him. The feel of her body in the throes of her orgasm took him beyond his ability to function. Every cell in his body came alive with the sensation. He wasn't going to last long, and he'd wanted to for their first time. He wanted to take her for hours, but he hungered too greatly for her.

He cursed himself for greedily tasting her as he brought himself up, hovering over her. Her cheeks were flush with satisfaction, her eyes the deepest navy he'd ever seen them. There was no shyness there, only unabashed confidence. She was everything he'd imagined, and he couldn't wait to experience the rest of her. At the thought, his length jerked. Her eyes flared as she brought her hand up and pulled him down for a kiss, licking herself from his face seductively. The groan it elicited from him was feral.

"My turn," she said against his lips before she gently pushed him.

Good God, he thought, rolling over with her. She rose above him, her auburn hair softly resting against his skin, and kissed him again. He could have kissed her all day, her lips were made for it, her kisses absolute perfection. Her mouth tasted of honey and nightfall. She drew her lips from his, her mouth taking the same slow trail his had until she reached his pants. His stomach trembled as she slowly removed them. The hitch of her breath when she came back up made him smile. He had a feeling his dick was the same length as Mark's—the man had an almost constant erection around her and lately around Crimson—but her reaction led him to believe he might have a bit more girth on him.

His smile faltered as her mouth met his length, all thoughts but her mouth and what it was doing to him fading. Her tongue made its way down his shaft and up again, encircling his head. When her hand gripped him, her mouth descending and taking him in completely he emitted a groan that rumbled deep in his core. Only Crimson had ever taken his entire length, and Skye made Crimson pale in comparison. It was no wonder Mark had resisted Crimson for so long. Skye was worth it.

Pete threaded his fingers through her hair, his climax growing closer. He couldn't help but thrust into her, tensing the more she enticed him with her mouth and her tongue. The sensations cascading through him had him on the edge until he could take it no more and he broke, his release flooding into her waiting mouth. She didn't let up, taking every bit of his essence as if she found him as addictive as he'd found her. He didn't know if he'd grunted or cried out, but he did know he'd never experienced a blowjob like the one she'd just given him.

Her mouth never ceased pleasuring him until he was firm again, a feat that had not taken long. Thoughts of her were enough to make him hard any time—he realized that now. His reaction to her had always been that way.

She crawled back up his body, her mouth brushing his stomach, his inhale an instinctual reaction. When her lips met his, he didn't hesitate to kiss her, bringing her in against him and knowing they were about to take the final step. His firmness pressed against her, twitching in anticipation. The thought of taking that step sent a rush of excitement through him. He drew back, brushing her hair from her eyes. He didn't need to ask; her expression said everything. Desire resided there, along with a vulnerability, one he would reassure, one he would claim as he claimed the half of her that was his. Their destinies had always been entwined by the heritage they carried, the gods they embodied.

He brought his lips to hers, feeling her melt into him, and moved them so that he was atop her again. She was his to take and he would take her, making love to her as they were meant to. He lined himself up, drifting back to look at her as he edged himself into her, just enough to watch her, enough to torture himself in her soaked opening. Slowly, he slid into her, watching her lips part in pleasure, her eyes lighting as she brought her knee up. Her hand drifted across his chest, her pelvis pushing upward, allowing him to slide further as he began to move. She entwined her legs around him, and he thrust deeper, a beautiful sigh escaping her, one he'd longed to hear.

They watched each other, each expression of pleasure driving him closer to the mounting release until her head fell back, her body failing to fight the rising tide within her. The feel of her tightening around him urged him on, his own need for release escalating. He increased his motion as his climax mounted with hers until, together, they were swept under, his power tearing from him and hers surging to meet it. With the tingle of her magic across his skin, his climax exploded, and with it, he lost all control of his body. Her muscles convulsed with his as the world around them shook, neither noticing anything but the total release of their bounds, their bodies overcome with ecstasy neither had experienced.

There was no going back, no returning from this. He was one with her in ways he'd never anticipated. As he took her again, falling deeper with every kiss, he didn't want to go back, no matter the consequence.

MARK

Mark stared at the ceiling, his mind too awake to find the sleep that Crimson had. Bormick lay beside her, out cold, his arm around her. Crimson's hand lay on Mark's chest. It was a strange feeling to not have Skye's hand on him, her body against him.

He wiped his face and sighed.

There was no explanation to how they had gotten to this place, with Crimson asleep next to him. He glanced at her, seeing the peaceful look on her face as she slept. He'd taken her and let his guard down, taking the permission Skye had given him, urged on by the fact that she was doing the same with Pete. But he wasn't certain it was the same.

Sure, he'd taken Crimson multiple times, starting in the hall where he'd pressed her against the wall, not bothering to remove their clothes, too driven by the need to have her and the jealousy that lay below the surface. He'd torn that revealing dress from her skin, the one that had pushed her voluptuous breasts at him the entire time she'd worn it. He'd wanted her with such intensity that he'd fucked her again in the hallway, then in the room

Bormick had found. It had only intensified from there as he brought all the repressed fantasies to life.

At some point, Bormick joined them. It was a strange experience, one he'd never had. Sure, he'd had more than one woman, but never had he joined another man. Bormick steered clear of him, satisfying himself with Crimson. He'd taken her from behind as her mouth had seduced Mark again. Bormick was rough and unapologetic, and she liked it. At one point, he'd pounded her so hard, Mark thought she might break. He couldn't help the arousal that had built from watching it. She'd climaxed with Bormick, her mouth still surrounding Mark so that her moans vibrated against his length in a way that he couldn't ignore. His release had come quickly after that, the orgasm leaving him so weak he'd required time to recover.

Bormick, however, was relentless, banging her again while Mark watched, marveling at the force with which he took Crimson. Mark felt guilty taking her as roughly as he had earlier after seeing Bormick with her and began to understand the dynamic he and Pete had with her. The next time he was ready for relief, he was gentler, allowing a certain degree of intimacy, putting the emotion aside, the jealousy and anger at the situation, and making love to her as close to the act as he could. He didn't think it was anything close to the way Pete would have handled her after Bormick had ravaged her. There was no love there, only an understanding between the two of them. And it was likely not something he would do with her often. What he and Crimson had sexually was nothing like Pete would have done with her. Nothing like he was likely doing with Skye.

Pete, who had seen that coming? He didn't think even Skye had. He prayed Pete was a gentle lover, like he was inclined to believe after seeing Bormick with Crimson. Skye liked it hard, but those were moments usually fueled by something, usually talk of Crimson, his own guilt and anger at himself spurring it. He saw now that his attraction to Crimson had been there all along, that damned need to have more of her, and he'd turned it into anger against her. She had been the reason he had lost Skye to Derrant every year. She had deserved his hatred, but he'd used it to cover the fact that no matter what he'd told himself, he'd wanted more of Crimson.

And now he had it, and Skye was with Pete. Doing the things she did to him, to Pete, and there was nothing he nor any of them could do about it. He'd sensed the moment Pete had taken her and she'd given herself completely to him. They had all stopped to look up as the room had shaken violently, a flow of power coursing through the room and in it, Skye's magic. He knew the feel of it when it spilled out unintentionally, when she was so lost that it escaped. Pete's power encased it protectively. The moment had come well after Mark's first, even his second orgasm, and cemented the fact that the two had climaxed together, that they'd made love passionately and emotionally.

He ran a hand through his hair, grimacing at the thought. He knew what it meant. The hurt that lie within him struggled against the acceptance that things were out of his control, out of any of theirs.

Crimson's hand drifted over his chest, and he turned his eyes to her.

"They'll come back to us," she said.

"Will they?"

She gave him a sad smile, her bright green eyes revealing that vulnerability again. The one that called to him to fix it because it wasn't who she was.

"Yes." He heard the hope behind the words.

Brushing a red lock of hair back, he asked, "And will it be the same when they do?"

"No," Bormick answered, rolling over. Mark tried to ignore the massive erection that protruded from him. "Nothing will ever be the same again."

"That's reassuring."

"It's the truth, Mark. The dynamics of our group have changed. You and Crimson are finally fucking, so I don't have to watch her ogle your ass anymore."

"Oh, you'll still have to see that," she replied, eliciting a laugh from Bormick.

Mark let his fingers fall from her hair and drift to her shoulder, gently tracing the curve of it.

"And Pete and Skye are now a thing none of us can undo. All of us, including them, will need to come to terms with that."

"And if we don't want to?" he asked.

"Then you'll have a wife who is no longer complete. She will be a shell of what she was because Pete has now claimed part of her. Same with us. If they're forced apart, he won't be his whole self."

"You're serious?" Mark asked.

"I am. They aren't ours completely anymore, Mark. No matter that the two of you have that Mage Warrior-Elite bond going on or we have our blood bond—this trumps it. Your goddess and our god have awoken and can no longer live without each other."

"Eliana and Derrant?" Crimson asked, as if she hadn't heard the realization earlier.

"Exactly, that's what Taenom meant—why he called Pete the Shadow King and Skye his mistress. Just like we suspected. That flux of power said it all."

"So I have to give Skye up because their magic is tied? Because they are some kind of manifestation of Eliana and Derrant?"

"It's not that easy and you know it. They're now tied to each other in every way and by the time they emerge, they will love each other with the same intensity with which we love them."

Mark's heart dropped. Discussing the possibility before had hurt him, but knowing it was now reality was soul-shattering. Skye had been the one to voice what he'd seen—that she looked like Eliana because, in a way, she was. But now, to know that it was the truth, to have confirmation, the pain was twofold. "How do you know all this?"

"Their auras, Mark. They've been reaching for each other since the moment we came to this place. You know that without seeing it. Those doors shattered not because of what we were doing with them but because their auras were seeking each other, their power and their souls."

"So, we've lost them?" Crimson said, the sadness in her voice palpable.

Mark thought about it. Unbreakable. Their love had always been unbreakable through everything. Suddenly, he wasn't sure that was enough. He wanted to believe that it was, that it was so strong that he could make room for her to love another man. It was unfathomable, but he'd done it before with Sam. Even if she'd never loved Sam to the same degree, she'd still loved him and slept in his arms every night for twenty years. No matter how much he hated the idea of her with Pete, the thought of losing her or having only a shell of her left him distraught.

"No," he answered. "They're still ours, but things will be different now, like Bormick said. We'll need to make room for whatever it is they have, what they need from each other."

"Wait, I'm in that we," complained Bormick. "How did I get the short end of the stick here? I have to give Pete up to Skye and Crimson to you. What do I get out of this?"

"I can guarantee you won't get Skye out of it," Mark said.

"No, from Pete's reaction when I kissed her, I'd say he's not sharing with anyone but you, and I don't think that's going to be sharing like Pete and I share."

Mark contemplated it. No, there was no way he could handle watching Skye with Pete. "That's going to be a hard pass."

"Well then, you're stuck playing with me, Mark."

"I'm not touching you, Bormick."

"Don't worry, Pete's the only one who gets that special treatment. My hands will only be on this beauty."

He leaned over and kissed Crimson, who purred as his hand fondled her breast.

"Give Mark a nice blow job for that hard-on kitten, then come satisfy me again." He rose and made his way to the food, grabbing a handful of fruit and sitting down to watch as Crimson climbed onto Mark. The move did nothing to keep his focus. She was difficult to resist as her breasts slid over his mouth. He grabbed one with his teeth, her groan sending a rush of heat to his now very prominent length. She lowered her body, his teeth scraping across her nipple as he released it.

Her tongue slid along his mouth. "Looks like you and I are going to get to know each other more," she cooed, nipping at his lip.

"I suppose that's not a bad thing," he replied, setting thoughts of Skye aside and raising himself to kiss her. If he was forced to share Skye, he'd satisfy himself with Crimson. No guilt this time, no hesitation.

Her lips drifted down his body until her mouth found his length, his moan uncontainable. Closing his eyes, he gave himself over to her seduction until he could no longer contain the pleasure that riddled his body. Her mouth was a salve that stroked his wounded heart. Every lick sent his hunger rising until his climax shuddered through him. His hand pushed her further down, his pelvis thrusting forward with the impact of it.

When the final current of it settled, she slowly let her tongue slide up his shaft, circling his head a few more sensual times before she rose. He watched her leave the bed and walk to Bormick, her hips swaying, her red locks drifting with the motion. Everything about her was erotic, a seduction he'd fallen prey to once before and had now given himself over to. She climbed atop Bormick's seated position, riding him with the same force he'd done to her earlier.

They were something with each other. A dynamic that was needy and demanding, matching the force that each had. Bormick fed the more feral side of her, the one that had likely driven her villainous ways in the past. With Bormick, she no longer needed an outlet for that ferocity. He was her equal to it.

Mark dropped his head, listening to their grunts and groans until Crimson's cry filled the room. Bormick's heated grunts followed. He looked the other way, only now noticing a shimmer to the wall that hadn't been there. Crimson and Bormick had begun again, but Mark ignored them, rising to look at the space. He put his hand out, feeling the magic, distinct but unlike Skye's or even Pete's. The magic took shape, a door appearing. Mark's heart leaped at the possibilities it held, of seeing Skye, of taking her back.

He didn't know how long he stood there staring at the door, contemplating what it indicated and what exiting through it would mean. Crimson's hand touched his back, and he turned his head, his hope dropping as he met her sad eyes. He glanced over at Bormick, who only shook his head.

"Don't, Mark," she said.

"But—"

She stopped him with a kiss. "There is no going back," she whispered against his lips. "You can't take her away from him ever again, not completely. I'm not ready to face that, are you?"

Dropping his head to hers, he brought his hands to her waist before bringing his lips back to her mouth. He wasn't ready. He needed more time, more from Crimson, until he would be. If he even could be. His hands took in her voluptuous curves as he pushed her to the wall and lifted her leg, penetrating her. Losing himself to her, he let her fill the hollowness, the need for comfort, the need to return to the past that was no longer in his reach, the need to control a situation in which he had no control. He took her desperately, her own desperation driving them both until he was drowning with her. The waves tumbled over them, burying the pain, filling the hollowness, masking the emotion.

He ignored the door, as did Crimson and Bormick, choosing each other over the tide of change that lay beyond it, waiting to submerge them.

SKYE

Skye woke to find herself in Pete's arms, his deep breaths melodic and comforting. She studied him, lifting back the black lock that had slipped onto his forehead. His beautiful blue eyes were hidden behind his sleeping lids until they slowly opened, stunning her with their depth as they always did.

They'd made love more times than she could count. Lost in each other, the world had disappeared so that only they existed. The situation seemed unreal. Yesterday she'd been a happily married woman with a man whom she loved with all her heart and now she was in another man's arms, unsure if Mark still held claim over her entire heart. The thought made her chest tight and threatened to break her.

Pete looked like he wanted to kiss her, but as if the same conflicted emotions were rushing through him, he drew back, removing his hands. Her body missed the warmth of them immediately.

She searched his eyes. What they'd done had been intense, especially that first time. Even with Mark, she'd never experienced anything like it. Pete brought his hand up and traced her face with his finger, lingering on her lips and tracing the outline of her bottom lip lovingly. Lovingly? God, it couldn't be...but it was. It was there like a freshly planted garden, waiting to bloom.

"I don't want to love you," she whispered, hearing the shake of her voice.

His eyes searched hers.

"I'm scared, Pete."

"I know. So am I," he replied.

Neither of them seemed to know what to say or what to do next. She rolled onto her back, her head turning from him. Something shimmered on the wall, and she sat up, clutching a blanket to her, suddenly self-conscious.

"Look," she said, pointing to the spot.

"What is it?"

"I don't know." She rose, taking the blanket with her and trying her best to cover herself. She didn't know why. He'd seen all of her, touched all of her, even tasted every inch of her. At the thought of his body against hers and of what they'd spent the last evening doing, butterflies flitted through her stomach. He'd felt so good, so perfect...too perfect.

As she approached the shimmering, it stopped and faded. She placed her hand where it had been, but could sense no magic from it. Pete moved behind her, his body against hers, his arousal pressing to her skin. She couldn't help but lean her head back against him.

"I don't think Taenom or whoever is responsible for this is ready for us to leave yet," he said, pulling the blanket from her hand. "Are you?" His hand brushed along her curves, her knees weakening at his touch. His lips kissed her neck, skimming her birthmark. A pleasurable shockwave skittered through her, just as it did each time he touched it. She'd always had a reaction to Mark's touches on it, but it was different with Pete, more distinct, more seductive. Like a call to the power that simmered below it.

"No," she said breathlessly, his hands magic on her skin. One caressed her breasts while the other found the mounting wetness that lay between her legs.

"Don't cover yourself up again. You're too beautiful not to look at."

His words left her weak and as his fingers swept over her clit before plunging into her, her knees buckled. He held her with his other hand, keeping her standing as he continued to pleasure her. She turned her head, kissing him, her body falling apart at his touch until she crumbled against him.

He didn't stop, bringing her arousal back in the midst of her climax, then removing his hand to spread her legs and plunge into her. He took her there as her climax faded, the second one building until she broke with him. The room shook again as their powers poured from them; her control was gone, everything absent save for his touch.

Picking her up, he brought her back to the bed and laid her gently down, rising above her. This time, it was her turn to trace the features of his face. His eyes closed as she reached his lips, gently sliding her thumb across them. She drifted to his chest, tracing the tattoos that covered the contours of his muscles and feeling the strength below them. His eyes opened as she reached the trail leading to where his firmness was ready to take her again.

The blue in his eyes was startling, the emotion in them over-whelming. She wasn't certain how they'd gotten here, but now that they'd arrived, she didn't think she could ever go back. Nor did she want to. There was a space in her that now belonged to Pete. She detected it, below Mark's claim, as if it had always been there.

She swallowed, feeling the emotion within her that matched his. They spoke no words, their eyes saying all they needed to say. And so she pressed her palm against him, moving it up his chest, her other hand pulling his head down. Their lips met, his body lowering as hers pressed against his.

He made love to her again, this time slowly, passionately, like their first time. With her rising arousal, her powers slipped through her grasp, meeting his. She fell deeper with each thrust, each moan that escaped her lips and as the power blanketed them, she climaxed with him. The room bled into darkness, her powers calling the hues in his, merging with them until the two danced in harmony across their bodies.

Breathless, her body quivered uncontrollably. She clung to him, his arms holding her tight as he shook against her. Their bodies settled, the aftershocks fading with the subsiding magic. Closing her eyes, she whispered against his ear, "I don't want to, but I do."

He nuzzled her neck, kissing it, and said, "As do I," before rolling her over with him so that she lay against his side. She fit so perfectly, as if the gods had designed her body for his. It was strange curling into him and not Mark, but it also felt right, like this was where she was meant to be. At the thought of Mark, her gut clenched. The guilt—the overwhelming sadness—barraged her until Pete kissed her head, bringing her back to his presence and erasing it all. His arm held her tight, his other hand drifting delicately across her breasts, sending a flush of warmth through her.

"Has it all been leading up to this?" she asked.

He sighed, his hand dropping to rest on hers. "I don't know. I don't honestly know how this happened or when."

She peeked up at him. His jaw was tight with tension that shouldn't have been there after what they'd just done. But she knew why it was there. Lowering her head, she took his hand in hers. Her thumb caressed the side of his finger, her mind wondering why her hand fit so perfectly in his, why it seemed so different from when she held Mark's.

"Is it this place, Pete? When we find our way out, does the spell lift and—"

"No, Skye. It's not a spell. I suspect it's always been there under the surface."

She dropped his hand and propped herself up to see him. "Why do you say that? You weren't attracted to me before."

"No? I told myself I wasn't. Everything with Crimson overshadowed everything else, so it wasn't obvious what it was. But"—he drew his hand up to touch her hair—"the moment I saw you...you were stunning, Skye. The most beautiful woman I'd ever seen."

"Compared to Crimson?" she asked scrunching her brows.

"You truly don't know how gorgeous you are. Crimson is beautiful, seductive, and yes, with killer curves but you're a goddess. Elegant, seductive in your own way, and your curves fit perfectly against me. Too perfectly. I wanted you then, and when you were teaching me, every time your magic touched mine, it called to me."

"I felt that."

"But you ignored it, as did I. You love Mark, and I love Crimson. We had to ignore it."

"We did." She thought back, realizing she'd done the same. Eyeing his body, his eyes that drew her in, the power that called to hers, the subtle rise in her arousal when he was near.

"We avoided being close to each other to compensate for it."

"But we love other people, Pete. What does this do?"

"Nothing. You will always love Mark. Has that changed?"

"No." It hadn't. She loved Mark no less than she had.

"And my love for Crimson and even Bormick hasn't changed. They're a different level than this."

"This is the undercurrent to the tide where they sit."

"Exactly." He smiled, his thumb tracing the corner of her eye. "Your eyes have changed. They look just like Eliana's."

"Changed?"

"The gold is gone. There are little flecks of silver there now, like hers. God, you look just like her now."

Her breath caught as realization hit her, Bormick's words

coming back to her. "The shadow god and his mistress. I needed you, Pete. I needed you to make me whole again."

It hurt to say it, to realize Mark hadn't been able to do that.

He frowned, turning to his side, her body shifting with his. "The power."

"Yes, it corrupted mine."

"But I thought Crimson fixed that."

She shook her head. "No, she didn't. The magic she took from you started it. My magic reacted to it because it held your shadows. I sensed it as I grabbed it and followed it with my own, finding my way out. But the residual touch of the foreign magic remained."

"Until we..."

"Yes, you needed to heal me because...because..." She couldn't continue, afraid to say the words.

"Because I'm your true mate in every sense of the word. Shit. You know why, right? It all makes sense now." His eyes sparkled, shadows within them. She didn't know the reason, but he did. "We were meant for each other, our lines tied to one another by our sires. Eliana is yours; Derrant is mine."

Her eyes widened as it dawned on her.

"We're not just the embodiment of them, holding their magic, their attraction to each other. We are them. We are their children just like Taenom said and they imbued themselves in us." His words should have shocked her, but she knew in her heart he was right. "What was it you told me? She created your line and he, out of spite, created mine? It wasn't spite, it was desperation because he loved her so much and she knew that. If Derrant and Eliana created both our lines at the same time, and she knew what Derrant had done, that my line was a piece of him and hers a piece of her—"

"She bound the two, ensuring that their love, although fractured at that time, would survive."

They stared at each other.

"Our lines were meant to mate," she whispered.

"Yes, but they never did. History didn't allow it."

"But Mark and I have a bond as Elite and Mage Warrior and you through the blood ritual with Crimson and Bormick. And Crimson is of my line, Bormick of yours. If that's true, why doesn't it tie him to me?"

"I suspect the bond connects only to the one who holds the Shadow Magic. My line started with one child, just as yours did, the power traveling only with one born each generation."

"And Crimson's line wasn't meant to be. Eliana said that herself. It's part of the reason the gods removed the Mage Warrior magic in her line. My line was the only one meant to carry it."

"And so you and I are the result."

"And the bond Mark and I have, or the blood bond with the three of you?"

"Unbreakable except by the gods themselves but formed by the same gods who formed ours. Perhaps out of envy or anger, but I guarantee the Elite bond didn't happen with the first of your line."

"No, maybe it didn't. The history is old. Derrant found her, stole her back, the dragons the result of him raping her, taking her against her will from the child and the king. She may have meddled with her own work and formed the link as vengeance on him later. I remember Mark saying she had blessed one of the guards and bound his line to mine, but I wonder if that wasn't as early as she led him to believe. I don't know the first instance of our line and the Elites."

"And the blood ritual was later, maybe even the same time as the Elite bond was formed. Perhaps they both tried to undo their show of love."

"But it didn't work," she said.

"No, but the shadow magic part of my line was removed from this world, so there was never a chance to test it."

"Until now."

"Until now. And here we are, in love with each other but loving the others who make us who we are, all of us tied by Eliana and Derrant."

"The two of us unbreakable? Just as Derrant and Eliana were?"

"The embodiment of them both, like you said earlier and, yes, unbreakable. I would die before I let someone take you from me."

Her breath caught, the reality of their situation crashing into her.

"As would Mark," she said in a whisper.

"And that is now the crux of the issue."

"The next step in this puzzle?"

"Yes. But, Skye, I won't take you from Mark, just as you won't take me from Crimson or Bormick."

"So what do we do?"

"I have no idea, but do you want to leave me?"

"No," she said without hesitation. "No, in fact, I want you to hold me. I want you to make love to me again, to touch me until we're ready to face that test because I'm not ready to face it."

"Neither am I."

He pulled her closer, his lips meeting hers, his heart racing against hers. She let all thoughts but him flee again, her body, heart, and soul his as they made love with a desperation that sent the walls of their room and beyond shuddering.

SKYE DIDN'T KNOW how much time had passed when she woke again. Time consisted only of sex and sleep, touching and kissing, longing that never seemed to wane.

Pete kissed the top of her head as her thoughts slipped to Mark. Crimson had him, and she would take care of him. Skye wondered how many times she'd done just that. There was no room for jealousy. What she and Pete were doing was bound to be harder for him.

Her fingers brushed along Pete's chest. She missed Mark, but Pete filled that part of her, distracting it. He owned a piece of her now that she could never give back to Mark, and that hurt. She'd always been Mark's. But that wasn't entirely true. Her heart had always been his but never entirely, her body never his completely. There was always a part of her that she had to keep free from his claim. Sam had taken it, Alex held part of her heart, Derrant had taken part of her body. There had never been a time when she had been completely his and now there never would be.

Pete removed his hold from her and rose from the bed. She watched him, eyeing what was now partially hers. With muscles lining his back and arms, the black tattoos that decorated his skin, and an ass that gave Mark a serious run for his money, Pete was beautiful. She was aroused just looking at him.

He brought a tray of fruit over with a glass of water, his eyes watching her knowingly. She dropped her eyes, letting them feast on the front of him, the arousal deepening.

"Eat," he said, but she saw the matching need in him as her eyes drifted back to his. "Are all the women in this world so insatiable?" He handed her what looked like a grape, its skin a golden hue. She sat up, taking it from him and studying it. "I thought Crimson had a sex drive, but you put her to shame."

"You're one to talk," she replied, biting into the grape and reaching her tongue down to lick the juice that had escaped.

"Good God, you make it hard to think."

"So I've been told."

He crawled in next to her, the tray between their legs. She didn't like the separation and wondered what that meant for them when they finally left the room. She pulled her knees up to her chin, the thought a conflicting one. The door hadn't reappeared, but it would. The memory of him taking her as it disappeared rushed back, and she nearly dropped the remains of the grape. Even thoughts of him unraveled her.

His fingers brushed along her leg, causing a flock of butterflies to soar through her. Turning to look at him, she asked, "What happens when that door reappears?"

His eyes sparkled a deeper shade. "I don't know, but I'm quite certain there's another test."

"The five of us?"

"Maybe."

She pursed her lips, pondering what would happen then. She didn't think they would return to their lives, not the way they had been before this deviation in their paths. The thought of Pete leaving gutted her, and with it, the knowledge that she'd experienced a small pang each time he'd left. She leaned her head back.

"What if..." She stopped. She knew Mark well enough to know he was insanely protective and jealous.

Pete brought his hand under her chin and forced her to look at him, his thumb caressing her cheek.

"There is no going back to how it was. They know that. Mark accepted that the minute he let you kiss me, the minute he kissed Crimson. He won't take you from me."

"And if he does?"

"I'll stop him."

A shiver ran through her. Two intense mates who were overly protective of her. There was no way this could work. "You can't hurt him, Pete."

"Shh, I'd never hurt him because that would hurt you, but I won't let him separate us."

"And Crimson and Bormick? I suppose they'll be easier to convince?"

"Don't count on it. Crimson may be assertive and fierce on the outside but she's soft, vulnerable even. She won't give me up, and I won't give her up."

"And I won't give Mark up."

"Again, the crux."

"Fuck," she muttered.

"How do you manage to make that word so sexy?"

She laughed, following it with a sigh. "How does this work?"

"I don't know." He dropped his head back, running his hand across his face.

Pushing the tray aside, she climbed atop him, straddling him, feeling him rise against her in reaction. He lifted his head as she traced the design of his tattoos, following each intricate pattern and hearing his soft moan.

"I didn't think it was possible to love anyone as much as I love Mark. He's always been the keeper of my heart. But you..." She paused the motion and looked back into his eyes.

His hand gently grasped her neck and brought her in to kiss her. "I love you, Skye."

Her lips parted with the hitch of her breath, his tongue moving to hers. Her body responded as he lifted her with his other hand and positioned himself before penetrating her. A cry escaped her, and her head fell back, his mouth taking her breast as it lurched forward. Warmth flooded her body. He brought her back, kissing her neck. Drawing his face to hers, she looked into those blue eyes that reminded her so much of Derrant's, but with a gentleness that was Pete. He wasn't her Pete, and she wasn't his, but they belonged to each other in a way the others couldn't touch, could never break.

"And I love you, Pete," she said, the words confirming the feeling in her heart and her soul, while the acceptance of it took over every part of her. She brought her lips to his and kissed him again, her emotion for him pouring forth.

A tingle of magic touched her skin, and she stopped, as did he, both looking at where the door had now formed.

"This test had been passed," he said, his voice low.

"Declaring our love for one another?"

He turned his eyes back to her. "Yes."

A weight grew in Skye's chest, one she knew came with the knowledge that what awaited them beyond the door could quite possibly fracture her heart more than it already was. She rested her forehead against his, not wanting to confront that future yet. The door waited and with it, their escape from the room, but she ignored it, refusing to look back at it. Instead, she held Pete's gaze, seeing the same resigned thoughts behind his eyes. Lifting her hand, she pulled at the dark shades of the room with greater ease than she ever had. His hands fell to her waist as she leaned back on him, letting the hues dance over her skin. She closed her eyes as his magic rose to touch it, the seduction in it almost unbearable.

Directing the magic to the door, she cast it in their shadows so that it was no longer visible. His eyes grew dark with hunger, a ravenous look overtaking them, one that set her body ablaze.

"I'm not ready to leave," she said. "I need you to fill me, Pete. I need you to claim me again."

His hand slid up her body, encircling her neck. He pulled her to him and kissed her, the force of the kiss nearly knocking her back. Below the need she sensed from him, lay the fear and desperation they both felt. Her power fled with his, enshrouding them as they took what they could, she giving him everything and taking all he gave. And as she broke with him, her body crumbling with his into an overwhelming ecstasy, she didn't want to ever be without him again.

BORMICK

Alrighty, you two, time to face the music," Bormick said.

Mark and Crimson were a tangle of naked limbs. Bormick had no idea how many hours had gone by. It may have been days for all he knew. After the door had appeared, they'd ignored it. Crimson and Mark going at it again in an insatiable way. Bormick had joined them a few more times, but for the most part, he'd watched and let them work out their feelings. Having someone there other than Pete was strange. He should have been jealous, but Crimson was enjoying herself too much and Mark was no threat. The threat was wherever Pete and Skye were. It was their sudden relationship that was the threat to the three of them.

He sighed, looking over at the door. Whatever lay beyond it would change them all, especially Mark. Bormick wondered if the man could take it. He supposed having Crimson as an alternative was helpful, but it didn't ease the pain completely.

He closed his eyes, unsure of how even he was feeling. As much as he loved the fact that Pete was finally getting a piece of Skye, he didn't know how he felt about the two being more than sex buddies. They were now lovers, no matter how any of them wanted to deny it. They were mates, in love, and inseparable. He'd seen it in their auras when they'd left, hovering, waiting for them to claim it. He wouldn't mind sharing Skye with Pete, but he didn't think that was going to happen. Skye was coveted, and both her lovers would fight anyone who threatened her or touched her.

"I think I'd rather not," Mark said, pulling Crimson to him and burying his face in her breasts. The man was relentless, and Bormick wondered if Skye had the same sex drive.

"Hiding in Crimson's breasts won't make it go away, Mark," he said, laughing at the squeal Crimson made when he tugged her nipple hard.

"Can't we stay a little longer?" she purred as his hand guided her leg up, allowing the deep thrust Bormick watched him give her.

He shook his head. "Fine, fuck her again, Mark, and then we leave."

He stood aside, watching the two, his own dick throbbing for release as Crimson came with a cry, Mark's release following not long after.

"I think Bormick needs some attention," Mark said, licking Crimson's neck.

Bormick stroked himself as Crimson turned and licked her lips, getting on all fours.

"Shit, that mouth of yours is too pretty to resist," Bormick said, bringing her head to his length and watching her tongue lick the pre-cum that had surfaced.

His eyes watched her, his dick aching. Mark moved behind her, caressing her ass and playing with her. It had taken some time for Mark to warm up to sharing but he was all in now. There was no doubt in Bormick's mind that sharing only pertained to Crimson. Skye was an entirely different matter.

Crimson's mouth opened with a gasp as Mark drove his fingers into her.

"Stop playing, Mark. You're distracting her mouth," Bormick said, pushing Crimson's head back down. It wasn't long before she was bucking against Mark's hand, her mouth tightening around him with the force. He wanted to come, but Mark had mounted her, gripping her hips tight and plunging into her mid-orgasm.

"Prick," Bormick muttered at Mark as her mouth left him again. "Fuck, Crimson, either finish the job or my hand will."

She took him again, and he shoved her down, driving her motion. As his arousal peaked, his orgasm flooded through him. He held her in place plunging into her with each wave of his release until with a grunt he let her go, stumbling back, his legs shaking.

"Damn, that was intense." Only Pete had ever made his legs shake like that. They needed to leave. There was too much sexual overtone in the room, fueling the uncontrollable urge that had taken hold of them.

Bormick grabbed his pants, watching as Mark finished, falling against Crimson and cupping her breast in his hand before moving from her. He laid on his back, Crimson going in for one more lick, as she was known to do.

"Enough, Crimson. Clean up. We need to see what's behind the door. No more delays. I want to see Pete."

"Do you?" Mark asked as Crimson crawled up to lie against him.

"I do. Don't you want to see Skye?"

He saw the flash of emotion. "I'm not sure."

"I want to see Pete," Crimson said.

"Why?" Mark asked.

"Because I love him."

"But he loves someone else. My someone else."

The doorway shimmered, losing its clarity.

"I'll be damned. Crimson, get off of him. Mark, man up and get dressed. You just fucked the shit out of my girl, for I don't know how many days. It's time to leave here and face our future, face Pete and Skye."

Mark pushed Crimson away, anger in his eyes.

"I love it when he's angry," Crimson swooned.

"Don't get angry with me, Mark. This happened. You took Crimson, and Pete took Skye. Everything has changed."

"I don't love Crimson," he snarled.

"Ouch, that hurts, Mark," she said.

Bormick shot her a look. "I don't like the fact that they love each other either, but I love Pete enough to make room for it, just like he made room for me with Crimson. He didn't have to. He didn't know me. He could have had me killed, but he loved her enough to know it would kill her in the process. If you really love Skye like I know you do, then you'll make room for Pete and Crimson will make room for Skye."

"I can do more than make room—"

"I don't think that will be an option, Crimson. You and I are left out of this when it comes to Skye. Neither of her mates will share her."

"Mate?" Mark asked.

"Mate. Both of you are her mates. You through your Elite connection, he through their magic, maybe more. I had a lot of time to think while you two were at it. I think their lines tie them, like the blood ritual ties us and the Elite blood ties you two. They are both direct descendants of Eliana and the Death God."

"But so are you and I," Crimson said, and he could hear the sadness in her voice. He'd meant to wake Mark to the reality but, in doing so, there was no way to protect her feelings.

"Only Skye holds original Mage Warrior magic, and only Pete holds shadow magic, both the most powerful, both directly from their sires. He is her mate on a level that goes beyond us. And I guarantee they've claimed each other, whatever part of themselves we weren't able to claim. Pete will be as protective of her, as coveting of her as you, Mark. He won't be sharing, just like you won't."

Mark's face fell, the anger gone. He walked over and grabbed his pants.

"Clean up, Crimson, then we go," he said, pulling his pants on. "How the hell is that supposed to work? I'm not having sex with her and Pete."

"And I can guarantee Pete won't like that idea either," Bormick said.

He glanced at Crimson. There was hurt in her eyes, and he didn't know how to fix it. Pete was the one who touched her soft side, not him. He was the one who fed the vicious side of her. He was out of his element and unsure how to handle himself.

"Goddammit," Mark cursed, pulling his shirt on.

"Do you love her enough, Mark?" Crimson asked. Her voice was soft, but Bormick could see her fighting to bury the emotion.

"Do you love Pete enough?"

"Yes." She hadn't hesitated. "If Skye makes him happy. Yes. You know what it's like to be torn from her, and I know what it's like to be torn from him. If we do that to them—"

"It will destroy them," Mark finished, looking defeated. He wiped his hand over his face. "So now I'm stuck working out a custody agreement?"

"What's a custody agreement?" Bormick asked. Mark and Pete both used strange terms, and he was glad Crimson was confused by them as well.

"A sharing arrangement like how Derrant gets Crimson five days a year."

"Seven," she corrected.

"Seven?"

She shrugged. "Derrant doesn't negotiate easily, and he wasn't that willing to give Skye up."

"Seven, huh."

"She sends us the tree nymph to play with while she's gone—"

Mark smirked. "I can guarantee that will stop. Skye won't like that idea at all."

"What's the difference between her and Crimson?" Bormick asked, not liking the idea of giving the tree nymph up.

"Skye doesn't like to share, either. She'll tolerate you two because he loves you, but she won't tolerate a random fuck. That you can count on, especially not with the tree nymph."

"Well, damn, this is getting more complicated by the minute," he complained.

"Oh, well, I'll play with her then," Crimson said. "Derrant's grown fond of her."

"I bet he has," Mark said with a smirk.

"Is there something I don't know about the tree nymph?"

"We'll let Pete tell you," Crimson said.

Mark furrowed his brow, thinking about something. "You said Derrant wasn't willing to give Skye up without bargaining."

"Correct. He's quite attached to her—reminds him of Eliana when she's gone, something I can't do because—"

"You don't look like her. But Skye does. You're right, Bormick. We have no say in this, as much as I don't like that. They were mates the minute Pete stepped into his powers."

"The Shadow King and his mistress," Crimson said.

"No, sorry, Crimson. As I said, I had a lot of time to think. She's his true queen. She's the Shadow Queen."

Mark leaned on the bed, his shoulders slumping. "But she's my queen," he said, the sadness in his voice nearly palpable.

"And now she's Pete's."

"That was my title," Crimson said, a quiver in her voice.

"No, it was never yours to take, Crimson, and never his to give to you. Skye is his queen. The rest of us are just lucky enough to be in their court."

CRIMSON

Crimson stared at Bormick, unsure of what to say. Looking away, she met Mark's eyes before he was able to mask the sadness she saw reflected in them. She was trying to be brave, but Bormick's words had almost knocked her to her feet. Being Pete's queen was something she'd loved and now the gods had stripped that from her, too. She was the mistress and they'd given her king to someone else.

"Looks like you'll be spending more time with us, Mark," Crimson said with a sigh, pushing aside the hurt. "I suppose it's not a bad consolation prize."

He gave her the hint of a smile. "No, it's not."

"Get dressed, Crimson," Bormick said. She could see that the situation had rattled him, no matter how he was trying to hide it.

"I would, but Mark ripped my dress off in the hall, remember?"

Mark looked sheepish, as if he'd forgotten; it was a cute look on him.

"What's that on the chair, then?" Bormick asked.

She turned to find a red gown on the chair, simple with straps that met a plunging neckline, and more her usual style than the previous dress.

"That wasn't there before," Mark observed.

Bormick looked around, his eyes squinting. "No, it wasn't."

"Do you think Taenom is watching us?" she asked, cleaning herself up before stepping into the dress which fit her perfectly.

"If so, he got quite a show," Bormick said.

"That he did," added Mark.

She fluffed her hair, lifting herself proudly. No matter what happened, she was a queen, a proud queen, one who wouldn't be broken by this.

"Ready, boys?"

Mark stood taller, tucking his weapon in his band. The weapon remained without its glow, without its connection to Skye. "Ready."

Bormick grabbed the door handle as Crimson moved next to Mark and opened the door. She hesitated for a moment before she left behind the room that had changed them and formed a new bond. Stepping through into the next test that awaited them, she was blinded by the brilliant sun.

Crimson raised her hand to shield her eyes, eyes that had been in the dim lighting of that room for what seemed like days.

"What the hell?" Mark said.

As her eyes adjusted, she saw Skye's castle.

"We're back. Why are we back and where are Pete and Skye?" she asked.

"We're in the courtyard. Maybe they're inside?" suggested Mark.

"Or maybe at our castles?" Bormick said.

"Shit. Let's look."

"No, we should split up. Mark, go in and look for them. We'll check Crimson's, then Pete's. If they're here, you can portal to us. Otherwise, we'll meet back up here."

"How long?" he asked. "I don't think it's wise to be apart."

Bormick looked at the sky. "It's morning here. When the sun spills to mid-day. That will give us time to look, and you to talk to your people. See if this has impacted the other Elite and if we're vulnerable to whatever Taenom has planned next."

"Good point. Okay." He hesitated, like he wanted to say more.

Taking the moment, Crimson kissed him. His hand reached around to pull her closer, then he gently pushed her away.

"I'm happily married still in this kingdom, Crimson. That will lead to more questions than I want to answer."

"You're still happily married, Mark—"

"To a woman who is not mine anymore."

"Fool," Bormick said. "Stop that talk. Remember, you're her mate, too."

"Yeah, look at Pete, Bormick, and me. We're all still mates. They both love me, and I love them both. Nothing's changed." But she saw the doubt in Mark's eyes and heard it in her own voice. She was trying her best to keep up the façade, but the uncertainty of what was happening between Pete and Skye—of how they would feel once they found them—made it difficult to maintain.

"Everything's changed," Bormick said, surprising her with his honesty.

"But it doesn't mean their hearts have changed," she said, hoping her words were true. "But it does mean Mark will be doing a lot more sharing."

"I'm not sleeping with Pete."

"You even try it and I'll kill you, Elite," Bormick snarled, but Crimson noted the hint of playfulness behind his words.

"Don't worry, I'm not taking your guy. Shit, my wife is already doing that. God, that's hard to say."

"I suppose we'll get used to it," she said, bringing her hands up and using her magic to form a portal.

"I suppose. Remember, be back by then if you don't find

anything or hear from me." With that, he ran off toward the castle.

"I hope they're not there yet. I think we need to be together when we find them," Bormick said to her.

"I think so, too." She was also certain she wasn't ready to face them and the consequences of all that had happened without Mark by their side.

She took Bormick's hand and stepped into the bedroom of her castle. It looked the same as it had the last time they'd been there which had been a while. They'd been in Pete's kingdom when they'd left.

"Not here," Bormick said.

She opened the door, running through the halls until she found Hentrom.

"My lady!" he shouted. "Sir." He bowed to Bormick, who was catching up to her.

"Hentrom, have you seen Pete?"

"King Peter? No, not since you were last here. You've been gone longer than we expected. Is everything all right?"

"Yes. You've been keeping the kingdom at peace?"

She'd made him an official advisor for his loyalty, leaving him in charge each time she left for Digremile or Kantenda.

"Oh, yes, my queen. Only up to your standards, always."

"Good," she said. "Are you tormenting the prisoners with your roaming hands again?"

"Only a spare few. Since you never let me have this one, I've had to settle."

"Hentrom, that was our secret," she said hurriedly, having never told Bormick the plans she'd had for him before he'd stolen a piece of her heart.

"Have this one? What does that mean?"

"Thank you Hentrom. I'm not sure when we'll be back, but the kingdom is in your hands until then."

He bowed as Bormick continued to grumble.

"Were you going to give me to him?" he asked as they stepped through her newest portal to Pete's castle.

"Only before I met you. I promised he could have you and Stavin once I'd taken you both down. You were both very cruel to him."

"Are you shitting me?"

She turned to him. "I thought it to be a suitable punishment until I met you and kept you for myself. I certainly didn't know you'd end up liking a man's lips around you or I would have offered you earlier."

He grabbed her roughly, pulling her close. "You will pay for that comment once this is over. I do not like a man's mouth around me, only your sweet lips—"

"And Pete's," she teased.

She noticed him grow against her and couldn't help but smile.

Smacking her ass, he replied, "Well, he's an exception. Now let's find him so that mouth of his can appease me."

"He's clearly not here."

"Then we need to look more, just in case."

She knew they wouldn't find him—knew that Pete and Skye hadn't returned. Yet they searched every part of his castle, asking the staff and the advisor Pete had delegated in his absence. No one had seen him since the day they'd left. After allaying the questions their search had raised, they returned to Pete's quarters.

"They're still there," she said to Bormick, staring at the rumpled bed where they'd lain not so long ago, oblivious to the future that awaited them.

"So they are, which begs the question of why."

"It's not over, is it?"

He laughed. "You can't have expected it to be."

"I was hoping it would be."

He pulled her close, kissing her head. "I can't imagine Taenom's goal was only to mate Pete and Skye. I imagine his original goal was that one that still lingers over us—our failure to accept them as a couple and in turn tear us apart—but there's more to this Crimson. I just have no idea what that is."

"We should get back to Mark. He seemed concerned about us being apart."

"Agreed, but go use that fancy waterspout Pete designed first. You need to rest."

"I've rested for endless hours—maybe days. We have no idea how long we were there."

"Go, I'll wait here for you."

"Not joining me?" she purred.

He gave her a crooked smile. "Aren't you worn out by now?"

"Don't you know better than to ask that?"

His laugh was refreshing. Turning her around, he slapped her ass and sent her to the washroom. Dropping her dress, she stood under the water that was magically tuned to their presence. She still marveled at it, sometimes insisting she bathe in the tub instead, missing the simplicity of it, the pleasure of soaking in it. For that reason, she had decided to leave her tub in place in her castle.

The shower—as Pete called it—did provide its own pleasures. She forced away the image of Pete taking her against the wall the morning they'd left, instead letting the water course down her body. She needed to dull the ache that remained in her chest. Mark had dulled it, quite fantastically, and her legs tightened at the thought. She chastised herself for the thought and her body's reaction. Mark had taken her so many times during their stay in the room that she really shouldn't have been anything but drained. That was not the case, however. Her stamina had always been enough to exhaust any man, but with as sex-craved as her men and Mark were, she was surprising even herself.

Pushing aside the thoughts of her recent sexual escapades, brought the reality of their situation back to the forefront. She didn't like the ache that had settled in her chest. The discomfort accompanied a fear of the unknown ahead of them. The unknowns were something she had always tried to avoid. They left her out of control and control was something she needed desperately. It stabilized her and right now she felt very unstable.

She stepped from the shower, drying herself before freeing the hair she'd pinned up. Bormick was sprawled on the bed, hands behind his head. She crawled next to him, expecting him to ravage her naked body, but instead, he brought his arm around her and pulled her close.

He held her, kissing her hair, his fingers caressing her arm.

Snuggling into him, she mused, "You know, this is more Pete's thing."

His chest moved with his chuckle. "Well, I suppose I'd best get used to it for times when he won't be here."

"Gentle isn't your thing, Bormick. Maybe Mark can take that role?"

"Ha! That man likes it rough and hard with you, Crimson. He's too bound to Skye to be the sensitive type with you."

He was right. Mark took her with a fury each time. She imagined his jealousy and discomfort with the situation fueled that aggression. He'd relaxed some, but he was still demanding, pounding her the way she liked it. Having Mark again had been amazing. She'd never hidden the fact that she'd wanted more of him. The way he'd taken her when she'd held him prisoner had left a craving for him that had never waned. Perhaps it was the connection Bormick had mentioned, Mage Warrior to Elite. Whatever it was, it had never faded. And the way he'd fucked her again had done nothing to calm that craving. He was rough and took her almost as hard as Bormick did, calling to that part of her that was wicked and lethal. She could feel herself growing wet just thinking about it.

"Stop thinking about Mark, Crimson. I can smell your arousal from here and you're going to make me change my mind on this sensitive thing."

Her fingers drifted along his chest, feeling the taut muscles beneath his shirt. Smiling, she let her eyes close. When she opened them, she was alone on the bed. She sat up, hearing the water stop in the other room. Bormick stepped out, drying himself.

"You let me fall asleep?"

"You needed to rest," he replied, toweling his hair. Her eyes perused his muscular body, her own body wanting it.

"Put the thought away and get dressed."

She was shocked, her mouth dropping. There was never a time he turned down sex. In fact, more often than not, he was the initiator and would relentlessly take her.

"I would say that rising reaction to me doesn't agree," she teased.

"Well, it's going to have to," he replied, pulling on a clean pair of pants.

She scrunched her mouth in confusion and he must have read her look.

"This is no longer our space, Crimson."

She sat back. "But it's Pete's."

"Yes, and Pete now has a queen. This space now belongs to them."

That ache grew in her chest again.

"They'll need someplace and that won't be the kingdom she rules with Mark, nor will it be the one you rule. I've ordered the staff to prepare it for their return, or his return. I have no idea how this is going to play out. You and I will deal with whatever the agreement is, but it's up to Mark and Pete to decide on that agreement."

"That should be interesting," she muttered. "And Skye has no say in that?"

"Skye wants them both and loves them both. She'll agree to whatever they decide."

"And we just go along with it?"

His face dropped. "Yes."

"That hardly seems fair."

"We still have each other, Crimson. Mark only loves Skye. No matter how many times he tries to replace her with your body, that will never change."

"Well, then, I suppose I'd better do a damn good job of distracting him then."

"That's my girl."

"I'm not giving up this room, however."

"Crimson." His voice carried a warning, one that she ignored.

"Nope. This is our space."

"I think you'll find it's not, whether you want it to be or not."

He handed her the dress she'd worn earlier, and she looked up at him questionably.

"Wear it. You look beautiful in it."

She couldn't help but smile, his comment warming her heart. As much as she loved the brutish, demanding side of him, his soft moments made her heart soar. She knew they were far and few between and reserved just for her. She leaned up and gave him a kiss, which he returned softly before pushing her away. "I'm quite adamant that I will not heed the call of my dick right now and bend you over that bed like it wants to. Get dressed before I change my mind."

Laughing, she gave up her attempts and put the dress back on. She lifted her hair and let him cinch the back of the dress up, smiling when his lips grazed her neck with a soft kiss. He moved from her too quickly, and as she let her hair tumble back down, she asked, "Ready to return to Mark?"

"Ready as I can be." His blue eyes held a seriousness she only ever saw when the warrior in him was present. They were evaluating her, and she tilted her head trying to determine what he was thinking. "When they emerge, things will never be the same again, Crimson."

She swallowed, ignoring the quiver in her lips that took hold. She didn't want to think about how she'd lost a part of Pete. Didn't want to fathom the pain it would cause to see love in his eyes that wasn't directed toward her. The thought threatened to destroy the façade of strength she was trying to maintain.

"I know."

Saying nothing more, she summoned her magic, forming the portal to Skye's kingdom. After taking one final look at Pete's quarters, she steadied her nerves. Drawing a deep breath, she prepared herself for the unknown that lay ahead of her and ignored the instinct that told her she'd likely never set foot there again.

MARK

You can't be serious," Noah said, his eyes wide as he leaned forward in his chair.

Mark had searched everywhere for Skye and, after not finding her, had called their council, all but Elspeth. She was too close to Skye, having raised her, to take the news without the emotional baggage. He also chose to leave Alex in the dark. He was the last one who needed to know, and Mark would leave that conversation up to Skye once this was over.

As it stood, he'd expected the rest of them to have strong emotions about the situation.

"Very serious," Mark replied.

Trent and Camin remained silent.

"Skye and Pete? Our Skye? Your Skye?" Noah asked.

"Yes, she's with him now."

Noah sat back in his seat, his eyes scrunched. "And how are you handling this?" he asked, his fingers squeezing the bridge of his nose.

"The only way I can."

"By fucking Crimson?" Camin asked with a raise of his brow.

"I didn't ask for judgement, Camin. The gods gave my wife to another man who is now her mate as well. I took what I was given in return. I don't know if any of us had a choice. It was all part of the test or trial that Taenom kept talking about."

"They tried splitting the five of you apart," Trent said.

"Yes, but we passed that trail."

"And now Skye is Pete's and yours?" Noah asked.

"Yes," he said, cringing at the words.

"Gods, how does that work?" Trent asked.

"That is a very good question and one we'll have to figure out. For now, all I know is that Taenom has the two of them locked away still in the other realm."

"And when they return?" Camin asked.

"Pete has our queen." Mark sat back, rubbing his face, the words still painful to say.

"One queen to rule two men and two kingdoms," Camin muttered.

"There's no way to just keep them separated?" Noah asked.

"No," Trent answered for Mark. "Not if the power that has mated them indeed courses through their lineage, connecting the gods to them. It would mean their bond is as unbreakable as the bond between Skye's line and the Elite or Pete and Bormick's blood bond to Crimson. Taking her from Pete would do the same damage to her as taking her from Mark."

"Does Pete know that?"

"I imagine so," Mark answered. "He, of all people, would understand it."

"Another unbreakable bond," Trent muttered. "One only the Death God himself can undo."

"Can the gods unbind Pete and Skye?" Noah asked.

Mark thought about it, a rise of hope in his chest at the thought. That hope receded quickly when he realized the consequences to Skye if he found a way. His shoulders slumped again, and he sighed. "No, it would hurt them to do that. I would never hurt Skye, no matter the cost to me."

"This is unprecedented," Trent said.

"Is it?" Camin asked. "Eliana loved a mortal and her Death God."

"A Death God who punished the mortal to an eternity of torment when he died, a god who stole her back and raped her before she could escape him," Mark grumbled.

"One she returned to because she loved him despite it."

"So, Pete's destined to steal her from me?"

"No, I don't think so," Camin replied. "This trial Taenom has set for you, for them—it seems to rest on mistakes the Death God made. He would never have shared her with the mortal. I imagine Pete could easily kill you, Mark. He could have in those tunnels but I'm guessing he wrestled with the feelings?"

"Yes."

"It's possible he can still return and kill you, failing the trial and following his sire's footsteps. You're weak without her magic and let's be honest, can any of us fight Pete? Even new to his magic, he's formidable."

"So the next trial is a face-off with me?"

"Well, unless the two of them have their own trials and that's why they haven't returned. You assume they've been off—how do I put this lightly—forming their mating bond?"

"Fucking," Mark spat out.

"The word I was trying to avoid," Trent said. "But that part of their trial may be over. I don't think that's all they'll face. If it's true that Taenom is a descendant of the Upper God, then this is about more than just causing a rift between the five of you or even you and Skye. This is about Pete."

"Pete? Not Skye?"

"Correct. Pete. The Upper God and the Death God have long feuded. Pete is the one who must pass the tests in order for all of us to survive this. Skye is only part of it—the part I imagine he's passed until he faces you again."

"Why would Taenom care if I approve of this? What does that have to do with anything between the gods?"

"I don't know, but I suspect these trials are not Taenom's doing. Just as you all have an intimate relationship with the Death God, so too may Taenom have one with the Upper God. What-ever they have planned for Pete will involve you and maybe the other two, but I'm more inclined to believe you suffer the greater loss with giving up a part of Skye."

"My thoughts as well," Bormick said.

Mark raised his head quickly. He hadn't heard them enter the room.

"I'll need to have a talk with the guards," he muttered.

"Don't be too tough on them. Crimson is hard to resist. You should know that well enough."

Mark glared at him.

"Do they not know that part?" Bormick asked innocently.

"Oh, we know," Camin answered.

"Jealous, Camin?" Crimson asked, her tongue making its way slowly over her lips.

Jesus, she never stopped, and his mind couldn't help wandering back to how that tongue had slid along his length. He sat forward, trying to hide the sudden growth in his pants. Maybe this could work somehow. His body obviously thought it would. Of course, Skye wasn't here to counter that reaction.

"I'm good, Crimson. Redheads were never my type, although I do like a well-endowed woman from time to time."

"Eyes off her breasts. I already have enough eyes and hands to share her with," Bormick grumbled.

"I'm sure Camin's wife would agree with that suggestion," Mark said, shooting Camin a look.

The situation had already disrupted his own marriage. He didn't need Camin's to be harmed as well.

Crimson sashayed her way to Skye's usual chair and sat. Mark eyed her, his lips thinning in annoyance.

"What? She's not here, and your queen now rules two kingdoms. I can keep her seat warm like I've kept you warm."

"Good gods," Trent murmured.

"My queen does not rule two kingdoms."

"Yet," Bormick corrected, resting against the wall as he was apt to do. "She will."

"Mistress, remember?"

"No, Mark. We determined Taenom only used that term because that's what we all call Eliana. Use the right term," Crimson said. "She's his queen, whether we like it or not. Just as Eliana is Derrant's queen. Denying it won't make it go away."

"I'm still her husband."

"I imagine that will change," Trent said.

"Are you shitting me? I'm not divorcing, Skye. No matter how this plays out."

"I'm not suggesting that, but Skye rules our kingdom, and Pete rules his own. A queen will need to be official and marriage—"

Mark stood quickly. "You are not suggesting—"

"Yes, he is," Camin said, an amused look on his face.

"Well, this just got interesting," Bormick mumbled.

Noah shook his head, looking completely miffed. "Pete can't marry Skye."

"He'll need to in order to confirm her place as queen and secure the throne for an heir."

"Christ, I can't believe you're even suggesting—"

"I am, Mark. Her throne will need an heir as well. The two of you hold the line of the Mage Warriors in your hands. The two of them hold the line of Digremile in theirs, as well as the continuation of the Death God's line."

"This is complicated on so many levels," muttered Noah.

"Complicated doesn't begin to describe how I feel right now."

"I'd venture that's the point. I suppose we should be thankful that this happened fast. If it had happened over the course of the years—"

"I could have gotten used to it."

"Really, Mark?" Crimson said. "You've been in denial about me, Pete about Skye, and I don't even know where to begin with Skye. It's better this way."

"Like ripping a band-aid off," Noah said.

"A what?" Trent asked.

"Never mind," Mark replied. He turned to Crimson. "You can't tell me the idea of Skye marrying Pete—I can't believe I'm saying that—and carrying his child doesn't bother you."

"Honestly, it doesn't. I'm not the marrying type and children, yuck."

"Then your line dies with you," Trent stated.

"Maybe, or maybe it continues with Bormick," Camin suggested.

"Whoa, me? You want to duplicate this?" Bormick gestured to himself, his eyes wide in what Mark could only read as horror.

"Maybe that's why there are three of us," Crimson mused. "Maybe you and I are aligned to carry on my line."

"Great, this just keeps getting better," Bormick complained.

"You've got quite a few hundred years to worry about that, Bormick," Camin said.

Mark had forgotten women developed differently in their world, their fertility beginning well into their lives. Typically, even centuries into their lives. Hopefully, by then, he'd be better adjusted to this strange turn of events.

"But Skye already has a child," Crimson pointed out. "Doesn't that make her fertile now?"

"Alex is a result of the effect the human realm had on her body," Mark answered. "Women cycle there early because they have short lifespans. We think it influenced her cycle. Her flows stopped when she returned."

It still irked him that she'd had a child that wasn't his, even though he loved Alex as his own. Now he'd have the possibility that she'd conceive Pete's child, experiencing that crushing blow again.

"I suppose you should be used to her carrying another man's child, Elite," Bormick said, rubbing salt in the wound.

"I should punch you for that remark, but it's not worth the effort of walking over to you," he replied bluntly.

Bormick let out a booming laugh. "You and I are going to get along just fine."

"So this means we get more of him?" Noah asked, pointing to Bormick.

"And me," Crimson said with a seductive smile.

"Oh, I've had my share of you, Crimson. Enough for a lifetime."

"Don't kid yourself. Once you taste her, there's no going back," Bormick said, "but touch her, and you die."

"My head is starting to hurt," Trent complained.

"Wait, you'll let Mark have her, but not Noah?" Camin asked.

Noah shot daggers at Camin with his eyes. "I don't want her, and if you say that in front of my wife, I'll kill you, Camin."

"Mark's different."

"Can we not talk about sharing me and focus on finding Skye and Pete?"

"We're not finding them, Mark, so this is what you get. Either that or we can go to your quarters and have some fun," Crimson teased.

"No! You are not setting foot in my quarters, and neither is Pete, for that matter. What the fuck?" He ran his hand across his face.

"Well, I think I've had enough for one day," Trent said, rising. "I'm going to see if I can find any mention of this other realm or trials like these."

The others stood, Noah shaking his head in disbelief before leaving.

Mark wanted to talk to him more, needing a friend, so he headed after him. Bormick grabbed his arm, halting his track.

"We need to stay together, and we need to talk."

"There's nothing more to talk about. We just talked about my wife marrying another man and having his child. I think that's enough talk." Mark cringed, thinking of how he'd had the same conversation long ago with Noah before Skye was his.

The energy fled him at the thought. He'd been fighting for Skye his entire life and now he saw that she would never be his entirely. She never had been, and it hurt.

Crimson rested against his back, her head pressed on his shoulder. He wasn't sure how he felt about the action. It seemed too intimate.

"We're all hurting, Mark. I think even they are. We see it from our perspective, but imagine how torn they both must feel."

The same way he'd made her feel by pushing her to Sam, the same she must have felt carrying Sam's child instead of his. Their past had been hard on them both.

"I know Pete well enough to know he's just as conflicted and scared as we all are," Bormick said.

"You scared? I thought you were the mighty warrior?"

Bormick chuckled. "You keep that between us, or I may go against my instinct and take your ass next time you're grinding into my queen."

"You touch my ass, and I'll ensure you never have the ability to grind anything."

"Stop it, you two. Bormick, we all know it's only Pete's ass you want. Stop taunting Mark with empty threats."

"Damn, Crimson, you take all the fun out of it. Just for that, I get Pete first when he gets back."

"That's if Skye gives him up when they get back."

"Oh, she will because I'm going to remind her whom she belonged to first," Mark said.

"Mmm, why don't you show me what you're going to do to her," Crimson cooed.

"Does she ever stop?"

"Nope, she's enough to drive any man mad. I'm up for some play time again."

"No," he said, resisting the rising desire within him. "We need to be ready for whatever test is next."

"What if it doesn't involve us?" Crimson asked, her hand grasping his newly formed bulge.

"Shit, Crimson," he complained as she squeezed him gently. "I thought Skye made it hard to concentrate."

She nibbled on his ear, her hand reaching down his pants. "You thought wrong."

"Jesus." There was no way he was walking out of the room like this. He wasn't certain what Skye would think if he took Crimson here. It wasn't their bedroom, but that table had seen its fair share of action over the years.

"You swear like Pete and that makes me wet," she purred.

"Fuck it." He turned around and kissed her, shoving her dress down to expose the full breasts he wanted to suck on before proceeding to take her against the table. The sound of Bormick shutting the door registered momentarily as Mark took what Crimson offered and more, replacing thoughts of Skye, of marriage, of children, and everything that hurt him with the pleasure of Crimson's body and mouth.

PETE

Pete watched as Skye dressed in the navy-blue dress she'd found in the room. The color made her eyes dark in the dim lighting. He longed to see them in the sunlight, to see her naked in the mid-day light and kiss every inch of her as if seeing her anew. He promised himself he'd do just that if they ever escaped.

Her breasts peeked out of the low v-line that ran down to her waist, the back plunging, exposing her delicate skin. The wisps of thin material that covered her legs left just enough light to make out the long thin legs that lay below.

His urge for her returned as she caught his eyes. She lifted her long dark locks, exposing her birthmark and the neck that called to be kissed. He let out a long breath before walking to her and bringing his lips to her neck. His tongue drifted over the birthmark, his body reacting to the call of the magic below. The pleasured sigh she released only caused his need to grow.

"We'll never leave this room if we don't stop," she muttered, letting her hair fall.

"Do you want to stop?" Pete asked, moving up her neck, his hands pushing down the strap of her dress to release her breast.

"No," she answered breathlessly, as his finger skipped over her nipple.

He kissed her, knowing he wouldn't let her go yet, the fear of losing her when they stepped beyond the door high on his mind. He walked her back to the wall and proceeded to take her again, unable to resist, no matter how his mind told him they needed to leave.

He held her, pushing into her with the final thrusts of his climax. Dropping her head back, she lowered her leg, the heat of her own climax still fresh on her skin.

"I thought you said you wouldn't take me like this."

Nibbling on her ear, he thrust one last time before pulling out —a move that elicited a sad moan from her.

"I did, but you're too hard to resist." His hand drifted down her neck, the soft skin calling him to kiss it more. "I don't know if I can hold myself to that promise in times like this."

The touch of her hand along his length threatened to tempt him again.

"God, Skye, we can't stay here forever."

Her eyes met his as her hand released him, and he missed the warmth of her instantly. "But if we leave —"

"We'll be all right."

"Will we?"

After buttoning his pants, he fixed her dress, pulling her strap back and kissing her shoulder. "We will. I won't let them tear us apart."

"But then we tear them apart."

"No, we can't do that either."

"So what, we share each other? You and Bormick take me while—"

"No," he growled. "Nobody touches you but me or Mark. I'll leave room for Mark, but no one else."

She furrowed her brow, her lips parting slightly in surprise. "But I have to share you with whom? Bormick and Crimson?"

"Yes. And there's no alternative option on that, just like with Mark."

He thought about Ash momentarily, frowning slightly. There was no way Skye would allow that. He was so possessive of Skye that he wouldn't even allow Bormick to touch her. She was bound to be the same.

"What?" she asked.

"I'm guessing my demon tree nymph is no longer in the picture?"

Her eyes grew dark, and he sensed her anger in the flux of her power. Her reaction should have bothered him but instead appeased him.

"All right, I get it, no tree nymph. Damn. I'll give her to Bormick when Crimson is gone. Maybe Mark can play—"

"No."

There was no hesitation in her response.

"You are quite possessive, aren't you?"

"No more than you."

"Point taken."

"So, now what?"

"Well, we walk through that door and get through the rest of these trials, then face your husband, my lover, and my mistress."

"Mistress? I thought I was your mistress."

He paused, unsure of why he'd used that term for Crimson. They'd established that Skye was his mistress. But that had been before they'd begun this trial, before he'd made love to her, before they'd declared their love. No, she wasn't his mistress.

"Damn." He let his magic flow, watching how it called to hers, and how hers pulled the hues automatically, empowering them rather than bleeding them. Their magic swirled around them. "No, Skye. You're my mate and my queen, not my mistress."

"But...but I'm Mark's mate."

"You're mine as well. You can see it in our magic, feel it in our connection."

Their connection was deeper than it was with Crimson and Bormick, and he suspected Mark.

"How can I have two mates?"

"Because we both claimed you. The same way I now have three mates. I claimed you and Crimson, Bormick claimed me."

Her lips parted in her shock, her eyes growing wide. "That changes everything, Pete."

"I know, but you know it's true, just like I do."

"Yes," she whispered. Her eyes reflected sadness before her gaze dropped. She looked broken for a moment, and he wanted nothing more than to fix everything for her. He brushed his finger along her cheek, knowing she was conflicted, just as he was.

"Skye." Picking her chin up, he forced her to look at him. Her blue eyes were deep with emotion. "We don't have a choice."

"But it hurts...all of us."

"I know. Neither of us asked for this, but now we have it. I can't turn my back on it. Can you?"

"No."

"Then all we can do is move forward and see what happens."

She reached her hand up to touch the magic hovering around them; the move caused a sensation to run through him as though she'd touched his soul. Her eyes sparkled like she'd experienced it, too.

He took her hand, drawing his magic back and watching as hers reached for it before drifting back to settle around her. They stood for an intense moment where his eyes held hers, their feelings soundless.

"We should go," he said finally, "before I take you again."

Her eyes shimmered. "Or I take you."

With a chuckle, he bent down and kissed her, moving her body close to his, and taking in the feel of her again, the way she fit perfectly against him.

Dropping his head to hers, he asked, "Ready?"

"No, but I have to be."

"Good."

He led her to the door, glancing at her once more before grasping the handle. Instinctively, he placed her behind him as he opened it.

"Pete, I have my own power, remember?"

"Yes, but you're still mine to protect."

He squeezed her hand tight, took a deep breath, and stepped through the door, making certain she was right behind him. His heart hammered at the unexpected. There was a chance he would have to fight Mark. Or worse, he would have to give her up. They might even all wake to find this had been no more than a dream. There were too many unknowns, and it did nothing to settle his nerves.

Her hand touched his back, and he continued to move down the darkened hall, feeling the magic of the door disappearing behind them.

"No going back now," he muttered.

They walked on, unable to draw the dark from the hall as they had previously, moving blindly until a light appeared ahead. Following the light, they came to a large bright and open room, Taenom standing across from them.

"Well, well," Taenom said. "I was beginning to think you two would stay in there forever."

Pete's power seeped from him in response.

"None of that, Peter. You'll fight me, don't worry. I guarantee it will be epic. But you need to pass the trials first, to prove you're worthy."

"Worthy? Why, you arrogant son of a bitch." He cast his power out, letting go of Skye and rushing Taenom, only to hit a wall, his power colliding with it first.

"I told you, we don't get to fight yet. They're not ready to make a judgement on you."

"Who's 'they'?" Skye asked.

"My god and his gods, of course. The Death God's champion must prove himself before my gods deem him worthy of their notice."

"I would say he already has their notice, given all the trials we've faced so far," she said.

She was smart, unafraid, and he realized those were some of the qualities he'd always admired in her. Now, he loved her for them.

"My, my, Skye," Taenom said, moving closer to her. "That was child's play. Well, play anyway. Now the games truly begin. Tell me, was it hard giving up one mate for another?"

"I didn't give anyone up," she spat.

The tone of Taenom's voice raised the hairs on Pete's neck, his magic stirring in alarm. He looked around the room, finding nothing, no threats he could determine. But still, he remained on guard.

"No, you spent days in a room giving yourself to another man, after giving your husband to another woman. Hours longer than they stayed, might I add, although he seems content filling your void with her body." He looked at Pete. "Your Crimson does like to please, doesn't she? And please she did, even after they were free."

Taenom was playing on their insecurities about the situation, trying to anger Pete and upset Skye.

Still, she didn't miss a beat.

"I gave Mark to Crimson and Pete gave Crimson to Mark. All of us accepted it, so don't even try—"

"Was it accepted? Will you accept watching him fuck her?" He stepped closer to Skye, and Pete's hackles rose. "Watching as she cries out when they climax together? Which mate will hurt you more when she's beneath them?"

She flinched slightly, a break in her façade.

"We know what we agreed upon. All of us do," Pete said, trying to take Taenom's focus from her.

Taenom turned his attention to Pete. "So willing to give your lovers up?"

"I didn't give them up. What does this have to do with your gods, or even you?"

"Everything." He brought his face close to Pete's. "Will you watch another man fuck your whore?"

Pete grabbed him. "Don't call her a whore or I will kill you."

"Which whore am I referring to? Your lover or your new mate?"

Pete punched him, picking him up by the collar as Taenom laughed.

"So protective, Peter. How will that help you now?"

The floor shook, and Taenom disappeared. Pete looked back at Skye as the floor split, all but the spaces they were standing upon falling away.

"Skye!" he yelled as her square moved further from him. He tried to use his magic to get to her, but it wouldn't heed his call. The silence that answered his command left him unbalanced. Without his magic, he didn't know how to get back to her or to keep her safe.

"Pete!" she yelled, trying to pull hues from the room that now lay in semi-darkness, save for where they stood.

"No, no. No magic, you two." Taenom appeared on his own square across from Skye.

"If you hurt her, I'll—"

"Threaten to kill me again? Save it for the battlefield. Now it's time for your next trial and this one should be fun."

"I don't care what you throw at me, Taenom."

"Oh, this isn't your test, Pete, it's hers."

A third square appeared near Skye, and Mark dropped with a thud against it. He looked dazed for a moment, then scrambled up, running to Skye.

"Skye!" The square moved further from her, sending him teetering on the edge.

"Mark!"

"Shit," Pete mumbled as Mark's eyes caught his and Mark glared at him.

"This is your test, Skye. Two mates, each with their own abilities, their own advantages. Which will you choose?"

"What?" she asked, as Pete stared at him, slack jawed. He couldn't have heard him correctly.

Mark swirled toward Taenom. "Choose?" he asked.

"Yes. Choose. Which will it be, Skye? Will you choose your Elite or your Shadow King?"

"I'm not choosing," she replied, crossing her arms.

"Oh, but you must. You hold the lines of two very powerful houses in your hands."

Pete's heart thudded uncontrollably, unsure of what Taenom was saying.

"With your Elite, the Mage Warrior line continues. With your Shadow King, the shadow line continues. You will bear an heir for your line or Peter's."

"Are you mad? That's what this is about? Well, I hate to tell you, but that ship has sailed, buddy. I have a son—"

"A son who does not hold Elite blood. Only an Elite can produce an heir to your throne, Mage Warrior."

"Well, then, the throne is lost already. Now let us out of here."

"No, it isn't, Skye," Mark said.

He knew something they didn't. Skye was too old to have children, even if she did look like she was still in her early thirties. Pete knew her real age.

"Mark, I can't have—"

"You will. Women don't grow fertile until well into their lives here. You stopped your period not because of your age but because your body adjusted to life here, to the way it should have worked if you'd grown up here. In a few hundred years, you'll be fertile again."

"Holy shit," Pete muttered. He'd never thought about it, had never even bothered questioning Crimson on it, assuming she was too old since she was older than himself and both Skye and Mark. He'd assumed once he'd found out her age that it wasn't an issue.

"I...I..."

"Will bear the heir to your throne or Pete's. Now which do you choose? Your Elite mate or your shadow mate?" Taenom said.

"You can't make her choose," Mark said.

"No? Do you like your wife in another man's arms, Mark? Like the idea of her marrying another?"

"Marrying?" Pete and Skye said in unison, but Taenom continued, "Will you watch as he takes her, listen as she cries out his name and begs him for more? What about bearing his child? Watching her stomach grow with life that didn't come from you?"

He was breaking Mark with his words, and it was pissing Pete off. He gripped his hands and glared at Taenom. "Enough!"

"Really? Will you watch her return to him, Pete? Let her go that easily? Or will you watch as they make love? Their love has existed far longer, and I guarantee they are quite intense to watch. The love between the Mage Warrior line and the Elite line is unbreakable."

"As is his line and hers," Mark hissed.

"Ah, then you have a conundrum. Now, choose your mate, Mage Warrior."

"Did you do this? Speed all this up just to make me choose?"

"Not I, only the gods have that power. Now choose."

"No," she said firmly. "I can't and I won't."

"Well, that makes it fun." Taenom's space joined with more pieces that moved as he walked to her.

"Don't touch her, Taenom!" Pete yelled as his fear grew. There was no way to reach her, no way to protect her.

Skye was trying to draw her power but, like his, it was silent. Mark was looking around frantically for a way to reach her.

"Pete, use your power!" Mark screamed.

"I can't! He has us both powerless."

Mark's face dropped. There was no way either of them could reach her. Taenom's hand went out, a stream of golden magic hitting her.

"No!" they both screamed. He could see the pain etched on her face as she fought against the magic. The sight gutted him.

"You will make a choice."

"I won't choose between them," she said, and he could hear the struggle in her voice.

She dropped to her knees and his heart pounded.

"Skye, go with him," Mark said. "It's okay."

"No," she said, her voice cracking. Taenom's magic stopped.

"She can't choose me, Mark."

"Why not? She loves you," he said.

"How?" she asked. Pete was just as baffled as she was that Mark knew.

"It's clear. You love us both, Skye. It's all right. Choose him."

"No, it will kill her, Mark. She can't choose between us, and he knows that. I won't let her choose me."

"I'm not choosing, Taenom," she said defiantly.

Taenom picked her up by her throat. He was going to kill her if she didn't choose, and the thought raked through Pete like a dozen razor blades.

"Let her go!" Mark screamed.

There was no way out. He would torture her until she had no choice but to decide and either decision would leave her hurting and empty. Pete looked at her, a wave of regret for ever stepping foot in this world, for coming between a love as solid as theirs, washed through him.

"I won't make you choose, and you won't force her to. I love you, Skye, but I won't force your hand, neither will Mark."

There was only one way, and he took it, letting his feet move past the solid space, hearing Skye's scream and Mark's yell as he plunged into darkness.

MARK

Mark yelled as Skye's anguished scream echoed around him, her heart shattered. He could do nothing more than stare at the space where Pete had disappeared, plummeting to his death. The fool had jumped, making the decision for her. He'd given his love for her up so Mark could have her.

"Dammit," Taenom snarled, flinging Skye to the ground. "He wasn't supposed to do that."

Skye was sobbing, but Mark couldn't reach her to comfort and hold her. The sound of her crying broke him. Taenom reached his hand out, a flood of magic fleeing down the dark expanse. It swept to the wall across from them, and a hard thud echoed from it. He dropped his magic, the space now lit so Mark could see Pete's body pinned to the wall.

Taenom walked away, the strange square pieces forming in front of him with each step he took. Pete lifted his head. Blood was running from his mouth, but he was alive. Skye was still in a ball, crying inconsolably, something that broke Mark's heart.

"Skye," he whispered loud enough for her to hear. "Skye, he's alive."

"I didn't think you'd pass that trial, Peter, but you did. You were meant to force her hand. To make her choose you. I was certain you would, but you are proving to be quite the unpredictable opponent."

"That was Skye's test," Pete said, spitting the blood from his mouth.

"No, that was your trial. I only said it was hers to mislead you. You love her so much that you would give her up to another man?"

"Yes, just like Mark did."

"Enough to die for her?"

"Yes," he said, his voice firm.

Skye had stopped crying, and Mark studied her. She was the same Skye he'd always loved, but she was somehow changed from her time with Pete. Her connection with him, her love for him had transformed her.

Her eyes met his, sad and layered with guilt. But the love was there, the same love she'd always had for him. It hadn't faded. She still loved him. That fact reinforced his heart, the one that still belonged to her. Like Pete, he loved her too much to lose her, but too much to hurt her.

"You people confound me. You were supposed to make her choose you!" Taenom screamed.

"And why would I do that?"

"Because the Death God did."

"And why do you assume just because his blood runs through me that I am him?"

The hold on Pete released, and he dropped to the floor with another thud. Pete glared at Taenom as he lifted himself.

"It's clear you've never loved another."

"And it's clear you make assumptions about me as well."

"Then you would know that you do anything to protect that person, no matter the cost to you."

"And your lovers—"

"I would die protecting any of them. Don't challenge me on this, Taenom. You will lose."

"Oh, I will challenge you, and I will win that battle, but first, you must face your next trial."

The room went black, and Mark felt himself moving again, falling hard against the floor. The new room slowly came to light. Pete rose from the floor across from him, rubbing his head.

"Where's Skye?" Mark asked.

Pete looked around, his eyes growing frantic. "I don't know." He started feeling the wall of the small room, trying to find a way out, Mark doing the same.

"Nothing. There's no way out," Mark said.

"And no way to Skye. Dammit, you're my next test."

"Great. So we fight each other while she's out there, not knowing if she's in any trouble?"

Pete slid to the floor, scraping his hands through his hair. "I won't fight you, Mark."

"You jumped so that she wouldn't have to choose. Asshole. I wish I'd thought of that." He sat across from Pete, his back against the wall.

"I don't think you were meant to. It was my test."

Mark looked him over. He seemed tired, which didn't make Mark feel any better. Mark crossed his arms, trying to calm the envy that was clawing at him. He had the urge to beat the shit out of Pete, but the defeat that showed in the way Pete's shoulders slumped stopped him. Crimson was right, as hard as this was on them, Pete and Skye were suffering as well.

"Why did you jump? Why not make her decide?"

He knew the answer. It was the same reason he would give— he would never make her choose. But he wanted to hear it from Pete, to have him validate his thoughts.

"Because I love her, Mark. I have no explanation, no fore-warning, no excuse, but I do. She needs you, though, and she loves you. I could never take her from you."

He leaned his head back. "Can't you be an asshole, Pete? It would make this easier."

"Would it?"

He laughed. "Probably not."

"Where are Crimson and Bormick? Are they safe?"

Mark heard the concern in his voice, the pang of pain.

"They're fine. Bormick was up her skirt when they brought me back here."

He'd left them after his last taste of her, heading up to his quarters, missing Skye the minute he'd stepped in. Being with Crimson had allowed him to bury his emotions,, but in the quiet aloneness the pain had come rearing back with double the force. Ignoring the need to break down, he'd washed up and changed, needing to be free of the room and the reminders it held of Skye as quickly as possible. As he was returning to Crimson and Bormick, ready to scold them for giving into their lust again, magic had taken hold of him and dropped him here.

"I suppose it's good then that your pants were up when they brought you here," Pete joked.

"True."

They were quiet for a moment. Mark had so many thoughts, but no words to voice them.

"Where do we go from here?" Pete finally asked.

"I'm not happy with you fucking my wife," he grumbled.

"And having your dick inside of Crimson isn't exactly something I like. You didn't touch Bormick, did you?"

"He's all yours. I have no interest in touching him or having him touch me, no matter how much he threatens it."

"He would have done it already if he really wanted you."

"That's reassuring. So...that leaves Skye."

"And Crimson."

"I'm not a threat to you and Crimson, Pete. Sure, she's amazing in bed and that mouth—"

"Is addictive, but no more than Skye's."

Mark grimaced from the claws of jealousy that dug into him, and he rubbed his face.

"It's different with Skye, and you know it. This isn't about what Crimson and I did, no matter how much it bothers you. It's about you and Skye. There's more at stake. I can go without Crimson again. Can you go without Skye?"

"No," he answered honestly. "But that stuff Taenom said...I don't want to take her from you, Mark. She's your wife, not mine."

Mark rubbed his eyes, thinking back on Trent's words.

"You don't have a choice. She's your mate now, too. You won't take another. Fate and our pasts connect the five of us. There will be no others in our circle. You'll need a queen, and Skye will fill that role. Everything Taenom said is true."

"Crimson—"

"Do you believe that? Does Crimson's magic call to you the same way?"

"No."

"Crimson is not your queen, and you know it. She knows it. Skye knows it. It's Skye who will continue both your line and hers with the both of us. Jesus, I can't believe I'm saying that."

"Neither can I."

"I want to tell you to leave her alone, to go back to your kingdom and never return, but I saw the way she crumbled when she thought you were dead. It would crush part of her, and I can't live with that."

"So what do we do? Some kind of custody agreement?"

"Thank you! I said that earlier, and Crimson and Bormick looked at me like I'd grown a second head."

"You can't use human terms with them," Pete replied, laughing. "Although Crimson does get quite fired up when I swear."

"So I noticed."

Pete's jaw clenched and Mark could see the anger before Pete shook it off.

"If I have to get used to you sleeping with my wife, you need to get used to me with Crimson. I'm not getting shafted on this deal. I get to play, too. I'll need something to take my mind off the two of you."

"So we share Skye."

"I guess we have to but...but not the way you and Bormick share Crimson. I don't think I can watch you touch her or, shit, watch her fall apart with you."

"Agreed. I'm not going for that either. And Bormick may be up for sharing Crimson with you, something I find surprising. Though he does nothing but surprise me. I, however, am not participating in that."

"It's weird enough with him there—"

"Takes some getting used to," Pete said.

"Hard pass on getting used to you with Skye. So what do we do about her?" he asked.

"I think we talk to her and we work out a way—"

The room shook, the wall to his left shattering. Both he and Pete jumped up at the same time. They stared at each other as Skye's screams filled the room. The sound hurt him worse than anything that had happened to this point.

SKYE

Pete and Mark had disappeared, but Skye was still on her knees, overwhelmed with relief. Pete wasn't dead. Her heart had broken into a thousand pieces when he'd jumped. She hadn't realized how deeply she loved him. She had suspected she couldn't live without him, but now she knew with certainty. The idea sounded mad. Love didn't bloom that quickly, like a door had been opened, love flowing through like a torrent that couldn't be stopped, filling a space that hadn't been opened before.

"So, it's true," Taenom said, walking to her, the squares forming before him with each step closer he came. "You love two men. Not desire, not lust, but love."

It was true. She loved two men, and she had no understanding of how that could be. It was something she couldn't fathom. But perhaps she could. She'd loved Sam, all the while continuing to love Mark. But that had been different. What she'd felt for Sam had been under the constraints of what she'd allowed herself, knowing her heart belonged to Mark. Nothing she'd ever felt for him came close to what she felt for Mark. Nothing ever had, until now. There was no denying she loved Pete to the same degree she loved Mark, and that terrified her. But she knew beyond doubt that she did, for even thinking she'd lost him had broken her.

"What have you done with them?"

Taenom was standing over her, and she didn't like it. She attempted to move, but he stopped her, his hand coming to her head. She jerked back, but he grabbed her hair, holding her in place.

"You know, I was in love once."

He yanked her head back painfully so she could see his face. Fire burned through her scalp where the hair was ripping. "You killed her on the battlefield, and quite viciously, I might add."

"That bitch was your mate?"

"Ha, no, but she was my lover and I think it's time you suffer for her death."

He jerked her harder, her hair ripping in the process, the move eliciting a cry from her.

"You are a beauty, aren't you? No wonder they both love you. You have a face that could shatter a man." His other hand grasped her skin tightly. "Maybe I should find out what makes you so irresistible."

"Don't touch me," she snarled.

"Or what? Your men will defend your honor? They're too busy killing each other to even notice."

Her heart dropped. It couldn't be true. They couldn't be fighting over her. If Pete killed Mark, or Mark killed Pete, she couldn't live either way.

"Each trial gets harder, each designed to challenge him."

"Why? What's the point of all this?"

Her scalp was starting to ache, and she wished he would release her. Instead, he tightened his grip, her tears sprouting in response.

"Because he must prove his worth, he must suffer the wrongs of the Death God in order to be his champion."

"Champion?"

"This is about much more than you, Mage Queen. This is about far greater. The gods will have their champions and if he proves his worth, he will face me."

Fear encompassed her, and she was finding it hard to breathe. Her heart was hammering so hard she could hear the pounding of it.

"Don't worry. He won't make it through the next trials."

Taenom let her go, and she slumped back to the floor, her head on fire. His words had only increased her heart rate, and she swallowed back the bile that sat in her throat at the thought of what Pete faced. Defiantly, she tried to draw the darkness from the room.

"Conserve your energy, Skye, your magic is bound for the moment. It's not your magic that's needed for the next test. It's his, if he passes this one. There's only one way to find out."

He drew his hand, and she was lifted from the ground. Desperately she tried calling her magic, but it wouldn't listen. Only silence and an empty feeling greeted her each time she summoned it. She fought the hold his power had on her, struggling against it.

"My, but you are a fighter. Let's see how you hold up against this."

A gold stream left his hand and hit her, slicing through her like a knife. It made its way into her, then exited her other side before plunging back into her near her shoulder, continuing to weave its way in and out of her like a ribbon threading itself through her.

She screamed with each entrance and exit, the pain nearly unbearable. When the magic had finished its path into her body, it began to slither within her, coursing its pain and heat with its movement. The scream that fled her was raw and unstoppable, just like the flow of the ribboned magic.

"Let's see if they can save you...if they don't kill each other first."

He walked away, shimmering from her sight. The pain continued, her screams reverberating across the empty space.

PETE

Pete ran, Mark next to him, both putting aside their current dilemma at the sound of Skye's scream. Nothing mattered but Skye now.

"What the hell?" Mark mumbled, halting his steps. Pete stopped, staring at the scene that was unfolding, his nerves pounding through him along with a feeling of terror he'd never experienced.

Skye was midair, thick ribbon-like streams of gold magic weaving in and out of her skin. She'd screamed so much her voice was raw and ragged, further breaking Pete's heart.

"Skye!" Mark yelled as Pete aimed his magic at her, the black of it enshrouding the room. He directed it to overlay the ribbons, but they resisted, her scream shredding him.

"Can you free her?" Mark asked.

"I'm trying, but every time my magic touches it, it hurts her."

"Fuck," Mark said, his face distraught.

A low growl came from behind them.

"Do I want to know what that was?" Mark asked.

Pete glanced beyond Mark, seeing the feral green eyes and the exceedingly large shape of a beast in the dark.

"Probably not," Pete answered.

"Great."

Another scream from Skye broke their trance.

"Looks like this is a trial for both of us again," Pete said.

"Right," Mark said, drawing his weapon. "You save Skye. I'll protect you from the creatures. With what little I can."

He pointed to the dull stone on his weapon.

"When I gave her up, I gave up her power to you."

He turned away and ran toward the beast, leaving Pete stunned by his words and the brutal reality of them.

"Save her, Pete!"

Skye screamed again, the force behind it weaker, so he focused his energy back on her. Sending his magic toward her, he let it coat the areas of her not affected by the golden magic, sensing the calm grow in her. He couldn't feel her magic, which explained how she'd been left vulnerable to the strands, strands he couldn't touch. They were an opposing source, striking out violently whenever his magic touched them. He could feel the sting of them as they struck back but it was Skye's cries that told him his attempts were causing her more pain.

He heard Mark fighting the beast, or maybe it was two beasts now. If that was the case, he needed Skye's magic, and fast. Pete calmed her screams, dulling the pain with his own magic, but he didn't know how to stop Taenom's magic. The more Pete thought about Taenom doing this to Skye, the more his blood boiled. He'd kill Taenom for hurting her.

The thump of a beast let him know Mark had downed one, but the growls continued, confirming his suspicion that there was more than one beast for Mark to fight. A separate thud resounded in the silence, followed by Crimson's cry of fear.

"Shit," he heard Mark mutter.

Pete swung his attention from Skye toward the sound. He searched for Crimson, unable to determine where she was.

Looking for Crimson drew his focus from Skye, and her screams returned.

"I've got her, Pete! Save Skye!" Mark yelled.

Pete spotted Crimson, seeing that several beasts had surrounded her. Mark jumped across one, slicing its head clear off and landing next to Crimson. He pushed her behind him, but now four beasts cornered them.

Skye screamed again. This time the sound was weaker, and it drove a dagger into his heart. He was torn. Both the women he loved were in danger. But Mark had Crimson and Skye was defenseless.

He turned his focus back to her, trusting Mark to protect Crimson. He was getting tired of trials. He clenched his fists in anger as a red-hot rage rippled through him. Taenom would pay for this, and Pete would enjoy every ounce of pain he inflicted on the man. Rolling his neck, he tried to calm his anger, knowing it wouldn't help Skye. The first tendril of his magic touched Skye, calming her screams. Ignoring the strands of golden magic that were so viciously embedded in her skin, he sent his shadows further into her, knowing her body would accept them and that they would strengthen her.

Once he'd calmed her, he cast a wave of magic to Mark, reaching for his weapon and binding it to him. Pete's power now fueled it just as Skye's once had. The flow of Elite power struck him in answer, Mark's eyes meeting his with a furrow of his brows.

He didn't know what exactly he'd done but he wouldn't let them die, no matter the cost, as long as that cost wasn't Skye or Crimson. He'd done the only thing he'd thought to do to save all three of them.

He turned from Mark's gaze, hearing the fight continue, feeling the connection, the power of the weapon as it cut the beasts down easily. He reached his magic back to Skye, this time letting it flow under the strands of gold, shielding her from them. Shadows wrapped around each strand, eviscerating each and turning the gold to ash. His irritation at Taenom and the situation he'd put them in, hastened the process. Every thought of killing Taenom in retaliation fueled his power. Beads of sweat formed on his forehead, he was concentrating so hard. Upon hearing the final beast fall behind him, the last strand eclipsing Skye faded. Skye collapsed and he ran to her, catching her before she hit the floor and holding her tight to him. He brushed her hair back and searched her eyes as they blinked open.

"Thank God," he said.

He'd been about to kiss her when Mark ran up to them, with Crimson behind him.

"Skye?"

Her eyes lit up, moving from his, and a slash of pain in his heart gauged his heart.

"Mark," she said, her voice a painful blend of relief, sadness, and guilt.

Pete helped her up, and the four of them stood there awkwardly.

"Well, this is fun," Crimson said.

"Fuck it," Mark said. "She's my wife. I can kiss her if I want."

He pulled Skye from Pete and kissed her. Pete couldn't help but notice how her body drifted further into his. Pete's heart ached at the sight. He met Crimson's eyes, which were lush and full of understanding. She gave him a smile that replaced the pain, and he went to her, drawing her into his arms.

"You can't stop what they have," she said. She kissed him softly and his blood stirred. "Do you still love me?" she asked.

"Never stopped," he replied, silencing any more words with his mouth. The feel of her against him was so different from Skye, but still perfect in every way.

The room shifted, transforming into a bedroom, similar to the one he and Skye had been in.

"You're fucking kidding me," Mark grumbled.

"Oh, they are deviants, aren't they?" Crimson said letting him go and clapping her hands in excitement.

He looked over at Skye, who was still in Mark's arms. Her eyes were sad, and he could only imagine she was feeling the same as he, seeing Crimson in his arms. The conflicted emotions—the tear of needing both her and Crimson—was almost too much to carry.

"This is not happening," Pete said, moving away and looking around the room, looking for any exit. Mark began doing the same, muttering his agreement.

"I don't think I can do this," Skye said.

"Not my idea of fun either, Skye, and, trust me, I'm always up for sex."

Skye sat against the bed, rubbing her arms, Crimson sitting next to her.

"So what do we do? You can't tell me they expect us to..." He couldn't say the words.

"To fuck Skye?" Crimson said.

"Yes."

"That's exactly what they want."

"But how does that solve anything?" Mark asked. "I don't want to watch Skye with him."

"Well, I don't want to watch her with you," Pete hissed. The thought made his blood boil.

"She's my wife!"

"Well, she's my queen!" He stared Mark down.

"Nothing like two men fighting over the other woman in the room to boost your self-confidence."

"Trust me, Crimson. I don't want to see either Mark or Pete with you."

"Thanks, Skye, because while I enjoy watching you and Mark, I'm not certain how I feel about watching you and Pete. I know it makes him happy, so I've come to terms with the idea of you sleeping with him and...loving him, but I don't want to see it."

"I really do love you, Crimson," he said, turning his eyes to her and softening some.

"I know you do, but you love Skye now, too. So that means I have to share your heart with two people now. Not as much room as I once had in there."

"That's not true, Crimson," Skye replied.

"No?" Mark asked.

"No," Pete and Skye said at the same time.

There was a rumble and a shimmer in the air, Bormick suddenly standing in the middle of it all.

"Gods, what…" He spotted Pete and smiled coyly, unaware of the others in the room. He walked straight over and, grasping the nape of Pete's neck, kissed him.

"That's something I still haven't gotten used to," Mark said.

Bormick drew away, leaving Pete winded. Bormick's intensity was a bit overwhelming at times.

"I'll take care of that later," he said, squeezing Pete's erection.

"Thanks, buddy, but I think you might have to stand in line."

Bormick turned around. "Well, well, this should be interesting." He made his way over to Crimson and kissed her with the same ferocity.

"I'm all right," she said.

"You disappeared."

"Mark saved me."

"Don't even think about kissing me," Mark said.

"What about Skye?"

"No," Pete growled in unison with Mark.

"The goddess doesn't get shared, Bormick," Crimson said.

"Damn, Skye, how did we get to this point? You now have Mark and Pete fighting over you."

"We're not fighting," Pete said.

Bormick looked around the room. "I think you might be if we can't get out of this room. Either that or you better start fucking her now."

"Nobody's fucking anyone," Mark said, scowling at Bormick.

"So we're stuck in here the rest of our lives and with no sex?" Crimson whined. "Should be fun."

"What trials have you faced, Pete?" Bormick asked him. He looked quickly at Bormick, the sudden change of topic throwing him off. He was always surprised how Bormick vacillated between boorish brute and intelligent leader. He would have found it sexy if they weren't in the situation they were currently in.

Rubbing his hands over his face, Pete thought back through the trials, He went on to detail what had happened since he and Skye had left the room.

"How did you escape the first room?"

"We did what they did," he said, feeling Mark's eyes on him.

"Nah, that wasn't the complete test because it didn't open after the first time or any time soon after that."

"How many times—" Skye started.

"Plenty to accept Mark as mine while you were occupied with Pete," Crimson purred. "I'd forgotten how voracious he is."

"Crimson!" Pete scolded.

"No, it's okay. We need to get used to this," Skye muttered.

Mark remained quiet. The tendons in Pete's neck were tight with tension. He didn't like thinking of Crimson with Mark, and didn't want to know how she'd enjoyed it. But Skye was right. As much as it stirred Pete's jealousy, Mark had every right to Crimson since Skye was now loving him.

"Our door opened when we all accepted that Skye was your other mate and you hers. Only when we all accepted it."

"I still don't like it," Mark grumbled.

"So when did yours open?" Bormick asked again, ignoring Mark.

Shit. He knew exactly when it opened, but he didn't want to hurt Crimson or Mark any further. Bormick could take it, but he didn't think the other two could. He met Skye's eyes, seeing the same thought in them.

"When?" Mark asked, and Pete heard the irritation in his voice.

They both stayed quiet.

"They don't want to tell us because they think it will hurt us," Crimson said. "Well, we're well past that. Everyone in this room is hurting, even you two. Whatever it is, it will only nudge the hurt that's there."

"When I said I loved him," Skye said, her voice soft.

"And I said I loved her."

"Fuck," Mark swore, walking away from Skye and rubbing his forehead. "Why was that easier when we were discussing it than actually hearing it?"

"Because it solidifies our suspicions," Bormick said.

"And now we have to deal with it," Crimson said. "Do you really love Skye, Pete?"

He turned to her. Her green eyes were rich with emotion. "I do."

She flinched slightly, then covered it. "Like you love me?"

He thought about it. "No…it's different, like it's…" He looked back at Skye. "It's embedded beneath what I feel for you and Bormick."

"The undercurrent," Skye said, using the term she'd used before.

"Undercurrent?" Bormick asked.

"Yes. Like the force behind what I feel for Mark, strengthening it, but solid and powerful on its own. He's the undercurrent to the tide I ride with Mark." Her eyes never left his, the blue sending a rush of need through him, as did her words.

"Undercurrent," Mark repeated.

Pete dragged his eyes from Skye, resisting the urge to kiss her, and watched as Mark sat next to Crimson.

"There long before the Elite tie or the blood binding. Ancient in its own right and something we can't ignore," Bormick said.

"You still love me, Skye?" Mark asked.

Pete heard the catch in her breath, sensed the increase in her pulse. She did and she always would.

"More than I ever did," she answered.

"More?"

"The undercurrent," Bormick said.

"Their hearts were partly locked, waiting to find each other before this but now they're complete," Crimson said. "So they love each other and still love us deeper than they did because the bindings have broken. Kiss her, Pete."

"What? Why?" he asked at the same time Mark did.

She turned to Mark. "I've seen you kiss her, all of us have. It's intense, Mark—otherworldly. I'd bet you anything it's the same for them now that they're mated."

"Is it the same for you and Pete?" he asked.

"No, we're driven differently. You two have a history that forged that intensity. We're good, but the two of you could make me orgasm just watching you."

Pete couldn't help but chuckle as Bormick let out a laugh.

"Kiss her," Mark said. "What the hell. We've already seen it once. Let's see what happens this time. Test her theory."

"Are you sure?"

"Shit, Skye, you just slept with him for days. You're going to marry him, and I'll have to watch you carry his child just as he'll have to watch you carry mine."

"Whoa..." Pete said, not understanding why this kept coming up.

"Shut up, Pete. You know as well as I do. She's your queen. We all know it. Even Taenom mentioned it," Mark practically growled.

"Mark," Skye said.

"No, Skye. It's my lot in life to share you with another man. It sucks, but it's what I've always had to do. At least this time you're still mine, too. If I lived through twenty years of you married to Sam, I can live through this. You're worth it."

She ran into his arms and kissed him. Pete wanted to turn away, the pain of seeing it was like a gaping wound to his heart. But he had seen them kiss before and he needed to deal with it, whether he liked it or not. He watched Mark's hand weave through her hair, pulling her closer. Crimson was right, what they had was powerful, sensual, and it spilled from them.

He looked away, catching Bormick's eye. Bormick gave Pete a sly smile.

"Go. Kiss him, Skye. Let's get this over with," Mark said.

"No, I get to kiss him first," Crimson said, rising from the bed and going to him.

"Is there a line forming to kiss Pete?" Bormick joked.

"Strange to think of that," Pete muttered before Crimson jerked him forward. Her kiss was passionate and demanding before she finally released him.

"Christ, Crimson," he said, backing up and catching his balance.

"Yeah, he still loves me."

Skye was glaring at her. "Oh, Skye, you're going to torment poor Mark. You might as well feel his pain, and here, both of you can feel our pain."

Crimson pulled Mark away from Skye, sending Bormick into a hearty laugh as she broke the man with her persuasive kiss, her hand making its way to his pants before Mark stopped her.

Pete's heart clenched at the sight, jealousy churning through his body. He wanted to storm over and rip her from Mark, just as he'd wanted to take Skye away from the man during their kiss. The intensity of the reaction was almost the same, but with Crimson it was surprisingly less.

"Really, Crimson?" Skye asked, her hands on her hips.

"Really, now kiss my lover before I finish your husband off."

Mark leaned back against the bed and Pete knew instantly what he and Crimson were like together—furious and needing, a replacement to cover the feelings they didn't want to deal with.

"I doubt Skye wants to watch that, Crimson. It might give her a view of Mark she's not used to. You bring something out in that boy that I don't think she sees often."

Pete threw Bormick an annoyed look, then glanced back at Skye who had turned to him, her eyes a heavy navy.

"She sees it enough, Bormick," Mark returned, but with a breathless quality to his voice.

"Your turn. Prove me right," Crimson said.

"Great," Skye mumbled.

Pete gave her a crooked grin, losing himself in her eyes before drawing her forward and kissing her. The world fell away like it always did, his magic draping over them, hers answering the call, unbinding from within her to reach him. Their draw to each other was a natural thing, instinctual, releasing without any thought, as if their magic needed to touch to survive. She pressed into him, fitting perfectly against him. His hand slid over her back, weaving through her hair as hers moved up his chest.

"Goddammit," he heard Mark, his voice breaking his trance.

He and Skye pulled apart, the magic dissipating.

"There's no competing with that," Bormick said.

"No, there's not," Mark grumbled.

The guilt in Skye's eyes matched his own, but he didn't know how to alleviate it.

"So what now?" she asked, drawing her eyes from his.

"I think that's as much as I can take," Mark said. "I can't watch anything more."

"Nor can I," Pete said.

"Maybe that's not why we're all here in this trial," Bormick said. "Everything you described has been a test of you, Pete. All tests similar to ones Derrant failed."

"Derrant? You're not going back to that again, are you?" Mark said.

"Yes, I am."

"But Derrant didn't love anyone but Eliana," Skye said.

"Yes, but this is about what he did to Eliana, not about Crimson and me. It's about the three of you. The Shadow God, his lover, and the mortal she loved."

"Testing his champion," Mark muttered. "That's what Taenom said. You are Derrant's champion. We've always suspected this was bigger than us."

Skye brought her hand to her chest, looking shaken. "Taenom used the same term. He called you the Death God's champion."

There was a moment where they remained silent, her words bringing a gravity to the situation that was ten-fold what it had been.

"So what does that mean?" Pete asked, not sure he was comfortable with the sound of that term or what it implied.

"It means you pass all the tests to prove to the gods that you're better than Derrant is, worthy of fighting for your true father," Bormick said.

"I'm not sleeping with Skye in front of Mark or even Crimson."

"And I'm not watching you with Mark or Pete, Crimson," Skye added.

"You've already slept with each other. You passed that test, you gained Mark's acceptance, and you left him alive, accepting his place in her heart."

"But Mark still holds claim on her heart," Crimson said. "As we hold claim on Pete's."

"We need to give up our hold on the two of you and—"

"I'm not giving up claim on Skye. She's still my mate."

"Not entirely," Pete said as it dawned on him. "She's mine as well, but your claim still holds."

"So, that's it?" Crimson said.

Bormick paced in front of them. "I don't think that's all of it. Let's say this is a battle of some sort, their trials leading to the final battle between the sons of the true gods, the Death God and his brother. Both gods choosing champions for it."

"Then Derrant would want Pete armed as best he could. He would argue for his own trial," Mark said. "One to equip Pete with the power he needs to fight Taenom and win."

"Yes, and all of these trails have revolved around Derrant and Eliana, Pete and Skye."

"All the regrets Derrant has," Crimson added. "And what would be the ultimate regret for a man who lost his love for countless centuries."

"That he never showed her he loved her by marrying her," Mark said sadly.

"Then that's it," Bormick said. "Pete marries Skye. Their union completes the trials, reinforcing his power through that union with her magic. You have to marry her Pete, that's the final test. That's Derrant's test."

SKYE

Her heart was pounding, but those words took Skye's heartache to another level.

Pete wore an expression of pure shock, his mouth opening and closing before he finally said, "What? I can't marry Skye. She's already got Mark."

"I can't. This is too much, too fast," Skye said, backing away, ignoring the sudden leap in her heart at the thought of becoming Pete's wife, of sharing his bed for the rest of her life. But her love for Mark countered that thrill, and the two were wrestling with each other. "Oh, my God, I can't..."

"Skye?" Crimson said. "It's okay."

"It's not okay. This just happened and really, really fast." She gestured between her and Pete. "We haven't even gotten used to that and you want us to get married? Christ, I have a husband. I can't have two husbands!"

"You can," Crimson said. "Revina was Mechon's third wife."

"What?" Mark said, turning to her.

"She was his third wife. He was married to three at one time, but the first two got into a fight about two hundred years after he married Revina and they mortally wounded each other, leaving her as the only one."

"See, that's exactly why this is not a good idea," Skye said.

"I'm not going to kill Mark," Pete countered.

"I might kill you," Mark mumbled.

"No, you won't," Bormick said. "Just like Crimson and I would never hurt Skye. It would destroy them."

"I can't marry Skye," Pete argued.

"You can if you have Mark's permission."

"You're in this, Skye, you love him enough already to marry him. He sacrificed his life so you wouldn't be hurt. He loves you enough," Bormick explained. "Mark is the one with the most to lose. You two have a history longer than ours. A love that existed longer."

"Mark, I can't—"

"Yes, you can," he said, and she recognized his tone. It was the same tone he'd had the day he'd stepped away from her, the day she'd married Sam. "There's no alternative, Skye, and we'll be faced with this at some point anyway, if he lives, and he won't live if the two of you don't marry."

She couldn't tear her eyes from his. They were sad but defiant, the hazel in them rich with emotion.

He sighed, rubbing his hand down his face. When he returned his eyes to her, she saw only resolution. His posture straightened, the commander in him taking over to control his emotions. "You will marry him, and I'll deal with it. I dealt with Sam, I dealt with Derrant. At least I know Pete will treat you better than Derrant. Now who here can officiate a wedding?"

She didn't know what to say and was too stunned to react.

"This is ridiculous—" Pete started.

"Maybe it is, but this is what the gods want. This is what would have happened somewhere along the way," Bormick said. "If you're worried about me and Crimson, we're fine. We'll do whatever it takes for you to survive and to be happy. Taking this step will do that."

"I can officiate as queen," Crimson said. "Not that I want to marry my king off to another woman."

"He was never your king, Crimson. She was always his," Mark said, the hurt that layered his voice like a knife through Skye's heart.

"And she was never only your queen." There was a slight quiver in Crimson's voice that further broke Skye.

"I'm sorry Crimson. I don't—" she started.

"I know, Skye. None of us do, but this is the way it's going to play out. You're going to marry Pete, he's going to win this battle, then we're going to figure out how to make this work. Oh, and don't think I won't be all over Mark every time you're with Pete."

"That's a given," Mark said. "I'm not suffering alone."

"There's no suffering with Crimson," Bormick joked. "Unless you mean sexually."

Skye sighed. "Okay, he's yours." The words hurt her to say, but she had to. Crimson purred and pulled Mark's mouth against hers. Watching them a second time was even more painful. Her heart wrenched before she reminded herself that this was necessary. If she was going to have Pete, Mark needed Crimson, and Skye would let him have her. Mark drew Crimson closer, his hand wrapping around her waist just like he did when he kissed Skye. She noticed how Pete turned his eyes from them, his own pain and confusion etched in his face. She could see it in the crease of his brow and the way his jaw was set in a grim expression.

"Guess you two will need to get used to that," Bormick said. "I was forced to."

Crimson let him go, leaving Mark breathless, just as she had earlier. He met Skye's eyes, and she saw the guilt in them.

"Don't be guilty, Mark," she said with a sigh. "We're both going to be with someone else. We'll need to adjust to it. At least it's Crimson, something I never thought I'd say."

"I can guarantee she makes him happy," Bormick said with a wink.

"That's reassuring," Pete grumbled.

"We all need to adjust," Skye told him.

"I know. Mark, she's yours, but you have to share her with Bormick."

"Oh, he's warming up to that."

"No touching him, Bormick," Pete warned.

"He already knows he'll lose a few appendages if he does."

Bormick grabbed his crotch protectively and grimaced.

"All right, let's do this," Crimson said. She moved to Pete, brushing her fingers along his cheek before kissing him. Skye's heart ripped at the sight, but she fought it knowing he was Crimson's, too. His arms gently wrapped around her waist, the kiss long and sensual. Skye turned away, meeting Mark's eyes.

"I release you of the claim I have on the part of you that belongs to Skye," Crimson murmured.

Skye's eyes flew back to them, catching Pete's look of shock as she stepped from his arms.

She stopped before Skye, kissing her cheek and whispering, "Be gentle with him."

Bormick stepped to Pete as Crimson moved away. Pete looked sheepishly at him. She experienced no jealousy when Bormick grabbed his neck and kissed him, the kiss just as passionate. It was more curiosity than anything.

"I release you of the claim I have on what belongs to Skye."

He let Pete go, threw a sly grin at Skye, then stepped to the left of Crimson, who nudged Mark with her elbow. "Go on, Mark."

"Damn," he muttered, slowly walking to Skye. "Why do I feel like I never get to have all of you?"

"Because she was never all of yours to begin with," Crimson answered.

His arms encircled Skye's waist, her heart leaping at his touch. His eyes softened. Threading his hand through her hair, he drew her in until their lips were touching. She fell as she always did with him, his touch taking her from everything so that only he existed again. The kiss contained the emotion, the love he held for her and as he dropped his head to hers, he whispered, "I release you of the claim I have on the part of you that belongs to Pete."

It didn't seem possible, but she felt the release, her heart freeing enough to completely accept what she had with Pete, making space for him along with Mark. She didn't know how to react to the sensation as it settled in her, her heart feeling complete as if it hadn't been before.

He kissed her once more, and that fear of losing him fled with it. She was reassured that he was still hers. Now they both would be. Each man owned a part of her.

Mark looked at Pete. "You hurt her, and I will find a way to destroy you."

"Understood."

Mark took her hand and gave it to Pete, then walked away.

"Let's get on with this. I'm about ready for this shit to be over and when we get through with this, when you beat that bastard, I'm making love to my wife. You've had her long enough."

"Fine by me, once we've worked out an agreement."

"Great," Mark muttered.

"Yeah, we're ready for some time with our mate, too," Bormick added.

Skye smiled, feeling relaxed and somehow whole, as if she were finally complete. She'd thought she was whole all this time with Mark, never realizing there was anything missing, but now she saw that she never had been. There'd been a space Mark had not accessed, just like Crimson surmised, but Pete had opened it. Mark's release had given it entrance to complete her.

"That agreement will involve all of us, not just the two of you boys," she told Mark and Pete.

"Well, let's get you two married. Anyone know how to do this?" Crimson asked.

"Are you shitting me?" Mark said turning swiftly to her, an expression of disbelief on his face.

"I didn't have much time for marriages in the past, Mark."

"You were too busy breaking them up," Bormick joked.

"Exactly."

"Just do something. You know, 'do you take this bride to have and to hold?'" Skye suggested.

"What kind of marriage ceremony is that?" Bormick asked.

"The normal kind," Pete answered.

"You all have strange customs in that other world. Here." Bormick ripped a long white ribbon that adorned the bedpost, and that's when she remembered that her wedding to Mark had been different.

"Forget that fast, Skye?" Mark asked, sarcasm coating his words.

"No, but it has been ten years, and I thought that was a royalty thing."

"It is. You and Pete are both royals. If it's not done right, the people will not recognize the marriage," he replied.

She couldn't think straight, and it was showing. Bormick talked Crimson through each step, how to use the ribbon to bind their hands together and to weave it up their arms with each word until it reached their hearts.

"How do you know all this, Bormick?" Mark asked.

"When I was a kid, the Queen of Digremile married. It was a big deal, but it was closed off from us commoners. I snuck into the castle and watched."

"And you remember from that long ago?"

Bormick shrugged. "I was a bit of a pussy back then. I liked the way the ribbons wound, and it stuck with me. That was the last memory I have of being happy. The mage wars began shortly after."

Skye studied him. There was so much more to the brute

façade he chose to have people see. The more she got to know him, the more she came to adore that side of him.

There was silence until Pete shook his head, saying, "So, a wedding was the impetus for your criminal life?"

"You never saw that queen, Pete. She was the kind who looks innocent on the surface but lets you fuck her like a whore in the bedroom."

"And now it all makes sense," Mark joked.

"You know, every time I come to appreciate you, Bormick, you go and turn it into something dirty," Skye said.

"It's that dirty side you want, Skye. Too bad these two have blocked you from it. You're stuck imagining how dirty I could be with you."

"Enough, Bormick," Pete said as Crimson giggled.

"Don't worry, Pete. I'll make sure I'm nice and dirty when I get to fuck you again."

"Can we just get this over with?" Mark asked. "It's bad enough I have to watch my wife marry another man, but now I have that image in my head."

"It's a good image to have, Mark," Crimson cooed. Skye could feel her cheeks growing pink as the image filled her mind. She wasn't sure why the thought turned her on so. "Even Skye wants to see that."

"I..." she started.

"Just get on with it," Mark griped.

"Fine, Mister Serious." Crimson pouted. "You need to relax again. I can help you with that."

"No!" Skye said. "No helping my husband relax with me in the room."

"Which husband?" Bormick teased, and both Mark and Pete shot him a look. "I'm asking a relevant question."

"Shut up. Crimson, do what you need to," Pete said, and Skye could hear the irritation that layered his tone.

"So serious, Pete," Crimson started, but he only narrowed his eyes at her. Skye couldn't help but think how cute the look was on him. He was so different from Mark when he was annoyed. Mark had that commander side of him that turned all business when he was serious. He became a demanding presence, and when he was annoyed, that same persona took over. It was sexy in a dominating way.

Pete was broody but with a boyish look, as if he didn't fully embrace that side of himself yet. The look was sexy as well, but turned her on in an entirely different way.

"I think you and Mark need to stop shooting us annoyed looks, because Skye is seriously aroused. Damn, you are hot when you're turned on, Mage Warrior," Bormick said, bringing her thoughts back.

Both Mark and Pete glared at him before turning their eyes to her. She felt the flush burn darker in her cheeks.

"I'm not—"

"The hell you're not. I know that look. Damn, I don't want to know if that was for me or him," Mark groused.

She crossed her arms.

"That's not helping your case, Skye."

"Shut up, Crimson. And, if you must know, it's for both of you. Now let's do this so I can take whichever one of you I get when this is done."

Mark's mouth dropped, and she looked away to see Pete's boyish grin.

"Are you sure I can't have just a taste of that?" Bormick tried again. "I mean, come on. That's sexy and I can only imagine what that brings to the bedroom."

"A lot," Crimson teased. "But leave her alone, Bormick. If we keep this up, she's bound to jump them both."

"And force them to do what neither wants to do—share her."

"Something I don't want to see!" Crimson said.

"And we don't want to do," Pete grumbled.

Skye's own irritation was growing, and she walked to

Crimson and snatched the cloth from her hands. "Marriage, now."

"Is it good to go into something like this that angry?" Crimson asked.

"Good point. Do you need a good fuck to get that aggression out? I'm happy to offer myself so they don't have to share."

"Bormick, if you don't stop, so help me I will bloody your face."

"Pete, you know you're a pussy. Now if that threat came from Mark, I'd be worried," he replied with a laugh.

Mark ran his hand over his face. "It's a wonder we get anything accomplished. Skye, calm yourself, Bormick, stop being you and, Crimson, let's get this over with."

"No advice for Pete?"

"No."

"Good," Pete said. His arms were crossed, and she could see his magic just on the surface of his skin, like it was ready to strike. Skye wondered if the target was Bormick or Mark. His magic tingled in the air around her and her own magic responded, drawing it to her. The warmth of its touch calmed her, and her tension fled. She met his eyes. He'd felt it, too, his own body relaxing with the connection.

"Can't argue with that," Crimson said, coming over and snatching the cloth back from Skye.

"What was that?" Mark asked.

"What?"

"That look between the two of you."

"Their auras, Mark. I told you, there is no stopping what they have. Even their magic knows it."

"You saw that?" Pete asked.

"Like watching sex. It's quite erotic, the way your magic touches each other."

"Not something I want to know," Mark said. "And, Pete, keep your magic and your hands off her while I'm present."

"I have no control over what my magic does, Mark."

"Damn. Let's get this done with. I think I'm ready for a strong drink about now," Mark griped.

"I think that's a very good idea."

They repeated the affirmations of their love for one another and their faith to their union, Crimson blessing it in the name of their gods. Upon her final word, the shadows slipped from Pete, Skye's magic fusing in answer, both seeping through the ribbon with a tingle as it turned black before her magic bled the color from it, disintegrating it. The hue swirled around them, growing as his magic surged to meet it. The force of it moved them closer.

She watched as a marking formed on the wrist opposite the one where her bond with Mark lie. This time, the black webs of the Death God weaved their mark, leaving a matching one on Pete's wrist. There was a sudden weight on her head, and she brought her hand up to feel the delicate crown that sat upon it. Pete's crown sat upon his, the same she remembered him clutching the day Derrant had sent him to this world. She remembered touching it, never knowing it was awaiting its mate or imagining the impact Pete's appearance would have on their lives.

"Time to kiss her, Pete," Bormick said, a bit of awe in his voice.

Skye's breath caught as he drew her closer, their eyes still locked. His head dropped to hers, and they both hesitated, knowing there was no going back once they kissed. But as the magic swirled around them, she thought they might be well past that point of return. His lips met hers and the world disappeared, leaving only the two of them and their magic. She sensed the change, the claim he had on her hearing his call, her body responding immediately. Their power danced in celebration, her heart reaching for his as he drew her closer.

"The others," she whispered, forcing herself from him.

"Shh, they're gone. I felt the magic the moment we kissed. We're alone now."

Sadness touched her heart before her awareness of him strengthened. She thought of who they were together, of what they meant to the future of their world, the final battle hovering near. All of it filled her consciousness. And she knew they needed to finish this step, to consummate their marriage, to own it, to take each other as mates, as husband and wife, as soulmates.

He brought both hands to her face, his eyes a darker shade of blue, rich with power. He kissed her again, and she released herself to his touch. Their clothes fell away, the crowns disappearing as their magic intensified. His hands were firm as they perused her body, passing over every curve like it was his first time touching her. And with that touch, he was claiming her again, each part of her coming alive with that claim. Her soul and heart opened to him, his conscious touching hers as he picked her up and brought her to the bed, entering her slowly. Each kiss of her neck, her mouth, her breasts left her weak and desperate for more of him. Her body was ablaze with flames that burned through to her very core, igniting a need for him that she didn't think would ever be satisfied. She was left begging him to enter her, pleading for him to be one with her. As he answered her plea and thrust fully into her, her orgasm broke, leaving her body a cataclysm of sensations that had her clinging to him. His groan filled the room, meeting her cries of pleasure, his moves pushing her over the edge a second time. His lips smothered her scream, and he continued kissing her until she was rising again. The ecstasy of him and of their magic was so intense that she could do no more than ride its tide.

He made love to her, worshipping her with his every touch, his every move, every thrust until her rising climax crested a final time, crashing over her, their bodies convulsing as one with the power of it. Even as she caught her breath and Pete's body trembled with hers, the need persisted. There was an insatiable hunger that continued to burn through her. Lifting his head from her neck, Pete grazed her skin with his lips until he kissed her again. He drew away, his bright blue eyes seeing straight into her soul. Her fingers traced his jawline, and he turned his lips to her hand and kissed it before trailing his kisses up her arm.

"Make love to me again, Pete," she said, her voice raspy.

"Tell me you love me again, and I'll make love to you the rest of the night."

She brought his face back to hers. "I love you, with every part of me that belongs to you. Every part that's always been yours, always been waiting for you to claim it. I love you."

"Good, because I love you, Skye, with every part of me that you own, the part of me that I gave you when I first saw you that night in the grove—alluring and powerful. You owned me then, before I even realized it, and you own me now."

They made love repeatedly just as he'd promised. There was a need within her, one she could sense was in him, that never quite seemed fulfilled until they'd given themselves to each other so many times that sleep overtook them. Pete's arms held her tight as she drifted off.

WHEN SHE WOKE, Skye was still in Pete's arms, his embrace tight as if he was afraid of losing her even in his sleep. She studied him as he slept. The thick black hair, the chiseled face, lush with the few days facial hair he'd sprouted. Below her hand, his toned chest rose and fell with his breaths. She let her fingers drift along his cheek, marveling at how beautiful he was, like a dark god, like the Death God himself. Replace the black hair with Derrant's blonde and one could easily mistake him for the god. It surprised her that she'd never noticed before, seeing it now so clearly.

His eyes blinked open, their bright blue finding hers as they adjusted. He took her hand and kissed it, fingering the ring on her finger.

"Morning," he said, his voice groggy.

"Morning," she replied with a smile, bringing her hand closer as his hand drifted through her hair.

On her finger was a black ring, gnarled vines escaping to wrap around navy blue stones that shimmered against the tiny diamonds that surrounded them.

"Pete, that's not my ring finger, and that's not my wedding ring," she said, sitting up slightly to show him where Mark's ring lay, this one starkly contrasting it on the opposite hand.

He took her hand, studying the ring before bringing his hand up, his finger now bearing a thick black band, no gems but spiky vines running through it.

"Guess that makes it official?" she asked.

"No, we made it official last night," he replied, touching her cheek and letting his fingers skim along her breast. His thumb brushed her nipple as a mischievous smile formed on his sexy face.

She bent to kiss him, pausing to look at the wall and spying two massive doors lined in gold.

A shiver ran through her as she swallowed loudly. "I think they're ready for you."

He turned to look, his hand dropping. "Yeah, I get that feeling."

Suddenly afraid of what lie beyond those doors, she turned back to him, fearful of losing him now that she'd found him.

"They can wait," he said, and her heart skipped at the seduction in his voice. "First, I'm going to take you in every position imaginable, ravaging you the entire time, and when we're through, I'm going to make love to you. If today is my final day, I want to go into it knowing I had all of you."

Her breath caught before he pulled her down, kissing her with a hunger she hadn't experienced from him before, her body reacting. Demanding yet still soft and the way only Pete touched her. He did as promised, ravaging her, doing things to her body and soul that even Mark had never done until her body was on fire and she'd had more climaxes than she'd ever thought possible.

She fell apart against him and with him until, when they were through, he took her in his arms and made love to her. Her heart soared with his touch, the ecstasy of him inside of her, his body enveloping hers as their powers shrouded them.

When he'd finally had his fill of her, leaving her weak and exhausted, he let her rest, holding her until she drifted off again. His touches filled her dreams, making them pleasurable and serene until a dark cloud drifted into them. With the cloud, the air turned cold, and fear tiptoed across her spine along with a sense of aloneness she couldn't fight.

Her eyes flew open, and she looked around, finding Pete gone, one of the doors cracked open from where he'd left to face Taenom. Above her, the ceiling shook with a powerful thunder. He'd left without her. He'd promised Mark he'd keep her safe no matter the cost, and so he'd left her in the only place he could keep that promise. Far from his side.

Another great force hit the ceiling, and she scrambled from the bed as bits of plaster fell onto her. The battle between the gods' champions had begun and was waging above her.

CRIMSON

The world fell from under Crimson's feet, both emotionally and physically. She caught her balance against Bormick, the castle grounds now under her feet again.

"Are we back home?" Mark asked.

"I think so," Bormick answered.

"Where are they then?"

"Back in the other realm. We're no longer needed," Bormick replied.

"Back there?" she asked.

"I would assume so, consummating their marriage."

"Goddammit," Mark cursed.

"They'll be all right, Mark," Bormick said.

"Will they? We have no idea what faces them. And I just officially gave my wife to another man, again!" She could hear his frustration, the anger pouring forth. She glanced at Bormick, who shrugged.

"Our man," Crimson said. "She married our man, and it hurts, but it's what needed to be done."

"Did it? Did it really?"

"Pete gave me up to you—"

"We don't love each other, Crimson, and I doubt we ever will."

Bormick crossed his arms. "Did you ever stop to think that you are not the only one impacted by this? Sure, you and Skye aren't used to sharing, I get that, but for gods' sake, I get the worst end of this deal. Pete's taken, you get Crimson, and I don't even get to try Skye because you and Pete are so obsessively protective. What do I get? To watch you fuck my girl and your wife fuck my guy."

Crimson turned to him and brought his head to hers. "He still loves you, as do I."

"I know."

"And I can let Mark go any time you want me to."

"Nah, the man needs a distraction and the two of you are a turn on to watch."

"Mark, she doesn't love you any less, and Pete doesn't love us any less. We just have to make room for them."

He pulled his hands up his face, then through his hair. It struck her that it was an action she adored. There was something vulnerable but sexy in the move. "Right."

"What now?" Bormick asked.

"I could think of a few things," Crimson cooed, thinking of Mark's body thrusting against hers.

"I bet you could, but we need to focus. Did you two see them when they kissed?"

"How could we not?" Mark answered.

"But did you see the power, the way it changed, the auras around them were black as night?"

"No, I didn't see that, but I felt it," he said.

"And I saw the crowns," she said.

"Yes, the crowns appeared."

Feeling like he needed it, she walked to Mark and pressed her lips to his. He pushed her away, but she stared him down.

"That's not what I need right now."

"No, but I could use it."

"You just had it before the gods pulled you there with us."

She pushed him against the stone wall. "It's what you need, Mark. Take me because you know damned well Pete's taking Skye."

His jaw clenched, his eyes hardening.

"Just do it, Mark," Bormick said. "There's nobody here and who cares if there is."

Crimson pushed her hand in his pants, coaxing his already growing length before freeing it, sliding to her knees, and taking him in her mouth. There was no reason for what she was doing other than to block out reality and replace it with Mark.

"Christ, Crimson," he groaned, his hands kneading in her hair.

"Now that's what I'm talking about," Bormick said, grabbing her hips and tipping her ass up before lifting her skirts and rubbing his hands over her ass. "I think we'll both take her, Mark. No harm in having a little fun to ease our frustration."

She gasped as his fingers plunged into her. The motion lit a fire within her that burned like an unstoppable flame. It was further stoked when Mark pushed her head back down. Moaning, she grasped his legs, his hands driving her rhythm as Bormick sent her to the edge. The stress of the day, the emotion of all they'd gone through, and the pain in her heart drifted away. Sex had always been the way she'd shielded her emotion. The pleasure coated it and as she'd aged, she'd let it fill the gaps, let it embolden her. That's what she was doing now. She didn't want to face the idea that she'd lost Pete to Skye, that she'd lost her title as his queen, that he was loving someone else. And she knew Mark didn't want to face it either. Even Bormick, who covered his feelings almost as well as she did, needed this. Sex would take it away, and so she let the feel of both men shroud the dull ache in her chest.

Bormick pulled his fingers free and thrust himself into her. Gods, he felt good and with Mark in her mouth, the intensity grew. Pleasure pulsed through her, sending tingles bursting in every part of her body. Each thrust sent her further over the edge. Mark swelled in her mouth as he lost control, his warmth filling her mouth, the taste sending her plummeting. Her own climax thundered through her and she cried out. Bormick's release followed, accompanied by his loud groan.

As her tremors subsided, she licked Mark clean of any remaining essence. Once Bormick freed her of his grasp, she stood and ran her tongue over her lips.

"You're insane, you know that, right?" Mark said as she leaned into him.

His hands squeezed around her waist, and she saw the matching look of want that shadowed his eyes. It was the same that she wore—that desperate need for more because the numbness hadn't completely found its way to her heart. She took him in her hand, stroking him until he was erect again, watching as that looked changed to desire.

"Fuck me hard, Mark. I want you to make me scream," she said against his lips.

"Good God," he said breathlessly. "Not here."

She pressed herself further into him, letting her tongue trace his bottom lip.

"Here."

"Dammit Crimson—" She covered his objections with her mouth, her tongue forcing its way in to play with his. His hands gripped tighter, the slight sting of pain encouraging her. He turned her so her back was to the wall and proceeded to take her rough and hard, just like she'd wanted. His emotions were fueling the act. Her body accepted the force embracing the way the pain of the stone against her back dulled the ache in her heart.

She met Bormick's eyes, catching the lust in them as he watched with no reservations. Mark broke, her own orgasm clinging just at the cusp. With each push further, ecstasy threatened to take her, cresting with the feel of his mouth on her breast, his tongue tantalizing her nipple until she could take it no more.

Her body was a thrill of pleasure and pain. He kissed her through her climax until her body calmed and he dropped his mouth to graze her neck, whispering, "Take me to Derrant."

She grabbed his shoulders, still trying to return from her high. Her mind was grappling to comprehend his words when her skirts fell back down over her legs in a rush of material. He stepped from her and buttoned his pants, never taking his eyes off hers.

"You do that and that's how you end it?" she complained, her breath still ragged.

He smirked, a look that nearly broke her again. "Why yes it is."

"You two together are something else," Bormick said.

"Mmm, the only one who fucks me that way is you, Bormick. Mark is raw and unrestrained sex."

"Derrant, Crimson," Mark said again.

"I can't take you to Derrant," she told him, reaching up and wiping his essence from her with the inside of her skirts. The temptation to leave it dripping there was high, but the sensation reminded her too closely of the act and that would only lead to her need for more. As it stood, her body was still feeling the after-effects of what he'd done to her. "He was very clear the last time, no more summoning him."

"She's right. I won't let her risk his wrath again."

"I need to talk to him. We know what's going on now and it's time he gave us answers."

Crimson bent over, still trying to stop the shaking in her legs.

Mark gave her orgasms like Bormick did, fast and lethal, ripping through her, causing every part of her to shiver.

"You did that to her, Mark? I'm impressed. I thought I was the only one who made her legs shake. Even Pete doesn't do that to her."

"No, Mark and Pete are very different. Or maybe that's just with me," she said, standing. "Are you a gentle lover with Skye, Mark? Do you just take your frustrations out on me?"

"I definitely take my frustrations out on you, Crimson, and I think we both like it that way. But I'm not necessarily gentle with Skye. She and I are pretty demanding in the bedroom with each other."

"Yeah, I've seen what you two are like when you go at it," Bormick said. "Maybe Pete's the soft side for both our girls."

"Don't forget, Bormick, there are times when Pete can be very demanding." Seeing the shift in Mark's expression, she added, "But those are rare."

She managed to stand; her legs still shaking slightly. Gods between the two of them, they were going to destroy her. She hoped this was all over soon so she could have a little soft time with Pete. That was if Skye gave him up right away.

"Call Derrant for me, Crimson."

"No, I'm not risking that again."

Bormick moved to her side, taking a protective stance. "She's not doing it."

"Dammit, we need to talk to him." He turned and yelled, "Derrant! We need to talk to you!" He sounded like a crazy man. Maybe the marriage had thrown him over the edge of insanity. "Derrant, I summon you through my connection to Eliana! I summon you!"

"Shit, you're going to piss him off, Mark," Bormick said in a hushed tone.

He was right, and a pissed off Death God was one even she didn't want to tempt. She'd been on his bad side once before and it wasn't an experience she wanted to repeat. A blanket of darkness took them, and a force ripped Crimson off her feet, sending her tumbling hard against a stone floor. She lifted her head, fighting the shake in her limbs. The fear of what she'd find before her gripped her body.

"You dare summon me!" Derrant raged, standing over Mark, who was just raising himself from the floor.

Crimson could see the ire in the power that billowed from him. He pushed his magic toward Mark and threw him against the wall, where he landed with a loud thud.

Mark lifted his head, challenging Derrant. "You dared give my wife to another man. I think that allows me some leeway." He stood, wiping the blood from the corner of his mouth with his sleeve. Bormick had taken a step in front of Crimson, always her protector.

"You think I did any of that?" Derrant laughed. "If I was going to give your precious Skye to anyone, I would have given her back to me."

"Tut, tut, Derrant. She's no longer yours." Eliana, who was perched on the stairs, stood, her beauty stunning Crimson just as it did each time she'd seen the goddess.

"Unfortunately."

"My, my, Bormick," Eliana said. "You look in need of some attention. Why don't you come with me?"

"Nice try, Eliana."

"I'm not trying, Derrant," she said, draping her fingers over Bormick's cheek. Bormick looked awestruck, and for the first time since Crimson had known him, was speechless.

Crimson furrowed her brows at Eliana, not happy with sharing another one of her men.

"You can come, too, Crimson, let them talk."

Her jaw dropped. She'd not expected that response.

"I'm fine with that," Bormick replied, looking like a happy kid.

"Of course you are," Crimson said, knowing it was the closest he would ever come to having Skye.

Derrant pulled Eliana away then sniffed, his eyes going directly to Crimson.

"I think they're all quite sated, aren't you?" He came closer to Crimson, and a need for him climbed its way from below. It was the same reaction she'd always had for him. One she could never ignore. "Have you been seducing the Mage Warrior's husband?"

"I wouldn't call it seducing."

He pressed her back against a column, one she hadn't realized he'd walked her to. Her mouth parted in reaction, and he shoved his mouth over hers, all her senses fleeing as they always did. There was no denying the Death God, especially when he owned her soul. And she didn't want to deny him. He was her wicked pleasure, and the things he did to her put all men to shame, even her lovers. It may have been the tie he had to her soul, or perhaps it was simply that he was a god. Whatever it was, Derrant called to a part of her that only he owned, and she would always answer his call.

"You're coming with me, Bormick. Let them play. He needs to get it out of his system. Mark, come," she heard Eliana say.

Eliana wasn't complaining which surprised Crimson, but she supposed the goddess had two other men to occupy her. Crimson didn't mind, Bormick needed the attention. She was curious to hear Mark's reply, however, knowing Bormick would jump at the chance, but Mark, regardless of what he'd done with Crimson, seemed too honorable to risk hurting Skye by sleeping with someone other than her.

"I...I'm really—"

Too tied to Skye, just like she'd thought.

"You don't turn a goddess down, Mark," Bormick said in a hushed tone.

Derrant diverted Crimson's attention from them as he untied her dress and let his tongue drift over her neck. His hands were on her breasts, fingers gliding over her nipples so that they heeded his command. His touch was magical, and she arched against him, feeling his need below his pants.

"Go, Mark. Eliana is worth the indiscretion, and as Skye is currently in the throes of orgasm with her new husband, I'd say you have time to find out where she gets her insatiability from. Only then will I answer your questions," Derrant said before his mouth took her again.

Her dress disappeared, the warmth of the marble pressing against her back.

She didn't know what happened to the others, her attention solely on Derrant as he penetrated her, a scream exiting her with the force. Her body bucked at the pain and exhilarating pleasure. He was enormous, and every thrust was an exquisite mix of the two.

"You are covered in the stickiness of other men, my little whore. Tell me, do any of them fuck you as hard as I do?"

"No," she cried with his harder thrust.

He picked her legs up, his pace quickening, everything around her fading as her body exploded in sensation, her need for release climbing.

"Are you going to come for me, Crimson?"

She brought her hands to her breasts, shivering at the touch, his pounding increasing in reaction. Unexpectedly, he took her breast in his mouth again, sucking and biting at her nipple until her climax soared through her with a fury. Her body trembled as he continued to pound her until he came, thrusting so hard the column cracked behind her with the force.

She couldn't breathe. Her vision was blurred as the quakes shook her. He'd brought her to climax, and it had been glorious. He squeezed her ass, tilting her pelvis as he sent his last stream into her inviting body. For a moment, he held her and she could feel the pounding of his heart.

"I think I need more of that as payment for summoning me," he said, his voice raspy.

"I didn't summon you. Mark did."

"Well, you'll pay anyway."

A shiver of expectation slithered through her, eliciting a laugh from him. The room disappeared, his bedroom coming into focus, and she knew there would be no talking until he had thoroughly taken all that he owned.

MARK

Mark sat on the marble steps of the throne room, his mind a mix of thoughts he couldn't flee. A few demons walked through, some in their demon form, others in mortal form. None paid him any heed, and he assumed Derrant or Eliana had commanded it. Either that or he looked tormented enough.

He'd snuck from Eliana's quarters, remembering the way she'd led them and returned to the throne room to wait. He could have participated like she'd wanted, he'd had every right to, but Eliana reminded him too much of Skye. Even watching Bormick with her had bothered him. It clearly didn't bother Derrant to let Bormick have her, and he wondered why. But then again, he'd had no qualms about taking Crimson right in front of them, so perhaps Eliana felt she deserved her own time with Crimson's mate.

He shook his head, bewildered at how this had turned into a sex thing when he'd just wanted answers. Hopefully, Bormick was enjoying himself. He deserved a little fun. He'd had to watch Mark with Crimson and share her with him, not to mention giving Pete up to Skye. Having Eliana to himself would be good for him. There had been no hesitation, either. Mark couldn't blame him—Derrant had been fucking Crimson so hard she'd been screaming when Eliana had pushed them from the room.

There was no claiming Crimson as Bormick's mate, no rescuing her from Derrant, and they both knew it. Derrant owned her. He'd claimed her long before Pete and Bormick had.

Mark lowered his head in his hands, wishing for once that they led a quiet suburban life in the human world. One where he'd make love to Skye each morning before he left for work, then at night after they'd tucked the kids into bed. Simple, uncomplicated, free of claims and magic and gods.

"Why so down?" asked a female voice.

He looked up to see a petite demon, green skin and horns, killer body standing before him. He scooted back on the step.

"Does this bother you?"

She shifted, becoming a black-haired woman with gray eyes and very full breasts.

"I'm good, thanks."

She brought her face closer to him, her breasts pushing against his chest, and sniffed. "You smell like Crimson and"—she sniffed again—"Pete's friend, the big one."

She backed up; her face lighting. "Do you know my Pete?"

He creased his brow, studying her.

"I'm Pete's tree nymph, Ash," she said with a giggle, her appearance changing to a pretty petite blonde with brown eyes, her breasts small but pert.

"You're the tree nymph?"

She was pretty, her brown eyes large and innocent on her round face.

"Yes! That's what he calls me." She plopped on the stairs next to him.

"Have you seen my Pete? I've heard talk. The master has been very preoccupied with the happenings in the other realm."

He wasn't certain what to say to the naked demon next to

him, who was chatting away. She seemed like a young, normal woman, not a vicious murdering demon.

She was waiting for an answer, her eyes wide with anticipation.

"Is it true he has a new mate?"

Mark bristled at the word. "Yes, I'd venture to say you won't be seeing him again. His new mate is quite possessive."

Her face dropped. "But Crimson lets me play when she's here."

"Yeah, I'm going to say that's not going to happen anymore. This mate doesn't like to share." He sighed, staring down at his hands.

"Why are you so glum? It is I who should be sad."

"His mate is Pete's new mate," Crimson said, entering the room.

"Oh. Then you can't have her anymore?"

"No, he'll have her. He just has to share now, and Mark doesn't like to share Skye."

Ash removed her hand quickly and rose. "The Shadow Queen is your mate?"

"And Pete is the Shadow King," Crimson said.

Ash stumbled back, her brown eyes wide.

"What do you know about it?" Mark asked, curious about her reaction.

She was quiet for a moment, then in a hushed tone, said, "*The Shadow King has claimed his queen and now he will fight for all. The shadow gods will stand in fear as Death's son decides their fates. The Shadow Queen will break as he does, the realms of old, now one.*"

Mark looked at Crimson, who appeared just as confused as he was.

"That sounds like prophecy to me," Crimson whispered. She looked behind her. "Come, Ash." She took the demon's hand, then turned to Mark. "Bormick is still with Eliana?"

"Yes," he answered, still miffed by the words Ash had spoken. Crimson's reaction didn't reassure him any. She looked desperate to escape.

"Good. Do you remember Pete's friend, my other mate?"

The demon's eyes lit up and a mischievous smile overcame her features. "He was very tasty."

"Yes, he is. Let's go give him some attention. I'm sure the three of us can soothe his aching ego."

"Crimson, wait," Mark said, wanting answers..

She turned back to him, her eyes deadly serious. "No one talks prophecy in the Death God's chambers, Mark. He forbids it, it's what led to him losing Eliana. Come Ash, let's find Bormick."

She led the demon out before Mark could object.

More prophecy. Mark was beginning to think talk of the gods not interfering with mortal lives was a mistruth. Skye's existence was muddled with prophecy and gods. He rubbed a hand over his face, running the words Ash had spoken through his head. *The shadow gods will stand in fear as Death's son decides their fates.* He couldn't even fathom what that meant. There was more to the trials and the impending battle with Taenom than they'd thought. Perhaps it wasn't only the title as Death's champion Pete stood to lose, it was everything. The fate of the world was in his hands.

"Fuck," he mumbled, praying he was misinterpreting the words.

He thought about the last line. *The Shadow Queen will break.* It took a lot to break Skye. But if something happened to Pete, she would break. That led him to believe there was a chance Pete wouldn't win. He should have been happy at the thought, but he wasn't. Skye would be devastated, as would Crimson and Bormick.

Pete was part of them all now.

He ran his hands over his face. Losing him would devastate them all, even Mark. Pete was a friend, he was a good man, one who hadn't asked to fall in love with Skye. Mark had seen him with the others, he loved them. There'd been no doubt there. Even if there had been some discreet longing toward Skye.

His death would hurt them and break Skye. He'd seen how she'd reacted to even the thought of his death. Losing Pete would crush her, and Mark would lose her. She'd be only a shell of the woman he loved. He raked his hand through his hair as an even more terrifying thought came to him. She was with Pete. If Pete lost, he would no longer be able to protect her, and Mark knew that's what he would do. He would die protecting her, just like Mark would. He was too like Mark in that aspect. Even Bormick had protected her. Without Pete to protect her and Mark unable to reach her...

His heart pounded, his mind drowning in fear.

"They will kill her," Derrant said.

Mark jerked his head up to where Derrant was standing in the doorway. "Can't you protect her?" He heard the plea in his voice, not caring that it was there.

"No," Derrant said. "That realm is not my domain. My brother rules it, which is why he and that mongrel son of his led them there. You all blindly rushed in to avenge the actions they had taken against your people. The connection Skye had to the portal was intact to serve a purpose. Taenom knew you would come. Knew you all well enough to know you'd strike at his father and leave him king. An impetus to the trials for which my brother has been waiting."

"He's been waiting?"

Derrant gave him a sad smile. "I tried to protect Peter, to prevent this from happening when my brother told me that mutt had been born."

Mark stared at him. Everything he'd thought they'd known, was shredded with those words and the implications they held. "You knew?"

"Perhaps. My brother likes to irritate me as best he can. This entire trial is his making, not mine. It's another attempt to show he's the stronger one. He had the upper-hand while Eliana was gone, that debacle Skye created when she first returned to this world giving him an unearned boost in his confidence. If she'd just let me bring my demons out to play, the table would have turned, and I could have annoyed him by breaking past his damned gates. He didn't care about the people or loss of life, only that my demons and I would have freedom."

Mark remained silent. He was suddenly aware of how small they were on the scale of these gods. Mortals were nothing to them, nothing more than souls to be dealt with.

"The trials were inevitable then?" he asked, not knowing what else to say, his mind too muddled.

"Yes. The bastard designed them all on the day that brat was conceived. Got a good kick out of it, too. Pissed me off to no end when I found out. He knew he couldn't beat me, so he thought he'd have fun with my son. Knowing I would have no control once you were there, that you'd be beyond my influence. I argued against it, but then he rubbed Eliana in my face, and I conceded with the ask that he give me only one trial to influence."

"The marriage trial."

"Yes, and you all passed, Pete passing by going through with it."

"Why? Why is it so important that my wife sleep with and marry Pete?"

"You must know by now that Pete's attraction to Skye and hers to him was inevitable. He has too much of me in him and she too much of Eliana. It was unstoppable."

"But Bormick and Crimson are your children, too."

Derrant shook his head. "Not like Pete and Skye. And you know that to be true. My magic runs through Pete and Eliana's through Skye."

"But she was mine," he said, hearing the desperation in his voice.

"By Eliana's hand when she tied the Elite to Skye's line. It was cruel and vindictive, but it did not undo the bind that was already in place. The day their ancestors were born marked the binding of Pete to Skye. They have always been one."

"Destiny?"

"You could say that. She belongs to him by all rights only to him and he only to her."

"They could break our claims on them?"

"Easily."

"That's what the trials were about?"

"Some. Others were to fracture the five of you, leaving them weak. You see, what I never realized is that Eliana's lover completed her. There was a part of her I couldn't please, couldn't hold. He brought that out in her, and I ignored it in my jealousy. Pete understands that you are another side to Skye, that your love makes her stronger just as his does. Skye recognizes the same with Pete and the others. Pete knows that to take her from you, to force her hand as I did to Eliana, will only break her and he will lose her in the end."

"Why are they so like the two of you? Why is this playing out as it did with both of you?"

"Because my brother is a jealous prick. He was angry with Eliana for choosing me. He always hated me because I was more powerful. He wanted Eliana to mate with one of his lesser gods and not me, but he didn't see that she loved me. He never saw it and assumed I forced her."

"He thought Skye would refuse Pete?"

"Yes, then he thought you wouldn't allow it, just as I wouldn't have."

"This gets more convoluted by the minute. Tell me, was this prophecy?" he dared ask. "Was it written when you and Eliana sired your lines?"

"Have they not warned you that I don't like talk of prophecy?"

"Maybe."

"You are bold, boy. I do not like prophecy, and this is the reason why. Yes, there was a prophecy from one of my brother's minions, foreseeing the fall of my realm. Prophecy is one-sided and can be interpreted incorrectly. My brother reads it as my downfall. I read it as an unknown. It does not say I fall, nor does it say my kingdom falls."

"He reads it the way he wants the outcome to play out."

"Correct. Thus, the reason I hate prophecy and my brother."

"What if Pete loses?"

The expression on Derrant's face grew dark. "Then my kingdom falls, and my people die."

"All of us? But we're his people, too."

"Only in the afterlife does he allow it now. Once Eliana returned to me, his protection of the people in our realm ended."

"That's why he came to Skye's defense when you threatened to bring your demons through the veil?"

"Yes, he promised Eliana he would protect the realm in her absence."

"But if it's your realm, why can you not cross into it?" Mark asked, sitting forward on the step.

Derrant gave a devious grin. "Oh, I once did. My demons wreaked havoc but as mortals flourished, their numbers growing, Eliana bent my brother's ear. Our first true fight, long before your lines were created. She is softer than I and didn't like the spilled blood, the stolen souls. We made an agreement that we would no longer cross our veils, that the three of us would oversee my realm, and protect the mortals. Eliana and her enticing voice soothed my brother, her stubbornness coercing me into accepting the condition."

Mark lifted a brow, thinking of Skye and the ways she would have manipulated him into giving in.

Derrant laughed. "Women hold sway over us, whether we think they do or not."

"So that moment reinforced the veils and locked you here?"

"Oh, no, I could still cross as could Eliana. Otherwise, none of you would be here today. It was only when Eliana fled to the mountains, my brother hiding her from me, that the asshole locked me here, angry at me for my indiscretions against her. I suppose I deserved it."

"You raped her. I think you deserved more than that."

There was a moment when Mark thought Derrant would punish him, but he only shook his head. "We all make mistakes, some worse than others, some that leave deeper scars. Eliana and I have left that in the past, as you and Skye left your mistakes in the past."

"Mistakes that were ignited by your doing."

"Do you really want to go there, Mark?"

"No," he said with a sigh. "So he locked you in the Shadow Realm and left our realm to fend for itself, only agreeing to welcome our people in the afterlife?"

"Correct. He cares nothing about what I have built. So, if Pete fails, my brother's people will purge my kingdoms just as they began to when this all started."

"Then we will fight them."

"How? Pete and Skye are your strongest fighters. If Taenom can defeat Pete, no one stands a chance."

Mark thought about it. He didn't know if Pete was stronger than Taenom. Taenom was a formidable opponent and had held his magic his entire existence. Mark was inclined to think he held an advantage over Pete.

"He did, but not by much," Derrant said, answering his thought. "Now, however, there's a high probability that my son can destroy that brat, unless my brother has interfered."

"Like you did?"

There was a gleam in Derrant's eye.

"The marriage consummation—that's why we had to give up our claim, why they needed to marry."

"Do not repeat that out of the Shadow Realm. I learned too late that Eliana strengthened me, that her power enhanced mine. That is why my brother fears her with me. The idiot thinks I want his realm. Gah, too much light there. I prefer my shadows."

"Skye makes Pete stronger. That's why we feel their power when..." He didn't want to say the words.

"When they're fucking?"

Mark growled, which made Derrant laugh.

"When they are in the throes of passion."

"That helps," he replied sarcastically.

"It's true. They can fuck all they want, but when they're truly connected, so is their power. Eliana may not have been born to the shadows as I was, but they seduce her and call to a part of her that's just for me, uninhibited and dark. It's the same with the two of them. What any of you have with them will never come close."

"You're not one for building confidence, are you?"

"You will never have what they have," Eliana's voice came from the other side of the room. She was stretching, her long body lengthening like a cat, her blue eyes striking like Skye's. "But that doesn't mean she loves you any less. The tie I bound your lines with is a strong one, a rare one, which makes it all the more powerful. Only my true daughter's line has ever mated with an Elite. The others do not feel that call."

"Not sure that makes it better."

She had walked to Derrant, and he touched her face tenderly before kissing her.

"You taste of Crimson and her lover, my dear."

"Mmm, yes, I had quite the experience. There is no doubt he is from your loins."

"Did he leave me any of you to satisfy me?"

"Did *they*?" she purred. "And I could ask the same of Crimson."

"Oh, there's plenty left."

"Can we get back to the crisis at hand, and where are Crimson and Bormick?"

"When I left them, he was riding Ash, as they have named her, while Crimson was riding her tongue. I think they may be a little longer. We seem to have blessed them both with a stamina that rivals ours."

Mark sighed, ignoring the rise in his pants at the thought. It had been years since he'd had two women and it was tempting to go participate. Especially knowing Skye's body was currently below another man.

"If I know Crimson, she can go a few more hours. Go play, Mark. The battle has yet to begin. Ash is quite a wonder with that mouth of hers and Skye would have no reason to be angry. She's in Pete's arms as we speak." Eliana had moved close to him and straddled him on the wide step.

"Taking another in front of me, dear?" Derrant asked as Eliana leaned into Mark.

"I'm really okay, I don't—"

Her hand gripped him, his erection belying his words.

"He passed up my first request, dear."

A mix of anticipation and nerves assaulted his stomach. He didn't know if there was a way to stop a goddess from what she was about to do, and the thought both tantalized him and frightened him.

"You turned down my Eliana?"

"Yes," he muttered as her hand stroked him, her lips sliding along his neck. She was tempting, very tempting. The motion of her hand feeding the need in him so that she was hard to resist. "She reminds me too much of Skye."

She stopped, sitting back to look at him.

"That's fair, my dear. You do look just like her."

She leaned forward, her lips finding his, and for a moment, it was like Skye was kissing him. He threaded his hand through her hair, deepening the kiss.

"Oh, I think that's enough torturing the boy, Eliana." Derrant's voice had lost its humor.

She ended the kiss and rose from Mark. "Shame, I would have liked to have experienced what my daughter experiences with you."

Derrant grabbed her arm. "Not with him and not with the other. Skye's mates are off limits to you. Just as Skye is now off limits to me."

"Ten years you fucked her, pretending she was me, Derrant. I don't get to have that?"

"No."

"Hmm, I do like it when you're jealous."

"Go, Mark, find the others, and have one of them take care of that hard-on Eliana gave you. We'll send you back when the battle begins. That's when we'll be watching, all of us. Until then, get your fill. It might be the last time you get laid."

He vanished, taking Eliana with him.

"Shit," he mumbled. If Derrant was right, and Pete lost, they were all dead, including Skye. Pete held the fate of the world on his shoulders.

He looked down at his hands, noticing the slight tremble to them. Everything Derrant had told him left him shaken. They were playthings to the gods. Skye and Pete in particular. The unspoken realization was that the gods had laid this path long before the two were born. With the moment the gods had created their ancestors. It was an overwhelming thought, one that led him to believe nothing in their lives had been by chance. Sure, he'd already figured out that Derrant had punished Crimson to the Forest of Lost Souls to ensure the blood pact came to fruition. That in itself had unsettled him, but now he saw that it was so much more. Pete's line had been punished to avoid this, hidden so that this would never happen. But that didn't make sense. He raised his head, narrowing his brows. Hidden until Pete was born. Until Skye was back in their world. Until the two could meet and bring about the start of the trials. The Upper God may have created the trials, may have spawned his own heir, but Derrant had played his own cards, ensuring his champion was where he needed to be when the time came and that his queen was with him.

"Holy shit," he muttered as the sheer power of the realization sank in.

Nothing in Skye, or Pete's lives had been random. The two had been careening down this course since long before they were born.

He stood, unable to think on it anymore and annoyed by the erection Eliana had left him with, the one that still persisted. It ached for release, and his mind ached for distraction. He walked in the direction of Eliana's quarters, unsure of what he thought about joining whatever they were doing. Unsure how Skye would feel about him fucking the tree nymph. It amused him that Bormick still didn't know what was under her skin. Knowing Bormick, he'd find it even more of a turn-on.

He opened the door, slowly peeking in for fear of what he'd find. Bormick was out cold, his legs spread wide. Crimson was sound asleep next to him.

"Have you come to play?"

"Shit," he mumbled again as Ash rose from the bed.

The temptation was there, but he was hesitant. He had every right. Skye couldn't say anything. He could hear her reaction and feel her hurt both of which caused his hesitation. But dammit, she was making love to Pete, married to him. And all he wanted to do was bend the vixen of a demon over and fuck her unapologetically.

She pressed her body against him, his dick throbbing to be

inside of her. He was just about to give in, to grab her and take her, when he heard Crimson's voice.

"Don't even think about it. He's off limits, Ash."

Her hand found his length and stroked it, further intensifying the need to give in to her. "Oh, but he wants a good fuck."

"Then I'll give it to him. Don't do it, Mark. No matter how upset you are with Skye. You and Pete are off limits to anyone but me."

"And me," Bormick added drowsily. "Come here, little nymph. I've got a little more in me."

She pouted but drew her hand away and leaped to Bormick, her perky ass drawing Mark's eyes. Mark shook the thoughts from his head as Crimson approached him.

"Skye entrusted you to me, and I will protect you from other women. Now, you abstained from the goddess, you can abstain from her."

Ash had Bormick in her mouth, her ass up in the air, waiting for him to take it.

Crimson grabbed his face and turned it back to her. "Fuck me, Mark. You want to bend me over, then bend me over, but you will not touch that demon," she whispered the last word so Bormick wouldn't hear.

He pulled her to him, his hands pawing at her breasts, devouring her mouth with his kisses. He turned her and forced her over. Nothing but need and desperation fueled his moves as he pulled her ass to him and unbuttoned his pants. He didn't stop to caress her, to make sure she was satisfied. He was ravenous, and all he wanted was to take her. Grabbing her hips, he penetrated her, hearing her wicked moan. His eyes focused on Ash's ass as it danced with the movements of her mouth against Bormick. He fucked Crimson hard, fantasizing that her ass was the demon's until he came with a fury that left him shaking. Fiercely, he pulled Crimson back up and took her again against a seat that overlooked Eliana's window, a fake scene of gardens outside of it. He plunged into her with no reservation, and she matched his ferocity as she always did, her cries filling the room.

If they were going to die and he couldn't have Skye with him, then he'd die pleasuring himself with Crimson, ignoring the need to take the fair-haired demon who was crying out passionately for more across from them.

PETE

Pete walked through the tunnel leading from the room where he'd left Skye. He had wanted to wake her, to make love to her once more, to tell her goodbye, but he hadn't. There had been no goodbye for Crimson or Bormick, and there would be none for Skye. He'd looked at her, taking her in one last time, cursing the fact that it had taken so many years of his life to find her, just as it had to find the others. His heart had tugged at the sight of her—she'd looked peaceful, so like a beautiful goddess as she slept. He'd touched her cheek softly, brushing her hair back as a smile curved on her lush lips. With a heavy sigh, he'd turned and walked away, leaving her and his heart behind.

Now he stood at the edge of the tunnel, a lush green lawn before him, the sun shining above. The clouds looked almost as if they could be touched. Taenom stood beyond, a bronze breastplate upon his chest, bronze arm cuffs adorning his wrists. Upon his head sat a golden crown.

Pete stepped out, his eyes adjusting to the brightness which left an uncomfortable feeling in him like it agitated his power. The clouds heeded his call, turning black above them as an ebony breastplate formed on his chest. Ebony arm cuffs encircled his wrists, and he felt the weight of the crown he'd left in the room with Skye upon his head.

The Death God was claiming his champion and Pete could feel his whisper through his soul, his power responding with a flare of fire that burned through him. He rolled his thumb across his new wedding band, feeling his connection to Skye under the surface of his power, like a slow rumble of thunder beneath an oncoming storm.

"Death's champion. Have you come to die?" Taenom shouted, his golden armor glistening in the sun.

"Not likely," he replied. "I believe you and your gods have tried besting me several times and I've prevailed."

"Not this time."

Taenom was like a bratty kid whom Pete wanted to punch. That annoying smirk on his face and cocky attitude needed to be remedied. It had been a very long time since he'd had a physical fight, aside from his roughhousing with Bormick, but Pete was sure if the power were stripped, he could take Taenom and his pretty boy looks down easily. Unfortunately, this was a magic battle. As confident as Pete was in this elevated magic he had, Taenom had been with his magic for a very long time in relation to Pete's mere months with it.

"Where's your pretty little bitch?"

Pete's jaw tightened.

"You know, when I've killed you and destroyed your world, I may keep her. She's quite a beauty and, from what I've seen, extremely talented in bed. Does she like it up the ass, Shadow King? Because that pretty ass looks like it needs me inside of it."

He was baiting Pete, but it didn't matter. Nobody talked about Skye that way. Even Bormick was more respectful.

"You won't touch her," he growled.

"And who will stop me? You'll be dead and her other mate

stands no chance against me. You are the only one standing in the way of me shoving my dick in that pretty mouth—"

He didn't have time to finish. Pete's power flared, his shadows wrapping around the man's neck, flinging him. Taenom soared through the air but landed on his feet in a crouched position. A flare of golden power tore through the air as Taenom struck back. Pete called his shadows to shield him, but Taenom's magic broke through, sending him across the open space, tumbling until he could find his footing again.

The battle had begun.

Taenom was powerful but not as strong as Pete, and it showed. The last trial had ensured it, his union with Skye elevating his abilities. He sensed the change in his power now, it surged through his being. Taenom's eye reflected his realization that Pete's power was now enhanced. Taenom picked himself up from Pete's last hit, glaring at Pete, his expression strained.

"It's over, Taenom. It's time to admit your defeat. Agree to leave our realm alone and send us home!"

"Never, this world needs to be purged of you and your kind. The Death God is weak, just as you are!"

Pete wondered what Derrant thought of that comment. He was certain the god would strike Taenom down for it if he had the ability to interfere.

"I'd hold your tongue. It's not wise to insult the gods. They're not keen on it."

The ground rumbled, and for a moment Pete thought the Death God was coming for retribution, but instead two large golden beasts emerged from the ground, shaking the dirt from their hides.

"This is our fight Taenom, man to man." He wanted to punch him, but couldn't get close enough.

Taenom drew his power and slammed it into Pete, one of the beasts leaping with it. Pete sent his shadows to stop the beast, but the magic penetrated his shield, pounding him into the ground so hard that it split. He lay there for a moment dazed. A beast was standing over him, drool dripping from his golden mouth.

"No!" he heard Skye scream. The beast whipped its head and bounded.

"Dammit." Pete jumped to his feet. She was supposed to be back in the room, safe and not in this mess. He turned to her, seeing her down the beast. Her magic ripped the gold hues from its hide, the gray left below turning to ash at her command. The gold swirled around her, giving her an angelic look. He'd underestimated her and should have known better, but he still didn't want her anywhere near Taenom or the battle.

Taenom took Pete's moment of distraction, barraging him with a round of calculated magic that he volleyed but not fast enough, his distraction costing him. The other beast leaped, turning to ash before it reached him.

Thank you, Skye, he thought as he missed a strike, the magic tearing through him like an inferno. He landed too far away to see Skye's reaction. Her magic, however, he could see and feel. Struggling to pick his head up, he observed how the gold darkened. Below his hands, the green from the grass dulled, and above him, the blue of the sky above turned black. She couldn't interfere with the direct battle, but that didn't mean she couldn't fight back at the gods who had forced them into this situation.

Taenom pulled him up, his golden eyes shining with victory.

"Looks like I won after all. Tell your mistress to stop, and I'll go gentle with your death."

"She's not my mistress, she's my queen, and trust me, I don't command her."

Taenom's face flashed with surprise. So, he hadn't known about the last trial. Pete wondered if the Upper God had known of it.

Pete drew his fist back and punched Taenom, causing his grip to fail.

"That felt good," he said, punching him again, and drawing his power before Taenom could, sending him flying across the storm-battered field. Skye was standing in a swirl of dark hues, her power reaching his, caressing him before drawing back with pieces of his. She was an angry goddess, a wicked storm that couldn't be stopped. He understood the anger and why she'd reacted, but he didn't know what she was doing now.

Pete countered a strike from Taenom, who drew his attention back to the fight as the ground lurched below them, lightning tearing through the field. Taenom was frantically battering him with his magic, sparks of gold glinting through the darkened air.

"Tell her to stop!" he screamed.

"I don't command her, and I won't start at your demand!" he yelled back.

"She's bleeding the realm! She's tearing at the fabric of the veil! I warned you all that she could destroy the veils of the very universe! I warned the gods, but they insisted we test you. Saying you were the threat! She will kill us all!"

He glanced at Skye, a fury of darkened hues encircling her. The air around her was shifting, warping as she continued to pull the hues, the sky above them stretching downward.

Taenom grabbed him. "Stop her now or I will."

Pete seethed at the command. "No."

He sent his shadows out to Skye, feeling the connection, sensing it strengthen his magic, an endless flow of it coursing through him with that touch. It fortified every cell in him, healing every bruise, every wound he'd received in the battle.

Taenom was running toward Skye, his power drawn, but Pete grabbed him with a stream of shadows, throwing him back.

"This is our fight, Taenom. You will finish what your gods started!"

"She will destroy us all!"

Pete stepped toward him. "It was fine to destroy my people, but when it's yours who are threatened, you change your tune."

Taenom fought back, his moves desperate and unchecked. Skye had him frazzled, and Pete intended to take full advantage of it. He just prayed Taenom was wrong, and Skye knew what she was doing. Otherwise, it wouldn't matter who won the battle, they'd all be dead.

BORMICK

When the Death God had returned Bormick, Crimson, and Mark he hadn't left them where Bormick had expected they'd be. They stood in the empty space that had once been the Kingdom of Eltander. Debris sat in small piles through the land, green grass sprouting through it in defiance. To the west lay the open sea, churning violently in the distance. The sky was empty, the dragons nowhere to be seen as if they, too, sensed the impending battle.

Bormick scratched his head and looked around, stretching to fight the weariness that still sat upon him. Sleep was something he needed, and he stifled a yawn, knowing he wouldn't be sleeping again until this madness was over. The tree nymph had been a delectable treat, but she'd worn him out, something he'd never thought possible. After Eliana, then all three of them, followed by Crimson and the nymph, he'd already hit his limit.

Good gods, he loved Crimson for giving him that. The goddess herself had been something he'd never forget, although he had to admit she reminded him of Skye. That had made it even more of a guilty pleasure. If he couldn't touch Skye, he had no qualms about fucking the goddess who was her spitting image. If

Skye was anything like her, then he understood why Mark had kept her to himself. He'd thought Crimson was seductive, but this took it to a whole new level.

And Ash. Ash had pleased him in ways he'd only fantasized about. She was a dirty little nymph, and he'd loved it. She'd been unrestrained when he'd taken her with Pete, but this time—

"Bormick!" Mark yelled. "Get your hand off your dick and help us figure out why we're here."

"Are you thinking about your treat again?" Crimson purred.

"I'll be thinking about that treat for years to come, baby."

"Head out of your pants, Bormick," Mark muttered.

Mark had no room to talk, there was no way his mind wasn't still back in that room. He'd fucked Crimson harder than he ever had. Bormick wasn't blind. Mark had wanted the nymph, and he'd taken Crimson instead, even then refusing to hurt Skye. Although he'd been tempted, very tempted from what Bormick could tell. If Crimson hadn't stepped in, Bormick had no doubt it would have been Ash Mark had pounded instead.

"Stop smirking at me," Mark groused.

"How long you think you'll be fantasizing about that perky little nymph, Mark? Even Pete's had many tastes of her and let me tell you, she tastes like nothing you've ever tasted, lush and rich. I could have licked her up all day if she hadn't been riding my dick most of the time."

"Enough, Bormick," Crimson snapped. "Leave Mark be and stop talking about Ash, or I won't let you play with her again."

Mark ran his hand over his face as Bormick gave Crimson a sour look.

"That's not very nice, Crimson," he complained, knowing her well enough to understand that her threat was real. He'd pushed too far and hit a nerve. It was hard to push her to the limit, but he had. If they made it through this, he'd make it up to her.

He grabbed her waist and pulled her to him, kissing her head and nuzzling her neck, feeling her relax. There was a sudden pull in the air, forcing his breath from his lungs. He let her go, but not enough that she wasn't within his grasp for protection.

"What was that?" Mark asked, his voice sharp.

The sky seemed to flicker, coming in and out of focus, the broken land before them shifting.

"Skye," Mark muttered.

The air grew thinner, the space beyond where they stood, morphing, blurring in and out of focus.

"Something's happening," Bormick said.

"It's Skye. I can feel her magic, but this—this is beyond anything I've ever felt before."

The blur flickered, stretching as a thunderous sound cracked the air.

"The battle has begun," Crimson said, clinging to his arm.

From the blurring field, a cold wind came, whipping across Bormick's skin, and sending a shiver down his spine. A billow of black shadows leaked from it, engulfing them, the sky above growing dark as the blue was leached from it.

"Pete's magic, the shadows. Good gods, how strong has he become?" Bormick couldn't fathom the power of drowning them in shadows from another realm.

"How strong have they both become?" Mark asked. "Skye is breaking the veil between the realms. She's bleeding the sky and everything in their world."

"Oh, that cannot be good," Crimson said, and Bormick could sense her fear. She was trembling against him, and he was trying his best to keep himself from doing the same.

"Can you use your power to move us?" Mark said, backing up, the blurred veil stretching both in front and above them.

"Good idea," Bormick said.

Crimson tried drawing her magic, but nothing happened.

"No, this is where Derrant wants us. This is where we stay."

"Dammit."

A force of air pummeled them and pushed them back.

"Holy shit," Mark murmured, the veil breaking open before them, the ground below severing with the force.

Bormick squinted. Something was coming into view as the veil opened. "Is that?"

Above them a massive land mass hovered, quaking every so often as if something were hitting it. A bolt of golden light streaked over them, the ground behind them exploding with the impact. That something was Pete and Taenom.

"It's the battle," Crimson yelled above the gale of wind that whipped around them.

"What do we do?" Mark asked.

"Nothing. We're here to witness. For confirmation that what we accepted and gave up was worth it and necessary."

The mass had shifted lower and hovered just above where Revina's kingdom touched the coast, the Dranth mountains precariously close to its tip. It moved no closer, breaking through the veil no more, hovering while the battle played out.

Shadows tumbled from the edge still, layered with ribbons of hues from Skye's magic. The mass quivered each time flames of shadow and gold lit the sky. Bormick pulled Mark back as the mass shifted lower suddenly. A blur of gold and black flared across the space, crashing to the ground behind them. Pete stood, yanking a very exhausted Taenom from the ground where they'd landed.

Crimson let out a cry when she saw him, but Bormick grabbed her, bringing her against him. Pete looked terrifying, every bit the Death God's son, every bit a Shadow King.

Behind them, a thunderous boom fell upon his ears, followed by a wind that nearly knocked them all over. Pete, distracted by it, gave Taenom an opening. Pete was sent tumbling back to the newly formed land, Taenom moving too fast and on him again. Bormick looked to where Pete's attention had turned to see that Skye had collapsed.

Mark was running to her, but they weren't close enough.

Taenom grabbed Pete, but Pete ignored him, throwing his power out to capture Mark and portal him somehow to Skye. Bormick's jaw dropped at the ease at which he'd moved Mark. His heart stuttered to a halt as Taenom took advantage of Pete's distraction and pounded him to the ground. Bormick held Crimson tight as her scream rattled his ears.

Taenom let out a roar and raised his hands to the sky. "I am your champion, Father!"

"Look," Bormick told Crimson, pointing to where Pete lay.

A flood of shadows seeped from Pete, the sky becoming even darker as if the shadows had snuffed the light from it.

"Don't claim victory until you've actually defeated me," Pete yelled to Taenom from the darkness.

Taenom turned quickly, but it was over. Bormick knew defeat, knew the sign of a true warrior. Pete's shadows drained from the space and drowned Taenom in an endless flood of darkness that suffocated him.

Now able to see him clearly, Bormick watched as Pete glanced toward where he'd sent Mark, as if confirming that he had Skye. Pete moved to Taenom, calling upon the shadows. Bormick's mouth fell at the sheer power of Pete, the shadows whipping around him in long tendrils before settling upon his aura. The arousal that grew at the sight was something Bormick couldn't stop. Pete's power only magnified the broody sexiness of his presence. He picked Taenom up and drew his arm back to punch him, but Taenom let a bolt of magic loose, sending it spiraling toward Mark.

Bormick couldn't take his eyes from the scene, feeling Crimson tense in his arms, her fingers digging into his skin. There was no way they could get to Mark or even warn him. He was focused solely on Skye, and the bolt of deadly magic would hit him without warning. Crimson let out a cry as she leaned into him. They were helpless witnesses to Mark's impending death.

Pete released Taenom, his fist meeting his jaw as he fell. A stream of shadows had fled his other hand before his fist met Taenom's face. Bormick's eyes grew wider seeing the magic overtake the golden stream, twisting around it before it sped past, and shielded Mark. The golden magic had slowed as the shadows dragged it down. When it reached Mark, it scattered in sparkles against the magic that had encased him.

Pete's eyes never left Taenom, his magic obeying his command with the simple directive. He grabbed Taenom again, pounding him with his fists. Grasping him by the back of his neck, like a cat picking a kitten up by the scruff, he dragged him further into the field.

"What's he doing?" Bormick asked.

"I don't know," Crimson responded, her voice shaky. Her fingers were still wrenched into his skin.

"Can you get us closer now, over to Mark?" he asked her.

Crimson released his arm, but her tension remained. He could see it in the crease of her brow. Picking her hand up, her fingers trembling, she formed a portal. He let out a breath that her magic was working again. Keeping her close, he ushered her through where they emerged a few feet from Mark. Crimson ran to him, kneeling next to Skye.

"She's alive, just unconscious. What's he doing?" Mark asked, nodding toward Pete as Bormick bent down alongside him.

"Besides saving your ass, I have no idea."

"Is that what that tingle was?"

"Tingle? That was no tingle. That was a very determined strike of magic that Pete took out without even looking."

Mark's astonished eyes said it all as he glanced toward Pete, who had dragged Taenom back to the broken land.

"Why hasn't he just killed him?" he asked.

"Not sure, but Taenom is hanging on by a thread."

Blood was dripping from his face, his body limp when Pete tossed him to the ground.

"You had your battle. Your champion has been bested!" he screamed at the sky.

Lightning tore through the sky, landing close to him, and the ground rumbled as if in answer.

"I will not kill him! I will be a pawn in your feud no more. I'm done, as are they. You fight your own battles!"

Thunder shattered the silence, another streak of lightning scorching the sky. Bormick could feel the electricity in the air. Mark handed Skye to Crimson and rose, his eyes seeing the same as Bormick's.

"The Upper God will kill him for his impudence," Mark said.

The wind stirred, streaks of gold tearing through the sky above. Pete turned and walked toward them, his back to Taenom and the Upper God. Mark ran to him, Bormick not seeing the stream of gold building in the clouds above Pete until it was too late. Mark dove, Pete looking up at the same moment Mark took him down. Bormick's breath froze in his chest, and he started running after Mark. The streak of power landed, cascading around Mark and Pete before he could reach them. The impact threw him back and he landed hard on the ground, hearing Crimson's scream echo in his ears.

He picked up his head, seeing only then the dark magic that surrounded them. It seeped up in heavy black shadows before the ground split in a plume of darkness. The Death God emerged.

"It's over Carzent! You will leave my son alone and put yours on a leash. I have let you control this matter for far too long!"

A stream of magic gathered across from Derrant. Carzent, the Upper God, emerged. Bormick scooted back closer to Skye and Crimson, placing himself protectively in front of them. Mark and Pete were still on the ground, staring at the two gods. Taenom had woken, his head barely lifting to watch.

The Upper God wore a scowl on his face. He narrowed his green eyes at Derrant who had emerged in his mortal form, to Bormick's relief. He'd heard descriptions of his true form and had been thankful when Mark had dragged them to the Shadow Realm that the mortal form had been present then, just as it was now. He didn't want to see what Death looked like when he was angry.

Bormick looked between the two gods. Their eyes were the only similarity. If anything, the Upper God favored Eliana's appearance. Carzent's auburn hair matched hers, but his features were rugged, less sharp than Derrant's. And he was massive, built like a bull. Derrant wasn't small by any means, but he had more of a sinewy muscular build compared to his brother.

"It is over when I say it is over," Carzent answered. "Your insolent brat will pay for your crimes."

"My crimes? For loving Eliana? It's been millennia, Carzent, she's not going back to your realm."

"Who had to protect her when you hurt her? When you hunted her down and abused her? Do not tell me it's over!"

"Then I will, Brother." Eliana appeared next to Derrant. "Derrant and I have made amends. My place has always been with him, not in your realm, not with one of your gods. Our children have proven their worth. His son has chosen the way Derrant now would. He has made the choices, passed all of your trials, and defeated your champion in Derrant's name. It is over, Brother. Let us move forward from here."

"Let us make amends now, Brother. You and I, and leave our children be."

The Upper God eyed his brother, and the look could have killed any mortal. Bormick thought that perhaps the people had it incorrect and that the Upper God was just as wrathful as his brother in the Shadow Realm.

He looked at Taenom, giving him a disappointed look and, in a dusting of gold, Taenom disappeared.

"Very well, your champion has won, your realm will be left in peace." He looked around at the newly formed convergence of land, his eyes landing on Skye. Bormick moved to block his view of her, and the god gritted his teeth, flinging Bormick away.

"No!" Pete and Mark rose at once, but Eliana stopped them with a look.

Bormick didn't know what would happen, but the god was focused on Skye. Crimson was still holding her unconscious body, drawing it closer. He wasn't sure if he needed to move her away. It was clear the Upper God wanted Skye, but there was no guarantee he wouldn't hurt Crimson if she was in the way.

"That one has broken the veil," he snarled, pointing his finger at Skye. "She was warned, and now she will pay for her arrogance."

His words hung heavy in the air and for a moment, no one spoke. Both Mark and Pete looked as stunned as Bormick was.

"But first we will talk, Brother," Eliana said, breaking the silence. "My daughter is not even awake to defend her actions. Let us leave her be for now. It has been too long since I have enjoyed your company."

Carzent eyed her, then looked to Derrant before disappearing in a glimmer of gold.

Derrant turned to Mark and Pete. "We will buy her time, but make no mistake, my brother will summon her."

"But she—"

His hand raised to silence Pete. "I am proud of you, son. You wear your power well."

He and Eliana disappeared, leaving them all staring at the place where the gods had been. Leaving Bormick to wonder what punishment lay ahead of Skye and how Mark and Pete would survive if she suffered the ultimate punishment.

MARK

As the last novice mage left the room, Mark watched Skye's chest move up and down with her steady breaths. She still hadn't woken. The novices had no answer since she was fine health-wise. The assumption was that it had something to do with the magic she had exerted during the battle. They'd moved her to her quarters, thinking the familiarity would help, but hours had passed, and nothing had changed.

Pete stood across the room, wearing that worried look he'd had the entire time, the same worry Mark carried. His eyes had not moved from Skye, and his tension permeated the air.

In all reality, Mark should have been terrified of him. The power he held was unimaginable, an endless flow of shadows at his command. But he wasn't. Even though Pete looked intimidating, his stance reflected a vulnerability, a fear for Skye, and a nervousness about being alone with Mark.

Pete met Mark's eyes. This was the man who had stolen Skye's heart from his grasp. The one who had made love to her for countless days, the one she'd risked her life for. The reason she was here, unconscious before them.

No, Mark, he told himself. He hadn't stolen Skye and whatever she'd done, for whatever reason she'd made the choice to do it, Pete was not to blame, the gods were.

"Do you want me to leave?" Pete asked.

Mark wondered if Pete could hear the thoughts in his head.

"Do you want to leave?"

"No."

"Then no, I don't want you to leave." Mark sighed and ran his hands over his face, then through his hair. "You saved me. Why? Why not let Taenom kill me?"

"The same reason you stopped the Upper God from killing me."

"Technically, Derrant did that."

"Well, technically, Derrant saved both our asses then."

He'd jumped the moment he'd seen the magic forming, knowing the intention. He hadn't thought. Instinct had urged him on and that need to protect Skye. Hurting Pete would hurt Skye, letting Pete die would kill her.

"I wouldn't have let you die anyway, Pete, even without this Skye mess. We're still friends, no matter how much I might hate you right now."

Pete laughed. "The feeling's mutual. So how do we do this?"

"I don't know. I guess we just accept that she belongs to both of us, that neither of us has sole claim on her, no matter how much that hurts." He paused. "You really love her?"

"Yes," he said, without hesitation. "As deeply as I love my other mates. And she still loves you."

"As deeply as she loves you." It irked him to say it—that what he and Skye had fought to have for so many years she now had with Pete after a matter of months. In reality, a matter of days.

"Yes, but what we have is different, Mark, and what you have with her is different."

"The undercurrent. That's what she called it."

"Yes, and that's exactly it."

"This is going to torture me, but what do you love about her?"

"Really? You really want to know that?"

"I need to know." Although he didn't know why. Perhaps it was the same curiosity that had always driven Skye to ask about Crimson. A need to understand, to rationalize.

Pete glanced over at Skye, a distant look in his eyes, a smile forming. He was in love, there was no denying the look.

"I love the richness of her eyes, the way her magic calls to mine, the way it mingles with mine when we're close. I love the delicateness of her, that fragileness beneath the strength, the softness of her."

Mark stared at him, uncertain what to say. Pete saw her in a completely different way than he did, loving parts that were opposite of what he loved about her—her strength, her fierceness, the intensity. Those were the prominent sides of her, the ones he'd grown to love more and more over the decades. But they weren't the parts of her that Pete loved.

"Although I will say I love that mouth of hers. I don't think I've ever had a woman who gives a blowjob the way she does. It's incredible. Not even Crimson is that good." He looked up quickly. "Don't tell her I said that thought."

"I should be angry about that comment, but I can't deny it. Jesus, she's good. It's been too long and yeah, Crimson is spectacular, but there's no comparing with Skye."

"Huh."

"What?"

"Well, we just talked about Skye giving us blow jobs, and neither of us got upset."

"Doesn't mean I'm not jealous."

"Nor does your mention of Crimson and her mouth mean I'm not jealous."

"Point taken."

"Were you good to her? Bormick is rough. Crimson needs a counter to him."

"Sorry, buddy, that's not me. I'm only gentle with Skye and I have a feeling from what you just told me that my gentle isn't the same level as yours."

"Hmm…why would you say that?"

"Because everything you love about Skye is the opposite of what I love about her. It's her fire, her fierceness that I love, and it matches mine. The warrior part of her that compliments the commander in me."

"And I love the mage side of her that compliments the mage in me."

"So it would seem. And as so, this might just work."

"Maybe, but we still have to share her and her body."

The anger flared like a raging fire in his chest; the thought of Skye making love to Pete caused his muscles to strain. He rubbed his eyes.

"Don't think the same thoughts aren't on my mind about you and Crimson."

"It's different."

"Is it? Take away the love part and it's the same."

"But you can't take that away."

"No, but you're still fucking Crimson, no matter what way you want to twist it, Mark. You and Skye, Crimson, and I are all sharing, cheating if you want. You on Skye, me on Crimson, and vice versa. Are you looking to assuage your guilt by turning your anger on us?"

Mark's anger took over, and he stormed toward Pete.

"That's it, isn't it? You enjoy Crimson, Mark. It tears me up just as much that she comes to your touch as it does for you that Skye comes to mine."

Pete's words stopped him.

"There's no going back, Mark. All we can do is accept it. You and Crimson have something together that never went away, Skye and I have something that is unbreakable. We're all pieces in this messed up family that we have. I love Skye. I love how it feels to be with her, to be inside of her, how she comes against my mouth, how she clings to me when we climax together. And you may not love Crimson, but I guarantee when you're pounding her or coming in her mouth that Skye is nowhere on your mind."

"Fuck you, Pete."

"I've got Bormick for that."

Something broke in him, and he couldn't help but laugh.

"You're laughing?"

"What the hell else is there to do at this point? You're fucking my wife; she enjoys it. I'm fucking your lover, and she's all for it. Christ, you're even married to my wife. God, it's like some polygamist nightmare I can't escape. So all I can do is deal with it."

"You gonna flip flop on this a few more times? Or is this it?"

"Likely," he answered.

"Great, something to look forward to. So, since you're dealing with it at this moment, what do we do now?"

Mark looked over at Skye. "We wait for her to wake, then we figure out how to make this work."

"And then we wait for her punishment."

Mark's heart dropped. He'd put aside the Upper God's threat, worrying about Skye. Now it was back.

"We can't worry about it yet, Mark. Let's worry about her first."

Pete pulled a chair from the fireplace and brought it closer to the bed with his magic, doing the same for Mark. They sat on either side of Skye, neither leaving her side for two days. Their proximity forced them to talk to each other, to talk about Skye and Crimson, the time relaxing Mark and easing his discomfort.

On the third day, Mark sent Pete away.

"You need to see Crimson and Bormick. They're waiting. She'll be all right."

"If she wakes?"

Mark gave him a sly grin. "I told you that I'm making love to my wife before your greedy paws get to her again."

"I do remember you saying something like that." His grin was cocky, but Mark knew he'd honor the request.

"Go spend the night with them. They need you and I'd venture you need them. If you don't hear from us by the morning, then you'll know she hasn't woken."

Pete stood, his eyes looking at Skye with love before he leaned over and kissed her forehead.

"Prick," Mark muttered in a teasing way.

Pete shot him a humored look, then left the room.

The situation was easier if Mark joked about it. Reality had settled more, and the humor helped soften its sting. He sat beside Skye, nodding off briefly until she touched his hand. Lifting his head quickly, he met her eyes which were a deep navy filled with love and longing. The gold specks were no longer floating among them. There was only the blue of them tinted with slight shimmers of silver. Another reminder of what Pete's new position in her life had done.

"Skye," he said, leaning closer to her and taking her in.

"What happened?" she asked, sitting up suddenly and looking around.

"He's fine. He defeated Taenom."

She relaxed, laying her head back down. Her eyes glanced at the empty seat.

"You both sat beside me? How long have I been sleeping?"

"Two days."

"You're kidding me."

"No. He sat with me until earlier this evening, when I sent him away."

"Wait, you sat here together? And didn't kill each other?"

"No," he answered with a laugh. "He's unharmed, as am I. I sent him back to Crimson and Bormick."

He saw the envy in her eyes, remembering Noah having said Mage Warriors coveted their mates, especially Skye's line. Well, she'd been able to give him to Crimson, it was only fair she do the same for Pete.

"You know you're going to have to work on that jealousy thing," he said.

"Like you are?"

"I am working on it."

She sat back up, pulling herself to the side of the bed, the straps of her nightgown slipping to reveal the curve of her breast. He couldn't help how his eyes lingered. He was hungry for her; he hadn't had her in what seemed like ages. But he wasn't certain she wanted him the same way anymore. Worry nagged him that things had changed, causing an uncomfortable ache in his chest. He didn't think it would ever be the same again. She loved another man, and he was sleeping with another woman.

No, things would never be the same. But as she reached for his hand and pulled him to her, spreading her legs so that he stood between them, he knew she loved him and wanted him no less than she had before. He leaned over her and slid his hand along her leg, pushing the gown's material up. Pressing his arousal against her, he felt the growing wetness as his hand made its way to her breasts, lowering her other strap so they fell free.

He should have asked if she was up to it, but he took her body's reaction as her invitation.

"I love you, Mark, nothing will ever change that, and nothing will ever extinguish the craving I have for you."

His fingers brushed her breasts, lingering on her nipples, feeling them harden below at his touch. "I want you, Skye."

"Then take me. Take me how you took Crimson all those times."

"No," he said.

She looked hurt, drawing back from his touch, but he brought his lips to hers and kissed her. She pressed against him, answering his kiss in a way that spoke of her need for him before he stopped and dropped his head to her neck.

"I will never take you that way. I don't think even Pete will. It's the same way I'll never take Crimson the way I take you. You're not Crimson, and the way I feel about having sex with Crimson is nothing more than that. I love you, Skye, and that will always be there when I make love to you."

"And Pete?"

"I'd prefer not to talk about Pete when I'm about to make you fall apart against me."

He slid his hand between her legs, feeling the warmth that waited there, and gently caressing her.

"You said—" she started, her moan interrupting. "You made it sound like he would be different with Crimson—"

He pushed two fingers deep into her, her head dropping back before he moved them in a rhythm that forced another moan from her. Her pelvis rocked against him, seeking more.

"Let's save the talk for later," he said, dipping his mouth to her nipple and teasing it with his tongue. Her legs tightened around him, her breathing quickening as he removed his fingers and rubbed her clit, her body bucking in response.

"God, I missed watching you come," he said, sucking her nipple in his mouth and biting gently.

He couldn't wait for her, his need for her was too great. It had been days since he'd even had Crimson, and Skye had been even longer. He wanted her like an addict needed a hit. He tore his pants open and, without hesitation, penetrated her, her body lurching into his. She clung to him, her pelvis pushing up into him. Reaching his hand under her ass, he tilted her, thrusting deeper as she tightened around him. She was ready to break, ready to fall over the ledge of release, and the thought enticed him. Together they fell, their climax toppling them both. Breathless, he held her close, feeling the shake of her body that matched his own.

After a few moments, he kissed her neck and pulled her gown from her. Her hands pushed at his pants, then his shirt. She slid down, kissing his chest, his dick throbbing again in anticipation as she wrapped her mouth around him. It was like heaven and as she brought him to climax again, he groaned, digging his hands in her hair and pushing further into her mouth until he was shaking so badly his legs were weak.

Rising, she gave him a naughty smile and kissed him, letting him taste himself. He didn't mind, instead pulling her in further when she groaned deeply. Maddened by the sound, he picked her up and brought her further onto the bed, climbing atop her and spreading her legs with his thigh. His need for her rose again, as if he hadn't just had release. The feel of her body against his called to him in ways nothing else did, his body answering as it always would.

"I'm going to make love to you for the rest of the night," he said, entering her again. Her eyes were heavy with her arousal, her body soaked and waiting for him to take her again.

He made love to her until they were too exhausted, both finally succumbing to sleep, wrapped tight in each other's arms.

THE NEXT MORNING Skye woke him, her mouth gently bringing him out of sleep's arms and into hers. There was nothing like having her wake him this way, and part of him hoped it was something she reserved only for him.

She brought him to climax too quickly and, as usual, he wanted more. He made love to her again, reveling in the feel of her, the touch of her hands on him, the arch of her back, the way his palm fit perfectly into the small of it when he brought her further to him. It was ecstasy that no amount of time with Crimson could replace. Skye was his mate, a claim that brought sex to another level.

He held her as his heart settled and the last of his final orgasm was winding its way through him, her body's residual tremor stirring his need for her again. Moving to his back, he brought her against his chest, kissing her head. His fingers traced her shoulder as she snuggled into him.

Her hand followed the ridges of his stomach muscles, something he loved. Staring at the ceiling, he let himself simply enjoy her body against his, the touch of her hand, and the soft rise and fall of her chest.

"I love you, Mark. I always have and always will. Nothing will ever change that."

He remained quiet, the thought of Pete holding her this way taking his calm away.

Pete.

"Shit, we need to tell Pete that you're awake and…occupied."

"Shh, I already talked to Crimson."

He peeked down at her.

"Before we fell asleep. It's fine."

"Did you interrupt them?"

He saw the color shift in her eyes, the grimace take hold of her lips before she answered. "No, they were done. He'd gone to find Bormick."

"I saw that, you know."

"What?"

"The envy."

"I'm not envious. She's his mate just like you're mine."

"Well, now she's my lover like you're Pete's. No, dammit, you're his mate." It was hard for him to say. He still wasn't certain how they'd come to this point and in only a few days.

Her eyes darkened again.

"Does that make you jealous? Hearing that Crimson is my lover?"

"I can't be jealous, Mark. You have every right to Crimson."

"To fuck her?" he pressed.

Her jaw tightened, and he couldn't help but laugh. It felt good to make her jealous. The thought of her with Pete still hurt immensely, leaving him with an ever-present pain that sat in his heart.

"Yes."

"Because that's what I do, Skye. I take her hard and rough and she likes it that way."

"Why are you telling me this, Mark?"

"Partly to irritate you—"

"Well, it's working. I can tell you how Pete makes love to me if you want to play dirty."

"Touché. But it does feel good to see that envy in you." He kissed her head, trying not to picture Pete with her. Sighing, he said, "Now's probably a good time for me to elaborate on what I mentioned last night, since we're talking about the two of them. I won't take you like I take Crimson. You and I are intense. We have our own level of roughness and, once in a while, it crosses the line. But that's rare. There's too much emotion there, and that's what fuels me with you."

"And Crimson?"

"That emotion isn't there and if it is, it's anger, or a need to cover my jealousy. It's hard, gritty sex, and it would be a rare day that I would make love to her. We both understand that. Pete's her gentle lover and although I don't want to imagine it, I'm guessing he's that for you, too. We both love different sides of you."

She was thoughtful for a moment before she spoke. "That makes sense."

"Good, because it makes it easier for me to think of it that way."

"You don't...you don't hurt her, do you?" There was an edge of fear in her voice.

"Jesus, Skye, I'm not Bormick and honestly, I don't think he'd ever do more than leave a few bruises, something I can't say I haven't done to either of you when I'm squeezing your hips or your tight ass."

He reached down and squeezed her ass, then followed the curve of her body. The move stirred his arousal, which had begun with thoughts of pounding into Crimson in Eliana's chambers.

"Shit, I need to tell you something."

"Uh-oh, what more could there be?"

"We went to the Shadow Realm to speak with Derrant. He wasn't happy and demanded payment from Crimson."

"He would do that."

"Well, Eliana didn't seem too pleased and took Bormick and me to her chambers."

She rose on her elbows to look at him, and he could see the concern in her eyes. "You slept with Eliana?"

"No, I didn't, but she wanted me to. I left while Bormick was distracting her. She looks too much like you. I couldn't, no matter how she told me you wouldn't mind."

"You turned down sex with a goddess?"

"While my wife was consummating her marriage to another man. Yes."

She smiled and leaned in to kiss him, but he stopped her. He didn't have to tell her more, but he needed to.

"I met Pete's demon. Well, his tree nymph, as Bormick thinks she is."

Her eyes narrowed.

"I guess someone needs to warn Pete that she's off limits now?"

"He knows," she said through gritted teeth.

"I didn't sleep with her."

She relaxed.

"But I almost did. I wanted to, Skye. Good God, she and Crimson and Bormick were all doing it while I talked to Derrant. Eliana was hard to resist. When they sent me to the quarters after Eliana told me I needed to indulge, Ash approached me. Christ, she's sexy, petite with perky little tits, and that ass—"

She was glaring at him.

"You married another man, Skye. I can check a naked demon out."

"You've got Crimson."

"But I wanted her."

She scowled.

"Crimson stopped me."

A look of surprise overtook her face.

"She did?"

"Yes. She said you'd left me in her protection so the nymph was off limits, and I could take her instead."

"Wow, Crimson protected you?"

"I wouldn't say she protected me; it was you she protected. I fucked her when I really wanted to take the nymph. I wanted to ride her ass while she was going down on Bormick. Christ, it was there, just up in the air begging for me to take it."

"That's not helping."

He reached down and grabbed his erection. "It's helping me.

She huffed. "So you took Crimson while you fantasized about her?"

"Damn right, I did."

"Jesus, Mark. Why would you tell me that?"

"Honestly, to rile you up." He turned on his side, pulling her against him.

"Don't come at me with the hard-on you got from thinking about the tree nymph."

Laughing, he wrapped his arms around her. "I didn't touch her."

"No, but you imagined you were while you were fucking Crimson."

"And you were fucking Pete."

She narrowed her eyes. "Does Crimson know you were thinking about the nymph while you were taking her?"

"I'm pretty certain she does. I don't think I've ever pounded her that hard."

"You're gross."

"Oh, come on. I can have some fun if you're off being fucked by another man."

"You're not touching the tree nymph. And when are we going to call her what she is—a demon?"

"When they decide to break it to Bormick. And you know Crimson sent her to them when she was with Derrant, right?"

Anger filled her eyes, her teeth clenching. Through gritted teeth, she said, "That will be changing."

"You can't keep her from Bormick."

"No, but I can keep her from touching either of you."

"What if I send Pete to you when Crimson's gone and I—"

She slapped his chest.

"God, I love it when you're jealous." He forced her into a kiss, but she pushed away.

"Eh, all right, no tree nymph for me. We live very long lives, Skye. Maybe you'll change your mind. Until then, I can always watch her with Bormick."

"I will be having a conversation with Crimson about the tree nymph."

She tried to move away, but he kept his arms tight around her.

"Where are you going?"

"I'm not going to relieve that erection you got from thinking of the tree nymph. No, the demon. I'm calling her what she is. A green-skinned, two-horned demon with a vicious tale."

"I don't think she's one of those, she was too perky. The way she rode Bormick after the blowjob she gave him...all right, all right, I'll stop."

"I'm still not satisfying that."

"Oh, yes, you are. I want you well sated when we see Pete again."

"And how do you know I won't be fantasizing about him while you're inside of me?"

Damn, she was good. She'd flipped the tables on him.

"In fact, I think I will," she continued.

"I don't think so, and I'm pretty sure you can't because you love me, too, and you're my mate, too. You can't, just like I can't. When I'm with you, Skye, no other woman could ever enter my thoughts. You're all I need. You put that demon in here with us and I would forget she was here because you become my world when I'm with you."

"Good try."

"It's true. I don't need anyone but you to satisfy me. It's just when you're not here that there's trouble now."

"I'm not sure that makes it any better," she said, smiling. "You might want to stop while you're ahead before you get yourself in more trouble."

"Then kiss me."

"And satisfy this?" she asked, her hand wrapping around him.

"Definitely."

"You'd better make it worth it for me since this"—she tugged on him, eliciting a grunt from him—"did not result from me."

He spread her legs and dropped his hand into her, massaging her. "I think I can do that."

Flipping her to her back, he proceeded to drive her mad with his tongue before he entered her, all thoughts of anyone but her long gone as release found them both.

PETE

Pete made his way to the chambers, where he knew Crimson and Bormick would be. After Skye had been his world for so many days, returning to them seemed strange and a flurry of nerves accompanied his every step. Only when he'd left Skye's side had he realized how much he'd missed them. Being torn between one part of his heart and the other two was a difficult place to be, and he wondered if he'd ever adjust to his heart belonging to another person. It belonged to three people now, to three mates, and he loved them all.

He opened the door slowly, never certain what to expect behind any door with as active as Bormick and Crimson were. He found Crimson asleep; the sheets covering her lower half, leaving her full breasts exposed. A wave of need swept through him as he closed the door.

Lifting her head, her eyes lit. "Pete."

She sat up; the sheet shifting to expose her limber legs. But her expression changed, her smile dropping.

"Why did you take so long to come to me?" She looked so innocent in that moment, almost fragile, and he knew it was the side of her she reserved for him, her exterior strong and fierce.

He pushed her red hair back, her green eyes wide with expectation.

"I do believe you made me wait several days as you sat by another man's bed not long ago."

A mischievous look claimed Crimson's face. "Ah, and now I know how you felt?"

"Not purposely."

"Skye?"

"Still unconscious. Mark is with her."

"So, you're—"

"Here for you and Bormick." He looked around. "Where is he?"

"He left to take his frustrations out in the barracks, rather than on me. Although he was more dominating tonight than usual. He misses you."

"Mmm." He let his finger drift across her breasts, her lips parting in response. "And do you miss me?"

"Very much so," she whispered.

"And I suppose since Bormick was so hard on you, you need a bit of softness."

"Yes, I do."

He pulled her close, but she stopped him.

"Do you still love me, Pete?"

Touching her cheek tenderly, he replied, "More than I ever have."

It was the truth. Loving Skye had deepened the love he had for them, showing him what it was he loved about them, what made them special to him.

"Good," she purred before relaxing into his hold.

He made love to her, hating that he hadn't touched her in days, not realizing just how much he needed her to complete him. Losing himself in her touch, her curves, her cries that were so distinctly Crimson. Being with her made him feel whole again, almost. There still was one piece of him he needed to reclaim.

He left Crimson to sleep, not knowing how late it was or how many hours they'd spent in the heat of their passion. Making his way through the castle, he avoided Skye's wing, knowing she had woken. Crimson had told him as much before she'd drifted to sleep. Skye was with Mark now and he knew they needed their time, like he needed time with Crimson and Bormick. Mark was a part of her, her other half, and she needed him now. They would all be together in the morning and then they would figure this new life out.

Pete stood in the doorway, watching Bormick. He was shirtless and sweaty, his muscles taut with tension and the workout he'd been giving them. From the looks of the training dummies, he'd had a lot to work out. Bormick walked to where his weapon had blown out the back of one of the dummies.

"I hope that aggression isn't aimed at me."

Bormick ripped the weapon out, the dummy torn in half from the force. Pete watched as the weapon returned to its dagger shape. He met Bormick's eyes, the blue vibrant but shielded.

"Decided to finally grace us with your presence?" he said to Pete.

"Ouch, that hurts." Pete moved into the room, closer to Bormick but not too close, knowing his temper. "I will remind you—like I reminded Crimson—that I had to wait longer while she sat by your bedside, my mind filling in the blanks, determining I would leave her here with you since she had clearly chosen."

Bormick snorted. "Too bad she was indecisive, now I'm stuck with you for life."

Pete moved up to him, getting right in his face. "And that's an issue?"

Bormick smirked. "Not if you keep sucking my cock the way you do."

Pete grabbed him by the neck, drawing him in for a kiss. He grasped his hairline, shoving his lips harder against him, knowing how Bormick liked it. Bormick kissed him hungrily, trying to take control, but Pete pushed him back, shoving him hard against the wall.

"Gain a new mate and new power and look at you. Are you claiming my role?"

"No," he said, kissing him again, his hands finding Bormick's erection. "But I am taking you."

"And Skye?" Pete stopped and looked at him. "She's one of us now?"

"No, she's off limits."

"Hmmm. Why?"

Bormick was pushing him, trying to anger him, but he wouldn't allow it.

"Because I don't need your balls breaking her. Crimson's the only one who can handle that."

"And your tree nymph. They both handled it while you were away."

Pete raised a brow. "You saw Ash?"

"I fucked her like she begged me to, and Crimson joined us."

White hot heat streaked through him, seizing his heart like a vice.

"Thought that would bother you. Bout time you feel what we've been feeling."

"We?" Pete said, backing off. "Crimson's been screwing Mark this entire time. You mean you."

"Maybe."

"You want me to say I'm jealous? That I don't like the fact that Ash took you without me?"

"Yeah, and you might want to get used to that because Mark says Mage Warriors are very possessive. We're lucky she lets us stay in the picture."

That was new, and the possessiveness turned him on a bit, though he didn't know why.

"Ash is all mine now, buddy."

Pete rubbed his temples, remembering how Skye had reacted to the mention of Ash in the trials. She'd made it clear there would be no more trysts with Ash. He could deal with it. He had three mates to pleasure him. He wouldn't risk Skye's wrath for another taste of Ash.

"I know," he said with a sigh.

"Don't worry, I'll take care of that fine piece of meat for you."

Pete bit his tongue. Telling the truth about her would alleviate the sting of jealousy, but Bormick was too happy about his consolation prize to ruin it.

"Great."

"I'll let you watch."

"I bet you will."

"If you let me watch you and Skye."

"No," he growled, his own possessiveness coming through.

"Damn, you're a dick. Well, let me gut you a little more. I had the goddess, too, while the Death God took Crimson."

"What?" Envy raged through him again, this time at Crimson and Bormick being taken outside his circle. And he counted Ash in that circle. He'd been jealous then, but now it was different.

"She's something. Good gods, even Crimson doesn't do that to me."

"Damn. And Derrant took Crimson?"

"Payment for bothering him."

"I think my *father* needs to keep his hands off my women."

"Good luck with that, although Skye is now off limits to him."

"Really?" Pete asked, a sense of relief slipping through him.

"Eliana doesn't like how closely she resembles her, and gods Pete does she ever. If Skye is anything like Eliana in bed—"

Pete slammed Bormick's head back.

"Oh, that jealous streak is sexy, Pete. You know how I like it when you're rough."

"Fuck you, Bormick."

"Gladly. Now tell me, is Skye awake?"

"She wasn't when I left, but Crimson said she is now."

"Mmm, so she's with Mark." He reached down into Pete's pants and stroked him. "Does that bother you?"

"No," he gritted, trying to focus as his length grew again. "He's her husband."

"So are you."

"They need their time."

"And you?"

"Needed you."

"Mmm. Then show me how much you needed me."

There was a glint in his eyes. He was ready to take control back, to make Pete prove he still loved him, still needed him.

He kissed Bormick's neck, dragging his hands down his chest. Bormick unfastened Pete's pants and grasped his length. Even after making love to Crimson, the mere touch threatened to send him over the edge. It was always that way, a hint of the forbidden that sat on the cusp of their acts together. It accelerated his arousal. He pushed Bormick's hands away, pinning them to his side. Pete licked at his skin, tasting the sweat and the scent of Crimson on him, trailing downward until he reached his pants. Unbuttoning them quickly, he freed Bormick's length, wrapping his hand around him and stroking upward. His need pounded within him as he ran his thumb over the pre-cum that glistened on his head before he swiped it away with his tongue. He plunged down, Bormick's groan breaking the silence. The sound stirred that part of Pete that was owned by him, one Pete reserved for him. His hand came to Pete's hair and gripped it, pushing him further.

Pete continued to take him, tasting Crimson on him, the taste and scent making him throb. As he sensed Bormick's release mounting, it intensified. Moving his pelvis, Bormick forced him lower, a grunt escaping when he succeeded. Pete's own length was pressing uncomfortably, ready to be satisfied again. Bormick's pelvis jammed him further down as he lost hold and released. The orgasm was intense, and he pushed relentlessly into Pete's mouth until he finally settled, empty except for the small remainder that Pete licked before rising to his feet.

Bormick wore a dangerous grin and grabbed him, shoving his mouth to his fiercely before he turned Pete over and pushed him against the dummy. He tore Pete's pants open and gripped his erection from behind. He was rough and demanding, claiming the alpha and asserting his dominance. A moan escaped Pete before he could stifle it, Bormick's hand working what was already close to release before he could hold it back. He came quickly, Bormick holding him around the waist, his length hard against Pete's back.

As Pete gasped to catch his breath, Bormick pressed his back down and readied himself. Pete wasn't sure he was ready, but Bormick was. He braced himself, knowing Bormick wanted to own him and that he would let him. As he entered him, Pete clung to the dummy, a mix of pleasure and pain searing through him. The sensation grabbed hold of him deep in his core until, as Bormick filled him, his own climax ripped from him, leaving him exhausted. Bormick had taken back his power, his alpha position in their relationship and maybe even in their circle. Although he had a feeling Skye was the true alpha Bormick would need to fight for that title.

He pushed the thought away, not wanting Skye on his mind when he'd just been used by Bormick, enjoying every moment of it.

They returned to Crimson, who soothed him, letting him take her with the force he needed, like he did each time Bormick stripped him of his power. The three of them spent the remains of the night pleasuring each other, making up for the days they'd missed and putting off what he knew was waiting for them—what they all knew they would face when the sun finally rose.

MORNING CAME TOO SOON, and Pete hadn't slept. They'd been up to the early morning hours, the others finally drifting to sleep, but his mind was too wired. Crimson woke first, climbing atop him and arousing him before he could protest. He left her with Bormick after that, rising and dressing after cleaning himself.

He needed some air, his mind still unsettled. Skye had ripped the veil, moving Taenom's kingdom, the realm of the Upper God, into theirs, and he and his radiant gods were not happy about it. There was a likely chance they would punish her for it. The possibilities of that punishment were enough to keep him on edge. He put his hands in his pockets and stared out beyond the castle grounds, the mage school in the distance.

"Is this normal for you? Standing and staring at nothing?" he heard Skye say.

He turned to look at her, the morning sun highlighting the gold and bronze strands of her auburn hair. Her eyes were a rich navy, startling in the daylight. The silver rays danced in them just under the blue. He gave her a small smile as she rubbed her arms, her light dress not heavy enough to fight off the morning chill.

"Not the usual. Just needed some air."

There was a moment of awkwardness. They were beyond the confines of the trial, no longer locked in a bedroom together. No longer answering the demands of the gods. He worried that would change the dynamics of what they were, place a barrier there that would be uncomfortable to remove.

She returned his smile, his heart thumping in response.

"I'm surprised Crimson let you leave."

"Ha, it's Bormick who posed the greater threat, but she was occupying him when I left."

"Did she occupy you before you left?" she muttered, hesitation in her voice.

He studied her. She sounded envious. But of course she was,

just as he was. "Are you asking me if I had sex with Crimson this morning?"

There was a subtle cringe to her face before she nodded.

"Did you have sex with Mark this morning?"

Guilt touched her eyes. Guilt. She shouldn't have felt guilty. Mark was her husband. But the guilt he saw there answered his question, and he couldn't help that it bothered him.

"I'm surprised he let you go. Does he know you're with me?" There was a tinge of anger in his voice, and he hated it.

"Yes, he does."

"Hmmm."

She looked away, staring absently beyond the castle walls. The dynamics had changed between them, making this more difficult than he had anticipated. He took her chin gently with his fingers.

"I still love you. This changes nothing."

She leaned into his touch. "But it does. You spent the night in Crimson's arms, Bormick's, and not mine. It hurts."

He started to state the obvious, but she brought a finger to his lips and stopped him.

"And I spent the night in Mark's arms realizing how much I'd missed him and loving every second of his touch like you did with them."

He kissed her finger, taking her hand in his and drawing her closer.

"But I still love you, Pete, even though I love him. Both of you fulfill me, just different parts of me."

"And I feel the same, Skye. This is happening. We are married now. There's no denying what we have even outside of the trials. I still want you. I would take you right here if I weren't in the open and worn out from the two of them."

Laughing, she said. "Mark wanted me to tell you he made sure to wear me out, too."

"Of course he did, the bastard." He wrapped his hand around her waist, the closeness of her stoking the fire in him.

"Doesn't feel like they wore you out enough," she teased.

"You have that effect on me."

She traced his cheek, her fingers soft against his skin. "I don't know if I can live without you now, but I can't live without Mark either."

He pushed her hair behind her ear, letting his fingers drift through it.

"And there's no way Mark and I are living with you together, and that's without throwing Crimson and Bormick into that mix," he said, knowing it was the truth. He would tolerate Mark's claim, but he would never be able to share a living situation with the man. He wanted Skye to himself.

"Is there any solution?"

"Probably. We need to talk with them."

"We do?"

"But not yet."

She raised her brow. "And what do you propose we do instead?"

He drew her tight against him and kissed her, realizing then how incomplete he was without her.

"I say"—he nibbled her bottom lip—"we find out who we are."

"What?" she asked with a giggle.

"I don't really know you, Skye. I mean, I know you, but I don't know you."

"Hmm, well, we have three mates in that castle waiting for us, mine likely wearing a track in the floor fretting about us out here so maybe we need the abridged version and save the extended for our first..." She paused, her eyes shining. "Date?"

He couldn't help but laugh. "Date it is then. I'd say we're going backward in our relationship progression if that's the case."

Her smile lit every inch of his soul.

"I suppose we are in a relationship. I mean, you are my other husband, after all."

"That I am. So, wife, abridged version?"

"Abridged version, then we go in and face our mates together."

He kissed her on the nose then slid down to her lips, unable to resist them.

"Mmm, we're not going to get far, are we?" she mumbled.

"No, I'm afraid we're not," he said against her lips, feeling the world fall away again and not certain he wanted to come back to the reality that lay around them.

SKYE

Pete's lips were like heaven against Skye's. Her heart was full and content as she stayed wrapped in his arms. She'd spent the morning with Mark, the same contentment in her soul, and only when she was with Pete again did she realize she'd been incomplete.

God, but Mark had set her soul on fire after she'd woken from her sleep. He'd stopped after the first few times they'd taken each other, concerned that it might have been too much, that he should have brought the novices back, but she'd shrugged him off. Her actions had drained her energy and now that her stores were repleted, Mark was all she'd needed.

She didn't really have an explanation for what she'd done. A sensation had come over her and she'd let the power take her, claim her as Pete had done, feeling his magic reach out for hers, strengthening it. Then the world had gone blank, and she'd woken to Mark's beautiful face.

Every touch, every kiss he'd given her had restored her and solidified her love for him. Loving Pete hadn't changed it. If anything, she loved Mark more now. The things he did to her and the way she made her feel, were different than how she felt with

Pete. There was a distinction between the two that when combined left her feeling complete, like she needed both men to survive.

She leaned further into Pete's kiss, her body responding to him as it did automatically now, as it may have always done. Mark had been right—there were distinct differences between her two mates and the way they loved her.

Pete dropped his head to hers, releasing the kiss, and she ached for more.

"I don't think that was a good idea," he said, his breathing ragged.

"No, it wasn't," she replied, her body needing him desperately.

He sighed and lifted his head. "Okay, the abridged version may be too long. How about three questions? We'll start small and walk. If I can walk."

She swallowed when he took her hand, wanting instead to relieve him, to have him inside of her again. Scolding herself for letting her mind wander, she tried to focus on anything other than the sensations that were currently assailing her body and the urge she had to kiss him again.

They started walking toward the castle at a slow pace which gave her the impression that he was just as impacted as she was.

"You go first," Pete said. "I'm having trouble thinking."

Butterflies flitted through her at the confirmation that he was indeed struggling, too.

"Okay." She chewed the inside of her cheek and thought about easy questions that wouldn't have them kissing again. The castle was upon them, so she stopped walking, not ready to go inside yet.

He looked at her, his blue eyes startling below his furrowed brow.

"I don't want to go in yet, not until we get our time to talk."

His smile left her knees weak, and she tightened her grip on his hand. "Fair enough."

For a moment, she forgot what they were talking about, feeling herself drawing closer to him before she stopped herself. He was waiting for her to speak, his eyes intently searching hers. Focusing, she tried to think of a question that would quell the yearning she had to kiss him again, saying, "Okay, question one: what do you miss most about the other world?"

"Geez, that's a tough one to start with. There's a lot I miss about the human realm."

"Just one." She watched him ponder the question. He was cute when he was thinking, his eyes dimming just slightly with the concentration.

"Besides the indoor plumbing?"

"You have a shower. One I hear gets used regularly," she said, trying not to grit her teeth, the thought of him with Crimson in that shower one that caused her hands to squeeze in tight fists.

He raised a brow and gave her a crooked grin. "It does, and I'd be happy to show you some of the wonders of a shower versus a tub. Because there are plenty of ways I could pleasure you there."

The rush of a shiver went through her, and his grin widened. Her legs almost gave out, and she wondered if he could hear the pounding of her heart, or worse, smell her arousal. She was wet before but now she knew she was soaked.

"There's quite a bit that can be done in a tub," she said, feeling the flush of her cheeks.

"Yes, there is." He was close again, too close, his lips hovering above hers. They were drawn to each other, like two magnets seeking each other out. "And I can't say I wouldn't mind sharing one of those with you, too."

His hand was on her waist, and she gave over to the pull, kissing him. She leaned into his body as his hand tightened on her waist. That feeling that she needed to be alone with him, to let him take her as she took him, swept through her again.

"Damn," he whispered against her lips. "We're not making it very far, are we?"

"No," she replied, forcing her lips from his. "Should we give up and just go inside?"

"No, we can handle this. We've had conversations before—"

"With chaperones and before we found out we were something more than..." She wasn't sure what they'd been, two people who had been avoiding being close to each other because of a strange attraction she'd buried, ignoring it because she hadn't truly recognized it. Even if she'd recognized it, she would never have admitted it.

"Two people hiding an attraction they weren't allowed to have to one another?" he said, voicing her thoughts.

"We couldn't have admitted it and I don't even know that I knew what it was more than infatuation."

"True. It wasn't meant to be admitted before we were ready."

"And you think we were ready now?" she asked.

"Ha, definitely not, but someone thought we were."

He brushed a strand of her hair back and she leaned into his touch, his hand trailing her cheek tenderly.

"And so here we are," she said, giving him a smile.

He looked lost in that moment, his eyes searching hers. "Here we are." He brought his finger to the corner of her eye. "You know, you have the most breathtaking smile. It lights your eyes up so they become this lush blue that rivals any other hue."

She didn't know what to say. His words called to the very core of her. She brought his head down and kissed him again, not knowing how they were going to make this work but knowing beyond any doubt that this man owned half of her heart and soul.

"You keep saying things like that and we will never make it into the castle," she said, her voice delicate.

"That would go over really well."

With a laugh, she stepped from his arms. "Yeah, we could

probably handle one unhappy mate, but three might be too many."

"So, where were we?"

"I believe I asked you what you missed most. And this time, no talk of showers or tubs."

"Understood." He was quiet again before saying, "My sister."

"Oh, I'd forgotten, sorry. I guess that was a way to break the mood, wasn't it?"

"No, I'm fine. I just miss her, although I'm glad she's not here for all of this. She was miffed enough about Crimson but add you into the mix, not to mention what's developed with Bormick, and she'd have my ass for breakfast. And if she found out we'd gotten married, and she wasn't here. Well, I think Mark would be quite happy because I would no longer be a threat. She'd kill me."

"Isn't she your *little* sister?"

"You'd think it would make a difference, but she's quite a force."

Skye laughed, realizing she'd leaned into him again. Instinctively, his arm had encircled her waist.

"It's like a natural position with us. That's going to be hard to manage when we're with the others," he noted. "All right, your turn."

"Hmmm." She thought about what she missed the most. "Simplicity, routine."

"Really?"

She nodded. "I miss the normalcy, the mundane routine of life. My morning coffee, my morning chat with Alex before he ran off to class. I even miss my boring day job sometimes. There was no threat, no impending doom."

"And you'd go back to that?"

"I don't know. I miss it, but where would that leave me? Pining for a cousin I couldn't have, an empty bed with only my fingers for company."

She felt his reaction at the same time as his eyes widened.

"Was that a regular thing?" he asked, his voice husky.

"The pining or the fingers?" she replied.

"The fingers."

"Pretty regular. It had been a long time, and I didn't want anyone else, so something needed to satisfy me."

"Good God, there's no way I can get that image out of my head."

He walked her into a shadowed corner near the castle entrance.

"Can I watch that sometime?" he asked, his hands slipping down to her hips, his mouth close to hers.

Her knees became weak again, and she didn't think they'd hold her up much longer. What he did to her was enough to break her. It was lethal and had her thighs twitching.

"Anytime you want, as long as you take advantage of me while I'm coming for you."

"Damn, you won't be able to keep me out of there."

There was an excited look in his eyes that sent a wave of anticipation through her.

"I want to feel you, Skye." Her heart hammered, need pulsing through her. "Are you wet?" he whispered against her ear.

"Very."

His hand moved the material of her dress. It skated up her leg, which lifted to greet it, before he spread her thighs. Her head fell back in anticipation. Dropping his head to her neck, his fingers gently slipped into her. His ragged breaths were warm against her neck, further stimulating her. The grip he had on her hip tightened in response and she bit her lip trying to stop the moan. His touch sent rivulets of pleasure tearing through her.

"God, you're soaked... Please tell me that's all you and not Mark," he said, drawing his fingers back. There was a quiver in his voice, and she could almost feel the desperation in it.

"It's all me."

"Good." He brought them to his mouth and licked them, his

eyes never leaving hers. The sight sent currents through her and she grasped his arm to keep from losing her balance.

That move hadn't helped him either. His length was bursting out of his pants and every part of her wanted it freed.

"I want you, Skye," he said, bringing her body against his.

"Then take me."

He weaved his hand through her hair, drawing her lips to his. Sparks soared through her, and she let her hands drift up his chest until they were wrapped around his neck. He squeezed her hips, his length digging into her as a groan slipped from him. She'd worn a loose dress, the material thin enough to feel his touch so when his hand caressed her breast it was as though he was touching her skin. He taunted her nipple, her body flush with a heat that was burning its way through her. Frantically, she tore at his pants, needing to feel him, to have him take her. He pushed her against the wall, pinning her so that her body shook with expectation.

"Skye," he mumbled against her mouth. The sound of her name in the hoarse whisper made her shiver. She was ready for him to take her, to satisfy the mounting need in her, but then he hesitated. Drawing his lips from hers, he dropped his head so their foreheads were touching.

"What?" she asked, desperate to have him kiss her again.

He lifted his eyes to meet hers, the blue she saw there was rich with emotion. There was a tremble to his body as he took a step back. "I want you, Skye, but not here, not like this. I told you. When I make love to you, it always needs to be the right way."

"You took me against the wall in the trials, Pete. Why is this different?"

"Because it is. That was private, and it was still gentle. This is not where I want you."

She swallowed back the mix of irritation and love. She was ready for him and wanted nothing more than to have him take her right here, but the way he wanted to treat her made her heart soar.

There would be no hormone fueled sex like she and Mark were prone to have in random places. No, Pete would always make sure it was a place that was perfect for what they were and what they had.

"I won't take my queen in a shadowy corner of a castle courtyard. You deserve more. You deserve for me to worship every inch of you slowly," he said, moving his lips along her neck. Her breath caught. "And that's what I want to do, is worship you."

He drew her away from the wall, kissing her again.

"Then take me somewhere and make love to me, Pete. I want you. I want you inside of me again."

He groaned and dropped his lips from hers. "You're killing me, Skye."

"Good," she said, her hand slipping to stroke the lump in his pants.

"Shit, woman. We don't have time."

"We do—"

He shook his head. "We don't. Because I can't make love to you once. There's no way I won't want to take you all day. Besides, didn't Mark wear you out?"

"Do I feel worn out?"

"No, you feel wet and waiting for me. Jesus, why can't this be easy?"

"Because we don't get easy."

He looked into her eyes, brushing the hair from her face. "We have to wait. We need to talk to the others, to figure this out and..." His eyes grew serious. "I think you're still in danger. I can't risk letting my guard down any more than I already have. I shouldn't have even left your side."

His words left her shaken, her knees trembling in an entirely different way than they had moments before. "You needed to see the others, and when I woke, I needed Mark."

"You didn't need me?" He looked a little wounded.

"Of course I did, but just as you missed Crimson and Bormick, I missed Mark. We all needed the time."

"Point taken."

"Now, why are you worried? The trials are over. You defeated Taenom."

"Mark didn't tell you?"

She stared at him blankly.

"Of course he didn't. Too busy getting his fill and leaving the responsible part to me." He ran his hand through his hair, his expression raising her concern.

"What's going on, Pete?"

"You broke the veil, Skye."

His words startled her. She remembered pulling at it, remembered the power, the world bending to her.

"I did?"

"Yes, and you brought Taenom's realm into ours. The gods are pissed."

"I severed the veil between two worlds? How are we still alive?"

"Nobody quite knows. You placed it over the western part of Eltander and it's just there now."

"That doesn't make sense."

"I know."

"Pete, the veils separate the worlds. If I compromised a veil, those two worlds would have imploded into each other, causing a chain effect that would destroy them all. That's why I scared them when I was first coming into my powers."

"That's why no one understands exactly how it didn't destroy our world. You didn't do it intentionally?"

"No, I remember seeing you and Taenom and fearing for you. Those beasts were huge. That's all I remember except for the power. There was so much of it. I was drowning in it, but something was urging me on. I couldn't stop."

She shivered, remembering how it felt—the lure of it, the

need for more. Pete rubbed her arms, his touch calming her instantly.

"So I severed the veil, something I was warned to never do. Now they want me punished?"

"The Upper God does. I think Derrant and Eliana are persuading him otherwise, if they figured out how to get over their strife."

"If we can, they can."

"We don't really know if we can, do we?"

He was right. They had yet to all be in a room together since the wedding.

Skye, Crimson's voice filled her head. *Are you seducing my mate again?*

Our mate, and no, we're talking.

Pete's expression held concern. "Skye?"

She brought her finger to his lips.

I'm sure you are. Whatever it is, Mark is growing impatient. Meet us in the dining room. If you're not here soon, you'll find me and Mark in a compromising position and I will not stop until he's thoroughly satisfied.

Trust me, he's quite satisfied.

As is Pete, but I'm sure he's hard again with you around.

You're relentless.

As are you. Get here soon or I will pleasure him.

She rolled her eyes in irritation.

"Crimson?" Pete asked with an amused smile.

"Of course. That link we have is a curse and a blessing."

"I'm going to rule no linking while we're intimate," he said.

"Intimate? That's a fancy word for you."

"Don't confuse me with Bormick, but if you'd prefer, no linking while I'm fucking you."

"Mmm, I like the way you curse, Pete."

"You and Crimson. Not sure why it's such a turn on."

"Not sure, but tell me you want to fuck me again."

"Good God, talk about sexy. Jesus, I think you need to be the one talking dirty to me."

She gave him a sexy smile and leaned her mouth against his ear.

"If that makes you fuck me harder, then—"

He turned his head and kissed her, his hands grasping her waist tight. His kiss was demanding, his hand coming around her neck as his arousal pressed against her. She was on fire. There was no question he could give Mark a run for his money, that he could be rough and dominating like she craved, and she wondered what that would be like. His tongue swept through her mouth, eagerly meeting hers before he pushed himself away.

"Shit." He ran his hand over his face. "No more of that, not yet. I need...I need slow and soft with you, Skye."

She furrowed her brow, not sure she understood. Mark loved it demanding, and it drove her to ecstasy. But that was Mark.

"Ah," she said, understanding. Gently she caressed his cheek, meeting his eyes, the need heavy in them. "What we have with them is different."

"Yes, I need to take you slow, Skye. It doesn't mean we won't ravage each other at times, relentlessly."

"Relentlessly?"

"Oh, yes, relentlessly. But for now, Mark and Crimson get that. You and I"—he drew her closer, gently encircling her back—"we enjoy each other deliberately, as if each time is our first. I want to make love to you like it's my first time seeing your body, touching it, kissing it, tasting it."

Goosebumps traveled across her skin. His lips had moved so close to hers that she felt each word as if they were touching her.

"And I want to touch you and taste you the same way each time, like I've never had you before," she said, "and I'll save the fucking for Mark."

The growl that escaped his lips gave her a chill. It was raw, protective, and instinctual.

"You said—"

"I know what I said. I just don't like hearing it from you."

"But I can tell you I want you to fuck me?"

"Jesus, Skye, you're killing me. Turning me hot and cold. You're doing that purposely, aren't you?"

"Maybe," she answered sweetly.

"You wait, next time you're ready for release, I'm going to make you wait until you're aching so bad that you're begging me to make you come against me."

She couldn't help the sharp inhale as his lips trailed from her neck to her breast. His hand had moved her strap down so that his mouth slid past the material, finding her nipple and gently sucking on it. She bit back the pleasured gasp, her eyes closing.

Skye, stop playing with—Shit, you are playing! Get in here now or Mark will be in my mouth when you walk in.

"Fuck you, Crimson," she accidentally said aloud.

Pete raised his head, the warmth of his mouth fleeing her abruptly. "That's a first."

"Sorry, she slipped in and yelled at me when she sensed my... reaction. We need to go. She's threatening to pounce on Mark."

"She's insatiable."

Skye pulled her sleeve up, covering her breast, her legs still clenching. "So are we."

"Mmm, I'd say that's true."

She leaned her head on his shoulder. "I don't know if I can walk now."

"You? I've got a raging hard-on and you can't walk?"

He rolled his neck, rubbing his hand over his face. "Okay, we walk slow, and talk about something that doesn't involve your body."

"My mouth?"

"Really?"

Laughing, she took his hand and started walking back to the front of the castle.

"Think baseball," he mumbled.

"Does that really work?"

"Never."

She couldn't help laughing again. When they reached the entrance, she dropped his hand.

"Probably, better if we don't—"

"Yeah."

They made their way to the dining room, but he grabbed her before they opened the doors.

"Remember, no matter what happens in there, no matter what you see or hear, I love you. You are my queen, my wife. There's no taking that back."

"I've seen you with them, Pete. The three of you have never been discreet about your relationship."

"I know, but we've changed. I have to remind myself of the same thing."

"Are you ready?"

"It can't be harder than marrying in front of them, can it?"

She thought about it. "Yeah, I think it could get a lot worse than that."

PETE

The doors opened quickly, and Pete found himself looking at the three mates, all waiting for him and Skye.

"I see you found him," Mark grumbled. He was sitting back in a chair, his arms crossed, an angry scowl on his face.

Bormick was sitting a few seats away, Crimson on his lap, his expression unreadable. Crimson had a façade of nonchalance, but he could see the vulnerability behind it.

Subconsciously, he moved further from Skye, noticing her do the same.

"She found a little more of him than she set out to find," Bormick teased.

"Leave her alone, Bormick, we were talking."

"Dirty talking with what I felt," Crimson cooed.

"Skye," Mark gestured to the seat next to him, his command clear. It irked Pete and his jaw tensed in response. He rubbed his neck, trying to alleviate the ire. Although she was Pete's mate, too, in this case, it was best they split up. This was going to be difficult as it was, but if it looked like it was the two of them against the three, the situation would worsen.

Skye gave him a quick glance, then made her way to the seat

next to Mark. Mark's hand went immediately to her leg, asserting his claim.

So, it was back to that again.

Pete stood close to Bormick and Crimson, preferring to stand, taking an authoritative stance to assert his power in the situation.

"Let the games begin," Crimson teased.

"I'm waiting to see who throws the first punch," Bormick said.

"Nobody's throwing punches. This is a civil discussion. So, let's talk about what we're going to do," Pete said.

"About custody of my wife."

"I still don't know what that means."

"Sharing her, Bormick. And she's my wife now, too, Mark."

He glared at Pete, the tension clear in his muscles.

"Vacillating again, Mark? Can you give me fair warning when you go back on your acceptance, so I know before walking into the shitstorm?"

"I'm not vacillating."

"The hell you're not. Yesterday you agreed, now you're going to be a pain in the ass again."

"I had her one night, Pete, and you can't keep your hands off of her?"

"Mark."

"No, Skye, I'm serious. One night and he's all over you again."

"We can't help it," she said. "And it wasn't just him."

"Goddammit, Skye."

"It's the truth. Leave Pete be," she said. "It wasn't only his fault."

"Did you go out there for that? I wasn't enough for you?"

She looked hurt, and that stung Pete.

"Enough, Mark. Leave her alone. Don't hurt her when it's me you want to hurt."

"I don't know how you two are going to get anywhere,"

Bormick said, scooting Crimson from his lap. "So, I'll take the reins. Skye, how long can you go without Mark?"

"At this moment?" she snapped. It was her fiery side coming out, the side Mark loved her for, the one Pete found slightly intimidating.

"When you're not pissed at him."

She relaxed a little and looked at Mark. Pete noted how Mark softened at the mere eye contact.

"Not long. This was too long. I missed him."

"I thought you were too busy to miss me," Mark quipped.

"You were quite busy yourself, Mark. Did you still miss me while your dick was in Crimson?"

Ouch, she was good, and he could immediately tell the dynamics of their relationship. Not that he hadn't always seen the way they were with each other, but now he saw them in a new light.

"As much as you enjoyed having Pete's dick in your mouth," he snarled back.

"It's a wonder you two are still married," Bormick said.

"I imagine the sex when we're through here is going to be incredible," Crimson purred.

Pete shot her a look.

"What? You want him to take that out on me or her?"

"Neither," he grumbled.

"Too bad, Pete," Mark said.

"Back to the question. What's your answer, Skye?"

"I don't know. Two maybe?"

"Two days is all you can go without him?" Bormick asked with a look of doubt on his face.

"Yes."

Mark seemed to relax a little again.

"All right, that's a good start. Pete, how long can you go without Crimson or me?"

He thought about it. Skye was right. Even though she had been his world when he'd been with her, he'd still missed them.

"Two."

Crimson smiled, her eyes losing their vulnerability.

"So, two for both of you."

"Yes," they answered together.

"Good, now how long can you be without each other?"

Never, his mind whispered, but he knew it wasn't the right answer. Her eyes flashed to his, the blue drawing him in. He was having difficulty breathing, and it was hard not to rush to her and kiss her.

"Two days," he said, relieved when she nodded.

"Yes, two," she muttered.

"So, two days. Then we start with every two days. Pete, you're with us two days. Skye with Mark, then you're with each other for two days and I'm stuck watching these two. I really think I got the short stick on this deal." He scratched his chin. "How about some of those days I go with Pete and Skye?"

"No," Pete and Mark said at the same time.

"You two are no fun. Hear me out, though. I don't have to touch. I can watch and Pete and I can play. I know Skye wants to see that." He winked at Skye, whose cheeks had filled with color.

"Are you blushing?" Mark asked.

She rubbed her cheeks. "No."

"It's cute," Pete commented.

"Skye doesn't blush," Mark's voice held a level of irritation.

"Well, I'd say she likes the idea. It's quite sexy, Skye," Crimson added.

Pete tried not to laugh as the color deepened. He wasn't entirely sure what he thought of Skye watching. There was a grittiness to what he and Bormick had, and he didn't know if he wanted her around that. Her presence did something to him, bringing out a protectiveness, a need to be soft and gentle with her. He was softer with Crimson than Bormick was, but nothing like he was with Skye. Having her around what he and Bormick did would either make him uncomfortable or turn him on entirely too much. Given his reaction to her flushed cheeks, the latter might be the case.

While he wasn't sure how he felt about having Bormick involved with anything to do with Skye, if it excited her, he'd think about it for future plans.

"You're shitting me," Mark said. "No, Bormick. Skye is off limits to you and whatever it is you two do. No watching."

"We'll work on him, Skye," Bormick said with another wink.

"I bet she's wet just thinking about it," Crimson teased.

Her comment sent Pete's mind back to how wet Skye had been when they were alone. The way his fingers had sunk into her, the breathless reaction she'd had. He ran his hands through his hair, trying to stop his thoughts.

"Enough, Crimson," Mark scolded, and Pete hoped that would put an end to the conversation. He could already feel the swell in his pants from the thought.

"Let's get back on topic, please," Skye said, avoiding his eyes.

"Sorry, Pete, but I'm off the table for now." Bormick grabbed his crotch and made a rude gesture to it.

"You're like a child, Bormick, you know that?"

He moved in front of Pete and grasped his neck, forcing him into a kiss before encasing the growth that had grown. "Two days without that, Pete. Think you can handle it?" he asked against his ear.

Mark let out an annoyed grumble. "Jesus, you two."

"Oh, no, don't stop," Crimson said.

Pete pushed him away, and Bormick laughed.

"Jackass," Pete muttered at him.

"You want more of that, Skye. You just let me know. I'll dominate him for you."

"I don't know how you three function, let alone run your kingdoms," Mark noted.

"With great difficulty," Pete replied, rolling his neck and trying to calm his arousal.

He met Skye's gaze. Her eyes were heavy with her own arousal, which did nothing to help his attempt.

"So we agree every two days?" Mark asked.

"Nobody asked us, Mark. Can you go without Skye for two days?"

"As long as he has you to occupy him," Bormick answered Crimson with a hearty chuckle.

Pete noted the lust in Mark's eyes. Crimson had him hooked. No matter how much he loved Skye, he still wanted Crimson. Pete fought off the envy that slithered through him.

"What about the week I'm with Derrant?" Crimson asked.

"Then Pete goes to Skye and Mark plays with the tree nymph—"

"No!" Skye yelled.

He knew how she felt about Ash. He would miss seeing her those days Crimson would be away and had been looking forward to the next time. Now it looked like there wouldn't be a next time. Although it was disappointing, he'd give up Ash's tempting body for Skye any day. There was no comparison, and Skye was well worth the sacrifice.

"My, my, then I guess Pete stays with me, and we get the nymph. Sorry, Mark."

Bormick was pushing her buttons, and it was working. The hues had begun to swirl when Mark was discussed, but now they grew.

"No tree nymph," she gritted.

"Ouch, Pete. I guess she's all mine. You two can watch, though."

"Skye." Mark took her hand.

Hues were swirling around her, Pete's own magic pulling from him, uncontrollably drawn to hers. It wrapped around them in a dancelike motion.

She turned to Mark and Pete could feel the hues calm, his magic pulling them from her as Mark talked to her. "It's okay. Pete and I will do without her. Right, Pete?"

"Right. We'll figure it out, but she won't be near either of us again."

Skye's body calmed, her shoulders relaxing as she leaned into Mark. Pete's magic sent the hues back out where they belonged before returning to him.

"I'm not giving her up. You two get another lover, so do I. Pete can stay with Mark and Skye those days."

"Oh, that should go over well," Crimson muttered.

"Let's table that conversation," Pete said, his jaw tight. He had no desire to watch Mark with his queen. He wondered if that would change in time. There was no way of knowing. This was all so fresh for all of them.

"So, two days with us, then Pete comes here and—"

"No." This time it was Mark. "Pete's not taking my wife in my bedroom. Off limits and there is no negotiating."

"Then she comes to my kingdom," Pete said.

Bormick shrugged. "All right, then we share Pete's castle."

"No, I'm not sharing. If Pete's castle is where we spend our time together, then that's our space. You two won't be using it anymore. And you won't set foot in the quarters I share with Mark."

"Now wait a minute, Skye," Crimson said. "That's our space. I don't care about here but—"

"No, Crimson," she stated firmly.

Crimson stood and Pete heard an "uh-oh" from Bormick. This would not go well if the two started fighting, especially after that last slip of Skye's power. Her magic was volatile when it came to him or Mark.

"I'm not giving it up, Skye. I'm already giving you Pete—"

Shit.

Skye stood, interrupting her. "And I'm giving you Mark. Now back down."

"It's fine, Crimson," Pete said, trying to diffuse the tension.

"It's not fine. That's my space, too, and she can deal with me there."

"Crimson, I warned you about this," Bormick started.

"And I told you. I'm not giving up my space. She can deal with me there."

"I'll deal with you in your castle, Crimson, and you're lucky you get that!" Skye's eyes were alive with flames of color. She'd stood as well, and the two were closing in on each other.

"Are you kidding me? You steal Pete from us—"

"I didn't steal Pete from you!"

The air was growing heavy; the colors seeping from the walls. He caught Mark's eyes, sensing the same worry that was now building in him.

"You did! Seriously, Skye, you married him!"

"Crimson," Pete warned.

"And you've been rolling around in the sheets and God knows where else with my husband!"

"Well, I guess now I get to fuck both your husbands," Crimson growled. "You're not taking that castle."

Colors sped toward Skye, swirling around her in a nightmarish scene.

"Why you bitch," Crimson started drawing her power, but Bormick dragged her back.

"Don't, Crimson."

"I'm not letting her take everything from us!"

Pete stepped from the wall as Mark rose. The room was aglow with hues, Skye's eyes a kaleidoscope of colors.

"I'm not taking everything. You'd know if I were taking everything, and you damn well know I could."

Crimson pulled away and hissed. "He's mine now. I'm taking

him back, Skye. I'm not playing this game anymore. I'm not giving any more up."

"You can't take any of it back, Crimson."

"Fuck," Pete muttered. "Would you two stop?"

"There's no going back, Crimson. It's done," Skye said with a growl.

"Then I keep the castle and I take Mark here."

"What?" Mark said. "I don't think—"

The color bled from the wall; the walls deteriorating.

"Uh, guys," Bormick said, grabbing Crimson and hauling her back again.

"Are you threatening me, Skye? I'm not caving."

"Forget the fucking castle, Crimson," Pete finally said, his voice carrying anger that was boiling over at the ridiculous situation. She turned her wounded eyes at him. "I'll build you another. Now step back. She's trying her best not to kill you right now."

He nodded to the faint stream of red that hung in stasis from her hair. Startled, she backed further into Bormick's arms.

Everything in the room was gray. Crimson's eyes widened, having not seen the full spectrum of danger that hung over them.

"Skye," Mark murmured, his hand on her arm.

There was no response. The grip of Skye's hands was so tight Pete worried she might split her skin. The outer wall of the room had crumbled, but thankfully the others still stood. Colors were bleeding from the hall now, and there was a quiver below his feet. Skye's power had compromised the stability of the castle.

His power was fighting to get to her, but he held it in, watching and waiting for Mark's move.

"Skye," Mark tried again.

Their clothes began to bleed. The power had overtaken her, just as it had during the battle. He thought about how she'd nearly lost control earlier, his magic surrounding hers instinctually, and how it had tried doing the same at the battle.

Mark was having no luck getting through to her. If she wasn't calmed soon, the entire castle would fall, and Pete didn't want to think of what she would do to the world beyond these walls. The gods were already pissed at her, having her unhinged was the last thing they needed. Heeding the call of his magic, he released his hold on it, watching it encase the hues and settle over them. She inhaled like she'd been holding her breath. As his magic embraced each hue, shielding it, calming her own magic, her body relaxed, the tension fading. His magic guided the hues back, the wall reforming behind them. He met Mark's eyes, an understanding crossing between them.

He was the calm to her fire, the gentleness to her fierceness. He met the other side of her, the one that could topple, taking her over the edge of sanity, of control. Her power had grown since the trials. He wasn't certain if their love had triggered it or if it had been lying in wait, the explosion of power within her triggered by the battle. Whatever it was, he was her match, the only one who could now assuage her completely.

She backed away, shaking.

"What in the gods' name was that?" Bormick asked.

Pete wanted to go to her, to hold her, but the situation was too tense.

"Go to her, Pete, finish doing what your power just did," Crimson said softly, "and Mark, you explain what that was."

Pete looked to Mark, who nodded, knowing this was now Pete's role. Mark may have been her guardian all these years, but Pete was now her protector, quite possibly their world's protector. The role was a heavy burden but one he would easily accept if it meant Skye was safe.

He went to her, pulling her into his arms, her body quaking against his. She seemed so fragile in that moment. Her magic called to his, and he answered it, letting his shadows embrace her, feeling how they affected her and strengthened her.

Mark turned away. "There's no going back, Crimson, no matter how much it bothers any of us. That's the reason."

"Fine, she can have the castle, but I want a shower in mine." She pouted, sticking out her bottom lip.

Pete smiled at her, his hands rubbing Skye's back. "A shower it is then. I'm sure Skye will oblige to help me build another one."

She nodded against him.

"Fine, now what was that, Mark?" Crimson still looked pouty, but Pete was glad she'd dropped the subject. Her power was strong in many ways, but it was a weak copy of what Skye's power once was. Even before the events of their marriage, Skye was the more powerful of the two. Now, however, Skye could destroy Crimson within seconds. He cringed thinking of losing one woman he loved to the other. The thought terrified him. With as fragile as the current situation was, he wasn't so certain it had been a wise idea to have Skye in the same room as Crimson. Both women were sharing him and Mark, both women giving up pieces of the men they loved. They were bound to be volatile which was not a good state for Skye to be in, especially now.

Mark was watching Pete, his eyes narrowed like he was thinking on something before he raised them and met Pete's gaze. That same understanding crossed between them again, and Pete could tell Mark had been thinking along the same lines as he had.

"I'm waiting for an explanation, Mark." Crimson crossed her arms and tapped her foot.

"I'd give her an answer soon or she'll go feral again and piss Skye off even more," Bormick joked. "That was hot, Skye, but slightly intimidating even for me."

Crimson shot him a look but he ignored it and pulled her into his arms.

Sighing, Mark said, "I'm not really sure, but I think it has something to do with the Mage Warrior in her."

"You think?" Crimson snapped.

"Not the power. Mage Warriors are extremely possessive of their lovers, especially Skye's line. They don't share. I suspect you and Bormick are lucky she does, but I also suspect it's ten times harder for her than it is for us, even though it sucks for us."

"So I should be thankful?"

"You should be thankful she let you live after touching either of us. What Skye's doing is a blessing and goes against everything in her code."

"But I'm a Mage Warrior—"

"No, Crimson, you're not," Pete said. "You're different and you know it. You wield the hues, but you don't own them, and you certainly don't own the shadows like Skye does. Your power is still a copy of Skye's. It always will be."

She looked hurt for just a moment, but Bormick wrapped an arm around her and nuzzled her neck, lifting the slight sadness on her face.

Skye looked up at him, drawing his attention from them, and he resisted the urge to kiss her with every ounce of his power. She looked away and freed herself from his arms, turning to the others. Her shaking had stopped, so he drew his shadows from her, leaving a light covering over her aura.

She rubbed her arms as if sensing the loss of them.

"I'm sorry, Crimson," Skye said, her voice soft.

Crimson raised a brow at her and put her hands on her hips.

"If I didn't like you, Skye, I'd kick your ass for fighting with me and taking my stuff."

"Stuff?" Pete asked. "Now I'm just stuff?"

"Sexy stuff," she added.

"Oh, that helps. Thanks."

She shrugged. "Thank you for not killing me back there."

"Trust me, I wanted to," Skye said.

"Bitch," Crimson returned, but he could sense the playfulness in it.

"I know, but Pete's castle is off limits. I'll help give you a shower. But I don't want to hear what goes on in that shower from any of you."

"Not even me?" Bormick said. "Pete's fun to bend over in the shower—"

"No!" Mark said, "That's more than any of us want to know and you will not be telling her about that either."

Bormick laughed. "I'll tell you sometime when we're alone."

"Good luck with that, Bormick. I have a feeling you'll never be alone with Skye, especially now," Crimson teased, and Pete was glad she'd relaxed. The tension in the air had dissipated.

"Christ, you lot are too much. So, we're agreed that we switch off every two days. Pete, you take your two, I take her for two. If I want to take my mind from the two of you, I have the freedom to take Crimson and this buffoon. If I want but not here…but then where? Pete, is that a problem if I'm at Crimson's?"

He thought about it. "No, doesn't bother me. I already deal with Bormick there."

"Fine, then I go to Crimson's. Here is off limits, Pete's is off limits. All of this is subject to change."

"Which I'm sure it will as you two loosen up about this and start sharing her," Bormick said.

"Not gonna happen," Mark said.

"We'll see about that."

Pete tuned them out, feeling a stir in his magic, a pull of it.

It's time, Pete, Derrant's voice filled his head. *Gather Skye. The gods are deciding her fate. I will call you to me.*

His heart crashed against his chest, fear ripping through him before he could stop it.

"It's time," he said, interrupting the others.

"Time?"

"The gods are convening to decide Skye's punishment."

The room was silent, all eyes on him. Terror filled Skye's eyes.

"Well, that certainly changes the tone," Bormick mumbled.

"I can't. I'm not ready. What if they kill me as punishment?"

She was freaking out. He could feel her fear, her anxiety permeating the air.

"Then I guess this conversation was for nothing," Crimson mumbled.

Pete gave her a scolding look.

"Sorry. Skye, they're not going to kill you," she said.

"They might. We all heard the Upper God," Bormick said.

"Oh, my God."

"Skye." Mark put his hand on her arms and rubbed them. "We don't know that, and Eliana won't let them kill you. I doubt even Derrant would. It's going to be okay."

The tension simmered, her fear abating some, and Pete understood now why he and Mark were meant to be her mates. Mark was the strength to her vulnerability, the support to her weak moments, Pete the softness to her fierce side. The two of them complementing each other, making her whole, creating her foundation.

"Huh," Crimson said, as if realizing the same thing. "She really does need both of you. One without the other leaves her unbalanced now that her power has changed."

Mark looked over at Pete, the awareness there, the mutual understanding that this had to work because Skye hung in the balance.

"Skye," Mark said, focusing back on her and picking her chin up. "You'll be all right. Where's my warrior?"

She gave him a small smile.

"Better. Now go with Pete."

She hesitated, then reached her hand to his and leaned in to kiss him. It should have bothered Pete, but this time it didn't. Mark wasn't any more of a threat than he was.

"Go," he told her.

She straightened her back, and Pete could see the strength return as she turned to him. He held his hand out for her.

"Derrant is calling me, we need to go." He could feel the tug at his power, knowing it was a warning. She walked to him, taking his hand, her other still holding Mark's. The symbolism did not go unnoticed by any of them as Mark slowly let her fingers go.

Bormick gave him a nod and continued his hold on Crimson, whose expression finally reflected the worry the others now carried.

Pete took Skye in his arms, the tug stronger.

"Protect her," Mark said, his face lined with fear.

"With my life."

The room disappeared, plunging them into a darkness that even he could not sway.

CRIMSON

rimson stared at the place where Pete and Skye had been. Her Pete, now Skye's, too. And Skye wasn't sharing well.

Bormick's hand curved around her waist. "You keep pouting those pretty lips. I'm going to put them to use."

He was teasing, but she knew him well enough to sense the worry in his voice.

"She's more powerful now than she ever was," she said, feeling the shake that remained in her hands.

The intensity of the situation hit her, and she took a wobbly step from Bormick's arms. She'd been so caught up in her jealousy, her mind a haze with white rage at Skye, that she hadn't seen the danger she'd been in.

"She is," Bormick said. "It sits on her aura now."

"But it's settled now, isn't it?" Mark asked, his eyes still fixed on the space where Skye and Pete had been.

"Yes, except when she's close to Pete and their auras touch. The same thing happens when you're next to her. She needs both of you."

And she did. Crimson had seen it, the way she had reacted to

Mark, then to Pete. Both of them calmed a different part of her, owning a piece of her and balancing the total of her.

Mark's gaze hadn't left the spot and her eyes fell to it, thinking of all that had changed in a matter of days. All she'd had to give up, the redefining of what she'd known, of what they'd all known.

"Will they be okay?" she asked, her voice low.

Bormick kissed her head. "Pete will keep her safe."

"But who will keep Pete safe?"

Mark turned his eyes to her. The fear that sat there was like none she'd ever seen him hold. "I don't think Pete's in danger. It's Skye who will need saving, and Pete's the only one who can do that."

His voice was sad but resigned.

"You can't always be the one to save her," Bormick said. "We're together for a reason, all of us. Maybe it was so those two could bring what they have now to fruition. Maybe it's for more than that. Whatever it is, we save each other, we protect each other. It's not up to just one of us anymore."

"Or maybe..." Crimson paused as the realization hit her. The thought that this was on a grander scale than she ever imagined, all of it revolving around Skye. "Maybe we're all here for her. To protect her and the power she holds. You protected her for years Mark, Bormick risked his life to save her. I pulled her from the brink of chaos. We've all played our part."

"And right now, it's Pete's turn to protect her," Bormick said.

"But why? Why does it have to be that way? Why is she so in need of protection?" he asked. "She's the strongest woman I know. Her power is immeasurable at this point."

"And unstable," she said. "The gods know that. Derrant would have seen that when he had her. Shit, he tried to make her his because he knew how strong she was. How she could bring this world to its knees. Mark, she has the power to crumble the entire universe."

"Which means she doesn't need protection."

"Fuck," Bormick muttered. "Yes, she does. It's up to us to keep her stable, particularly you and Pete. In doing so, we keep the world and universe safe."

Mark's mouth dropped, understanding lighting his eyes. "I thought the two of us just kept her powers in check."

"You do, but that in turn keeps everyone safe."

He leaned against the table. "If the Upper God sees her as a threat..."

Crimson went to him, lifting his face to force him to look at her. She didn't know how to reassure him. She was good at seduction, at sex, but not at comfort. But this wasn't the time for those things, and she knew it wasn't what any of them needed at this moment.

"Pete will protect her."

"And who will keep Pete alive?" he asked.

A trickle of fear ran through her. She couldn't lose Pete. Giving up a part of him had been hard enough. Losing him completely was inconceivable.

"Derrant will. He's too invested in all of this not to keep his son safe. He won't let his brother touch Pete, and Pete won't let anyone hurt Skye," Bormick firmly stated.

She clung to his confidence, knowing if she didn't, she would break.

"Is it safe for me to ask what in gods' name is going on here and why the castle started falling apart?" Noah asked, peeking his head through the door. He took in Crimson's proximity to Mark, his eyes narrowing.

"Oh, get over it, Noah. I'm fucking Mark now and Skye is fucking my lover. We're not doing anything right now...but if you want to watch later, I'd be happy to put on a show that will have you orgasming like you used to."

The daggers in his eyes were rewarding. He'd been fun to play with and he'd given in much faster than Mark had. He didn't touch Mark's ferocity, but she'd had her share of pleasure from him.

"Leave him be, Crimson," Mark scolded her, a commanding tone to his voice.

"I love it when you command me, Mark. Can you do that when you're—"

"Crimson," Bormick said in warning. She turned her eyes to him, understanding the warning. Bormick's command she did heed, she always would. He didn't do it often, but when he did, it called to that feral part of her.

"We're fine, Noah."

Noah looked between him and Crimson again. "Where's Skye?"

The mood in the room dropped again, the unknown hanging over them.

"With Pete. The gods are deciding her punishment," Mark answered. His tone was dry, but she knew it was only to hide the emotion below the words.

Noah's demeanor changed, fear reflected in his eyes, before he pulled himself together.

"Well, then, you've got time. You've been absent and I'm getting tired of commanding your troops, commander. Get your ass out on the training field and give me a break."

She saw the change in Mark, Noah's redirection of his attention bringing him back.

"If my ass is on that training field, it will not be giving you a break."

"Can I watch both your asses on that training field?" she cooed, enjoying the lightened mood, and having her mind on something besides Pete.

"My ass is off limits, Crimson," Noah said. "But you can watch Mark's all you want."

Bormick squeezed her ass, adding, "As long as my hands are on yours while you're watching, Crimson."

"That can be arranged."

"No, it can't. If I'm working, Bormick's working."

"What?" he asked, following Mark from the room, grumbling about not being one of his Elite.

Crimson shook her head. She glanced back to the space where Pete and Skye had been one last time before following them from the room. As she left, she sent a prayer to Eliana to protect them and to bring them home, knowing somehow that Eliana would hear her.

SKYE

The breath fled from Skye and she clung to Pete. They were in a dark, nearly sightless space.

"Pete?"

"Shh, I'm not letting you go."

Her heart hammered in her chest, but his magic touched her skin, calming her.

Reeling from all that had happened—the conversation, her loss of control, nearly killing Crimson, and now this—she leaned further into him. Pete tightened his hold on her in reaction.

The blackness ahead shimmered, revealing a dimly lit tunnel. Sconces lined the walls, throwing out the low light. Upon closer inspection, she saw that no flame was present. Only magic fueled them.

Pete led her through, never removing his arm from her waist. He hesitated at the opening into a vast room, the brightness of it causing Skye to squint. The Upper God stood within the light, flanked by the radiant gods. She remembered him from her early years, warning her to avoid the Shadow Realm, and wondered if he'd known that Eliana was her sire, that Pete was in her future, that she would come to welcome the shadows.

Across from him—in a dimmer setting contrasting starkly to the golden lit side—stood Derrant and Eliana, flanked by the shadow gods.

Gods. All the gods had gathered. The three ruling gods and their lesser gods, all gathered to pass judgement on her.

Pete ushered her in, all eyes trained on them. The Upper God scowled at her. Eliana smiled, lovely and warming to Skye's heart. Derrant remained expressionless.

To the far end of the radiant gods stood Taenom. Pete tensed beside her, and she leaned closer to him. When they were in the middle of the room, Pete stopped with her. Her breaths were short and strained, but she refused to show her fear.

"We have summoned you to judgement, daughter of Eliana. With Taenom, son of mine, and Peter, son of Derrant, as witness."

Witness? She glanced at Pete, but his eyes were locked on the Upper God, his grip firm around her waist. The thought crossed her mind that he'd be forced to witness her death sentence and her execution.

"Peter," Derrant said, gesturing for him to stand with them.

"I prefer Pete, and I'm not leaving her side."

Derrant glared at him.

"Obstinate like you, Brother," the Upper God noted.

"I see you've worked out your differences," Pete said.

"And mouthy. Mind your manners or I will punish you with her."

"You'll have to, anyway."

Power flared through the room, gold and angry, pushing Pete from her over to Derrant. He struggled against the magic's hold trying to get back to her.

"Let her be, Pete," Eliana said, placing a hand on his shoulder. "She must stand judgment. We have no choice. She's lucky we argued this much, or she would already be dead."

Skye's heart skipped, and she saw the fear etched on Pete's face and in his eyes. He stopped the struggle.

"You stand accused of shattering the veil between realms—of breaking the laws of nature and wielding magic as only gods should," Carzent bellowed. "What do you say in your defense?"

Skye didn't know what to say. She barely remembered anything from that day and certainly didn't remember doing what he'd just described. She had, though. Pete had told her. They'd all witnessed it.

She couldn't defend herself against something she didn't even remember doing.

"I have no defense..." She thought back to the moments before it all went blank. "It was instinctual. At first it was reactive, a response to the attack on Pete, but then something took over and it just happened."

"Just happened?" a radiant god asked. He was tall and thin with a beautiful face topped with auburn hair that shimmered with gold. But the sour expression he wore marred the beauty of his appearance when he spoke.

"I don't know how to explain it."

"Because you were out of control. You are dangerous and, if left unchecked, will destroy our world and those beyond. The veil is fragile," Carzent said.

"Punishment is due," another radiant god said. This one was just as striking but with a head of blonde hair and lips that snarled with his words.

"Why punish her for something she doesn't remember doing?" Pete asked.

"What if she loses control again and shatters the veils that separate our world from another? Will it matter if she doesn't remember?"

The gods were right, but it still didn't make sense. She was missing something. They all were. She had moved another realm into theirs and done it with ease. Sure, it had drained her, but it hadn't killed her. And it hadn't done any more damage than to fracture that veil. Only the one and no other. There had to be a reason for how she'd done such a thing and not destroyed their world.

"That veil was meant to be shattered," she mumbled.

"Realms are separated for a reason," one god said, but she didn't know which one. Her eyes were trained on the ground as her mind worked it out.

"But this one wasn't as strong as the one that separates your realm from ours, or even the Shadow Realm from ours. It was pliable. I remember touching it before, sensing it, brushing it in the past." She looked up at the Upper God. "Why didn't it collapse before?"

"Because you held less power. Your final trial enhanced your powers—"

"Bullshit. I nearly collapsed the veil to the Upper Realm, nearly brought the Shadow Realm into ours when I first discovered my magic. Why did this one fracture so easily and why did I never do it before? If I reached into your realm, why would that one not have folded at the time?"

He looked irritated, confirming her accusation.

"Because you weren't in the right place to sense it and break it," Pete answered.

"What do you mean?"

"You said you brushed it, but you reached into the veil separating their realms. You weren't anywhere near Upendum, were you?"

"I...no, I wasn't." Then it dawned on her what he was saying. "That veil *was* meant to be shattered."

"It was, wasn't it?" he asked the gods. "It fit perfectly over the edge of Eltander, not touching any of our kingdoms."

"I think they've got you, Brother," Derrant said smugly.

"She will be punished for her disregard—"

"Of what? Our stubbornness. Let them go," he argued.

"The Shadow Queen will break, the realms of old now one," Pete said, and she looked over at him, unsure as to what he was saying.

"You dare quote prophecy to me, boy? Derrant, I'm surprised you allow that talk."

"Shut up, Carzent, and let him speak."

"Those are the words Ash told Mark and Crimson. But neither of them knew what it meant. I didn't either when Crimson told me, but now it makes sense. Skye was meant to merge Taenom's land with ours, wasn't she?" Skye's mouth dropped as her eyes met Pete's. "You were. That's why you did it so easily, although your easy and mine are two very different definitions."

She smiled, even through the nerves.

"Brother, it is time we tell these three the truth," Eliana said.

"It is time for punishment," he grumbled.

She left Derrant's side and went to Carzent. Skye realized then that Eliana was the bridge between the two brothers. She could traverse both realms, soothe both tempers. She was the balance to their world.

"Brother, it is time. Skye did what she was meant to. She united us."

"We are not united," Derrant grumbled.

Eliana shot him a look.

"Why do you insist on living in his shadows, little sister, when you are so attuned to the light?" the Upper God asked.

"Because the shadows comfort her. They calm the overpowering touch of the light and make her whole," Skye answered for her, thinking of her reaction to Pete and his magic.

"We are too alike, my daughter," Eliana said with a coy smile. "You know me almost too well."

"The shadows have always been my home. I just never realized how deeply rooted I am in them." She exchanged a look with Pete, feeling his emotion from where he stood.

"Tell us why the veil was broken."

"Because it was never meant as a permanent divide between the realms we created," Eliana answered. "When we formed our world, and I decided to stay with Derrant, my two brothers began arguing viciously. We decided it would be safer to create our pieces of land separately, and that's exactly what we did."

"The land beyond the Eltander Kingdom is an endless ocean. No one has ever traveled beyond because there is nothing beyond, is there?" Skye asked.

"Correct. There is a void that surrounds your kingdoms just as there is a void surrounding Taenom's."

"The two were waiting all that time to be merged," Pete mused. "And now Skye has finally merged them, doing what your brothers were too stubborn to do."

"He should be punished as well," Carzent growled. "Enough talk—"

"No, Carzent, that is not enough. You started this. You dragged my people, my son, and Eliana's daughter into this with your pompous son's overly ambitious ideas. If anyone is to be punished, it is he who breached the veil in the first place to annihilate my realms."

"In my defense that was my father's doing," Taenom said.

"Shut up, you insignificant flea," Derrant raged. "You made this mess, then tormented them with trials that only strengthened them, and for what? To have your champion fight mine? To show that you are the stronger of us? Well, you're not Carzent, and you never have been."

Carzent transformed to his true form, towering over them in a brightness that was nearly blinding, his face distorted and frightening. Derrant morphed to his true form, his demon-like features terrifying in the dim light, even more so when he stepped into the light.

Skye stumbled backward, Pete catching her, then backing her up.

"I think we struck a nerve," he whispered.

Just having him close calmed her. She caught sight of Taenom, who looked horrified, and she wondered if he'd ever seen the true side of the gods as she had.

"Enough!" Eliana bellowed. Her form grew but without the distorted features, instead a glowing aura billowed from her, her hair streaming with shadows and gold. She was every bit as enchanting, like the true goddess that she was. "You will calm yourselves now. Carzent, Derrant is right. Your people started this by attacking ours. The trials were cruel and unnecessary. You pushed them into what should have been slow and beautiful, risking everything they hold dear to make it happen at your pace so that you could have your fight."

"He didn't care about the battle. He was hoping Pete would fail long before he got to that point and never claim his true place or his queen," Derrant said.

Skye squeezed Pete's hand. So they'd been meant to be. Their love would have happened regardless, only gradually. She didn't know if that would have made it any easier on any of them.

Derrant stared his brother down. Eliana returned to her mortal size, looking up at them.

"Please," she said.

Derrant broke first, returning to his normal form, then Carzent. Both continued to glare at each other.

"Regardless of whether it was meant to be or not, she is still reckless, with no understanding of her true power or control of it. She is a threat to the veils, our world, and our universe. If we cannot decide a punishment, I will bring the others in and I assure you they will not sit well with a threat that large to their worlds."

"Others?" Pete asked. "I thought you were it."

They turned to him.

"Our world is one of many, Pete," Eliana said. "You should know this since you came from a neighboring one. We have countless brothers and sisters who created their own worlds and people. They are all connected to us, the veils between our worlds all that separates us."

"And as so she threatens more than just our world," Carzent finished. "She must be punished, Eliana."

"What if I can guarantee she won't lose control again?" Pete asked suddenly.

Skye looked at him. She didn't understand how he could guarantee such a thing when she couldn't.

"And how would you propose to do that?"

"My power calms her. It soothes her hues. I've seen it work. If she ever loses control, I can stop it."

"If what you say is true, how can you guarantee it? This would require you to be by her side nonstop."

And that would never happen. Mark would never allow it.

"Because both of us calm her in different ways. Her other mate has the same effect if she's not completely lost to it."

"But if she is?"

"Then I will soothe her. One of us will always be by her side."

"But you will not."

"I will be often enough. Please, we can protect her and the veils. You made us mates for a reason, you forced us into this. You should trust me to ensure she never severs another veil."

"Even if I accept your offer—"

"We," Derrant corrected, eliciting a dirty look from Carzent.

"I still want proof."

"Proof?" Skye asked. "How does he prove it?"

"Yes, brother, tell us how."

"This way."

He raised his hand, and Mark appeared in front of them.

"What the—Skye?" he said, confusion clouding his eyes.

Carzent's power grabbed him before she could react, crushing the life from him. Skye watched in horror as his limp body fell to the ground. She screamed and the world around them broke into chaos, her eyes fixed on his body, her mind fixed on the pain and a need for retribution.

PETE

Pete watched in disbelief as Mark's life was snuffed out as easily as one might blow out a match. His heart broke for the loss of his friend and for Skye. The room erupted in a chorus of voices, a cacophony of sounds as the gods screamed at each other. Skye's scream rippled through it all and silenced them. The hues bled from the walls, the black encircling her like a snake, the golden light snuffed out, streaming to her in vinelike waves. Her hair was blowing back with the force of her power, a vortex of color creating a world within her prison of color.

The radiant gods backed up, the Upper God standing still, watching her intently and not fazed by the storm she had created.

Her power had bled the wall, turning it to ash, the cavernous ceiling above them doing the same.

Save her, Peter, Derrant's voice echoed through his mind. *Otherwise, my brother will have his way and force us to kill her.*

But he had no idea how to stop her. This wasn't a fight between her and Crimson, this was the loss of the love of her life, her other mate, a part of her. He didn't know if there was a way to stop something this damaging to her psyche.

The walls had now completely crumbled, leaving them in an

open space. Pete looked down, seeing stars below them. They were in the Upper Realm. The space to his left began to quiver, the same to his right, the stars below growing blurry.

Skye was breaking the veils, just as they said she would. She would lead to the death of everyone and destroy every world in the process. Or the gods would kill her first.

"There is no stopping her!" Carzent boomed.

Pete tuned him out, turning back to Skye. She was terrifying in a breathtaking way, seductive and deadly. The power swirling around her was throwing shadows over her.

Shadows, that had been his intention. He listened to his power, hearing its call to hers, then releasing it, not directing it but letting it follow its own course, trusting its instinctive draw to her. The shadows streamed through her hues in ribbons, encasing them, calming them, binding with them. An endless flow of shadows poured from him, dancing with her power. There was a sensuality in the way they merged that touched the piece of his soul that belonged to her.

Drawn to her magic, he stepped through the vortex into the eye of her storm, her magic swirling around them. He tipped her chin up, forcing her eyes to focus on his, the kaleidoscope of hues within them settling to the rich navy he loved. He wanted to kiss her, but her heart was broken, and he knew the action would only bring confusion to her already volatile state. Instead, he pulled her to his chest, letting his shadows flow over her and wrapping them both in its touch. Gently he settled her, calming her as her body responded and the storm abated.

The shadows guided the hues back, repairing the damage, and rebuilding what had been there. She broke, her body quivering as she fell apart in his arms, tears breaking through the damn. An anguished cry escaped her as he held her tight, her body convulsing with her agony.

"He has passed your test, Brother. Now fix the damage you have caused and let our children go."

"Fine," Carzent grouched.

The world shifted from under his feet and Skye was no longer in his arms, no longer crying uncontrollably, Mark's body gone.

She looked around wildly.

"It didn't happen?" Pete asked.

"No. It was in your heads. Look."

He waved his hand, Skye flinching slightly. She was shaking, so he brought her close, feeling how weak she suddenly was. It may not have been real, but that didn't mean she hadn't exerted the energy and experienced the emotion. The floor cleared to an arial view of Mark, Crimson, and Bormick. Noah was there, as was Camin, both talking to Mark while Crimson draped herself over him. Bormick was shaking his head and watching from the side.

"She never stops, does she?" Skye whispered, leaning into him further, her body relaxed finally.

"No, she doesn't."

Crimson's hand slid up Mark's thigh, and he pushed it away.

Pete knew Mark's mind was on Skye, and no matter how Crimson tormented him, he wouldn't take her invitation until he knew Skye was safe. This wasn't like the last trials. This was a sentencing and he stood to lose Skye to more than just Pete.

"That's enough," Skye said quickly.

Pete looked away from the scene and back to the Upper God. "You tortured her, made her think that was real, just to test her?" Ire burned its way through his body. He was pissed that Skye had suffered. He let her go, tension rife in his muscles, and stormed over to the god. "Was that entertaining?"

"Would you prefer I had actually killed him?"

"No, I'd have preferred that you hadn't tormented her and had trusted me."

"Trusted you?" Taenom snapped, interrupting the god's comeback.

"Mind your place, Taenom," Pete growled, his patience with the man long gone.

"Mind games, Shadow King." He sneered the titled, grating further on Pete's nerves.

"I defeated you once. Don't make me do it again."

Taenom came closer so that he was in his face and Pete held back, his power stirring to break free.

"You only defeated me because your slut decided to break the veil."

Pete punched him, and he landed on the floor.

"I thought I made it clear you were not to insult my mates."

Taenom glared at him, rubbing his jaw. Blood trickled from his lip. He began to rise, but Derrant stopped him. "I'd stay down if I were you. Retain some dignity." He looked to Carzent. "You need to keep your insolent brat in check, Brother. And if he insults Eliana's daughter again, I will bleed him out myself and feed his soul to my demons while he's dying. They do so love a living soul."

Skye touched Pete's back, his fists relaxing in response.

"What happens to me now?" she asked.

"We will return you, but know this, Peter, you are the only thing that stands between her and death. If she so much bends the veil an inch, I will kill her where she stands, no matter how it hurts my sister," Carzent answered.

"Carzent," Eliana started.

"No, Eliana. The veil between the worlds must stay in place. If she becomes a threat again, I will not hesitate to spare the multitude of carnage she will invoke."

"We submit to that request," Derrant said.

"What?" Pete couldn't believe what he'd heard.

"You are her protector, Mark her guardian. Between the two of you, she will be safe. Work out a way to ensure she remains that way. Now, what do we do with this fool?" Derrant pointed to Taenom. "And your damned realm that now sits within mine."

"It is the way it was meant to be," Eliana said. "It will remain that way and Taenom will rule his realm alongside our children."

"I don't think so," Pete argued, Derrant complaining as well.

Eliana gave Derrant a look that silenced his complaints.

"You will get along and my brother will ensure that Taenom is a gentleman."

"Will I?"

She stooped next to Taenom and ran his fingers through his golden hair. "If you do not play nice, I will show you why I favor the shadows." The hues of his hair bled from him along with the gold in his eyes. No stream of color came from him. Instead, the color simply faded, turned by her shadows, ones that now covered her. The darkness on her side of the room billowed around her like a cloak. Taenom's eyes were wide with fear, the color of his skin turning gray.

"Enough, little sister."

"Oh, but Carzent, she's having fun. Isn't that what you did with our children?" Derrant replied.

Eliana stood, Taenom's pallor returning, his hair becoming its normal shade again. She held her hand out to help him up. Tentatively, he took it.

"Behave," she said.

Pete furrowed his brow, studying Taenom. He didn't trust him. "He and his people breached the veil and attacked our people, annihilating an entire kingdom. Why is it you've made us suffer?"

"It's a fair question," Derrant said. "And one I will answer since my brother will not. Because my brother felt the need to punish us through his children, knowing damn well we couldn't interfere."

"You had too many kingdoms," Carzent complained.

"Are you serious?" Skye asked.

"Don't make me regret leaving you alive. You will rule alongside my son as he rules his kingdom."

"And he will stay out of our lands unless invited," Pete snarled. "Otherwise, I will finish what I started. I don't need magic to beat the shit out of you."

Taenom rubbed his jaw again.

"Send them back. We're done here," Carzent announced. "Keep them in check, Shadow King, Son of the Shadows, or I will take her from you."

"What was all this for?" Skye asked.

The god turned his eyes to her.

"What was the point? Countless people lost, the two of us jumping through hoops, Pete battling Taenom. What did all of this accomplish?"

Pete put his arm around her waist and brought her close, worried about their reaction.

"Was it anything to do with us? Or was it all about you?'

"She just keeps pushing, doesn't she?" Taenom said, his eyes darting around.

"She's clearly too comfortable with my brother and sister."

"I think she deserves an answer. There was a prophecy tied to this. What was its point?" Pete snapped, having had enough of the insulting tone the god had toward Skye.

"It was a test for the two of you and a way to reconcile with my brother."

"Eliana," Carzent said. "What are you saying?"

"You know what I'm saying. You two needed to talk again. Our world was severed, and it should never have been."

"You guided Skye that day," Pete said, seeing it now. That's why Skye hadn't remembered. Eliana had taken over her.

There was a glint of acknowledgement in her eyes.

"I love Derrant, but I missed our brother."

"Sly, little vixen," Derrant mumbled with a proud smile.

"And the prophecy?" Skye asked.

Derrant eyed her before sighing and saying, "Was about Pete, although you know how I hate prophecies."

"As do I," Carzent said.

"What about me?" Pete asked with a raise of his brow, his curiosity now piqued.

"The fate of the mortal realm and the Shadow Realm was on your shoulders. Had you lost, your defeat would have meant the sacrifice of all of the kingdoms., My brother would have stripped me of Eliana and my realms, subjecting them to his rules. What he failed and continues to fail to see is that I am the stronger one, as is my heir."

"You laid all of that on my shoulders?"

"*He* laid all of that on your shoulders," Derrant answered.

Pete stared at the Upper God. "I didn't like you before, and I definitely don't like you now."

"Good, because you have no place in my kingdom. You are Derrant's heir. The Shadow Realm is now yours to claim when you are ready."

"To claim?" Skye asked.

"Yes," Derrant said. "When Pete passes from this world, my crown becomes his. I am ready for a successor, ready to take Eliana and step into the shadows."

Pete couldn't breathe, his knees shaking from the confession.

"The Shadow King," Skye whispered, a quiver to her voice.

"And his queen," Eliana said.

A small cry escaped Skye, and she clung to Pete's arm.

"You're putting him in charge of the Shadow Realm?" Taenom whined.

"When he is ready, and Skye will rule with him, leading the souls as Eliana does."

"But—" Skye started.

"Shh," Eliana said. "Do not worry, child. It is a very long time from now for you. And your loved ones will have a place in your court. It is your court, after all."

Pete thought he might be sick. He would rule the Shadow Realm, this world's version of hell. The idea was surreal, and a shiver ran through him. "I'm not a god. I can't rule the underworld."

"Underworld? Isn't that what Lucifer's people once calls his domain?" Carzent asked.

"Lucifer? Jesus—" Pete started.

"Now you don't want to drop that name around either of our brothers. The one is still upset about that fiasco, split his places of worship, damned humans. Regardless, yes, we will train you, and you're already equipped with the power. For now, the kingdoms are yours above the Shadow Realm, all yours for the taking, except your wife's, of course."

"I don't want kingdoms, nor do I want the Shadow Realm."

"An eternity with your queen? Is that worth giving up for your fear?"

He glanced at Skye, who looked sick herself, her lips quivering.

"That's what he won when he defeated me?" Taenom asked. "Would I have won your kingdom?"

The Upper God laughed, a sound that echoed through the space.

"No, I will not be surrendering my realm. And I doubt my brother will enjoy the life of a wandering god. I would wager a bet that he will tire of that life."

"I may take that bet, Brother."

"Shit, you two are joking around about this? You can't be serious. I can't rule the Shadow Realm. Even saying it sounds ridiculous."

"Gods can do what we want, we give power to whom we want, immortality to whom we want. In some worlds, they invite those immortals to rule with them. That is what you won as you fought for me."

"An immortal life in the Shadow Realm?"

"As a god, Pete, with your goddess by your side."

The world fell from under him. The words shocked his

system, his mind not comprehending what the gods were saying, what Derrant had just said. His knees were suddenly weak, and he was having trouble keeping himself standing. A god. This couldn't be real. And Skye would be a goddess. Both of them then living for eternity and ruling a world of demons and the dead. An eternity with her by his side and in his arms. Skye squeezed his hand, her presence drawing him back.

"We have a long time to get used to the idea...to those titles." Her voice trembled as she spoke.

He searched her eyes, seeing no fear, only acceptance.

"You'll make a good god, Pete."

"Not too good. We save good for Carzent. You'll ruin the realm's reputation if you get too goody."

"And what do I get?" Taenom said. "I fought for you! I risked everything for you."

His last word came out as a squeal, his face turning bright red before he vanished, his clothes tumbling to the ground.

"Eliana, make sure you keep him in your realm. I don't think I can take any more of him. Inconsiderate brat," Carzent said.

Skye had inched closer to Pete, and they both stared at the pile of clothes.

"You could have let me take him alive. My pets do love a treat from time to time," Derrant said.

"He's still from my loins, brother."

Derrant looked at Pete. "Any more complaints about my gift?"

"No, none at all."

"Good. See to it that the five of you choose a better king for Taenom's kingdom."

"Or queen," Eliana said.

"Or queen, my dear. Now, you two need some time. Take it."

The room shimmered and Pete grabbed Skye, pulling her to him and holding her tight, not knowing what faced them next.

PETE

The light gray walls of his quarters shimmered into view, but Pete still clung to Skye, savoring the warmth of her body. She had linked her arms tight around his waist, and he soaked in the closeness.

His mind was still reeling from all of it, from almost losing her, to finding out Eliana had used her to break the veil, to hearing their destiny. He lowered his head, kissing her hair, and rested his cheek against it. They stayed that way, unmoving for longer than he could count until she finally tilted her head, bringing her lips to his. Her kiss was laced with love and desire, relief and hope. He threaded his hand through her hair, then drew back to see her face. Her eyes were a lush navy, silver specks sparkling behind the color.

She brought her hand to his chest, resting it there, a sly smile forming at the corner of her lips. He squinted his eyes, trying to decipher the look.

"So, you're stuck with me for eternity, huh?"

Laughing, he replied, "Couldn't ask for anyone sexier to be stuck with."

"I think Crimson would disagree with that."

"Likely."

He looked around at his quarter. Their quarters. "Tell Crimson to let the others know we're safe, and that it's over. Have her tell Mark I'm taking my two days. After everything we've been through, we need it. Then we can deal with the new kingdom, and I'll give you up for two days."

Her eyes darkened slightly, the silver sparkling in a sensual way before she closed them and sent the message. He watched as she cringed, knowing she was on the receiving end of Crimson's rage, likely all three of theirs.

"Tell her I'll make it up to her."

She raised a brow, peeking an eye open, her lips pursed before she opened her eyes completely a few moments later.

"They're not happy, especially Mark."

"Oh, well."

"So, you'll make it up to Crimson?"

He heard the note of envy in her tone, the downward turn of her lips emphasizing it.

"Jealousy is not your best feature, Skye, although it is sexy. Besides, I'm certain you'll be making it up to Mark as well."

"Hmmm, perhaps. So, what do you intend to do to me for the two days you have me, Shadow God?"

His lips drew to a coy smile, a heavy pull of need tugging at him. "I'm going to worship you like the goddess you are." He pulled her against him, meeting her lips again as they parted for him, his tongue exploring and dancing with hers before he drew it down her neck. With his magic, he untied her dress, pushing it down, his hands lingering at each curve that awaited him. "Every single inch of you."

She inhaled sharply as he kissed her nipple, luring it out quickly. Tugging at his shirt, she broke his connection to her skin and smashed her mouth against his greedily. He groaned, squeezing her waist and thrusting her pelvis against his hardness, needing to be inside of her.

"Slow, Skye," he said, pushing her mouth away. "Jesus, woman, you'll have me coming in my pants. What did I tell you?"

She nibbled on his neck, her hands unbuttoning his pants. He grasped them and picked her up, bringing her to the bed and pinning her arms above her head, relishing the deep exhale it caused her.

"Remember, I want you slow and deliberate. I want to feel every move, every quiver of your body as you break against me. I want it to last for hours, Skye."

She shivered, her breath drawing in.

"Now," he started, brushing his mouth against her birthmark and feeling the responding tingle, "I'm going to make you come so hard you'll plead for me to stop."

He leaned into her, her legs spreading in reaction as her pelvis reached for him. Dampness pressed against his pants, his dick throbbing in response. He didn't know if he was torturing her or himself more.

"I'm going to let go of your hands now, and you're going to lie there and let me ravage you like you deserve to be ravaged. Like my queen, my goddess should be taken."

Her lips parted, and he had to fight the thought of them around his length. He kissed her, the feel of her breasts against his chest only worsening it.

"Shit," he muttered against her lips as she tipped her pelvis further, a sigh escaping her beautiful lips.

He slid his hands down, brushing her breasts, his thumb taking time to feel the still taut nipple, then grazing her stomach, the curve of her hip arousing him further. He spread her legs even more, slipping his fingers into her and feeling how ready she was. Her lips parted seductively as the breath left her. As her back arched into him, he pulled her breast into his mouth and sucked gently on it, flicking his tongue against her nipple. The moan that escaped her when he further sank his fingers into her made his length jerk, and he contemplated just taking her right then.

She felt almost too good to resist, too wet, too ready to have him deep inside of her. Where he wanted to be. He removed his fingers, grazing her swollen clit, then raised himself up and kicked his pants off. Coming back down, he couldn't help dipping his tongue into her, moaning when her legs clenched as she reached for her climax.

"Not yet," he whispered, trying to maintain his breathing and calm the storm that touching her stirred within him.

She dug her hands into his shoulders, pushing him back down, her release close. He obliged, taking one more lick of her sweetness and feeling her body start to tremble as it reached its peak. Bringing himself up, he slid into her with a deep thrust that sent his groan out with her cry. He grabbed her ass, tilting her, and sending himself deeper. Each thrust was like an electric current cascading through his body.

His power surged with every move, hers seeping out to meet his. Within moments, she broke, her cry further calling the rising storm that threatened to explode in him. He continued to move, her muscles clenching around him so tightly that it brought him closer to his own release. Lifting his mouth from hers, he looked into her eyes, the blue of them so intense that he couldn't look away. It was just as it had been their first time. Just being in her presence, being this close, this bound to her took him to the edge. Her body began to tremble, another climax swiftly overtaking her. He let himself go as she lost it, the tide of his climax sweeping him away. Holding her hand, he kept his eyes locked with hers as they drowned in their bond to each other, their reality that this was destined and there was nothing they could do to fight it. And he would never fight it again because he never wanted to be without her. Dropping his head to her neck, he swiped his tongue over her birthmark as the final tremors of their release drifted through them.

He began moving inside her again, his erection still raging for more of her, even after the power of his last release. His body craved her like sustenance and satisfying that craving would always mean making love to her more than once. It would forever be like that. He needed her too greatly to take her only once.

She wrapped her legs tight around him, and he lifted his head from her neck. Her beautiful eyes were brimming with love, and he kissed her passionately before drawing back to watch their magic as it made its own love around them.

"I love you, Skye. I think I've always loved you. It's been there, in that space in my heart, right near the others, waiting for you to fill it."

"And now we've both filled that space. I'm yours, Pete, that part of me that's always been yours is there for you to claim."

"Then I claim your other half, just as I did the first time I kissed you. I'll take every part of you I can, Skye."

"And when you are god of the Shadow Realm?"

"Well, then I'll take all of you."

He kissed her again, relishing in her touch, the feel of her against him, and how she filled every space the others couldn't reach. His undercurrent, his magic, his soul.

SKYE

FOUR HUNDRED YEARS LATER

Momma!" a little girl squealed as she ran to Skye, followed by the patter of matching feet from her brother. Skye picked her up and gave her a big kiss on her rosy cheek. Her blue eyes sparkled with their depth as Skye rubbed noses with her. She reached down and scooped up the boy, whose hands reached to touch her face, his hazel eyes shimmering with humor.

"Fedhem was teasing me."

"Lyra started it."

"I did not!" she shouted, her auburn curls bouncing with her words.

"Did you two come in here to argue or to say good morning?"

"They came in to say goodbye before you leave," Mark said, leaning over their heads and kissing Skye.

He took Lyra from her, and she put her hands on his cheeks before saying, "Can we send Fedhem to the Shadow Realm?"

"Lyra!" Skye scolded, letting Fedhem down to drop to his height. "No teasing your sister while I'm gone."

He gave her a mischievous grin, the very same one she'd seen on Mark countless times, and knew he wouldn't be heeding her words.

"You need to stop picking them up," Mark said, leaning over and kissing her again. The warmth of his lips was welcome, as if she hadn't made love to him earlier that morning.

Lyra giggled at them, and Skye parted from his mouth reluctantly. It was always hard leaving either of her mates, but leaving the twins was especially difficult.

"They're much too heavy for you to carry now. Especially this little beast," he said, rubbing his hand in Fedhem's hair.

There was a shimmer in the air, and she sensed the pull to Pete's magic as he stepped into the room, no portal needed as his shadows dissipated quickly.

"Mark," he said, greeting Mark before pulling Skye in for a deep kiss. She melted as she did each time, his touch so different from Mark's, both men meeting her soul like a moth drawn to a flame.

Lyra giggled again, and Fedhem gave her an elbow.

"How's the feisty Lyra today?" he asked, drawing his mouth from Skye's and giving Lyra a smile.

"Uncle Pete!" she cried, reaching her arms out for a hug.

"And our commander in training?" he asked Fedhem, whose little eyes shone with pride. He was every bit his father. He gave Pete a big smile, saying, "I get to use weapons today."

"Oh, that's not frightening when it involves a three-year-old."

"Training starts early, Pete. You don't get to be me by playing with shadows," Mark said.

"Funny, Mark. Lyra, are you causing any trouble for your father?"

She nodded enthusiastically.

"Good, make sure to give him plenty of trouble while your mother is away. Maybe try pulling some color from his hair, give him a little gray," he said with a wink.

"It's you who will give me grays before anyone," Mark griped at him, with a bit of humor layered in it.

"I keep telling you I'm going to outlive you, Mark, so I can have her all to myself."

"Enough, you two," Skye scolded.

Pete put Lyra down just as the nanny came to collect her and her brother. Skye noted the eyes that lingered on Pete as Lyra and Fedhem gave Skye and then Mark another hug goodbye.

"Be good for Miss Marcy, you two. Not too good, though."

"Yes, Mommy." They took the woman's hand and walked with her from the room, but not before Sky caught the glance back that Marcy gave Pete.

With a hue of brown from the stone floor, Skye whipped the door closed.

"You know it's bad enough she flirts with you all the time, but now she's flirting with Pete, too?"

"She's just looking, Skye."

"No one looks," she grumbled, "and she better not lay a hand on you when I'm away."

"I don't go anywhere near her. Besides, my hands are kept busy when you're gone," Mark said with a smirk.

Pete laughed, then placed his hand over Skye's stomach, rubbing it gently. "And how's my son doing today?"

"Ready to exit my swollen body."

"I'm ready for that as well," Mark said. "As much as I love your backside, I'll be ready when I can easily take you from the front again. Pete, your son is in the way."

"I remember quite distinctly having to work around your twins, Mark, and trust me, there are plenty of ways to take her from the front."

Arousal overcame her, her hormones overactive. Shadows spilled from her belly.

"Didn't wear her out this time, Mark?" Pete joked. "Skye,

you've got our son worked up. Ready for me to release that need that's stirring from between your legs?"

"Yes," she said as her stomach fluttered with the baby's movement.

"Care to join us, Mark?"

"I'll let you two have your alone time. I'm going to pay Crimson a visit."

"Good luck with that. Bormick was going to town on her in the throne room when I left. Couldn't even bother to say goodbye."

"Did they forget you two are together until the baby comes?"

"Likely, you'll have to make it up to her. I'm sure she'll be fired up when she realizes it."

"That's the way I like her."

"You two really should have been the mated ones," Pete joked.

Mark pulled Skye away from him, kissing her. It was a long sensual kiss, and she took everything she could from it. The baby would be here any day and just as Pete had done when the twins were born, Mark was giving them the time with their new son. It would be weeks before she'd be in his arms again.

He drew away, brushing her cheek with his fingers.

"My invitation still stands, Mark, if you want to join me while I take our mate."

The thought was a tempting one. They'd moved past their hesitation to share her after all these years. The two of them together lit a fire in her like nothing she had ever experienced.

"No, you have her, Pete. Just protect her."

"I always do."

"I love you, Skye."

"Love you, too. And no flirting with the nanny," she said, kissing him once more.

"I'm sure Crimson will keep an eye on me. Besides, she's the only one who comes close to you, or did you forget that?"

"No, I didn't," she replied, as he stepped away.

Pete formed a portal for him to Crimson's. He looked back at her once more, then at Pete.

"I'll be glad when that pesky son of yours is out of her. He's got a temper, and those shadows don't play well when I'm trying to make her come for me. When this is over, I get her for a full week, and you can babysit all the kids."

"Deal," Pete replied, laughing.

Mark gave her a final smile before he disappeared, the portal closing behind him. He'd be preoccupied spending time between here and Crimson's. Crimson would keep his attention, she was good at that. Bormick would ensure he kept his eyes on her and no one else. She was certain the twins would go with him some of the time. They loved Crimson, although Bormick frightened Lyra. He did it purposely, something Fedhem thoroughly enjoyed.

"So," Pete said, dropping his head to kiss her belly. "My son is torturing Mark already?"

"Just a bit."

"Good boy." He leaned over and kissed her, his hand threading through her hair. Her body lurched as desire whisked through her. She ached for him, and he knew it. She always melted for him, her body needing him like it needed air.

"What do you say we break Mark's rule and I take you here before we go home?"

"You know how he is. He only lets you in here when he's part of things."

"But you know how I love to make his life difficult."

He nuzzled her neck, his hands tracing her body and sending her need flaring.

"Let's go home and you can take me every second of every day until this baby comes. But before you take me, I'm going to let my tongue taste every inch of you until you fill me."

"Shit, that sounds good to me."

She licked her lips, her hand reaching down to feel his growth.

"You sure we can't just do that part here?" he asked, his eyes laced with yearning.

"No, because you're not going to be able to walk when I'm through with you."

"Isn't that supposed to be my line?" he teased.

"Maybe neither of us will be walking when this day is over."

He drew her against him, his shadows stretching to take them to his kingdom. "Have I told you how much I adore you?"

"Maybe, but you can tell me again."

His lips drifted to her neck, his kisses sending shocks along her spine.

"Well, I adore you, every bit of you, and I will love you until the end of time."

She closed her eyes, knowing the truth of his words, her heart singing as his shadows took her from the one half of her soul, Mark, to the other, him—her Shadow King, her Shadow God for eternity.

About the Author

J. L. Jackola discovered her passion for writing in grade school when she wrote a short story that earned her a spot in a local writing work-shop. She has been creating fantasy worlds ever since. When she's not weaving tales, she can be found logging miles in her running shoes, watching movies with her family, or curled up with a book. She resides in Delaware with her husband and three children.

To learn more, visit her website at
www.jljackola.com